CW00663037

International Praise for David Brierley

Tough...witty...in the best tradition of suspense fiction.
New Yorker

Super skilled graft of fiction onto history...an authentic winner.
Sunday Times

Unusual, exotic and tantalising.
Irish Times

Has the rancid strength of a distillation of the best of Le Carré
and Deighton: an authentic winner.
Sunday Times

In the top flight of thriller writers.
Natal Mercury

Smashing action scenes...superb entertainment.
New York Times Book Review

Espionage in the le Carré class
The Observer

Brierley's style is first class, and his evocation of external
bleakness...is superb.
The Jerusalem Post

One is definitely hooked from the first page
BBC French Service

Also by David Brierley

Novels
Cold War
Blood Group O
Big Bear, Little Bear
Shooting Star
Czechmate
Skorpion's Death
Snowline
One Lives, One Dies
On Leaving a Prague Window
The Horizontal Woman
The Cloak-and-Dagger Girl
Death & Co

Short Stories
To El and Back

Dead Man Telling Tales

David Brierley

SAFE HOUSE BOOKS

www.safehousebooks.co.uk

Safe House Books Ltd
London, England
www.safehousebooks.co.uk

Published by Safe House Books, 2022

DEAD MAN TELLING TALES

Copyright © 2022 by David Brierley. All rights reserved.
David Brierley hereby asserts his right to be identified
as the creator of this book.

Cover design by Stuart Polson

A catalogue record for this book is available from the British Library

9781739754013 (paperback)

This novel is entirely a work of fiction.
The names, characters, and incidents portrayed in it are
the work of the author's imagination. Any resemblance to
actual persons, living or dead, events or localities is
entirely coincidental.

All rights reserved. No part of this publication may be
reproduced, distributed or transmitted,
in any form or by any means, without prior
written permission of the publishers.

Typeset using Atomik ePublisher from Easypress Technologies

For my lovely
the crazy weed lady

Beyond this stone the earth groans

Eizens Ververis

England, January 2001

Chapter 1

One step inside the room he pulled up short. Instinct warned of danger, something that would knock his life off kilter. *You know*, Sam had said, *you're paranoid, bloody paranoid*. Paranoids live, but he didn't tell Sam that. Perhaps he should have done.

Ahead of him were conspirators, two of them, heads together over something on the desk. Look at them. Conspirators know better than everybody else. That's what they believe. A click behind him made Clough turn his head. Someone closing the door, that's all. No danger. This room made him on edge.

'Ah now, you'll be Clough, Mr Matthew Clough. Correct?'

The bald one had spoken. His colleague looked like a frog, with those bulging eyes. Could have a thyroid condition. Note something physical, Clough had been taught, because sometimes you only caught a glimpse in a crowd, sometimes you only had seconds to escape. Frog was perched on one of those typist's chairs with wheels and was gliding back from the desk. He keeps out of the light. Interesting.

Why hesitate? This was a police station in one of England's oldest market towns, a room for interviews. No decorations, no pictures. Then he spotted a printed sheet on one wall. *My rights*, he thought, *if I have any*.

'And you…'

Clough didn't finish. The bald man put two fists on the desk and pushed himself up. He was a man to be careful of; a head taller than Clough, chest of a heavyweight wrestler. Bruiser, that's him. Feel the power in him, like a dynamo. Energy contained.

'Superintendent Beckett,' Bruiser said. His mouth cracked open enough to show darkness inside. It was a smile, perhaps. He thrust out a hand for Clough to shake. 'Have a pew. No, man, bring it closer.'

Clough dragged a chair up to the desk. 'And he is…' He nodded towards the man he thought of as Frog, still and watchful.

'A colleague. Now Mr Clough, did you bring some ID with you? Something with a photo? Got to make certain I'm dealing with the right man.'

Clough patted side pockets, first left, then right. See how the superintendent frowned, as if Clough had forgotten.

'Yes, that will do nicely.'

Clough had drawn a passport from inside his jacket and the superintendent reached for it. Eyes on the photo, up to Clough's face, down to the photo again.

'It's me,' Clough told him.

'Passport photos make crims of us all, but yes, it's you. Name Clough, Matthew Leopold. Touch of class, Leopold. Date of birth about right, I'd say.'

Now Frog reached out for the passport and withdrew into the shadows. From a pocket he produced a hooded flashlight that threw a violet glow across the back pages.

'What's your colleague doing?'

'Having a look. No harm in that. Not hiding anything are you, Mr Clough?'

A murmur from the shadows could have been 'Kosher.'

'I'll have it back.' Clough held out a hand which Frog ignored. He turned the pages, twisting the passport as he inspected the immigration stamps. What was making him frown?

'Well, well, quite the rover, aren't you?' the superintendent said. 'Most of us go on holiday and collect the odd stamp – Turkey, Morocco, so forth. You'd say the travel was in the line of business.'

'Give it back. Tell him to give it back.'

'Praha – that's Prague to the unenlightened… Budapest…

Budapest again… Otapeni? Oh, Romania… When you see them all together, all these trips to eastern Europe…' He didn't finish. 'Same when you had the old blue passport, was it? Always travelling behind the Iron Curtain? Passport bursting with stamps of the communist countries? Business took you there?'

The policeman's bantering tone had left him. He sounded colder but that could have been his normal style. His colleague had finished his study of the passport and tossed it on the desk.

'What line of business is it exactly?' the superintendent went on.

'Exactly? You mean I might be inexact?'

Bruiser stared at him. 'I'm implying nothing, sir.'

Silence. Then from his inside pocket Clough produced an envelope and held it forward. 'You wrote to me. My home address is also my business address. In Vino Veritas.'

'I don't have the advantage of your education but I concede – hang about. What do you think you're doing?'

Clough was swift about it, on his feet, gathering up his passport. 'This is England. I don't like being summoned to a police station, no reason given, accused of…'

'Accused?' the superintendent broke in. 'I've accused you of nothing. Bloody hell, where do you think you're going?'

Out. But Clough didn't say it. Scrape of chairs, raised voices, but Clough kept going. For the first time Frog in the shadows spoke directly to him.

'Listen. We had to establish your identity beyond any doubt so stop flouncing out. Your father – or the man who claimed he was your father – is dead.'

The superintendent opened the door and called outside, 'Bring us three teas. Milk. And a sugar bowl. On a tray. Thank you.'

Clough had come back and was sitting in the chair again, perched on the edge. Father? What father?

The superintendent was giving Clough a steady look.

'Sorry to be the bearer of bad news but there are *circumstances*, you see. So they got on to me. I'm not from the local cop shop, I'm from Oxford.'

'My father, he said.' Clough ducked his head towards Frog who'd moved back out of the light again.

'Correct.'

'But I have no father.'

'Ah now,' the superintendent ran a hand over his smooth head. 'Everybody has a father. Fact of life. We all have an old man. I do. You do. Or did. It's been a shock but thank God you're not a cry-baby.'

'My mother died giving birth. On my birth certificate where it says *Name and Forename of Father* there's a blank.'

'Hold on a minute,' the superintendent said. 'So who brought you up?'

'My aunt. My mother's sister.'

'Well, he did exist. Had to.'

'I asked about him.' Clough stopped. Why was he telling these two strangers? Sometimes a memory demands to be shared. 'Other boys had fathers – why didn't I? I asked my aunt, "Where's my daddy?" This is what she said. "The devil has him." I'll always remember that.'

'The devil has him? What made her say that?'

'Some happy-clappy hallelujah chapel had snared her, so I didn't ask again. To me what she said meant he was dead. Now it looks like it was her judgement – let him be dead and in hell.'

'Silly cow,' the policeman muttered.

'We only have his say-so,' said Frog, 'that he was Clough's father.'

Clough looked across at him. 'Who *are* you?'

'He's from London,' the superintendent said, answering for him. 'Drove down specially. Early start so he's a bit tetchy.'

'But why did he come?'

'Because of the situation which I shall tell you about.'

There was a knock at the door and a middle-aged man in a brown sports jacket and black trousers came in with a tray. Retired bobby, Clough decided, now part of the civilian help.

'Tray over here.' The superintendent tapped his desk. Silence for a few moments and then, 'that'll do. No interruptions. No telephone calls, no heads round the door. Thank you.'

'I'll be mother,' the superintendent said and poured the tea. He picked up a sheet of paper. 'Listen, this is what I can tell you. Five days ago your father…' He broke off at some gesture from his colleague. 'All right, all right, the man who *claimed* he was your father was found dead in Riga, which is the capital of Latvia, so I'm told.' Nod towards his colleague.

'Latvia?' Clough asked. 'You said Latvia?'

'Your father – let's assume that, we'll make quicker progress. Your father was Latvian. That is our information. Mother British, father Latvian. She had the sense to return to England before the birth, otherwise there might have been a question mark over your nationality.'

'I might have been Latvian?'

'Bloody sight worse. It was part of the Soviet Union. You'd have been a Soviet citizen, done your stretch in the Red Army, married some Svetlana with hairy legs. By the way, you're not married, are you?'

'Latvian?' Clough had fixed on that. He let out a grunt of suppressed laughter. The idea was preposterous.

'A wife can get emotional when things like this pop out. You've been hiding something so what other secrets are you keeping in the dark? No wife, then?'

Clough shook his head.

'No live-in girlfriend? I'm not being nosy, but a lover can also be upset. No regular partner?'

'What was he called? The man who claimed he was my father?'

The superintendent frowned at the paper. He ran a finger along the name. 'Krisjanis Kulbergs.'

'So I am Matthew Leopold Kulbergs.'

'Your birth was registered in your mother's name, Clough. You can be Kulbergs if you wish. Call yourself what you like provided there's no intention to defraud.'

'He died five days ago?'

'So we're told.'

'What from?'

'Cause of death, cause of death…' He frowned again as he scanned the document. 'Not given.'

Clough reached out a hand. 'Let's have a look.'

'This is not a death certificate. Free country or not, we do not show police documents to the general public.'

'What the hell do you mean? I'm not the general public. If it's about my father I have the right to see what's written.'

'The *right*? Hear that?' He seemed to be addressing his colleague, though without looking round.

The colleague stirred. 'It deals with matters other than the simple reporting of your alleged father's death.'

'What do you mean?'

'He means it is our business, Mr Clough, not yours.'

The superintendent put the page on the desk and laid his hands on it to form a wall.

'Let me explain,' Frog said.

The colleague from London stayed where he was, a voice from the shadows. No, not a colleague, Clough decided. They barely seem to know each other.

'This is how it is. Five days ago the Latvian Krisjanis Kulbergs died. He left a communication with a lawyer in Riga. With unlawyer-like speed this man went to the British Embassy. There was some kind of problem, so they passed him on to the Foreign Office in London. He informed them that the deceased had a son living in the United Kingdom, apparently his heir. In order to trace you the FO got on to the Passport Agency. Why did they do that? No idea. Anyway, they produced your particulars: name, date of birth, address, emergency contact a woman in Folkestone who I guess is your batty aunt.'

The superintendent was a man who liked to have the last word.

'So you received a letter from me, hand delivered yesterday afternoon, no bloody time lost by us.'

He uncoupled his hands and brought one down on the desk like a guillotine blade.

'So there we are, Mr Clough.' The superintendent stretched upright in his chair, rolling his wrestler's shoulders. 'Broken the news to you. Duty done. My colleague can return to the fleshpots of our wonderful capital and I can hurry back to the dreaming queers of Oxford. You've gained a father and lost a father before lunch, but I'd say you were bearing up.'

Bearing up? Should he be showing signs of mourning? Someone he didn't know had died.

'The form,' came a murmur.

'Ah yes, the form.' The superintendent shifted documents and pushed a sheet of paper across the desk. 'May I trouble you for your signature, sah?' he ended with a military bark and a slap on the desk.

Sign nothing until you've checked what's hidden between the commas. Clough had learnt this the hard way.

This is to confirm that I have been informed of the death on 12th January 2001 of Krisjanis Kulbergs, allegedly my father, in the city of Riga, Latvia. Imparting this information to me does not imply authentication of the relationship, nor does it confer any obligations on Her Majesty's Government, nor on any of HMG's departments, agencies or authorised personnel.

A pen was thrust forward. When Clough didn't take it the superintendent waved it in front of his face.

Clough frowned. 'What's this about?'

'It's about bureaucracy, Mr Clough, showing some pen pusher that we have come to the ancient chartered borough of Wallingford today and broken the sad news to you.'

'This bit about not conferring any obligation on HMG...'

'We suffer a plague of lawyers. Suppose I tell you your father is dead. Suppose the shock brings on a heart attack. Suppose, furthermore, that...'

'But I haven't had a heart attack.'

'Bloody sign it, my advice,' was the murmur from the shadows. 'Don't be a bore.'

Clough signed.

The superintendent pulled the form back, slipped it into his colleague's outstretched hand and searched for another sheet of paper. 'Here's the lawyer's address in Riga. Will you be visiting soon?'

'Should I?'

'What?' The superintendent ran a hand over his bald head again. 'Chap pops his clogs and says you are his son and for all we know his sole heir. There'll be an estate, maybe a big one. According to Our Man in Riga, the lawyer is a stickler for rules like the rest of the tribe. They go by the book, but they like to have sight of a live client.'

Clough stared up at the ceiling. Year-end accounts, VAT returns, Sam's desertion on New Year's Day. There was too much to do, a life to sort out.

'Possibly,' he said. 'I'll think about it.'

The superintendent raised his eyebrows. 'Think about it?'

The man from London shook his head. 'Hold on. Maybe it's not about money. Maybe the lawyer has something else for you. That's what you should be thinking about. For the first time your father wanted to make contact with you. Odd that. Why did he do it? That's what will nag at you. Is it a document? Something else entirely? Why did he do it? What's the big secret? Here, shove this along to him.'

He tossed a sheet torn from a small spiral-bound notebook on the desk. The superintendent glanced at it and passed it to Clough. It was a mobile phone number.

'Direct line, no secretary saying I'm tied up in a meeting. I'll take care of the details. You know, flight, hotel, car hire. If you're going at short notice we have strings in our clammy little hands we can pull.'

Clough stuffed the papers and his passport into his pocket and stood up. Why were they watching? Did they expect him to give something away? He frowned.

'What's the matter?' the superintendent said.

'Is something wrong?' the man who liked the shadows said.

Wrong? Yes. Questions came into his mind in no logical order. Who were these men? Was this the normal way to inform next of kin? Why did it take two of them? Someone had to drive down from London. Why? Why did they study his passport? How did his father know his name? He remembered his aunt's pursed lips – *the devil has him* – and turned away.

'Mind how you go,' the superintendent said.

Was that a warning?

Clough's face showed nothing as he walked to the door. Could they read his thoughts? Why had they lied? What were they hiding? Why were they worried?

Chapter 2

Clough stepped out from the police station and began running. And he really could run. It was important to him. People stared. An escaping prisoner, is that what he was? But nobody tried to stop him. Running was part of his life, keeping fit. Get away from them, that was the important thing. A bruiser from Oxford. Why? A superintendent wasn't enough so someone had driven from London. He kept to the shadows, face hidden. A man with no name, his department a secret.

Clough turned right into the town centre. In Vino Veritas – his shop and the flat above – was just beyond the High Street.

He ran and his mind turned. They had Special Branch in Oxford but not dear old Wallingford. Yes. How about the man from London? He had a secret life. They wanted to have a look at Clough because they knew nothing about him. How about that document absolving the British government from all responsibility? That was to impress him. Childish. Or maybe – a bad thought, this – they wanted a copy of his signature. Suppose he'd refused to sign it. Then what?

He ran faster.

God was on holiday. Clough had closed the shop to go to his interview. He unlocked the door, paused a moment. Just checking. He stepped inside and it hit him. It always did. This was something he had created. Godfrey was the money man but he was the wine man. Posters covered the walls. Customers liked looking at them. Aerial shots of vineyards. A Mad Ludwig schloss. *Look, isn't that*

President Havel, drink in hand, sharing a joke with Clough? How about this - a blonde, head tilted to one side, offering a tray of glasses? She offered more than that, Clough remembered, her floral print blouse eager to burst open and join the party. There was a menu from a banquet at the Premiera restaurant in Bucharest. That had been a night. Bottles from Paulis, Jidvei, a remarkable Cotnari and a headache from Murfatla.

He was a niche wine merchant in a market town. The business would never grow into a national chain. Who wants to be a link in a chain?

That meeting… it nagged at him. No, more than nagged. It was a warning that something was going wrong. The superintendent had put on his uniform to impress. It wasn't him. It was the other one who stayed in the shadows and took the document Clough signed. He was the important one.

A father he had never known had appeared. For Clough he had been dead. His aunt had made him think that. He was going to have to speak to her. No getting away from it. He took a breath. He told people about her and they laughed. *Matt, Matt, come on. Nobody is like that.* Wrong. She was beyond satire.

He stood at the window, eyes on the shop window across the road. A woman was arranging fancy sweaters. He stared at her, telephone in hand. The ringing tone stopped. Silence. He waited. Then came a sound like a spade shifting sand. His aunt had cleared her throat.

'Yes?'

Suspicion in a single syllable.

'Hello, Mona.'

'Who is it?'

'Matt.'

'Who?'

'Matthew.'

And she was off. Not Matt, his name was Matthew, tax collector, then disciple of Jesus, evangelist, more, a torrent of words. What had

Frog who kept to the shadows called her? His batty aunt. Clough waited until she fell silent.

'You're well, I trust?'

'I am not well. You know how pain afflicts me in winter. It is God's will that I should suffer and it is the strength of His love that lets me bear it.'

Hallelujah, he shouted to himself. Out loud: 'Taking one thing with another, God's love countering God's will, I'd say you were bearing up.'

Was this pious fervour? Sarcasm? Uncertain, she hesitated and Clough jumped in.

'I've just heard – an hour ago – about the death of my father.'

'Your father?' Briefest of pauses. Off she went again. About his mother being a sinner who was led astray by a monster. On and on. His mother was a poor soul, weak, falling from grace. 'He had his way with her and you dare to talk about him.'

'You told me - I was six or seven years old - you said the devil had him. I thought you meant my father was dead. Now it turns out he died last weekend, not all those years ago.'

'The man who begat you had the devil in him. So did your poor mother. Valerie was a fallen woman in the sight of the Lord. I pray for her still.'

'My father was a man called Krisjanis Kulbergs.'

'Stop. I don't want to hear any more.'

'I don't know any more.'

He waited, leaving a silence. Stalemate? Not for long.

'He was Russian,' his aunt said at length, 'from a Godless land. Your mother was at our embassy in Helsinki. Oh, we were proud even though she wasn't a proper diplomat. She was something in the chancery. She never really explained what she did.'

'What happened?' he prompted.

'She was tempted.'

She sighed and then came a rambling account of a department store in Helsinki and meeting the monster there. Or not meeting him. She didn't know. She didn't want to know. Oh, she remembered, it was in the record department because Valerie loved music.

'She played the piano beautifully and it is my opinion she could have played the organ too, used her talent in the furtherance of the church.'

Furtherance? Clough blinked.

'What was he doing in Helsinki? Was he a diplomat?'

'She was vague about that. In their foreign service, she said.'

'Did he know she worked at the British embassy?'

'You mean when they met in the department store? How could he? They don't wear a uniform.'

'They know things like that.' Clough thought of this morning's meeting. Now he knew why Frog, in the shadows, was worried. 'What happened?'

Silence. Was he pushing too hard? He heard another sigh.

'Your mother was alone. They shouldn't send a woman without an escort to a place like that. It was very unusual in those days. She must have had some special skill. She said she hated Finland. It was dark in winter and in summer she was eaten by mosquitoes.'

'Aunt,' he said. She responded best to being called Aunt. 'What happened?' he prompted again.

'She told me the man didn't live in Helsinki but he visited four or five times from Russia. Only four or five times? She was being miserly with the truth. On each occasion he came to Helsinki he sinned. She got with child.'

'Me.'

'Yes.'

'And then?'

'Her condition began to show. No hiding it. She was sent back to England. I didn't see her for weeks because she was being questioned. Somewhere near Watford. A facility she called it. She wouldn't talk about it. All I got out of her was that they wanted to know who the man was, how they met, when, where. They didn't ask why, because she was a woman alone and didn't have the strength of faith. She lost her job. I thought there would be a big scandal, but it was hushed up.'

Aunt Mona's little mouth snapped shut. Her church was the New Tabernacle of Holy Light, though Clough's memory of it was of a low red brick building of Victorian gloom.

His mother had died giving birth to him. As a teenager he had felt he owed his existence to her in some mystical way - her spirit flowing out of her body and into him. Puberty has alarming effects. Now a father had appeared and vanished.

'Did you ever see him?'

'If he had rung the bell and announced who he was and demanded to see the baby I would have slammed the door in his face. He was an evil man, an emissary of Satan.'

An emissary of Satan – there was a phrase to be shouted in the Tabernacle.

'Now you, Matthew. There is something of your father in you. You are lost to the church. It is only in church that one truly under-stands the beauty of God's love. He is the light of the sun shining through a stained glass window showing the passion of our Lord. It is our sins that are the stains in the glass and only God's love has the power to shine through the stains. I shall pray for you.'

She was gone, except Clough could still see her. She was in the front room of the terraced house in Folkestone. The telephone was on a narrow table in a corner. Three china ducks flew up the wall as it startled by its ringing. Net curtains on the window had a pattern of a thatched cottage. To one side was a large potted fern. *Reader's Digest* Condensed Books filled a bookcase. When the sun slanted through the window there were dust motes floating in the air. They were germs. That's what he thought.

Clough needed a drink. He stood in front of a poster, glass in hand. Look at that vineyard, rows of vines so neat they could have been knitted. In the background was a building where vineyard equip-ment was stored. It could have been anywhere but he knew it was

16

in Hungary, near Eger. He stood close, eyes edging up the rows, searching for something, say a man desperate to hide. Instead he saw the figure of the man from this morning's meeting, the secret man who stayed in the shadows.

Why?

Bloody year-end accounts. VAT returns. Sam's thin-lipped exit. So much to do. His thoughts skipped to his mother's clandestine meetings with a man in the Soviet foreign service. No wonder that secret man had been worried. His father had left something for him with a lawyer. What? The lawyer wouldn't send the something. He had to pick it up in person. He thought about this and could feel the change inside him.

He dug the passport out of his pocket and two pieces of paper fluttered to the floor. The sheet with the lawyer's name he tucked back in the passport. The page torn from his notebook by the man from London he stared at. The mobile number would always reach him. Ring him. Don't ring him. No difference. The first time he showed his passport at the airport an alert would flash.

But he remembered what Martin had said: make the other side believe you are co-operating.

He punched in the number.

Latvia, January 2001

Chapter 3

It was the next day. Clough, telephone in hand, listened to the ringing tone, staring out of a window streaked with rain.

'Godfrey Lewis cannot take your call right now. Leave your name and number and he'll get back to you.'

'Does God have a hangover this morning?' Clough spoke into the telephone. 'Or is it one final swoop down the slopes? Bit early. It is…' Clough consulted his watch. '…6.35 here, 7.35 in Swissieland. God, I'm phoning to say I'm on my way to Heathrow. Something quite extraordinary has come up. I'm flying to Riga, returning next week. Not sure when. Depends. Simply too bizarre to explain on the phone. Sorry to leave you with the VAT returns, otherwise everything's in good shape.' He glanced at his watch again. 'By the way, did you get to taste the Yvorne?'

Clough arrived in Riga on Saturday afternoon. Lawyers don't work at the weekend. Later, much later, Clough knew that if he'd seen the lawyer and made decisions, his life wouldn't have been thrown into turmoil.

And five people wouldn't have been murdered.

'You're booked in at the Konventa Seta.' That was the Man with No Name. 'It's quite decent,' he went on in a lolling tone, 'or so I believe.'

'You haven't stayed there yourself?'

'Good God, no. Latvia isn't my concern.'

Seizing his chance, Clough jumped in. 'What actually is your concern?'

'Seeing the world stays on the straight and narrow, as I believe you have done in your time, Mr Clough.'

It was spoken softly, almost a tease, showing a little something, hinting at more. No goodbyes. There wasn't a click but the telephone went dead. Funny sort of dead, Clough's view, more of a watchful silence than a disconnection. But maybe he was listening for things that weren't there.

The Konventa Seta had two receptionists, both blonde. First one smiled, then the other. They've only got one smile, Clough thought idiotically, and pass it between them. Yes, there was a reservation for Mr Clough. How long would he be staying? Mmm, not sure.

From his room he dialled the lawyer and that was when his plans fell apart: the phone wasn't answered. For several minutes he stared at the telephone. Don't call England, don't try to speak to her, don't ring her sister in Bath. That's where Sam would have gone. He closed his eyes so he no longer saw the phone. Instead he saw Sam's mouth, her slow burning smile when he touched her breasts.

I'm flying too high today, he told himself, and got out of the hotel as fast as he could. The sound of a saxophone drew him left to a cobbled square. He checked the name – Filharmonijas laukums – because that is what he always did. The jazzman was playing sweetly, cap on the cobbles spotted with coins. Clough dug into his pocket and as he peered at his handful of change he sensed a presence behind him, heard a sleeve brushing a coat, and felt himself slip back in time. It could have been Prague or Bucharest or East Berlin in the old days. The murmur would have been 'Dollars? Deutschmarks?'

'You want postcards, mister?'

These were not even nostalgic ones from *La Vie Parisienne* but views of a museum, the opera house, churches, statues. He settled into a restaurant and spread the cards on the table. A man with a shield and a sword – is that me?

Postcard from the dark, he wrote. *You said that all the time we'd been together you never found out what went on inside my head, that*

22

I wanted to please but not to share. Some things in life it is impossible to speak of but I'll share this with you now: I am hurting.

Would he send it? No.

Sam wouldn't give a rat's arse.

Her words.

In the night a scream woke Clough. He lay rigid in bed, pulse racing. Finally he accepted the scream was from his nightmare, the scream of a woman he'd known years ago. He'd heard it once, never again. It was a scream of passion but it could have been her dying scream.

Certain parts of our life haunt us forever.

'Your friend must be an important man,' one of the blonde receptionists said. 'That address is in Mezaparks.'

'He is dead,' Clough said, 'or so I've been told.' He'd given her Krisjanis Kulbergs's name and she had looked it up in the telephone directory. 'Where is Mezaparks?'

'It is a suburb. Rich people built houses by the forest. You can take a taxi.'

She wrote the address on a sheet of hotel notepaper which Clough showed to the taxi driver.

'Mezaparks,' the driver said.

'How far is it?'

'Mezaparks,' the driver said again.

Clough stared out of the window. The taxi passed car repair shops, derelict land, drifts of old snow, factories with tall chimneys belching pollution even on Sunday, a cemetery with flower stalls at the gate, a colony of communist-era apartment blocks. Clough had seen just the same in Warsaw; the concrete flaking and crumbling. Nothing looked like the postcards he'd bought last night.

'Mezaparks,' the driver said, pointing ahead.

Clough saw a pine forest, trees as tall as the masts of a clipper. The forest had been cut back so houses could be put up, big ones, two storeys plus dormer windows under the eaves where the maids had slept. It was a competition of styles: Alpine, art nouveau, neo-classical, Marie Antoinette rustic, Bauhaus. There were no gardens, just frozen mud, dead weeds, chairs and tables abandoned until summer.

The driver pulled up where a side street met the main road.

'Gatartas iela,' he said.

He pointed at sheets of ice, shaking his head. Clough wanted the taxi to wait but the driver refused to understand, tapping the meter. Clough paid and began to walk. The second house had a mailbox with the numeral 4 surrounded by a heart daubed in white paint. No numbers on the next two houses. Number ten had its lower windows boarded. Number twelve had its garage door open. A woman stepped out of the gate of number fourteen and began a slow jog. Outside number sixteen a car was parked. Clough wanted number eighteen but the next house had no number.

Krisjanis Kulbergs had lived here? Clough walked to the next house, saw 20 in large wooden numerals and returned to his father's house.

It was enormous, three storeys. This hadn't been enough so a circular tower had been tacked on one corner. Above the front door was a date: 1928. Why hadn't the idea of a family occurred to Clough before? Nephews, nieces, cousins, squabbles, legal disputes. No wonder the lawyer made contact. Disputed wills made happy lawyers.

The garden was drifts of snow and a pine tree. An old summer house had been brought to its knees. The wooden fence by the road sagged. Wire net fencing on either side cut the neighbours off. An empty bottle had been tossed in – Bailey's Irish Cream. Bailey's? In Latvia? The yard was from a shanty town. The house spoke of money.

The gate opened with a screech. Sudden brightness drew his eyes upward. The sun had found a break in clouds heavy with snow. His eyes moved down to the bedroom windows. The curtains were closed. His eyes dropped to the ground floor. That window to the left of the door. The curtain had twitched. Or had it? He tried to picture a face, half a face, in the crack between the curtains. Maybe a fold in the material? He moved forward. There was a single step up to the door. As his hand reached out to the bell the door pulled slowly open. Two men filled the gap, the one in front with a pistol pointing at Clough's chest.

'*Policija.*'

He stepped outside the house. That's not right. Even in his distracted state Clough knew that. A cop would have beckoned him inside. Clough stared at him: about twenty-five, thick sweater with a turtle neck, baggy blue trousers.

The other man moved up. '*Militsia,*' he said.

Was this different from being the police? Seeing the doubt in Clough's face and realising he was foreign, the man added, '*Polizei. Sprechen Sie Deutsch?*'

This one was older. No coat. The cold didn't trouble him.

'English, actually.'

The man glanced down at Clough's shoes. Has he walked from England in the snow?

'Where is your car?'

'I came by taxi.'

'I hear no taxi.' His English was slow but serviceable.

'It dropped me at the end of the road.'

The man turned his head a little, listening for a retreating taxi, then stepped past Clough. 'Come.'

'Hold on a minute,' Clough said. 'Show me your identity card.'

The man halted. His eyes switched from Clough to his colleague who made motions with the pistol for Clough to get moving. Clough felt the sweat coming. Never just do what they tell you, Martin had said. Get in the habit and you won't stop. Easy advice but that pistol told another story. Clough's throat was tight.

He swallowed and said, 'You're not in uniform. Maybe you're burglars. The curtains are…'

The man cut him short. 'Maybe you are burgle-rer. We see you look at all the windows. We see you look at side of house. We see you look if neighbours are watching. Show me your identification.'

Clough hesitated then gave him his passport. The man glanced at the cover. 'So you are British burgle-rer. Come.'

He slipped the passport in a pocket and moved off.

'Not so fast.'

'You go,' said the young man. Clough didn't budge so the man jabbed the pistol into his ribs. Clough staggered and found himself moving.

It was a procession going down the path, the man with Clough's passport leading, Clough next, behind him the man with the gun. Where are nosey-parker neighbours when you need them? Why hasn't the woman jogger looked back? They turned right but only to walk to the parked car. It had no police marking. The older man opened a rear door.

'Get in.'

'Show me your police ID.'

The man hissed some word in Clough's face then gave an order to his colleague. There was a stabbing pain in Clough's right leg as the gunman aimed a kick at the back of the knee. He folded forward across the car seat. Two pairs of hands grabbed and shoved at him and Clough found himself inside the car, head down on the back seat, feet tucked in, the door slammed. Squirming round he reached for the handle. Locked. Sliding across the seat his way was blocked by the older man getting in the other side. The young man sat behind the steering wheel, twisted round, the pistol on the back of the seat aiming at Clough's face. Don't argue with a man pointing a gun at you. You won't be a hero. You'll be dead.

'You're not police. What do you want?'

The older man gave an order, the pistol was laid on the front passenger seat, the driver started the engine and the car moved off, slithering on the ice.

'Who are you? Why am I being kidnapped?'

No answer.

'Where are you taking me?'

'Not far.'

'What for?'

'We go somewhere we can talk.'

They passed the jogger, eyes fixed on the icy pavement. At the main road they turned right towards a hut that served as a café. Next to the café was a track and they turned down that into the park which was more like a forest. They bounced over frozen mud and stopped at a clump of bushes.

'We talk here.'

'What do you want?' Clough said.

'No, not what we want, what you want. Why you try get in that house? You see curtains closed, you think people away, you think you can get inside?'

'No.'

'Why you come from England to that house? Big house so rich people live there. You want to steal. You are a burgle-rer, yes?'

'My father lived there.'

'Your father?' He shook his head. 'Now we will see you are lying.' He dug the passport out of his pocket and checked the photo. 'It is you. You have British passport and it says your name is Cloog not Kulbergs. Cloog is English name, I think. You are Mr English.' He pinched the bridge of his nose to help him think. 'You have English name. You have British passport. You are not born in Latvia. You do not speak Latvian language. You are not Latvian citizen but you say the man in that house is your father.'

Clough took his time. This was a stupid thug and they have no imagination. He shifted to get a better look at the man. His face was like gravel, pocked and weathered, a face that had spent time on the street.

'That's what I was told.'

'Who tell you?'

'My father left a letter with a lawyer in Riga. When he died the lawyer contacted the British authorities.'

'One moment. The lawyer thinks Kulbergs has British son. How does he know?'

'Ask him, don't ask me. Most likely Kulbergs told him. The Foreign Office in London found me and told me on Friday morning.'

'Friday is… two days. When did you arrive here?'

'Yesterday.'

The man flicked through the passport until he found the immigration stamp.

'The ink is not good. I cannot read the date.' He turned more pages. 'You visit many times Hungary… Czech Republic… Romania… All were communist countries. Why you visit these countries so much?'

'Business.'

'What business? Is same business that brings you to Latvia which was part of Soviet Union, could be, I think so. I am wondering very much about your business. What is it?'

'I am a wine importer. I buy wine in all these countries and sell it in England.'

'You make a lot of money? You are rich capitalist?'

'I am a poor capitalist.'

'You are poor. That is why you come to that house.' His lips had a hint of a smile – here was a motive he could understand. 'Because Kulbergs was rich man. How does he get rich?'

'I don't know how he got rich. I never knew him. I didn't even know he was rich.'

The smile had vanished. 'But you come. Why?'

The driver had been watching. Now his head jerked towards the window. Clough glanced out. The track they'd driven on divided and a woman was walking away down the other path. A carrier bag dangled in her hand as she took long easy strides. Shout for help? What could she do faced with a pistol? Clough turned back to Gravelface.

'My mother died when I was born. I never knew who my father was until Friday morning. I wanted to find out about him.'

The answer brought a violent shaking of his head. 'If you know your father is dead, why come to *this* house,' he jerked a thumb back, '*this* morning – *you*. Tell me.' He jabbed his finger in Clough's face.

28

Clough took a moment, deciding what to say. 'To see where he lived, what kind of house. Perhaps he was married and had a family. Maybe I have half-brothers and sisters.'

'If he had wife, maybe she gets his money.'

'It's not about money.' Anger came to Clough's rescue. 'Can't you get your bloody head round that?'

In the silence that followed the driver lit a cigarette and opened the window to let out smoke. Gravelface stared at Clough with dead eyes. They are the eyes of a night worker, Clough thought, with a drenched look from lack of sleep, someone who didn't see normal life. He turned back to the passport. He held up a sheet of paper, read it and showed it to Clough. It was the address in Gatartas iela the receptionist had given him on hotel paper.

'Konventa Seta. You have room there?'

It's back and forth, back and forth, always another question. Clough held Gravelface's eyes until movement made him look away. The woman with the carrier bag was walking back. The policeman – if he was a policeman – took Clough's silence as an answer.

'What number?'

'What business is it of yours?'

The man returned to the immigration stamp, tilting the passport one way, then another to catch the light, shaking his head. He looked up at Clough with those eyes that seemed to have seen everything, every trick, every crime, every betrayal. 'Maybe it says you come yesterday, maybe it says you come a week ago.'

'What bloody difference does it make?' Clough said.

'What difference?'

The man spoke to the driver who handed him the pistol. He held it two-handed, raised it in one swift movement to Clough's face, the black hole in the barrel aiming between the eyes. Clough was frozen solid.

'Krisjanis Kulbergs is dead one week. Now listen to me, Mr English, listen carefully. I explain it as a friend. Are you listening?'

A friend who points a gun in your face. A friend who watches with dead eyes. Clough opened his mouth and couldn't speak.

'I repeat: Kulbergs is dead. It can be accident, it can be suicide, it can be murder. You understand what I am saying? If you come to Latvia yesterday, you cannot kill Kulbergs. If you come one week ago, you can kill him. Or you can be part of an international gang. So I shoot you now…' He paused, turning it over in his mind. 'Do I kill a murderer? Or do I make a mistake? Hey? That is the fucking difference. You understand, Mr English?'

Clough was hugging a pine tree. He tapped his forehead against the bark. A point of light pulsed between his eyes where the muzzle of the gun had aimed. He had been close to death. The feeling wouldn't leave him. Gravelface had spoken in a flat voice. Squeeze the trigger, don't squeeze the trigger, he didn't care. With one eye closed he had aimed down the barrel, looking into Clough's face, into his eyes, measuring him. Then the pistol had been lowered.

'Here, Mr English.' He tossed the passport into Clough's lap. 'You want a friend's advice? Go back to England, drink some wine, be happy.'

What was he? Plain clothes cop, friend of K.K., enemy, burglar, madman? Clough had been pushed out of the car and staggered to the tree. *God, I'm old*, he told himself. *Didn't even get the car's licence number.*

The knee where the driver had kicked him still hurt. He reached the main road. No taxis. He turned left and began walking. With each step his anger grew. He'd been passive – why? You got into the rhythm of answering, Martin would say, your own stupid fault. *Go back to England*, he heard the flat voice, *drink some wine*. Clough was disgusted with himself. *Mr English*.

People were running as a tram passed and pulled up at a stop and waited. *Centr* said the destination board. There was ice on the pavement but Clough joined the runners. He climbed into the tram and sat down. He was sweating and his leg throbbed. Why was this woman standing in front of him, bending down, saying something? A fake fox fur was round her throat, plastic jaws biting its tail, glass eyes fixed on Clough.

It was the conductress wanting money. He dug coins out of his pocket, thrusting them out for her to help herself. One slipped out of his palm and rolled under the seat. *Dear God, look at my hand, shaking all over the place*, Clough thought. *But I never closed my eyes when he pointed the gun in my face.* Mr English didn't.

Chapter 4

He was alive. The shakes stopped.

Clough got down from the tram and wandered by a frozen canal. There was a line of winter-bare trees and beyond that a column topped with a statue. Looking up he could make out the figure of a woman holding something above her head. Sports trophy, funeral wreath, sacrificial head, no telling. Above the statue was the sky, clotted with grey clouds.

Why did those men try to frighten him? Why tell him to go home? So he wouldn't see the lawyer?

Two soldiers formed a guard of honour. An officer marched up and stood nose to nose with one. The soldier never flinched. His uniform looked ironed to his body, his buttons winked, his boots were a mirror, his rifle stood to attention. The officer's duty was to find some fault so he fiddled with the soldier's collar. This is how wars are won, with soldiers who have neat collars.

Clough turned back to the flowers laid on the ground. Roses came from the florist, a posy of snowdrops from someone's garden. *If Gravelface had shot me*, he thought, *who'd put a wreath on my grave?* He twisted his head to make out the inscription at the base of the statue.

'Tevzemi un Brivibai.'

Clough turned to see who had spoken.

'For Fatherland and Freedom, in plain English,' the woman said, 'if that's what you are. English I mean, not plain.' She had a big open smile.

Beyond her shoulder the officer went striding to check the other soldier's uniform. Clough kept his eyes steady on the woman, on her face. It was four or five seconds, but she held his gaze, didn't look away.

Well hello, Clough thought, *could be*. But he wouldn't probe.

'Thank you for not asking what part of America I'm from,' she said. 'People do because they can't tell the accent is different. So I reply, "The civilised part." The US doesn't own all of North America. We don't salute a flag that was sewn out of Cousin Bertha's bloomers. We salute a maple leaf. We don't colonise space or elect convicted cocaine snorters to be mayor of our capital or need metal detectors in school classrooms or – Hey, why are you grinning?'

This was his introduction to her way of speaking, a Niagara Falls of words, on, on, drawing him into her current, making him swim with her.

'I asked where you were from,' Clough said, 'and I get a state of the world speech.'

'That's not the state of the world, just the state of Uncle Sam. Tronno, that's where I'm from.'

'Tronno?'

'Toronto to you.'

She gave him another smile, showing perfect teeth. She stirred her coffee. They were in a café within sight of the Freedom Monument. Clough didn't suggest it. Perhaps she had. Or it was an unspoken joint decision. They'd started walking away from the Monument, seen the plate glass windows and a table inside that was free and they'd turned in. She was drinking her coffee, holding the cup with both hands, raising her eyes over the rim to his eyes.

'My name's Matt,' he said.

'Matt? That's your given name?'

'Matthew.'

'Sure. My name's Debbie.' She put out a hand and they shook as solemnly as diplomats. 'What do you do, Matt?'

'I buy and sell wine.'

'Hey, that's neat. I dated someone once who said he was in money. Turned out he worked in a bank in a shopping mall and he had the soul of a bank clerk, if bank clerks have souls. You'd have to dig pretty deep to find one, down past the checking account and the credit facility and the premium loan. Only thing worse is a lawyer. Their souls are hidden under layers of heretofores and wherebys and notwithstandings and party of the third part. You reach what you think is their heart and it turns out to be a plea bargain.'

'Give me one guess – you're not a lawyer or a bank clerk.'

'I take pictures.' She raised both hands to her eyes to form a rectangle and clicked the shutter of an imaginary camera.

'A pro? What sort of photos?'

'Well, not weddings or passport mug shots or graduations.' She paused a moment. 'OK, that's what I don't do. A little while back I did a backwoods feature. Have you been up to Georgian Bay? On Lake Huron? You do know Ontario, don't you? Admit it, you've never been to Canada.'

'Guilty.'

'OK. I was up at Georgian Bay with a "friend",' she made quotation marks in the air, 'only Bob and I aren't so friendly any more. I took the photos, Bob wrote the text, and what do you know, *National Geographic* bought it. This is almost without precedent. They nearly always *commish*, don't take walk-ins.'

'Congratulations.'

'Thank you, sir.'

She put a hand up to tuck a wayward wisp of hair inside her hat. It was an extravagant hat, deep purple, with a brim that dipped low over her forehead in a piratical way. Practical too, made of soft velvet, easy to fold up and tuck away.

'So you're here on another photo shoot?'

'No.' She paused. 'Call it family business, a roots trip. There's Latvian blood flowing in these veins. And you?'

'Same really.'

'No kidding?'

'Hm-hm,' Clough murmured. He stopped, still feeling a shadow from the encounter in Mezaparks. She was waiting but he didn't go further.

'Look,' she said, suddenly full of movement, her body, her face, a hand fiddling with the hat. 'I've got to beat it now. But it seems a shame… we have stuff in common…'

So, a dinner date. That's how it was.

Off she went towards the Opera. *Look at her go. Look at those long strides.* Clough tried to place her in Mezaparks, long strides down a track while he had a gun pointed between his eyes. The extravagant hat transformed her. It could have been in the carrier bag. Did she catch the same tram? He'd been too shaken to notice.

Was that it?

My afternoon as a tourist, he thought, *bloody do it. But do it like the old days just to see if you're in the clear. Walk the cobbles, dodge the scaffolding, stare at red brick churches. Take an interest in shop windows and the reflections in the glass. Change your mind and turn abruptly round. Check people's feet, if they falter.* In another life that is what he would have done. He was alert now. That pistol had sharpened him.

Darkness came and he was standing on the corner outside the Hotel de Rome. He stamped his feet against the cold and turned to stare at the Freedom Monument just across the way.

'A penny for them.'

She'd been watching from inside the hotel's double doors.

'Let me guess,' she went on before he could reply. 'You're puzzling what Milda is holding up.'

'Milda?'

'Top of the column. Lady freezing her ass off. Her arms go straight up in the sky, then her hands are kind of flattened in a way that looks painful to me. So what's she holding?'

The column was tall, the floodlights weak, Whatever Milda held was lost against a clouded night sky.

35

'The official version,' Debbie went on, 'is she's holding stars representing the three regions of Latvia. Ho-hum, bureaucratic mind at work.'

'In your version?'

'Milda's stormed into the penpushers' attic and she's had a ball. Grabbed files of tax forms and import licences and letters in duplicate and economic stats and official reports and government fiddle-faddle of every kind and she's hurling the lot out into the street and crying Freedom.'

Her talk was relentless, like everything she did, her energy driving her.

'So where are we going for dinner?' she said and went straight on, 'I know a place.'

The extravagant hat had gone. Tonight Debbie wore a scarf, Latvian style, knotted under her chin. Other women it turned into grannies but it gave Debbie a gamine look. Their walk up the path to the restaurant was lit by its sign – a nude woman with tresses of blonde hair swirling over her body. Debbie stuffed the scarf in her coat pocket as they went through the door. Her hair was dark and short, the sort you don't brush, just run your fingers through. Their table was in the centre of the room.

'The place is called *Palete*,' she told him. 'It boasts modern Latvian food, whatever that means. Also it's not far from your hotel.'

How did she know? He hadn't told her. He was staring at his menu but thinking about Debbie. He'd got out his wallet to pay for their coffee this morning and the key-card with the hotel name had flopped onto the table. She noticed things. He flicked through the pages to the wine list. *Well, what did you expect, chum? Romanée-Conti?*

Why were you at Mezaparks this morning, he wondered, why did you trail me back to town and pick me up, why did you want this dinner? Why the blouse tonight with the top three buttons undone? Clough had a button code: one button undone was fashion, three buttons undone were a promise.

'We'll use the random selection procedure,' he said and stabbed a finger at the list. 'So, a wine from Navarra, an honest peasant.'

'OK, my turn.' She stabbed at the menu. 'We're having *Karbonade*. It's a local dish.'

'It's local in Belgium. Beef and beer stew.'

'Matt, the Latvian blood is weak in your veins. Here it's pork chops done with potatoes and stuff. What's your surname?'

Now she's digging, he thought. He hesitated a moment. 'Clough.'

'Clough.' She ran fingers through her hair. It was a gesture women had, meaning see how relaxed and open I am with you. 'I can't think of a Latvian equivalent.'

'My mother's name. She died in childbirth and I was brought up by my aunt. My father, I didn't know who he was until I was told on Friday morning. Suddenly I had a Latvian father and he was dead.'

'So your father's name wasn't Clough, right?'

'No, Kulbergs. He used to visit Helsinki and that's where he met my mother. Who ever thought of Helsinki as a city of romance?'

The waiter brought the wine and dribbled a little in Clough's glass. He tasted it, making a face.

'Perhaps the peasant was not so honest.' But he nodded to the waiter.

'Are you a linguist, Matt?'

'Linguist is stretching it.'

'Latvian?'

'No.'

'Russian?'

'*Nyet.*'

'So you're deaf and dumb here. OK, I have Latvian from my mom and she got it from her mother but in Riga half the population is Russian, which I don't speak. It's a problem sometimes. So what languages do you stretch to?'

'German and French.'

'Where did you learn your German?'

'School. Then university.'

'Is it really good? Latvia was occupied by the Nazis. Could you have survived here?'

'Yes. There were a lot of different accents in the Greater Germany.'

'To learn a language well,' she said, 'you must love it or love the people.'

'I had a great teacher at school. His parents were refugees from Hamburg who'd escaped in '38.'

'Jews?'

'Socialists. German had a kind of fascination – that thing about the verb at the end of the sentence. It bothers the English. But for me a sentence constructed like that has a certain tension, it delivers an impact.'

'Sure. You wait and in the end comes the punch. That is *so* German.'

At that moment the Karbonade arrived, putting an end to the cross-examination.

Had the city darkened while they were in the restaurant? No, his mood had. The evening had held a promise – even a three-button promise - and it had come to nothing. They lingered a moment outside the entrance.

'No need to escort me home, Matt. I'm just a stroll away.'

She moved a step closer so he wondered if after all she would kiss him. She said in a quiet voice, 'You're seeing your father's lawyer tomorrow morning, you said.'

Why had he told her? He nodded.

'Matt, you don't speak Latvian. Does he speak English?'

English is the international language.

'I assumed that…'

'Hey, you think you've arrived at some outpost of the British Empire and the natives have all learnt English? He'll know Russian but you don't speak that either. I better come with you. So where's he at?'

Did he want her muscling in? But odds were he'd need an interpreter.

'Valdemara Street.'

'Valdemara iela, got it. We'll meet up at the Freedom Monument. What time's your appointment?'

'I don't have one. No one answered the phone.'

'Nine-thirty then.'

No kiss. She was gone, walking with swift strides. There was purpose to her. Now it was to reach her room, tomorrow morning to go with him to the lawyer, afterwards to uncover her family's roots. *You can't imagine how tough it is,* she'd said. *I want to find where the family lived but the house was bulldozed when the panzers rolled in. Old city plans are unclear. People I want to talk to are dead or missing or have gone gaga. Nothing is simple.*

It was three blocks to his hotel. At the first corner he stopped. Down a side street a neon sign promised *Bars*. Some quirk made the Latvians add 's' whenever they could. He was drawn. Why not? The evening with Debbie had left him feeling empty.

Half way there the neon sign went out. He stopped. Pitch black, no light in the alley. On his left was a hulking warehouse. On the right, nothing. Perhaps a building had been knocked down and now it was used as a parking lot.

Close by there was the crunch of gravel. Rats in the parking lot? Then a prick on the nape of his neck and he froze. Mosquito bite? Here in Latvia, in the capital Riga, on a freezing night in January with drifts of snow shovelled against the buildings, there were no mosquitoes.

He felt sweat under his shirt. He couldn't move, just his imagination kept leaping. *This is tropical Latvia*, he thought desperately. Jungle creepers twined round his arms and held him tight so he couldn't slap away the mosquito. *Cry for help.* Good plan but he should have thought of it long ago – a second or two – because some disgusting jungle creature clamped itself over his mouth. Other jungle creatures were invading his clothes, inside his coat, inside his jacket, searching his pockets, jabbing, poking, groping. He went limp. A convulsive heave could throw them off. But…

He was free. The knife didn't prick his neck. The hands had gone. Turning, he saw three men at the street corner, scarves hiding their faces, hats pulled down, looking back before they split, each down a different street. He opened his mouth to scream.

What's the Latvian for 'Stop thief'?

Chapter 5

Monday morning. Sky sullen with clouds.

He tipped his head to look at Milda. The memory was suddenly vivid, a flashback to childhood. Milda became Mona. Every child has a fantasy. This was his.

The time: the darkest days of the war. Britain stood bloody but unbowed, alone against the forces of evil. Each man knew his orders: the enemy must not pass. Sometimes the supreme sacrifice was demanded.

The mission: to discover the secret the enemy took such pains to conceal.

The place: the jungle, mysterious with shadows that hid the soldier. He crawled on all fours through hostile territory the enemy believed was impenetrable. The enemy was wrong. On his stomach he squirmed closer. His ears picked up the sound of the approaching enemy. He froze. The enemy had come on silent feet, wearing flimsy footwear. He dared not breathe. Slowly the soldier lifted his eyes, up the legs, past the thighs, the hips, the belly, the chest… His lungs were bursting. The enemy's arms were raised, lifting something towards heaven. This was it, the moment of revelation, the secret the brave soldier had risked his life for. He gazed, mystified, but committing every detail to memory. Now he had to wriggle backwards to the safety of his own camp. But the agony was too much for his lungs. His breath exploded in a great sob and the enemy cried out in alarm.

'Are you worshipping Milda? Hey Matt, it's me.'

The jungle vanished and Clough returned to a freezing morning in Riga. The rendezvous was outside the Hotel de Rome, as it was then called. Again she'd been waiting inside, watching him.

'Not worshipping Milda.' Why hadn't he seen her spying on him? 'It's Mona lifting off her dress.' Her eyebrows rose. 'My aunt.'

He could have left it at that but Debbie wanted more.

'I was a boy – eight, maybe – and I crawled into her bedroom to watch her undress. I was a soldier sent out through the jungle to spy on the enemy. When I was discovered she said Satan had got into me. Religion is big in her life, the New Tabernacle of Holy Light. I remember looking up her body, up and up, while her hands pulled her dress over her head. That's what Milda reminds me of.'

'What happened?'

'She walloped me, beat the devil out of me, she said. Or else I was set on the path to eternal damnation. I was wearing pyjamas and she made me take the bottoms down so she could beat me.'

'What with?'

'A hairbrush but it flew away under the bed so she went on smacking with her hand.'

'Did you cry?'

'I was a soldier,' Clough said. Which wasn't a complete answer.

'This was after she'd hauled off her dress?'

'She was wearing a bra and knickers. A shoulder strap slipped and a cup of her bra hung loose but she didn't stop smacking me.'

'Well, well, well.' Debbie shook her head. 'What would Freud have made of that?'

The lawyer was called Birznieks. His office was two blocks up Valdemara iela. The brass panel also listed a London accountancy firm, a Swedish engineering company and MAD: Munters Advertising and Design. A plaque announced in German that the sculptor August Volz, deceased 1926, had worked here. Another plaque had it in Latvian.

Above the door was a frieze of vine leaves and bunches of grapes. Look higher and it was more interesting: carvings of voluptuous naked women stretching their arms out in welcome.

'The guy enjoyed his work,' Debbie said.

The reception area was a hotel lobby from the '70s: mirrors and spotlights and an empty desk. A curving staircase led to the first floor. This had the offices of the accountants and the advertising agency. MAD's door stood open and the sound of Spring from Vivaldi's *Four Seasons* drifted out. The next staircase was meaner as if servants had lived above. The engineering firm was on the left, the lawyer on the right.

Reaching Birznieks was not easy. First there was the secretary. Clough had years of experience of the type. She glanced up and returned to her typing. Computers had not been invented. She hacked at a vintage machine that pinged at the end of each line. Returning, the carriage made a noise like a train crossing points.

'Good morning.'

No effect.

'I want to see Mr Birznieks.'

She hammered out another sentence. Concrete Bust, he decided. You'd bruise your hand if you ever made a grab for her.

'Do you understand English? *Sprechen Sie Deutsch?*'

The typewriter clattered.

Hands on his hips moved Clough to one side. Debbie bent low over the desk, chin just above the upright typewriter. She spoke, softly, then louder. He caught his name which in the Latvian way became plural, Cloughs this, Cloughs that. The typing faltered and stopped. Concrete Bust's face reddened. Debbie delivered a closing speech, Cloughs here and there, *Angliski*, God knows what. Concrete Bust said nothing. She pushed up from the desk and disappeared through the door behind her.

'Impressive,' Clough said. 'She was the worst kind of Soviet apparatchik. What did you say?'

'Oh, this and that of a social nature.'

The sun was shining and Clough felt his mood lift. He was in the lawyer's office where he should have been on the first day.

Then the clouds closed over the sun again. The brightness had lasted seconds.

Birznieks appeared out of a cloud of smoke. An ashtray wasn't big enough for him. A ceramic bowl on his desk was littered with stubs. The cigarette packet beside it was called *Millord*. Clough checked. Yes, an extra 'l' for extra class.

Birznieks came round the desk, a slight figure with a gaunt face, grey eyes behind spectacles, thin lips. Clough put out a hand to shake but Birznieks ignored it. He launched into a monologue. Debbie had a stab at interrupting but he waved her to silence. He spoke some more and then returned behind the desk and reached for another cigarette.

Debbie turned to Clough. 'He says we are not behaving in the correct manner. He says that Mrs Gerasimova is deeply upset by our attitude. Speaking personally I find that difficult to believe. Does a T72 tank have feelings?'

'Tell him I have come about Krisjanis Kulbergs. I want to know where he is buried.'

Debbie translated. 'He says he is not buried. The body is held in a mortuary on the orders of the police. Why? Because there is doubt about his death. Not about the fact of his death but about the manner. Is it from natural causes? Is it murder? Even suicide?'

Clough felt a tightening in his chest. Gravelface had said that, pointing a gun between his eyes.

Birznieks was talking again. Debbie translated. 'He says we have made no appointment to see him and are interrupting him in work which is of an urgent nature. Oh yes. He says that he has many distinguished clients. With democracy and capitalism and the horde of businessmen flooding in he has a full engagement diary. Tycoons from Sweden and Germany and Switzerland and Japan all need his help. In any case he wants to know who you are because you haven't said your name, though it is hard to slip in a word when he has mastered the art of speaking without drawing breath. Also, who am I? Am I your boss, your wife, your secretary, your close and constant companion? There could be legal implications to his saying anything to you in my presence. I might be subpoenaed as a witness. It is doubtful whether the confidential nature of discussions between attorney and client extends to a third party unless I was an accredited interpreter licensed by the Latvian authorities, in which case I would not he held to be a third party but *in loco* something-or-other for you. Oh yes.'

'He said all that?'

'That is the condensed version. Oh yes.'

'Oh yes?'

'He says "Oh yes" as if we have raised some objection.'

'Tell him who I am,' Clough said. 'Tell him I am Kulbergs' son.'

Debbie did. It made no impression. Birznieks drew on his cigarette and blew out smoke.

'He has no client with him,' Clough said. 'No one was waiting outside. Now we have interrupted his urgent business he might as well deal with us.'

Debbie made this reasonable suggestion. Frowning, Birznieks put out his cigarette. It was half smoked and instead of stubbing it out he folded it over and pressed it to death. The bowl was a mass grave of bent-over cigarettes.

Debbie raised her eyes to the ceiling. Perhaps inspiration was there. She sighed and reduced the lawyer's speech to a single sentence. 'He says he does not know you in a legal sense.'

'Well, tell him.'

'I did tell him. He says that is who you say you are. That is different from actually being that person. Oh yes.'

Birznieks was speaking again. Debbie translated.

'He says you could be an impostor. You could have stolen a letter or listened to a telephone conversation. You could even have killed the real Clough. Proof is what he needs.'

'What does he want? A character reference from the Archbishop of Canterbury?'

Debbie said, 'The same objection would apply. The Archbishop would have to prove who he was.'

'For God's sake.'

'Sorry, God, you have to prove who you are too. How about your passport? Easy-peasy. Name and photograph together. Problem solved '

Clough stared at the window beyond Birznieks. The view was the tops of trees hacked back for winter. Bare tree trunks, drifting cigarette smoke, Clough imagined the remains of a forest devastated by war.

'Go on,' Debbie urged. 'We're not making any progress here.'

'I don't have it.'

'It's at the hotel, go get it.'

'Last night after I left you I was mugged. They took my passport.'

Oh bloody yes, Clough said to himself.

Nothing unlocks a lawyer's heart better than hearing of a crime. There could be a fee. They were invited to sit, offered cigarettes. Birznieks took one for himself, cleared a space on the desk for his elbows and positioned his hands close to his chin. He delivered himself of a short lecture, gesturing once at some files he had pushed aside.

'What's he talking about?' Clough muttered.

'Crime.'

'What about it?'

'Since the communists were booted out it's gotten worse.'

'Worse for him? Lawyers make money out of it.'

'Don't try to get smart. He asked if you've reported the loss of your passport to the embassy.'

'When's there been time?'

'And the police. You've got to get a written statement from the police. The embassy will demand that.'

Clough nodded.

'Did you shout for help?'

'There was nobody about.'

'How many were there?'

'Three. One had a knife.'

Birznieks's eyes flicked from one to the other until he seemed to lose patience.

'He says – Matt, you're not going to like this – he says, when you've got your new passport, come back and show it to prove who you are and *then* he'll hand over whatever it is.'

'Christ, I've got a business to run. Tell him that.'

'I said you weren't going to like it. But face it, how could you board a plane without a passport?'

There was no answer to that. He stared at her and then at Birznieks. Perhaps the lawyer understood some English. He nodded his head and pursed his lips. Something in that gesture infuriated Clough. Bloody lawyer. He looked round the office. What could it be? Letter, will, title deeds? He came to a wall safe, German from the manufacturer's panel, an antique with a dial the size of a dinner plate.

'It's in there, I bet. At least he can get it out so I know what to expect.'

Debbie asked Birznieks who shook his head.

'This is one stubborn lawyer.'

'How about if I hold him out of the window by his ankles?'

Debbie said nothing.

'All right, is it to do with the house?'

Debbie put the question. 'He asks, Which house?'

'There's more than one?'

'He says there are three houses. He can give you this information because it is in the public domain.'

'Will he give me the addresses of the houses?'

'He says he will give you the address of the house in Mezaparks and the house in Sigulda but not of the third.'

'Why not?'

'He says first he must see your passport.'

'Is it in Riga? Maybe it's in England.'

'He won't say.'

'OK, so I'll have the addresses of two houses – well, I already know Mezaparks. I need the keys to the houses.'

There was a brief exchange and Debbie sighed. 'No. He says you do not necessarily have the legal right of entry.'

'Is there a wife?'

'He says a woman certainly shared a house with your dad but her status is unclear. Could be his wife. Maybe a mistress or housekeeper. Even a tenant. She hasn't approached him.'

'Lawyers, don't you love them?'

He stood up. Time to start down the bureaucratic trail.

Birznieks folded another cigarette in half in the ceramic bowl and turned his pinched face towards them. His lips parted. It was the grin on the face of the Cheshire cat, fading while you looked at it.

Chapter 6

The trouble was that Matthew Clough had history. And for him history didn't repeat itself as tragedy or farce but as danger.

'*Labdien.*' He'd picked up the greeting from Debbie.

'*Labdien,*' the receptionist replied.

Nobody smiles like a blonde. It sent him a little warmer on his way. Then, by the glass doors to the street, he knew, absolutely knew, that history was stalking him. He'd known it in Wallingford, that sleepy market town, when Frog, the man in the shadows, had trawled through his passport. He'd known when Gravelface had pointed a pistol between his eyes.

On the way back to the hotel he'd come across a sports shop and bought running shoes. Cobbles and scaffolding ruled out the old city. He'd take the bridge over the river. There was a tree-lined avenue he'd noted on the way in from the airport. But first there was this thing, a sign, a warning, a problem. Time to find out more.

Today the busker in Kalku wasn't playing a tenor sax but something deeper. He must take it easy, Clough decided, up two blocks to where he'd been mugged last night, pausing at the junction with Kalku, turning abruptly. *Oh yes,* he said in Birznieks-speech. Ahead was the busker, playing a tuba. A solo on a tuba was eccentric. *When the Saints go Marching in* wasn't attracting a crowd. The street broadened into a square with market stalls. There were brooches made of amber – or orange plastic, he couldn't tell - carved wooden bears, thick mittens, Russian dolls you take apart, each hiding another doll. He took his time strolling towards the busker. Beyond him were the golden arches of McDonald's, and in the distance his aunt hauling off her dress.

Clough dug in his pocket but had difficulty selecting a coin so he went past the busker to the dress shop and stood a moment, peering at the coins in his hand and at the reflections in the window. He wheeled about to drop the coin in the busker's case and now he was certain. The man in the leather blouson turned aside. Don't rush things, don't make a scene. Seven steps and he caught up with the man.

'Just a minute.' Clough wrapped a hand round one arm. 'You speak English? Why have you been following me?'

The man swung round. There was something of a bull about his head, wide nostrils, direct stare. He said nothing.

'You one of the muggers from last night?'

'Don't be a fool, Clough. We're on the same side.'

He gave a shrug and Clough's hand fell away.

'Who are you?'

'You want to talk, we'll go somewhere less public, somewhere out of the cold.'

'How did you know where I was staying?'

The man was walking off. When Clough didn't follow he swivelled round.

'You coming? Listen, it doesn't matter if you change your hotel. I can always find you.'

Clough caught him up.

'What do you mean we're on the same side? What side?'

No answer so he stopped again. The man walked a few paces before turning round.

'That café in the next block – see it? That's where I'm going. You can suit yourself.'

Clough followed. The man knew he would. *Vagners* was the name on the sign over the door and a piano stood in one corner where perhaps, late at night, someone might get in a drunken muddle over a bit of Parsifal. There was a man behind the bar, a waitress, a couple of tourists plotting over a map. The waitress wandered over as they sat down. Clough ordered coffee. The man said he would have a beer. He spoke English to the waitress, who nodded. His English was fluent with the sort of accent that's called mid-Atlantic. He could be Latvian, perhaps Russian, but wanting the waitress to believe they were Western visitors.

'What's your name?' Clough asked. Pointless, Clough knew, as the man could have a file of names to choose from.

'Finnis.'

'Is that your first name?'

'It's what you call me.' He unzipped the blouson and it opened onto a blue sweater patterned with rows of brown pine cones and white snowflakes. 'I am Finnis, OK?'

'How did you know I was staying at the Konventa Seta?'

'I knew.' Finnis shrugged. 'Smart of you to notice me.'

'I saw you get up in the lobby.'

'I held back.'

'I saw that in the glass door. You weren't standing up to go about your business. I was your business.'

'Sure.'

Finnis wasn't put out at having been spotted. He nodded as if it was what he expected of Clough. He got out a packet of Marlboro and offered it to Clough who shook his head. Finnis used a battered Zippo, cupping the flame with a hand. You did that if you were standing in the street, shielding the flame from people's eyes.

'Why were you following me, Finnis?'

'I wanted a word with you. Then I had a thought: let's just see where Mr Clough is going, who he's meeting.'

'I was going to run.'

The cigarette on its way to Finnis's mouth paused. His eyes roamed Clough's face, searching for a secret message. 'Run? Who from?'

'I was going running.' He moved a foot under the table, showing a Nike shoe.

'Oh.' Finnis pulled on his cigarette. 'Where were you going to run?'

'There's an avenue on the other side of the river.'

The waitress brought their drinks. Finnis raised his glass and tipped it towards Clough.

'*Prieka*.'

'What's that? Cheers?'

'Sure.'

'In Latvian?'

'Why not? We're in Latvia.'

At this point Clough should have showed caution and hung back but there was a cockiness about Finnis that riled him.

'Why did you say we're on the same side?'

Finnis drew on his cigarette and blew the smoke out through his nose.

'I was never in the army,' he said. 'I was conscripted but,' he waved the inconvenience away with his hand, 'nothing came of it. You were never in the army either, not really. We're brothers, right?'

Finnis smiled while Clough hoped he kept his poker face. Hotel, name, link to the army. How much did Finnis know?

'1985, spring, when a young man's fancy does whatever it's meant to. You weren't in the army, you were *attached*. Your job – I'd say it was more dangerous that any regular soldier's.'

Clough felt numb. How did he know this? Finnis had the wit not to stare at him and see his confusion. He was staring at his hand as if thinking his fingernails needed cutting.

'I'm full of admiration. Strange for you, a civilian. Should you salute the officers?' He took a swallow of beer. 'Strange for the officers too. Could they give you orders? Polish your shoes. Get your hair cut.'

Just a little joke. Finnis smiled. Clough stayed stony faced.

'Near Düsseldorf, right?'

Now Finnis was staring at Clough. Clough looked away. Memories came flooding back. Some moments in life are fateful, changing it forever, and there'd been one at Oxford. His German tutor had been a man called Shields. In his last year, before he'd even sat his Finals, Shields had asked, 'What are you going to do next? Your spoken German is exceptional, never mind what mark the examiners give you. And you have a quality I call *awareness*. Just a moment ago – I'd heard nothing – you turned your head because you registered footsteps on the stairs. You notice things. So, after Oxford…' He gave Clough a final scrutiny. 'Of course some bank would snap you up, send you to Frankfurt. On the other hand the Foreign Office is always on the look-out for linguists. They're snobs, happiest with chaps who know ancient Greek but what they really need is people with Russian or Mandarin or German. So…'

They didn't advertise for spies in those days. Someone who knew someone spotted a likely one and there was a chat and hints and that was that. Clough never talked about it. It was something so secret it never happened. That was how they told him to look on it.

'Yes,' Clough said. 'Düsseldorf it was.'

'Ach, memories,' Finnis said. 'They can ambush us. You think of a woman you once loved and you think of what might have been. And there *was* a woman, not that you loved her.'

'Rose,' Clough murmured.

Finnis seemed to know so much. Who was he? What did he want? *We're on the same side.*

'It was you who found her,' Finnis said.

'Eventually.' He was entering the black zone. Finnis was right: memories ambushed him. 'Baader-Meinhof was gone but there were still the groupies.'

'Groupies for sex?'

'Sympathisers. Helpers.'

He'd met them, the middle-class revolutionaries. Shoot a pig, kidnap an industrialist, bring on the workers' paradise. These romantic free spirits were all over Germany, offering a safe haven, transport, cash. Rose was a sister under the skin, fighting capitalism. She puffed up their self-importance and put them on the world stage.

'But she did use sex, didn't she?' Finnis said.

A woman had been drinking with a soldier and left the bar with him and then he was shot. A second soldier was shot and that was when the authorities got a name for her. The soldier called her Rose as they left the bar. After the second shooting there was a media frenzy. Our brave boys were being murdered. What was our government doing? What were our spies doing?

'Keep away from girls offering sex was the order. Did they really expect young soldiers to refuse?'

Someone telephoned the BBC in London and said the International Brigade of the IRA did it. They were striking a blow against British imperialists wherever they were. Then it went quiet but nobody thought that was the end of it. *You've got a place at Düsseldorf University,* Martin told him, *doing post-grad work in cultural studies. Find your way into the radical circuit.*

Clough was tiptoeing further into the black zone. Bad times, lies, deceptions. It was a lonely life. Visits to London were out, personal meetings were out in case he was being checked. He met the army CO just once, an uneasy courtesy call. The CO wouldn't look him in the face. Calling in an outsider seemed to diminish him. *Damn, damn, damn,* Martin said, *you're too green. We shouldn't be asking this except there's no one else.*

'Work my way in. Get accepted. I had to do that.'

The words were shrivelling inside him. Here were things he had sworn to forget.

'It became urgent when the third soldier was killed.'

Find her, Martin said, *seduce her, whatever. Just find her.*

'And you found her,' Finnis said.

Rose was twenty-three or twenty-four. Auburn curls, pretty face, full lips, eyes that said *Yes.* One Sunday afternoon at a funny cigarette party Clough was introduced to her. This is Clare, his host said, but Clough knew it was Rose. They had a few scraps of information. She put up a hand to hide her mouth when she laughed as if laughter was a sign of weakness. She bit her fingernails. In the bars she had ordered Jägermeister.

Clough told her he was running away from his class, his petty bourgeois upbringing, the whole rotten system. I'm trying to become a virgin again, he'd said, perhaps you can help me. She'd laughed and when she'd raised a hand to her mouth he'd seen the bitten-down fingernails. *Foolish boy*, she'd said but such foolishness caught her fancy and later he went home with her, which the soldiers had been warned never to do. She drove a battered old Beetle and here was the thing: she didn't live in Düsseldorf, she'd rented a one-room flat across the border in Holland. Rose had screamed when they made love.

Next morning Clough had a callbox-to-callbox talk with his controller. 'Holland?' Long silence. 'Damn, damn, damn,' which was the extent of Martin's swearing. 'Legal nightmare.'

He'd said nothing more, just thanked Clough and cautioned him to behave absolutely as normal. For Clough it was the end of the assignment. That night, some time before dawn, Rose's neighbours had heard a scream and called the police. Rose was found on the floor. She had been garrotted by a wire coathanger. A quantity of heroin was discovered and the police issued a statement that they thought the crime was drug related.

'Yes, I found her.' Clough stopped. He couldn't say more. He'd found her, he'd made love to her, he'd passed on her address, she'd been strangled. He'd seen her naked body, but not with a coathanger round her throat.

He'd killed her.

You won't open up, Sam had said. *Something deep inside is damaged and you won't share with me.*

Don't be a fool, Clough. We're on the same side.

Finnis had said that and never explained. Instead he'd prodded Clough's memory until Clough talked. You keep the past buried but sometimes the earth heaves and it escapes.

'So who are you, Finnis? How do you know about me?'

'Because I worked for the same outfit as you.'

That stopped Clough. The same outfit. Said so coolly, as you might say we were at the same school.

'Where? London? Here?'

'Not so fast. First I'm going to tell you about New York. You're going to say why is Finnis telling me this old history, who cares? Because I want you to understand I'm not one of those cheap joes after an easy dollar. It's from the time of the old Soviet Union, of which I was a citizen, which you no doubt guessed.'

He put a cigarette in his mouth, cupped the Zippo with a hand as he lit it.

Then he told Clough a tale of working at the United Nations in New York, a small cog in the Secretariat, and how he was approached by a man – CIA, FBI, who knows? He dropped a note on Finnis's table at lunch in Pizzarama making a rendezvous for a drink that night. Finnis went, just to hear his pitch, and said no. Sure, life was better in New York than Moscow, but no. And yes, he had trouble with his wife, but no. And the money was tempting, but no.

'Look, I told him, do you think the KGB just sit on their asses and twiddle their thumbs? Do you think they don't have their sources in Langley? Do you think I want my name to be flashed to Moscow as a traitor? Do you think I want to end up on a slab in the mortuary? Thanks for the beer but no thanks to the rest.'

Why tell him this? To show he was honest and open, Clough decided, not a cheap joe. They were walking along a road by the river. Clough had never seen such a dead river, no boats at all.

'I've never been to Britain.' Finnis decided to get to the point. 'Funny, right? Working for a country that is just…what?…an abstraction. Why do it?'

A red light held them up. It turned green and cars started to move. Finnis looked over his shoulder and it could have been to check the traffic.

'Listen, it wasn't a rational decision. I was working for the Foreign Ministry and I was sent to The Hague. One day I had to drive some big cheese to Schiphol for a flight back to Moscow. Should have been a gorilla with me but at the last moment he got food poisoning. So I was returning home alone, sunny day, spring in the air, and I saw a sign to Keukenhof. I thought, I'll just take a little look, perhaps I'll meet a pretty girl. You've been to Keukenhof?'

'No.'

'Big gardens, millions of bulbs blooming. Pretty girls like pretty flowers, but it wasn't a girl I saw, it was someone from the British embassy. Smith let's call him. I'd shaken hands with Mr Smith on the cocktail party circuit. We nodded and took different paths. I saw snowdrops and crocuses. We crossed paths. More nods. When we met a third time it was as if the gods were prompting me. I said, "How are you, Mr Smith?" "Not well," Mr Smith replied. "On such a gorgeous day, why not?" "One of our soldiers has been murdered in Germany. The IRA is spreading its wings. I came here to look at something beautiful." I have left out the diplomatic chat.'

'Just a minute,' Clough stopped walking. He wanted to break Finnis's flow. 'You were driving from Schiphol to the Hague. Keukenhof's not on the route, is it?'

Finnis hesitated. He shrugged. 'Small country. Nowhere's out of the way really. Anyway, couple of weeks later a second British soldier was shot and I remembered Smith. I thought: I'll just see. I gave my gorilla the slip and drove to Keukenhof. Daffodils, hyacinths, anemones this time. He was standing not far from the entrance. He could have been staring at the flowers but I had a hunch he was hoping I'd come. "It's a woman," he said. "We'll get her sooner or later." Then a third soldier was killed. I drove there again. Tulips, tulips, tulips. Mr Smith was waiting for me. "We've got a man who's getting close," he said. I said, "If there's a fourth murder we shan't be able to meet like this. Keukenhof closes next week." Smith put a hand under my elbow to pull me closer. "Are you recruiting me or am I recruiting you?"'

Finnis laughed. Clough did not.

'You understand?' Finnis said. 'The British sense of humour. Maybe that's why I spied for your Queen.'

'How did you know it was me who found the IRA killer?'

'Mr Smith told me.'

'That is incredible. Intelligence agents simply don't – '

Finnis swung in front of Clough.

'Don't tell me I'm lying. I was there. You weren't.' He had that stony stare again, his eyes not wavering. 'It was after the police found the IRA woman's body. I met Smith for a drink one afternoon. We were in one of those Dutch cafés with squares of carpet on the tables drinking *Jonge Genever*. He raised his glass. "A toast." "To the Queen?" "To Clough," Mr Smith said. "He's the one who got in close to the IRA killer." Finnis nodded. 'An emotional moment for Smith, you understand, relief.'

They got walking again. Sleet had started, the afternoon darkening.

'So I joined the twentieth century's great growth industry, the spy trade. I was a spy of a kind already. Everybody in the Foreign Ministry was. Not full time, it was just in the air. Now I was reporting to a British Intelligence officer. At first it was a nothing kind of job. What is there to spy on in The Hague?'

Clough felt he should say something. 'You wouldn't be there forever.'

'Exactly. Nor was Mr Smith. He got called back to London. We had a farewell drink. It was in a place looking out over the sea. We were in a glassed-in terrace, no one near us. Mr Smith was what he called demob happy. We drank silly toasts. To the Queen's corgis, to Castro's beard. "This is a serious one," I said. "To the man who pointed the finger at that IRA killer. What was his name again?" "Clough," said Mr Smith, "Matthew Clough. But he's resigned. He only lasted a month after that and then threw it in."'

Clough didn't speak. He could not believe – absolutely could not – that a British Intelligence officer had used his real name, not even if he was drunk. And how would he have known? They walked in silence.

'Then, and this is Mr Smith, more than a little pissed by now or he would never have said it, raising his glass, "And here's another toast: to Matthew Clough's father, because he still works for us."'

* * *

No.

Time was suspended. Clough was floating in limbo.

No, no, no to everything Finnis had said.

Finnis's face was purple, then jade, then yellow under a neon sign. When he spoke his mouth gaped like a goldfish. Words came out in bubbles. Smith saying, 'Like father, like son.' Smith saying, 'It must be in the genes.' According to Finnis.

Not possible, not his father. Search for another explanation for the sorties to Helsinki, the liaison with a lonely woman at the embassy, what she might have told him or shown him. Finnis was lying, laying a false trail, leading him on, about to unwrap the big con. Clough could feel his chest heave, a great shout of denial welling up.

Then he thought: *Grow up. Krisjanis Kulbergs being a spy explains a lot.*

A suspension bridge heaved over the River Daugava. Half way across they stopped. Below was black water and grey ice floes. The river was empty, no boats, no fishermen, no lovers strolling in the dusk. No traffic passed. The area could have been cleared so they could talk in peace. Once again Finnis got out his cigarettes, put one in his mouth, flicked the Zippo until he got a flame, cupping it with a hand. Melting sleet glistened on the shoulders of his leather blouson.

'And now you're here,' Finnis said.

'So are you.' Clough felt he should say something, just to show he was functioning. 'Riga must be like The Hague.'

'I never put you down as a comedian. Riga is *nothing* like The Hague.'

'I mean what can you spy on here?'

'I'm out of all that. No more Mr Smith. No more Russian Foreign Ministry. I never want to see Moscow again. A lot of people think the same way, people who don't like Moscow politicians and Moscow corruption. And they hate Moscow crime, Moscow guns, Moscow contract killings.'

The knife pricking his neck last night wasn't in that league so Clough kept quiet.

'Matthew – you don't mind if I call you Matthew?'

Aunt Mona called him Matthew. And Martin – well, Martin had said he was Matt and Matthew was only to be used in certain very special circumstances. He didn't tell Finnis that.

'Matthew, a number of people I used to know have moved here. I keep in touch. I hear things. For instance, that your father died. And that you'd never known him. But you came quickly because there was something for you.'

Clough stared at the river.

'You're his heir,' Finnis said.

'That's possible. But there's a woman who lives in one of his houses.'

'Ah yes, I did hear he'd gone into property. His Mezaparks house is impressive. I don't think his woman lives there.'

'Maybe in Sigulda,' Clough said.

Finnis drew on his cigarette.

'Sigulda would make sense. None of the pressure of the capital.'

There was the third house but Clough said nothing about that. Well, he knew nothing about it.

The cigarette brightened Finnis's face. He said, 'Look, you may need help. This isn't gangster city but you could run into trouble. A man like your father dies…' He left the sentence hanging but pressed a page torn from a notebook into Clough's hand. Clough glanced down. He could just make out a telephone number. Finnis had come prepared with it already written. Clough was reminded of Frog in Wallingford, also a scrap of paper torn from a notebook. 'You staying long?'

Clough tucked the paper into a pocket. 'I have things to sort out with my father's lawyer.'

'That could take half your life.'

'I'll give it this week then I'm going home. I'm not going to play games with lawyers. I've got a business to run.'

'What business is this?'

'Wine.'

'You make the world a happier place. I wish you a speedy return to your work. If you still want to do your run,' he pointed across the river, 'it's not far. Take care. Don't slip in the dark. Come to think of it, that's a good motto for people in our trade.'

'Just a minute,' Clough said. 'Why did you make contact? What do you want?'

'I have everything I want. I've met you, Matthew Clough, the man who cleaned the world of a bit of scum. I wanted to give you my contact number because you may need it, because of who you are: spy son of spy.'

He flicked his cigarette out into the darkness, sparks spinning then disappearing into the river below.

It was full dark, too treacherous to run. Clough began the walk back to his hotel. Sleet was turning to snow, a halo round street lamps.

His thoughts stayed on Finnis. He had the head and features of a bull. He told tales, some true, others from the imagination of someone who always had a cover story.

Bullshitter. That was Finnis.

Chapter 7

Clough chose the restaurant. It had provincial decor, stag's antlers, waiters who bowed. *Gemütlicheit,* the German side of him said. The head waiter could have been a Viennese diplomat, bowing and fussing over Debbie as he pushed in her chair. So why did she frown? In a post-Samantha mood Clough blamed himself. Something he'd done. Or hadn't done. He did not understand women. Women were the unfair sex.

'You wanted to know about Bob,' she said after her first glass of wine had vanished.

'Bob?'

'The one who wrote up the *National Geographic* piece.'

'I never asked about him.'

She wagged a finger. 'I know you, Matt Clough. You're a man and you want to know who's gone before you. That's normal, embedded in your genes.'

Clough was at a loss. *You want to know who's gone before you.* She'd fast-forwarded in their relationship.

'It was like this. A reporter I knew on the *Globe and Mail* threw a Halloween party. You had to go wearing a mask. I hate fancy dress. You're a guy, do you put on Mickey Mouse ears? Does a gal put on Marilyn Monroe's face, never mind what she's got below the neck? This fella comes up to me – gone eleven o'clock – a pumpkin with cut-out eyes over his head. "Pardon me, did you drive to the party? You see, it's not even midnight and my carriage has turned into a pumpkin and I'll need a lift home." Truth is I don't go for men who are short, which Bob was. They all have a Napoleon complex and feel they got to invade every woman they meet. Bob said, "Hey, I don't get it. What are you?" "I'm a snapper," I told him, "so I took a self-portrait and glued it on a mask. I've come as myself. I'm the only person here who isn't a fake."'

Does she have a script? Clough had never known anyone like her. He said: 'So did you give him a lift home?'

'No sir, I did not. I didn't see him for an age. Come spring – this was last year, OK? – he telephoned. My *Globe and Mail* friend must have given him my number. He said, "I'm the guy whose carriage turned into a pumpkin on Halloween and you're the honest woman." Honest? I said I wasn't a fake. Anyway, we got together.'

She broke off while the waiter brought their starter of lampreys and the maitre d' fussed around. When they'd gone she leant forward.

'Have you any idea what it is like to spend two weeks in a tent with a total asshole? Of course not. You're civilised Matt Clough who spends his life with wine, lives in Sleepy Hollow and whose claim to the exotic side of life is being the bastard son of a Latvian mystery man.'

A bastard? He'd never seen himself like that but there it was. Right. Get business cards printed: Matt Clough, bastard.

'You see I'd read an article he'd written and liked it so he said we could do something together: piccies by me, text by him. Some Canadians with Attitude. I called it, grizzly bears, skunks, moose, you get the scene. Remember I told you yesterday about going up to Georgian Bay? We found a crummy motel for one night then he said we should camp, get the *real* wilderness experience. We bought a tent, sleeping bags that zipped together, fishing rods and drove up a dirt track to somewhere called Crooked Pine Lake and stayed two bloody weeks; me, Bob, the mosquitoes, the tent.'

'Why didn't you get out if it was so bloody?'

She gave some thought to that.

'Maybe I couldn't believe he was an asshole through and through? I dunno. In the beginning I guess I was attracted even though he was short. Cheerleader hormones leaping up and down hollering *Go girl, go*. Wow, do we make mistakes.'

'You survived.'

'Yeah. The *National Geographic* bought the piece and I told Bob that was it. The end. Finito.'

She made shooing movements with her hands which brought the head waiter to the table, snapping his fingers for minions to clear the plates, murmuring to Clough. He seemed convinced they were German tourists, reinforced by Clough's replying in German.

'What was he saying?'

'The usual. Was everything to the *Gräfin's* satisfaction?'

'*Gräfin*? What's that?'

'You. Means countess.'

'Countess? Nothing but a German countess will do?' She gave the head waiter a look then shook her head as if to clear it. 'Something I've puzzled about, perhaps you can help.' She moved the candle aside so she could lean closer, arched an eyebrow. 'Matt, is it your experience we get the lovers we deserve?'

The metal gate to the street was icy to Clough's touch. He held it open while Debbie passed through. She swung round, laying a hand on his chest.

She said, 'Can you hear it?'

There were muted sounds of traffic and distant laughter. 'What?'

'The *Horst Wessel* song, faint, like an echo.'

Clough was baffled. There was no brass, no male chorus.

'I have different ears, Matt. I hear different things. Why did the maitre d' call me *Gräfin*? Why did he speak to you in German? Why was he so delighted Germans were coming back?'

'A tip?'

'I don't want to be a German countess. What did German countesses do during the war? Cheer Hitler on, drop their pants for Goebbels? What did the maitre d' do during the war?'

'He wasn't born.'

'What did his father do? Which side was he on? Nazi, Soviet? Was there any difference?' She shivered. 'Hold me, Matt, I'm cold.'

Clough held her and even through her coat could feel her body shake. She hugged him as tight as she could, her head tucked into his chest.

'There,' she said, 'better now. Sometimes you have to hold onto another person just so you feel human. Thank you, Matt. Wonderful man.'

She kissed his cheek, just a peck.

Neither of them spoke for a while. The street was narrow with snow on the cobbles. She took his hand and tucked it between her arm and her body. His fingers nestled against softness.

'Good,' she said, 'your hotel.'

She followed him into the Konventa Seta. They made their way through the lobby to the lounge which had a bar at one end and a pianist at the other.

'Coffee?' Clough suggested.

'Why?' she said.

It wasn't the answer Clough was expecting.

'Well, a drink?'

She looked round. It seemed every male eye was looking back.

'Don't you have room service?'

She laughed, at herself, at Clough, at the situation, and then she stopped. Her eyebrow was arched, just as it had been at the restaurant.

'Great tent,' she said when Clough pressed the light switch. 'Curtains to keep the bears from looking in. Desk so you can write up your nature notes.'

Her voice was bright. She could have been an estate agent showing off a property.

'TV for the latest disaster brought to you courtesy of CNN. And this.' She sank her fingers into the duvet.

She turned to him, put her hands on his shoulders and he thought it was to draw him closer, that first kiss. But she said, 'Shall I tell you a secret about women? Let me do that. You seemed so hesitant while we were standing in the lounge and that pianist was playing the tea dance version of *I Can't Get No Satisfaction*. So I'll share this secret with you if I may.'

Why such formality when the bed was just beside them?

'Why do you have to ask my permission?'

She pondered. 'Your aunt would consider it sinful and she brought you up.'

'Tell me.'

'It's a simple truth about women but first I'll tell you about men. Men are not devious – I'm not saying that – but my God they work hard at finding a reason to do something, particularly if the world sniffs and says it is naughty. But we women, well, we decide what we are going to do and only afterwards search for a damn good reason why we did it. And the crazy thing is we search for justification even for doing the right thing. That's it really, how women are. So I decided a long time ago – while we were at table, somewhere between the lampreys and the venison – I decided I was going to bed with you.'

'And the justification?'

'Making love is its own justification.'

She talked and talked and Clough couldn't decide if she was laying out her philosophy of life or delaying the moment before they sank on the bed. In case she had more to say, he kissed her. The first kiss was a hello sort of kiss. The second was serious.

They undressed each other, their clothes dropped in a muddle on the floor. Now they were naked she took a step back and stared at him, head on one side.

'Damn you, Matt Clough, you are beautiful.'

Nobody had ever said that to Clough. He wasn't a young man, no point pretending, and he was lost what to say. So he kissed her again. That was the best response.

They made love. It was the same as it always is and different as it always is.

'Yes,' she breathed, 'oh yes.' And then, 'Do that again, just the same but different.' Her eyes closed and then a howl came out of her and she screamed words in his face he didn't understand. She wrenched the pillow from under his head and hurled it across the room. It thumped against the wall and dropped on the pile of clothes. She died with a sob.

They were at peace, side by side.

'What were you shouting?' Clough asked.

'What? When?'

'You reached a peak and screamed something and threw the pillow over there.'

She lifted her head to look.

'I don't remember,' she said. 'It was nothing.'

'It wasn't nothing,' he said. 'It was something I couldn't understand.'

'If you insist,' she said. She was staring up at the ceiling. 'If you have to know, I was cursing you. I was cursing you in Latvian so you wouldn't be offended.'

'What did I do wrong?'

'Nothing.'

'Then it was something I said?'

'It was nothing.'

'Debbie… '

She hauled herself round and laid a hand over his mouth.

'I told you we women had a secret, that we made up our minds what to do and justification or morality or whatever fancy word you want came trailing after. So I knew I wanted to go to bed with you but I imagined myself in control. Instead I was overwhelmed so I was swearing at you. Now do you understand?'

'Not really.'

She laid a hand against her cheek as if there was a pain. 'You've made me want you.'

Clough couldn't make out her expression. It wasn't commitment.

It wasn't love. It was as if she was troubled, that such passion was a diversion from her chosen path.

It was the small hours of the morning. She came back from showering and stood with her hands on her hips. Clough looked at her down the length of the ruined bed.

'Stay,' he said.

She shook her head. 'I'll see you in the morning.'

'Stay and it would be first thing in the morning and all night too.'

'I've got my own place. I rented a small apartment for a month. I decided I needed a place I could feel was home.'

Clough swung his legs over the side of the bed. 'Why don't I – '

She sat beside him. 'I need space, Matt. I'm hell to be with all day and all night. I give so much of myself when I'm with other people I'm like an actor, I need to wind down. I need time on my own. No offence. It was *wonderful*.' She laid a hand on his thigh. 'So what's on the schedule for tomorrow?'

'Nothing I can do until the passport is issued.'

'Sure there is. Be positive. We'll go out to Sigulda, have a look at your dad's property.'

It had become *we*.

Chapter 8

Latvia, land of clouds. Clough stared through the train window and remembered his aunt. Clouds were a punishment from God, she said, dampening the ardour of sinners. *A strange idea but there you are*, he thought.

They had the carriage to themselves. They were passing the tower block of the Science Academy inspired by that mighty Soviet architect Stalin in his own image: a brutish giant with flamboyant touches, a sort of imperialist Gothic style.

We're going to see my father's property, he told himself. *We're doing it together, Debbie and me. We are. We.*

The train passed vegetable plots, junk yards, an iron foundry, a Gulag of Soviet era apartment blocks planted in a wilderness of scrub. Our ancestors were cavemen and here were concrete caves in the sky. This was progress?

'What are you thinking about?' Debbie asked.

'You,' he lied.

'What about me? My charm? My wit?'

'The way you threw the pillow.'

She moved to sit beside him, linking her arm through his. The conductress entered the carriage and came towards them, swaying to the train's movement, bumping each hip against the seats in turn, left, right, left, right. She stamped their tickets on the back and moved on. Debbie called after her. The conductress half turned to reply.

'What was that about?'

'The next stop is Sigulda.'

Snow began to fall. A lake was frozen. Look at that man in the middle of the lake. He'd cut a hole in the ice and sat on a folding stool with a stubby fishing rod in his hands, as still as a garden gnome. Clough's mind flashed back to the anglers on the Thames path and how he jumped over their rods like a hurdler when he was running. Wallingford was a different world.

Why was Debbie quiet? After forty-eight hours Clough wouldn't say he knew her, but of one thing he was certain: normally she was not silent.

An hour after leaving Riga the train stopped and Debbie leant across Clough to look out. No platform, no sign, just sidings and a squat building.

'We get out here.'

'How do you know?'

'She said the next stop.'

An old couple had climbed down from another carriage and were making their way across the tracks. Clough and Debbie followed. Small pellets of snow like frozen drizzle batted against their faces.

The snow told a story. It had come during the night, then earlier today snowploughs had pushed it to the side of the road. Now the snow was returning, only a dusting so far. Wheels of traffic made twin tracks through the light covering. The pavements showed prints of the ribbed soles of boots.

He looked at the sheet of paper Birznieks had handed over. So where was Lacplesa? A police car drew up in a parking slot outside the post office.

'I'll ask the cops. Or you'll ask them.'

'Look - there's a town plan on that board,' she said and took his arm. 'We're here.'

She pointed at the corner of Pils and Ausekla iela. So where was Lacplesa? The plan gave the names for the main streets. It marked the bus station just round the corner. Clough learnt more Latvian: *Karavanu Parks*.

Lacplesa wasn't marked.

'Come on, the cops can tell us.'

But when he turned, the police car was driving off, a puff of exhaust like breath in the freezing air. The little icy pellets had changed to lazy snowflakes. They went to a café, ordered coffee and chocolate cake and Debbie questioned the woman behind the counter.

'No problem. We go down the street and it's on the left before the church,' she said. 'We can't go wrong because there's a traffic circle with a statue in the middle. Modern, she said.'

Drifting flakes hazed the trees of a park on the right. They reached a roundabout with a large metal construction.

'That's so modern I'd say it wasn't finished,' Debbie said. 'What is it? A mosquito on stilts?'

They turned left down Lacplesa towards half a dozen concrete apartment blocks. Number 21, the house belonging to Krisjanis Kulbergs, was down a spur that ran at right angles off the street, perhaps eighty metres long.

Part way down was a hut with a blue van parked outside. Beyond was a house on its own. They started walking. The hut was a pumping station. You could see where the pipes were buried, the snow melting on the ground above so it seemed grassy paths led to the hut. Five metres away from the hut the door was flung open and a man staggered out, stumbling in the snow. A second man emerged, swinging a toolkit in slow motion. The one on the ground scraped together a snowball, scrambled to his feet, pulled his arm back and stopped. The one with the toolkit turned sharply, the fun draining out of his face.

'*Labrit*,' Debbie called out, giving her all-Canadian smile.

They were overgrown puppies enjoying a romp. Their eyes slipped to Clough and back to Debbie.

When they moved off Clough asked, 'What did they say?'

'Just chat.'

'About what?'

'Big snow up around St Petersburg. Could be going to hit here.'

The house stood four-square in front of them. They hadn't talked about how they were going to get in and Birznieks hadn't given them a key but Clough hadn't come all this way to stand and stare at stucco. Smash a window, kick in a door panel, whatever. There was a slamming of doors, the rasp of the van's diesel engine, silence.

They weren't the first visitors. Tyre tracks led towards the house and back again. It had snowed sometime past midnight and the car had come after that. When they reached the gate to the house they saw where the car had done a three-point turn so it faced back along the street. One pair of footprints went towards the house and came back.

The house stood alone, isolated. The blocks of apartments were out of sight. Away on the left was a Ferris wheel frozen in winter stillness. To the right was a cable car station. You live here if you want to be private.

The gate was open. They walked up the path. At the front door Clough used a knocker in the shape of a clenched fist. No one answered. He hadn't thought they would.

'So?' Debbie said.

Whoever had come before them hadn't bothered climbing the step to knock at the front door. Footsteps led straight to a path of concrete slabs that ran to the left past a bed of last summer's dead flowers poking through the snow. They went round to the back of the house where there was another door. Now they were out of sight of the street, overlooked only by a line of pine trees and the cable car station. The town plan had shown a river valley and a hill with a castle, but the falling snow hid that.

'No one home,' Debbie said. 'Now what?'

Birznieks wouldn't commit himself, but the house now belonged to him. Well, probably.

'I'm going inside.'

'Matt, someone's been here in the night. Did he get in?'

The snow was scuffed on the step by the door.

'No telling,' Clough said. Only destroy evidence, he'd been instructed, if it incriminates you. 'Best we can do is record the fact that someone was here before us.'

She got out her camera and lined up a shot of the footprints leading to the back door.

'Zoom in,' Clough said. 'Get the pattern of the boots. Now a shot looking back that shows our prints.'

She showed him the viewing panel. 'Our prints are clear. His are muzzy with snow.'

'Good.'

Snow was useful.

'Matt, Krisjanis Kulbergs owned three houses. The one in Mezaparks is bigger than this, right?'

Clough waited.

'What kind of man got rich in the old Soviet Union? Who didn't have to obey the rules? Who could piss all over that Marxist crap? Your ordinary factory worker? Some pen-pusher? What kind of person?'

Finnis had already told him what kind of person.

'Come on, let's go in,' he said.

Clough rapped with his knuckles, just for form's sake. The footprints had come and gone away. Whoever it was wouldn't be inside. But you never knew what you were walking into.

'Matt?' she said, meaning what are we waiting for.

How had it got like this? She had picked him up at the Freedom Monument and then it had just rolled: dinner, the lawyer, the police, the embassy, dinner again, bed. After that she'd said *we*, as if they were colleagues. Who was she?

'Hey Matt, what is it?'

'Just thinking.' He pointed at the door. 'No scratches on the woodwork, no broken glass. Whoever went in had a key.'

'Or the door wasn't locked. Or he picked the lock.'

'Or that.'

He dropped his hand on the handle and the door eased open. Just a crack, then enough to see the cooker, a work surface, a microwave, finally a view of half the kitchen. The open door let in that flat white light that reflects off snow.

'Shit,' she said.

Cupboard doors stood open, shelves ransacked, packets of sugar and dried beans spilled, saucepans dropped. They could see all this from the doorstep.

Someone in a hurry. Snowmelt showed footsteps.

They stepped inside and saw more. Cookbooks were swept off a shelf, mop, bucket and broom pulled out of a closet, fridge door open. The fridge light showed milk, orange juice, lettuce, a tub of margarine, other stuff in paper bags.

'Camera?' he said.

While she recorded the mess he moved close so he could put his mouth to her ear. 'Someone's living here, right? Not just the fresh food, the heating's on.'

'Can't hear anybody. Gone out?'

'Let's see.'

They passed from the kitchen to a passage, from tiles to wooden floorboards. More snowmelt. Debbie stepped past him to look through open doors.

'Jesus, like the worst party ever.'

To Clough it was a rampage by someone in a fury. One room had a desk with the drawers pulled out, contents dumped. A metal cabinet had spewed files. In the living room a painting had been taken down – looking for a wall safe? Ordinary loot was ignored. A carriage clock, a pair of antique pistols, a heavy silver candlestick – no interest.

Clough tapped Debbie on the shoulder and pointed up. Then he thought about a weapon. He took the silver candlestick, solid in his hand.

There's always one board in the stairs that creaks. There's always some movement in the corner of your eye but when you swing round with the candlestick raised you find the movement is yourself in a mirror.

Upstairs a passage ran the length of the house with three doors each side. The door to a linen closet was open, sheets, pillowcases and towels littered the floor of the passage. The other doors were closed. Why? What would jump out when he opened a door? He opened the first door. A bathroom. Untouched. A separate lavatory. Untouched.

It was in the first bedroom they found her.

'God, I can't…' Debbie didn't finish. 'The blood,' she said, as if that needed saying. She dug her fingers into Clough's arm.

Clough stared. The old woman was sprawled on the carpet, her head wrenched round to the right. She had been bludgeoned to death.

'I'm going to throw up,' Debbie whispered. But she didn't. She put her shoulders back for courage, took a step into the room, bringing Clough with her, then another step, bent over, just to check the old woman wasn't breathing. They stared at her in silence. Now Clough had confronted the worst he wasn't afraid or nervous, just angry. She was killed because of my father, he knew. Because he was rich? Because of his past?

She wore a patterned nightgown, yellow daisies blossoming among her blood. She had straggly grey hair, arthritic hands, skin with the brown splotches of age. The bedclothes were thrown back, the rug she lay on rumpled.

Work out the timeline, Clough told himself. Intruder thought the house was unoccupied? No, the heating was on. Night time, so he would have come straight upstairs, looked in a bedroom, killed the woman, and gone back down. She had been asleep until something woke her. She had got out of bed and reached for the telephone. It lay on the floor beside her body. She had got as far as holding the handset when the first blow came.

How many blows had there been? No telling. The attacker had used a heavy silver candlestick – it had been dropped on the floor

by the body. Its pair was in Clough's hand. The blood on her temple
looked tacky but Clough didn't touch it. He didn't know about
blood, how quickly it dried, how central heating affected it. But
she hadn't been dead long. Melted snow from the killer's boots was
still on the kitchen floor.

Her eyes were open, unseeing.

'We sit in separate carriages,' Clough said when they got to the
station. Debbie didn't want to be on her own. He shook his head.
'It's better no one sees us together.'

He thought about his father and what Debbie had said. Three
properties made him rich. He was too old to be one of the bucca-
neering new *biznezmen* so he had acquired his riches when Latvia
had been part of the Soviet Union. To do that you had to have
powerful connections. Something in the house had been worth
killing the old woman for. Assumption: the 'something' had not
been found because every room was a shambles. And Finnis had
said he was a spy.

Now Debbie… she wanted to come to Sigulda, she wanted to
get into the house. The sight of the murdered woman made her
pause. She'd rallied as if another person inside her issued an order:
come on, girl, shape up. When they left the old woman's bedroom
she'd gone to open the doors of the other rooms. 'Just in case,' she'd
said. In case what?

Murder changes everything. He couldn't handle this on his own.

At Riga Central they walked separately down the steps from
the platform, through the tunnel, across the booking hall. Debbie
kept a few paces behind Clough as they emerged on the concourse
outside. The clock showed mid-afternoon but the night-time
trade had started. Women with too much make-up stood around,
smoking cigarettes. Men in leather blousons eyed Clough and one
gave his girl a push. She clipped over on high heels and stood in
front of Clough so he had to stop. Cherry red lips were parted in
a smile for the foreigner.

'*Guten Tag, Liebling.*'

There was the smell of alcohol on her breath.

Debbie caught up with Clough. 'Hands off, kid.'

Why had she spoken English? Was it the German that riled her? She linked her arm through his as she claimed ownership and swept him away.

Clough felt the pimp's eyes on them and thought of all the witnesses who'd come forward when the murder made the news: the conductress on the train, the woman at the café, the young men at the pumping shed. At the house Debbie had said, 'no police.' In her voice was the assumption that in such-and-such circumstances you did so-and-so. As if he, Matt Clough, would assume it too. So, no police. Police would demand to know why they were in the house. Police would be scratching round for a motive. Had the old woman been married to Krisjanis Kulbergs? Living with him as his wife? She might inherit, motive enough for Clough to have killed her.

'No police,' Clough had agreed. It seemed a good idea at the time, as people said.

A broad avenue separated the station from the old town. There was a subway but they avoided that. They dodged between buses and trucks and when they reached the other side Clough turned to check no one had followed them across the road.

'I'll make prints,' Debbie said. 'There's an internet café I use.'

The prints would be evidence: footprints in the snow, rooms tossed upside-down, bloodstained corpse.

'Send the prints to yourself, *poste restante*,' Clough said. 'They'll be at the post office if we need them.'

'I'll delete the exposures on the memory card,' she said.

Steady eyes rested on him. A conspirator's stare, in this together.

Chapter 9

Half-way across the square she did something strange: she came to an abrupt halt and turned to look back. Why? Why stop and look back? So she could wave goodbye? Checking he wasn't following?

She walked on, legs striding, hips moving. In his mind he had an image of his first sight of her, moving away down the snowy track in Mezaparks, the curve of those hips, those long strides. A second image was of those long legs in bed last night, binding him to her. Sex with a woman changed everything. You saw her in a different way, your judgement was skewed. She reached the corner of a building and disappeared but he could still see her naked body. Making love made her part of his life. He knew that, knew he had to guard against it and yet…

There was a café on the far side of the square and he sat down at a table inside and ordered coffee. He needed time to get his thoughts in order. Through the café window he could see the corner of the building she had disappeared round. It was a *Jugendstil* apartment block, flowing lines, streamlined, the German answer to *art nouveau*. Then the image of Debbie came flooding back. He saw her flowing lines as she walked towards him in the bedroom, naked. Goddam it, stop letting her image cloud your brain, just stop it.

He'd left the Firm after Düsseldorf but there are certain things in life you never quite say goodbye to. It was some time after when the doorbell tinkled at Wallingford and he looked up and saw Martin.

Martin had been his Controller when he first joined the Firm. Clough was fresh from training.

'You're a virgin,' Martin had said, 'you don't know what it's all about yet.'

But Martin had picked up that same awareness the Oxford don Shields had. He'd sent him on little jobs to Bratislava and Prague ('because Czecho is fun') and Berlin ('because you're wet behind the ears until you've done Berlin'). Then came Düsseldorf. Clough had brooded on that. Her scream when she made love, her murder. He couldn't stomach the idea that sleeping with a woman would end with her being garrotted. He quit.

Then came the day of Martin's visit to In Vino Veritas. Martin was framed in the doorway, an eyebrow raised, uncertain of his welcome. He was just as Clough remembered, his charm and diffidence. A back office wallah, you'd say. You'd never guess he could shoot a man in cold blood. Clough opened a bottle for old time's sake and they gossiped about people they'd known. On the third glass Martin came to the point. Clough travelled a lot behind the Iron Curtain, though it was crumbling by then. Wine buying was perfect cover. Martin wasn't suggesting he came back to work full-time but he might be an Irregular. Just the occasional little job, nothing scary. Clough should have turned him down flat, but Martin was so off-hand about it that Clough asked what he was suggesting. Oh, collecting a little packet to pop in your suitcase, having a wee chat – the personal contact gave them a warm glow. No big deal. That was what Martin said.

True enough. Until Eger.

The time was the mid-80s. The satellite countries were drawing deep breaths before taking the plunge into freedom. Gorbachev was in the Kremlin, the Soviet Union was in ferment, nobody believed the Red Army was going to stage a lightning strike across Europe except certain dinosaurs in the Ministry of Defence. Martin was apologetic. Would Clough terribly mind contacting this fellow Lajos, some lowly Major in one of the Hungarian armoured divisions?

They were doing autumn manoeuvres east of Eger and he had some papers to pass over. Martin didn't say what the papers were.

Clough went to Budapest then Eger. He did some buying. Godfrey didn't like the wine but Bull's Blood on a label always found a taker. Clough made a useful contact for a private venture that was going ahead so it was not a wasted journey. He kept a day clear to meet Lajos.

A country ramble, that's what the briefing made it seem. Local bus to some village with an unpronounceable name, admire the church with its onion dome, spot of lunch, then wander back towards Eger on lanes and farm tracks through vineyards to a barn. The barn was the rendezvous.

And it was the country ramble that saved him. He should have come direct from Eger, that's what they were expecting, not to be returning there. The rendezvous time was close and Clough was hurrying and then he stopped, mid-stride. Just ahead, four jeeps were tucked away behind bushes. One jeep could have been Lajos. But four? Instead of approaching from the front he worked his way round to the back of the barn. Through cracks between warped old planks he caught glimpses of movement, uniforms and guns. He froze. He heard mutters, a sharp order, then absolute quiet. He knew at once that Lajos had been betrayed or that Lajos had been playing a double game.

It was silent in the barn, silent outside except for the cawing of a crow. Clough took a step back, and another, then knocked into a wheelbarrow carrying a pitchfork. Metal rang against metal. Clough froze, his body, his brain, until shouts erupted inside the barn. He ran. Someone fired off a couple of shots and then he was in among the vines. The grapes had been picked. The leaves were yellowish brown and shrivelled. There had been a frost during the night and whenever he brushed against them they fell.

Then he heard it. Jesus, a helicopter. Just for him? How could he be so important? Where had it been warming up? He was a pawn in some Hungarian chess game. Show the world or the Kremlin or some faction in Budapest the scheming nature of the West, sending spies to steal secrets. Or possibly that Hungary was able to look after itself and didn't need Moscow leaning on it. With Hungarians you never knew what was going on in their heads.

Clough ducked and ran and stood still and ran some more while the helicopter searched for him. He glimpsed it between leaves, then it swooped down out of sight, rose again. The roar of its engine was terrifying. It came from everywhere, a skyful of aggression. Run, don't run, take cover, don't breathe, don't panic, get to the next row of vines, wait, count to ten, move to the next row, wait, run again. He made it to a shed. Bugger, its door was padlocked. Flatten yourself against the wall, he told himself, it's your only hope. He edged his way round all four sides while the helicopter made a slow circuit.

There's an arrogance to helicopter pilots, thinking that they are God looking down and if they can't find someone then he isn't there. The helicopter swooped off to a far corner of the vineyard. Clough listened and there was no sound of soldiers. He scuttled between vines, keeping the sun to his back. The vineyard stretched to the horizon. Don't try to hide, he told himself, the soldiers will come searching. My God, my footprints, they'll follow my tracks. But when he looked down no footprints showed in the dry soil.

He came to a road, tarred a long time ago, now potholes and dirt. He darted across to a patch of waste land. There was no cover but he could see no one looking for him. Calm down, he ordered himself, act normal. He walked on to a suburb of concrete apartment blocks. A couple of women carrying shopping were too deep in gossip to notice him. Further on was a man with a hose washing a car. He'll want to stop and chat and ask what I'm doing. Clough crossed the road to the other pavement.

The dog worried him. It had latched on to him when he crossed the patch of waste land. Sometimes it was at his heels, then when he turned and raised his arm the dog retreated, cringing, but never went away. *The dog limps and people will think I've been brutal,* he worried. *People will shout to keep my dog on a leash, don't let it wander loose in town, except I won't understand. Police will stop me, demand my papers.*

A spy on the run worries about the smallest things.

He turned round and found the dog had disappeared.

Clough walked into town as nonchalantly as any spy could who's just had his meeting betrayed and the army after him. *The army is a closed world*, he reasoned to himself. *They won't have alerted the police beforehand. They'll want the kudos of catching the spy themselves, especially since one of their own is involved. So stop worrying. Just get out of Eger fast.*

At his hotel he changed into clothes that weren't smeared with dirt and checked out. Or tried to. At the front desk was a woman built like a sack of potatoes, with hair wound into a bun.

'Es ist verboten.'

Forbidden? What did Potato Sack mean? His worries swarmed back. Had the police put out an alert?

'Ihr Gutschein zahlt für eine Nacht, so dass Sie nicht verlassen kann. Es ist nicht gestattet. Es erfolgt keine Rückerstattung.'

There was a pause. Eyes sunk in piggy cheeks gazed at him. Clough had made her day and he thought he saw a glint of bureaucratic triumph. Clough was at home in German and hated the way she spoke it, like a Nazi baddie in a war film. He didn't want to spend the night that had been paid for, he didn't want a refund, he just wanted to get out of town.

Verboten he muttered to himself. He hated that word. *Verboten.*

Sometimes when you are stressed and the bad men are after you and betrayal is in the air it only takes a word and your caution, your training and your secret nature are overwhelmed. *Verboten.* You're trying to get away, the helicopter is going round in your head, you really think you've made it and at the last moment some bureaucrat with a bosom like a hippo's backside bars the way. Just for an instant your control slips.

'Ich will nicht mein verdammtes Geld zurück.'

Clough had barked it and she pulled herself upright and glared. Who was this foreigner who didn't care about money? No honest man wastes forints. Clough dropped the key on the counter and to cover his tracks he asked Potato Sack about buses to Debrecen, how often did they leave and where from. Then he walked to the railway station and took the first train to Budapest.

He resigned when he got back to England.

Memories. He stared in the empty coffee cup.

He'd had Christmas cards from Martin. You may have left us again, Martin was hinting, but I haven't forgotten you. Once he called at In Vino Veritas after he'd been to see some don at Oxford. Another time, near to Christmas, Clough got a parcel in the post. On the outside was written: *I spy with my little eye something beginning with P.*

He opened the box and found a brace of pheasants. There was a note: *I can still shoot straight.* It wasn't signed.

Quit the Firm and it was a clean break, that was the diktat. Martin shook his head. The job they did couldn't be done according to a book of rules. Hence, have a brace of pheasants. Still thinking of you.

It was a long time since that scare in Hungary, dodging the helicopter, skipping out of town. When he thought about it, he hadn't done these jobs for the government or for love of his country, he'd done them for Martin. Martin made certain the link wasn't broken. So…

Martin's phone number was in his little book. Not under M, that wasn't secure. It was listed under Yellow Submarine.

Clough paid and left the café. Outside he fumbled with the bill and it fell on the cobbles. As he stooped to pick it up he glanced all round the square.

England, January 2001

Chapter 10

Martin hadn't retired, he'd been retired. The rules insisted on it. He despised rules but there was nothing he could do. Hobbies did not take the place of work. Memoirs? What was the point? The interesting bits would be censored.

Fourish on a drab London afternoon and the telephone rang. One moment he was thinking there was something post-coital about London in January: festivities over, hangovers over, the day shutting down at teatime. The next moment everything changed.

He had two telephones, one landline, one mobile. It was the mobile that warbled. He cleared his throat and gave his number. A pause, a slight crackle then the sound of whistling. *Yellow Submarine*. Just the first few bars, ten seconds, then silence.

He said, 'This is Martin. I'm at home.'

The connection was cut.

Martin glared at the phone, daring it to ring again. It maintained an operational silence. His mind raced back decades ago to his first posting in the field.

He was in Poland, had just recruited two fishermen to haul certain boxes out of the Baltic and was reporting to an embassy contact in Warsaw. Martin was in the men's toilet in the Grand Hotel and the contact had marched in, metal tips on his heels ringing out, taken up a position at the next urinal and whistled *Yellow Submarine*. Perfect recognition procedure, much better than scraps from a Pinter play. 'Did you send Martha a get well card?' Pause. 'She says there's nothing wrong with her old well.' Longer pause while no one laughs. Whistle and there's no problem with speaking English in a foreign environment. There were certain people who did odd jobs for Martin and he said: 'If your cover is blown, if the dogs are after you, if you can't make it to the embassy, get to a public phone and call me, whistle this ditty and follow the protocol.'

Martin put on his winter coat and hurried out into the fading day. Sometimes you couldn't trust your own phone. You knew who you were calling but you didn't know who was listening.

The telephone box was towards the bottom of Upper Street, a stroll away from Angel tube station. A rash of open kiosks was spreading in London, cheaper, less welcoming to lovers, but hopelessly insecure. This was the old-fashioned red kind that British Telecom was selling off to canny American investors. Every time he walked to the tube station he checked it was still there.

He wasn't as slim as he had been at the Grand in Warsaw and he was wearing an overcoat. His bulk hid his right hand depressing the cradle while his left hand clamped the receiver to his ear and he conducted an animated conversation with himself. Out of the corner of his eye he saw a woman watching, young, black, in a fake leopard skin coat. She was glowering until he gave a beaming smile and she turned away in a sulk. Above the telephone thrusting entrepreneurs had stuck cards advertising their wares: French lessons – strict discipline; Have fun – will travel; Lovely Swedish Model (not a Volvo). He snatched his hand from the cradle before the first ring had finished. He checked his watch: exactly twenty minutes.

'This is Martin. Over to you.'

Yellow Submarine.

'All right this end,' Martin said. 'Careful, Cheltenham could be listening. Who is it? Give me a clue.'

There was a pause and in the end the caller said, 'It's what you put on the table under a plate.'

There was a matching hesitation in Martin until he made the connection. Of course Matt. Matt Clough was self-sufficient as an only child tends to be, damn near bilingual in German, alert to every nuance in the environment, a mite too agreeable to women though that could be a plus, had called Martin 'sir' until Martin put a stop to it. All of which came to him in a rush.

'And I sent you a card last Christmas of the nativity scene and wrote: Mary had the best cover story ever.' Contact confirmed. Martin went on, 'What is it?'

'Trouble.'

Martin said, 'I'm out of the Firm, didn't I tell you?'

'I didn't come here on the Firm's business.'

'Where are you?'

'Riga.'

'Riga?'

'Capital of Latvia.'

'I know where Riga is.' It was just, as Martin didn't say, that Latvia had been bundled into the Soviet Union which he'd never touched. Europe up to the Soviet border had been his patch.

'You're someone I can trust,' Clough said. 'Understand what I mean?'

When you were in badlands and identities and loyalties were blurring, a desperate hunger for a fixed point took over. Martin understood.

'Why are you there?'

'My father was not known – remember?'

'Yes.'

'Turns out he was Latvian. It's hard to get my head round that. Anyway he just died. You got a pen and paper?'

Martin fumbled in an inner pocket. 'Go ahead.'

'Krisj – '

'Stop. You better spell it.'

What names were in the Cheltenham computers? His own for sure, Matt's less likely. The dead Latvian? That depended. Martin tucked the receiver between his shoulder and head. He pressed the notebook against the glass of the phonebox and found the ink in the pen wouldn't flow at that angle. The girl in the fake fur had come back, scowling. He transferred the notebook to a tiny ledge and held it steady while Clough spelled the name.

'A copper gave me the news last week. Name B-E-C-K-E-T-T. Superintendent, Thames Valley Police. Another man had no name but gave me his phone number. Always reach him, he said, no cut-outs.'

'What kind of man?'

'Somebody who preferred the shadows. Somebody you might have come across.'

Martin's view of life brightened. The crawling traffic of Islington could have been in any of the cities he had stalked when Europe was divided. He asked for the telephone number, read it back to make certain he had it right.

'Where are you calling from?'

'Central Post Office.'

'Secure?' Martin was eyeing the black girl who was standing off by the kerb. It had started to spit with rain and she opened an umbrella, white with a pink elephant blowing bubbles from its trunk.

'Yes.'

Clough outlined his weekend: the lawyer who wasn't available, his father's house in the suburbs, the pistol in his face, the woman who picked him up. He spelled her name. 'She lives in Toronto, photographer, got a feature coming up in *National Geographic* in the autumn. So she says. Visiting Riga to research her roots. So she says.'

Was that it? Not enough for Matt to have made a distress call.

'More?'

'I've been mugged and my passport taken.'

'Bona fide mugging?'

'I don't know. The lawyer has something to give me but he needs to see my passport first. I should have a new one by Friday.'

'More?'

'I was followed from my hotel so I challenged the man and we had a chat. F-I-double N-I-S. Here's the nasty thing. You listening? He knew about the Düsseldorf job all those years ago.'

F-I-N-N- Martin paused then went on. –I-S.

'And?'

'Told me my father worked for the Firm. Do you hear me? My father.'

'I hear you.' Martin was full of wonder.

'It goes on. The Russian said that he too worked for us, recruited by a man called Smith. No need to spell that. The Russian admires the Queen and kneels before a picture of Thatcher.'

'Well, well, well.' It was just a holding remark. He moved the receiver away from his ear, staring at it as if it puzzled him. The black girl edged close to the box and was making winding up motions. She'd painted her eyelids pink and her lips gold. Shouldn't it be the other way round? He jammed the receiver back to his ear.

'Today we went to – '

'Which *we* is this?'

'Debbie speaks the language.'

Martin thought about this but his silence seemed an accusation.

'Martin, don't get shitty about this. You're there and I'm here. It's a pig of a language and she's incredibly useful.'

Martin noted how he reacted. Matt and the woman were together. Only a minute ago he'd been suspicious of her. That was Matt.

Clough said, 'We went to another town about an hour away where my father owned a house. He has three houses, did I say that? The back door was unlocked. All right, I know what's going through your mind. Door unlocked? Why didn't Matt turn round and get the hell out?' Clough stopped and Martin said nothing. 'I should have. The house was ransacked. One man did it. One pair of footprints in the snow. Whatever he was looking for he didn't find.'

'You know that?'

'The rooms – every one was trashed. If he'd found it – money, whatever – he'd have stopped. Also – listen – he murdered an old woman, wife, mistress, housekeeper, I don't know. Bludgeoned her to death.'

Martin raised his eyes like a man who had heard the first thunder of an approaching storm. Murder was reason enough to make an emergency distress call. Again he had the sense of being no longer in London but elsewhere in Europe, and the glistening headlights on wet tarmac and the people with their heads down and coat collars up were the same he'd known in Dresden and Gdansk and a dozen other cities. The murder he'd been told about could have been that of anybody. Friend or enemy, it scarcely mattered. A killing marked a shift to a different order of things. The tightening of his nerves was not fear but an alertness, like a tonic.

'Where are you staying?'

'The Konventa Seta. It was that secret bod who booked me in.'

There was a draught of cold air and Martin looked round.

'Oy, haven't you finished yet?'

It was the girl with the elephant umbrella. She stood glaring at him. He could smell her perfume, something that came in a fancy bottle from a market stall.

'I won't be long,' he said.

'I'm not hanging about no longer.' She thrust her hand at him. Martin saw rings like knuckle dusters and a piece of card. 'You fucking stick it up then.'

Making a grab for the card, Martin let the phone slip. It dangled, twisting round on its cord, Clough's voice swelling and fading. 'Martin… Martin…'

'Don't worry,' he said. 'Just a girl.'

'What girl?'

Martin looked at the card. *Want to Stroke a Black Pussy?* he read.

'Martin?'

It was the voice of a man marooned a long way from home. Martin was suddenly brisk, knowing the London working day was winding down.

'What's your hotel phone number?' He wrote it down in his notebook, tucked the girl's card in to mark the place and stowed it in a pocket. 'I'll be in touch. Watch your back.'

* * *

The evening rush had started early because of the rain. Martin teetered on the pavement's edge like a man delaying a suicide dash. His mind was on the telephone box, its smell of a thousand cigarettes, and the sound of Clough's voice. The tone had swung from determined and logical to defensive. No blame in that. He was out in the field even if he was no longer a spy.

Also listen – Martin was listening again – *he murdered an old woman, wife, mistress, housekeeper, I don't know. Bludgeoned her to death.*

Martin heard the emphasis in Clough's voice. *Bludgeoned.* A word straight out of the tabloids. Like slayed. He slayed an old woman, bludgeoned her to death. Was she still lying there? Clough wouldn't have reported it.

With the rain set in and the rush hour under way looking for a taxi was futile but today was a day for miracles: one came dawdling towards him.

The pub was round the corner from the Old Vic. Martin was nursing a whisky. The pub was empty except for two men at the bar, stage hands from the paint dribbles on their boiler suits. There again they might be the Jackson Pollocks of the new millennium. No-one else was in the pub, too early for the pre-theatre crowd. Canned music came from hidden speakers. Musical sawdust in his opinion but good security.

Heather came in from the street, coat collar turned up against the weather and hiding half her face. She spotted Martin at his table against the wall but her gaze went all the way round the room before she came over to him.

'You found it all right,' he said, getting to his feet to help her off with the damp coat. 'Sorry I couldn't remember the name.'

The pub was far enough from the Fortress so Heather wouldn't run into disgruntled toilers, close enough so it wasn't a trek. He'd forgotten his mobile so he'd rung her from a telephone box near Holborn while the taxi waited. Martin kissed her on the cheek which was wet as if she'd been weeping. She stood back a step.

'I have to say, you don't look troubled.' She peered into his face as if it was a puzzle to her. 'There's a glow to you as if…' She didn't finish. A smile dashed across her lips and was gone.

'I said there was trouble, not that I personally was in it. I need your help.'

She said nothing.

'I really do,' he said.

'You're out of the game now, Martin. You're not one of us anymore.'

Her expression told him nothing. Was this Heather speaking or somebody else? Her eyes were steady, staring into his. He said, 'You've been warned off me?'

She shook her head.

'Just talking to you like this, I could be sent to Siberia.'

But she sat down.

She worked in Records, the neon-lit shadowless basement in the Fortress where the archives were buried. Siberia was an unlovely building in a Watford industrial estate where files were sent by armoured van to be put on microfiche.

'What can I get you?' Martin was still standing.

'I have to go back. Plain tonic, ice and lemon.'

Martin was looking down at her with his most sincere smile. He tried to coax an answering smile out of her, some sign of complicity, but her face was unbending. It was as if he had jilted her and was trying to sneak back in her favour. She was a brigadier's daughter beating a slow retreat towards middle age, petite with a body that was still trim. Martin knew that. They had made love, just once, and she had led the way.

He returned with her drink. He lifted his glass, still the same whisky, still the same smile.

'Happy New Year. Is it too late to say that?'

She shook her head as if she was still puzzled. Finally she lifted her glass.

'Happy whatever it is.'

They took modest sips. The pub door opening made them both swing round. It was one of the down-and-outs who'd set up cardboard home on the church steps.

'So how are you?' he asked, straining to get warmth into his voice.

'Oh, I'm fine,' she replied. 'Thank you.'

They could have been talking across a crowded room.

'It's wonderful to see you again. You're looking blooming. Is there a lucky man in your life?'

Even to Martin's ears it sounded forced.

She continued gazing at him and he felt he was a stranger to her and had no right to ask. But if he didn't make it right at the personal level, how could he move onto the real business?

'If there isn't,' he ploughed on, 'I mean if there isn't anyone special, it would be wonderful to have dinner.'

Wonderful, wonderful. He seemed stuck for another word.

She went on gazing. Am I still smiling, Martin asked himself, am I fixed like this for life? Speak to me.

'Or a theatre,' he tried. 'Isn't there a new Ayckbourn?'

No response. She's thinking of when we made love, Martin decided. He'd gone to Poland, nothing urgent, more a nostalgic tour of old 'assets', as they called agents. But the world had changed. Communism had vanished. Poland had joined NATO. So when he was observed with a certain colonel it was thought Martin might be spying for... for whom? The new masters in the Kremlin? For Ghaddafi? Maybe for Mossad? Martin had not been officially arrested. He thought of it as being kidnapped by unsmiling thugs of the state and it took forty-eight hours of pressure from London before he was bundled onto a British Airways flight to Heathrow. At the Fortress the Top Floor was steaming with fury. For Martin the worst feature – absolutely the worst – was that during the two days he was in limbo his wife died. It was their cleaner who found her body in bed. Cardiac arrest was on her death certificate. Guilt overwhelmed Martin; perhaps if he'd been there her life could have been saved.

Months passed. One evening Heather had fallen into step beside him as they left the Fortress and murmured something about supper. Martin, not quite catching her words, asked what she was having.

'I'm inviting you for supper and you're demanding to know the bloody menu?'

So they went back to her flat. When supper was finished and the dishes were washed, she took his hand and led him into her bedroom. Quite naturally. And made love to him, not with passionate desire but with loving care, bestowing light kisses like a butterfly landing all over his body and murmuring *Martin... Martin*. Afterwards, while their sweat cooled, she lay sprawled with an arm across his chest and spoke to the ceiling.

'I'm not in love with you,' she said, 'but I care about you. Mourning is one thing, guilt is something else. Mourning is right and proper and has its place but don't let it take over your life. Blaming yourself doesn't change the past.'

'But if...'

'Hush,' she said. 'Stop brooding. Look outward. I'm not taking you on full time. You'll find another love. What we've done is just to get you started.'

It was an astonishing pep talk, delivered by a naked woman who had just made love. When she saw him in the Fortress a day or so later she gave him a cheery 'Good morning,' as she passed by, brisk and military again.

She'd said she wasn't taking him on so he didn't follow up that night. Was that his mistake? Maybe she hadn't meant it. Did any woman? She was looking at him now, puzzled, and shook her head. 'Oh Martin.' He searched for meaning in those two words. Perhaps it was: It's too late.

Is the past ever over? Give it up, Martin told himself, lay out the problem. Keep it simple.

'There's an occasional I used for little jobs. This is back a few years but I have kept in touch with him. This afternoon he sent a distress call from Latvia. I know I'm out of the game but an emergency is still an emergency. Matt didn't go there on the Firm's business but because his father died. It turns out there was another side to his father and matters in Latvia have taken a murderous turn. There are things I have to know. Latvia and the Sovs were never my target but it's possible his father used to work for us. Well, more than possible.'

Heather's gaze was fixed on his face. His smile was gone. His frown seemed to say: I'm not trying to get back in favour, just asking for a bit of help. She hadn't agreed to give it but she was listening.

He broke off at the sound of a chair scraping. The homeless man had sat at the next table with a pint and a packet of peanuts. He raised his glass.

'Cheers. How's it going? All right?'

Martin nodded to the man and leaned closer to Heather.

'Names. I'll give you three names. I need to know about them, I really do. And a telephone number – who it belongs to.'

He took out his notebook and wrote on a piece of card tucked into it: Finnis, Deborah Brown, Krisjanis Kulbergs. He added the phone number of the man who had no name.

'Finnis is Russian. I don't know about the name. It sounds false, just a workname, but he might have used a corruption of some operational name like Phoenix. Deborah Brown is supposedly Canadian. Again no telling if the name is real. She says she has a feature coming up in *National Geographic*. And K.K. is Matt's father, Latvian. If it's true he used to work for us there should be a lot in the old Soviet section.'

She took the card, studied the names and nodded. She lifted her head and there was something of defiance in her face but it was the authorities she was defying not Martin. He could see a light in her eyes: I'll fight your battles for you like once I took you to bed, just to get you started again. She'd said she wasn't taking him on full time but again Martin wondered if he should have believed that. She turned the card over and read the printed message on the other side. Perhaps one eyebrow twitched but the brigadier's daughter made no comment.

'I'll work late tonight,' she said.

Sally, Martin's wife, once said that the telephone spoke with forked tongue. A call before midnight was a lonely waif wanting a chat. After midnight it was bad news that was too urgent to wait until morning.

The midnight chimes of Martin's long case clock were joined by the warble of the telephone. Midnight. It was the landline not the mobile. Not *Yellow Submarine* sending him out into the London rain to loiter in the telephone box.

He cleared his throat.

'Hello.'

'Thank you for the tonic water,' a voice breathed in his ear. 'It's important I see you. I'm at my flat.'

'You've found…'

She didn't let him finish.

'Come round now.'

She hung up before he could say anything. He was left frowning at a barometer on the wall that forecast *Fine Weather*.

Latvia, January 2001

Chapter 11

Debbie's clothes mingled with Clough's on the floor. The duvet was shoved to the end of the bed. A pillow crashed against the wall. The bedside clock told Clough it was 2.32.

From the bathroom came mock curses of 'Dangbat,' and 'Footle me fods,' followed by a real one, 'Why the fuck does your shower go from freeze-my-ass cold to burn-my-tits hot? Why is there nothing in the middle?'

Now she was humming while she washed away evidence of their love-making, the smell and feel of his skin on her skin. He hadn't joined her. 'If you won't stay the night at least your perfume will.'

'Ah, what a cutie,' she'd said.

'What are you thinking about?'

Debbie stood naked in the door from the bathroom. The workings of Clough's mind made her curious.

'You never can tell,' Clough said.

'Tell what?'

'You, me, here we are.'

She was picking through the heap of their clothes, smiling to herself, when the telephone on the bedside table rang. Clough frowned at it, an intruder in their intimacy, and for no particular reason noted the clock had moved on to 2.44. He had never met Sally, Martin's wife, and hadn't heard her warning about bad news that wouldn't wait until morning, but his face hardened.

He jammed the receiver against his ear.

'Hello?'

A pause was followed by whistling, then silence.

'Hello? Matthew Clough speaking. Can you hear me? This is Matthew Clough.'

He gave his first name in full, a warning, his old tradecraft returning. It's not secure, I'm not alone.

'Matthew Clough,' he said a third time. 'Who is it?'

But the telephone had gone dead.

Debbie had got as far as putting on lacy black unmentionables, as aunt Mona would have it. She wandered across the room while Clough was talking and rested a hand on his shoulder. When he put the phone down she said, 'Who was it?'

'Didn't say. Wrong room, I suppose.'

'I thought I heard whistling. What was he whistling for?'

'Plastered if you ask me.'

Clough summoned up a smile while inside his stomach muscles tightened.

He was running the way he ran to Benson lock in winter along the Thames towpath, with short steps because of the ice. He passed aunt Mona floodlit in the night sky, the guard withdrawn to barracks. In his head he heard Martin's whistle, rough, as if he didn't have enough breath in his lungs. Why the urgency? Traffic lights were at red and he hesitated, running on the spot, fumbling in his pocket for a phone card, then bolting across the intersection, lights still red.

Thirty-five minutes and counting.

He pushed open the door of the Central Post office clutching the phone card. He should have got another. International calls ate cards. He dialled and listened to mysterious clicks: this one in Riga, that one in Islington and now one in Cheltenham where bored listeners were glad of a diversion.

In faraway London the telephone was ringing and then it wasn't. Nobody spoke. The etiquette was that the caller made the first move. Clough whistled *Yellow Submarine*, needing to break off twice to draw breath.

'You weren't alone,' Martin said.

'I had to wait for her to leave,' Clough replied.

'You're not calling from the hotel?'

'No.'

Clough turned his back to the wall so he could sweep his eyes round the room. There was a group of four men, drunk. Two girls who were part of the party were sharing a telephone, one speaking, then the other. They're trying to hustle up a girlfriend or two to make up the numbers, he decided.

'I've been getting help from a toiler in the Fortress,' Martin said. 'Your father *is* well known to the Firm. There are bulky files not yet reduced to microfiche. The whole lot is embargoed – understand my meaning? Anything dangerous to the Firm itself is buried there. For Top Floor and God only, provided God knows this week's password which is Scandal. *However*,' Martin seemed to take a deep breath, 'when engineers came to check the security system my friend found out, accidentally on purpose, how to bypass it. Tonight she accessed the files. Here's the bottom line. Your father worked for us for decades. He also worked for Them.'

Clough listened to the words and the spaces between the words and whatever it was the words couldn't say. He repeated, 'Them?'

'Them. Don't be thick.'

A sense of anti-climax settled over Clough. He knew this. All right, here was confirmation from the Firm's embargoed files. But he'd already heard it from Finnis, a Russian spy now in retirement, so no hallelujahs sang out.

'Matt?'

'I'm taking it in.'

'There are other facts, I'm afraid, very…'

There are silences, and an art to interpreting them. If any listener in Cheltenham had the interrogator's art he would say Martin's pause was pulling back from sharing a confidence, and as the pause developed into silence the confidence turned to concern, worry, even fearful worry.

'Let's say the facts mean trouble. I'll move on. Your bedmate I have nothing on for now. Nor F-I-double-N-I-S. There's something you can do about that. Fax me a photo and I'll see if I know him. If not, I'll ask a helpful pal who dealt with the evil Bear to cast an eye. Got a pen and paper handy? I'll give you my home fax number.'

'I don't have a photo of Mr F.'

Weariness, irritation, possibly even a rebuff from Heather caused Martin's usually calm voice to harden.

'Damn well get one.'

That same Wednesday morning, after not much sleep, Clough picked his way with care through the frozen streets of the old town. Men with axes attacked humps of compacted snow on the pavements. Finnis was waiting for him, stamping his feet outside the Opera House.

'Jesus, it's cold. Let's go and have coffee.'

That wasn't Clough's idea at all.

'I prefer to be outside.'

'Listen, after God created snow, He made up for it with warm cafés.'

'So people could sit at the next table and spy.'

'What do you mean?'

Clough was already walking away. Finnis would follow. Clough aimed for the strip of park behind the Opera. Leafless trees stood like stage props. Ducks skidded on the frozen pond. Finnis hurried to catch up.

'What spies? What do you mean?'

Clough stopped. A bench had been provided by a thoughtful city so old ladies with shopping bags could rest. He brushed away a sprinkling of snow and sat. Finnis checked all round and lowered himself.

'It's urgent,' Clough said. 'I told you that but it's not something to discuss on the phone. I don't trust telephones, not anymore.'

Finnis moved his head in a circle like a man easing neckache, glancing to each side. The face Clough remembered as fleshy looked pouchy in full daylight. The eyes that fixed on Clough were veined. They flicked over Clough's shoulder then came back. He frowned and blinked. He was edgy. Bad conscience? Clough wondered about accusing him then went right the other way.

'We're on the same side, Finnis. This is why I'm telling you, alerting you. Day before yesterday, late afternoon, we talked. We went to a café. There were a couple of other customers but they were there already and they weren't close. How about the waitress? Do you know her? Is she all right? Could she have overheard?'

Finnis had half turned towards Clough. He frowned, running a gloved hand across his mouth.

'Overheard what?'

'Afterwards we walked.' Clough ignored the question. 'People passed us. You talked about being recruited, same side as me. Half-way across the bridge we stopped. I don't know but someone could have tailed us. It was sleeting, a bit murky. Someone could have followed and then crammed himself behind a beam and overheard what I said. It could have been - that is all I'm saying.'

'Nobody was behind us. I checked.'

'You checked at the lights. Did you check after that?'

Finnis frowned.

'You can never swear you haven't been overheard,' Clough said. 'Could have been someone with a directional mike at the end of the bridge.'

'What are you getting at?'

'My father had a house in Sigulda. I told you that.'

Finnis had a glove off. He put a cigarette in his mouth, snapped his lighter a couple of times for a flame, drew in deeply. Was he working out his response? He looked at Clough.

'So?'

'So I went to Sigulda yesterday but I was too late.'

'Too late for what?'

'Someone could have overheard and got there before me.'

'What are you getting at?'

'Footsteps in the snow. Back door unlocked. House turned upside down. Somebody had been looking for something. Upstairs do you know what I found?'

Finnis stared at Clough, waiting.

'I found Krisjanis Kulbergs' mistress or housekeeper.'

Finnis took a deep pull at his cigarette. His expression didn't change, not a flicker.

'Dead?' he said.

'Dead. She was on the floor by the bed. She had been beaten about the head by a heavy silver candlestick. Her face was a mess and there was blood on her nightdress, blood on the rug.'

'Jesus, it's early in the day for details.'

Finnis looked away to two young girls in a hurry, exercise books in mittened hands, late for school. Across the frozen water a tourist had a camera to her face, lining up a shot of the Opera House. Clough waited until Finnis met his eyes again.

'It can't have been somebody who happened to overhear us talking,' Clough said. 'Too much of a coincidence. It had to be someone from K.K.'s past who knew he was dead but wasn't expecting the old woman.'

'What was he looking for?'

'You tell me.'

'Me? Why me?' But he gave some thought to it. 'He wouldn't keep much cash in the house. A bit of run-money is all.'

'It had to be someone who knew him and wanted some special thing.'

'The police have any ideas?' Finnis asked.

Clough didn't answer.

Finnis took a final puff before tossing away the stub. Three or four ducks came waddling, then quacked disapproval.

'I get you.'

'I saw it like this,' Clough said. 'Am I the sole heir? Maybe not. I might have had to share his property with the old woman. But not if she's dead. There's a motive the police mind can grasp.'

'So you tiptoed out? Fingerprints?'

'I hadn't taken my gloves off.'

'A pro.'

'You gave me your telephone number. So…' Clough got to his feet. Leave it a moment or two so Finnis begins to wonder. '…I'm giving you this warning.'

Finnis swung round. 'Warning?'

'It wasn't money the intruder was after. A list of names? You were in the same line of business so is your name on the list?'

Finnis stared at Clough and muttered something sharp in Russian. 'I'm going for coffee,' he said, 'and something stronger.'

Churches I have prayed in, Clough thought, praying the contact would come. The windows down one side had stained glass. On the other side all the glass was plain as if a wartime bomb had cleared the lot. Clough walked down the nave and back along the aisle by the plain windows. Slabs of stone were stacked beside a heap of sand. Nobody was working. The church was empty.

He took a seat where he could be seen from the entrance. Go for a church if you can – the gospel according to Martin. Keep away from bars. Your accent gives you away the moment you order a drink. Strangers will talk to you and remember you. In a church you can be a believer, you can be a tourist, you can be resting your feet. No one talks to you.

'Matt Clough, bastard, praying for forgiveness.'

Debbie dropped into the seat beside him. A knitted bobble hat covered her short dark hair. She wore a padded jacket. Snowflakes on her shoulders were turning to glistening drops of water. Her lips were pressed tight, her brows knotted with anger as if she'd uncovered some infidelity.

'You got a photo?' Clough asked. She carried nothing, no bag, no large envelope.

'Damn right I got a photo. Whether you get it is another fucking thing altogether. You tell me what's going on. Who was the bad man on the bench? And who…' her voice dropped to a conspirator's whisper, '…are you, Matthew Clough?'

Not Matt but Matthew as in Martin's warning signal: watch out. It was a marvel how her voice changed, how she played with it, showing her range like an actress at an audition. Now her anger… He was listening not to her words but to what was behind them, unspoken. She had insinuated herself, wormed her way into his life. *We can do something. We can go to Sigulda.* Her anger was because she felt she had been duped. It wasn't as a lover, it wasn't as a friend. It was something else.

'Why the hell don't you answer me?' she said.

'Because I don't know what's got into you.'

He looked in her face and saw the same frown. She was saying nothing, waiting for him. What the hell, he thought, I am innocent, I am wrongly accused of unknown crimes, I can show a little muscle too.

'I come to Riga. We meet and become lovers. I ask you to do me a favour and you attack me as if I was Hitler and Stalin rolled into one. Asking you to take a photo - what the hell's wrong with that? Who are you, Deborah Brown?'

Her eyes held his, looked away, and when they came back they were still shadowed with suspicion.

'I thought we were friends and you go round hiding things from me.'

Clough took the opening. 'We are friends, Debbie. That's why I asked you to do this. Man found out – don't ask me how because I don't know – that I was staying at the Konventa Seta. He said he had known my father and wanted to shake my hand. Con artist I thought, after a chunk of my father's money. I still can't figure out why he wanted to meet me. Maybe the con is still to come. So I decided a photo of him would be useful. I could show it to the lawyer or the police. OK?'

She looked away again. Your call, Clough decided. You accused me, I answered, so what do you do now? They sat in silence. After a while Debbie took a small breath and blew it out.

'Saying sorry is the hardest thing.'

Was that an apology? Clough said nothing.

'I didn't get enough sleep last night. Or the night before, I guess.'

Leaning across she gave him a sisterly peck on the cheek. As part of the same movement she winkled a brown envelope from under her jacket and slid it onto his lap. Done like a pro in a hostile environment.

At the front desk of the Konventa Seta Clough smiled at one of the blonde receptionists.

'Can I send a fax to England?'

'Certainly sir.'

'A photograph?'

'No problem.'

The print showed Clough and Finnis seated on a bench. Clough was half turned inward but Finnis was taking a cigarette out of a packet and staring straight at the camera. Across the bottom Clough scribbled: *Here I am enjoying a joke with a friend.* Neither of them was laughing.

A fax was safe, wasn't it? You couldn't overhear a fax. No voice recognition program could monitor it. No key words would trigger the computers at Cheltenham. Yes, I'm all right, he decided. He was just inside his bedroom when the telephone rang. A fax had come, the receptionist said. A reply already?

He went back down and took the sheet of paper. *Afraid I didn't get the joke so I'm going to ask a pal who knows all the old ones.* Signed *M.*

Chapter 12

Clough looked at the interpreter and looked again. About his own age, he decided. Clough had a hopeful attitude which placed many women in this category. Maybe a year or two older but she'd determined to stop right there. Not another line would define her face. Her body would stand firm against the years. And her eyes - when she spoke her gaze held his, wouldn't let go.

'The captain is pleased you came so quickly.'

Pleased? The captain's face showed no pleasure. This was the same police station where he had reported his passport stolen. The captain wasn't in uniform but wore one of those lumpy grey suits left over from communist days.

'So the captain is pleased. That makes one of us.' The woman didn't blink as Clough stared at her. 'I'm here because a policeman knocked at my door at the hotel. "Great," I thought, "my passport's been found." The policeman spoke phrasebook English. "You come, Mister." He didn't understand anything I said.'

When the captain spoke his lips scarcely moved. His voice was a growl. The interpreter said, 'Have you found your passport? The captain wishes to see it.'

'The captain knows it's been stolen. Or maybe he doesn't. I reported it stolen at this police station on Monday. I signed a statement, one copy to give to my embassy, one copy to rot in your files.'

'He thinks maybe your passport was only misplaced and you have found it again.'

'Misplaced? You tell the captain I reported that I was mugged at knifepoint by three men. That is a new definition of misplacing.'

'The captain wishes to know when you entered Latvia and what is the purpose of your visit.'

The captain hadn't spoken. She had an open pad on her lap but never glanced at it.

'I've answered these questions already. Why do I have to go through all this again? Ask the captain why he doesn't speak to his men.'

The woman translated and at a query seemed to translate again. They both stared at Clough.

'Mr Cloff,' the interpreter said, 'the captain desires that you should explain. Who are "his men"? He hasn't spoken to any men. He hasn't given orders to any men.'

Mezaparks, Clough explained, the house of his father. Yes indeed – in response to her query – his father was Krisjanis Kulbergs. Then there were the two police who came out of the front door, kidnapped him, took him in a car, the questioning, the pistol in his face.

'The captain desires to know why you are lying.'

Keep your temper under control because you give away less. That had been drummed into Clough during training but it was difficult.

'I am not.'

'These men you say were police, were they in uniform?'

'No. Nor is the captain.'

'Was it in a car marked Police?'

'No.'

'Did they show you identity? Did they tell you their names? Did they say what department of police they were from?'

Clough didn't answer.

'Mr Cloff, what did these men want with you?'

'I don't know.'

'But you went in their car.'

'I was forced to. Perhaps it was to frighten me.'

'Mr Cloff, are you easily frightened? You seem – I read the phrase in an American magazine – a cool customer. Even now you show no fear.'

'Why should I be frightened? I have committed no crime.'

'You have nerves of steel – I have read that too. Let us go back to these men.'

'I'll tell you this – I was frightened by them. A pistol pointed between the eyes has this effect.'

'They must have wanted something.'

'Like the captain, they asked to see my passport.'

'Did you show it to them?'

'Yes. They wanted to know when I came to Latvia.'

'But they could ask Immigration at the airport.'

'Perhaps they couldn't,' Clough said.

'Explain please.'

'Perhaps you are right and they did not have the authority. If they were impersonating police officers, that is a crime the captain could investigate.'

The woman's face was in sudden movement, her lips pursing, an eyebrow rising. She translated. The captain growled something, several things.

'Mr Cloff, save us the trouble of asking Immigration, tell us when you came to Latvia.'

'On Friday afternoon. I caught a flight from Heathrow to Stockholm, changed planes, Stockholm to Riga. SAS. Ask them. It'll be in their computer.'

'Oh we will, Mr Cloff. Last Friday? Not the Friday before?'

'No.'

'Mr Cloff, are you married?'

'No.'

'Did you come to Latvia alone?'

'Yes.'

'Then who is the woman seen coming out of your room?'

This had to be a bluff, a trick. But instinct warned him not to deny it. 'Madame, it is not unknown for a man on his own to find a woman.'

'Where do you look in Riga?'

'You can make friends in one of your many bars. If you are desperate, you can pick up a woman outside the station.'

'You have been to the station?'

'I have walked round the city. I have seen the station.'

'Mr Cloff, you took a train.'

Never help the other side, never give them an opening. Martin had drummed that into him.

'Why don't you answer?'

'You didn't ask a question.'

'Mr Cloff, you took the train to Sigulda yesterday. Is that not true? The woman who inspects tickets on the 10.34 train remembers two foreigners. The man did not speak. The woman spoke Latvian but with a foreign accent, maybe Swedish. What do you say?'

'I don't speak Swedish. I don't know any Swedish women.'

'That is a trivial objection. Maybe she was another nationality. She could even have been British like you. Be careful how you answer.'

'I did not go to Sigulda,' he said flatly.

Did she believe him? Her eyes had fixed on him, trying to get inside his head. *I got it wrong*, he realised. *She's not the interpreter, she's the captain's superior.* He had launched into a rumbling sort of complaint. Abruptly he pushed back his chair and left the room. When the door opened Clough caught the sound of an old manual typewriter from the secretary's office, and from further off a ringing telephone.

What's this? It was as if the captain's exit had changed her. She leaned towards him.

'Mr Cloff, you must tell the truth.' Her voice had softened. 'We are not monsters in Latvia. We know human weakness can lead to mistakes and we are capable of forgiving. We are happy to be free after years of Nazis and Communists. We see you – an Englishman – as a particular friend because your government never accepted that Latvia was part of the Soviet Union.'

Turning out nice again, Clough thought. The good cop/bad cop routine.

She went on, 'The captain suffered when the Russians ran our country, so he can be merciful. No, I don't mean merciful, perhaps I should say understanding. He was not a captain then. We were a colony and the Russians were our masters. They kept the senior posts for themselves. Police, army, ministries, television, radio - to be a boss you had to be Russian. Latvians swept the streets and stood back when a big black Zil drove by. Latvians died on the battlefield but did not give the order to attack.'

She came to a halt. She reached into a handbag for cigarettes then held out a lighter to him. He pressed the lever three times before he got a flame.

'You're not in the police, are you?'

He couldn't think what made him say that. She looked in his face.

'I thought you were the interpreter but you're not. You're more. I think you are much more.'

She drew on the cigarette, blew out smoke, then waved it away as if she wanted to see him more clearly.

'You're from one of the ministries. Let me see. Interior? No?' She didn't reply. 'How about the Foreign Ministry, is that it? Your English is so good. Were you in London? Maybe you weren't diplomatic, maybe you were on the trade side. Or Aeroflot? They had a huge office in Piccadilly though I never saw anyone in it. Who would choose to fly Aeroflot?'

None of these questions did she answer. She continued drawing on her cigarette, studying him, his face and his gestures.

'Where has the captain gone?'

Her answer was a warning.

'If you are lying the captain will be very angry. I know the captain when he is angry. Sometimes he forgets his manners. It is because of the years when he was…' She pressed down with her thumbs. 'Too much pressure. So now sometimes…' The hands opened, the fingers flying upwards. 'The volcano erupts.'

Clough regarded those hands, how the fingers splayed like an explosion.

She was gazing at Clough again, her eyes unblinking. She could have been a trial lawyer or an interrogator, some close observer watching for tics and hesitations and evasions. Then, in a flash, he turned it round. She hadn't been an interrogator; she had been on the receiving end, watchful for sharp questions, wary of traps, alert for tricks.

'At some time you've been a prisoner here,' Clough said. 'I'm right, aren't I?'

'Mr Cloff, we were all prisoners, our whole nation. We were economic prisoners and political prisoners. We had life sentences. In the worst times, death sentences. Then in 1991 the prison doors were flung open. And now? I would say we are prisoners of our own freedom. We shake the bars in desperation but there is no escaping our own failings and weaknesses. Our sentence is to bear responsibility for our acts.'

The captain burst in, flinging the door open so it banged against the rubber stop nailed to the floor. He wanted to get at Clough. He was across the room in four paces and leaning down to shout in Clough's face. His jacket fell open so Clough saw the pistol in its holster.

'I told you he would be angry,' the woman said. 'I warned you not to lie.'

'What's he saying?'

'He is swearing, Mr Cloff. He is swearing in Russian because it is more satisfying than swearing in Latvian. If he knew English he would swear in that too. He says you fuck your mother, Mr Cloff, and much else. It really is very bad. I won't translate for you.'

The captain gripped a fistful of Clough's shirt. Maybe he was lining up a punch in the face with his big fist. A vein throbbed along one temple. A scar along his jaw showed white.

'Oh, I hope he doesn't, Mr Cloff. For a man like you it would be terrible.'

Clough's heart was racing. He heard the captain's bellows but he heard the typewriter clacking as well. Nobody came. Nothing unusual here. The telephone was still ringing. Perhaps these reminders of the outside world penetrated the red curtain of the captain's anger. He dropped Clough, kicked the door shut and slumped into his own chair. He slammed a fist on the desk and another outburst followed.

'Jesus Christ, he is saying. Also that he will… Oh, that would be most painful. You poor man. Are you frightened?'

Clough took a moment thinking what to say.

'Yes.'

'That is what the captain intends.'

'What have I done to make him angry?'

She spoke to the captain and listened to his reply, nodding her head.

'He says you and a woman went to Sigulda. The man you say was your father had a house there and you went to that house. You were seen by two men who were checking some pumping equipment. The captain has just been speaking to these men. They remember the woman very well but the man less so because they didn't look at him so much. This is normal in my opinion. In your father's house a corpse has been found. An old woman has been murdered. Also the house was in an uproar caused by burglars.'

Don't challenge her, Clough knew. Focus on the captain.

'And the captain believes I did that?'

'You did not report it to the police. A terrible crime. Only the guilty would close the door and walk away.'

'Does the captain believe I would kill an old woman if I had been seen by two witnesses? Does he believe I would steal something from a house that belonged to my father and which now belongs to me? The captain is a policeman, maybe a captain of detectives. Doesn't he believe in logic?'

'There is a time for logic, Mr Cloff, and there is a time for emotion. In my experience it is not in our nature to have both at once.'

The captain was talking in bursts and she paused to listen.

'He says the house has none of your fingerprints which means

116

you were wearing gloves. The logic, if you like, is that you went in prepared. You broke into the house with the intention of committing a crime.'

'How does the captain know my fingerprints? He is making it all up. He has gone mad.'

'Possibly, Mr Cloff. Possibly you are mad too which would account for such behaviour. It is a mad world we live in. I am not the first person to remark it.'

'I want to speak to someone from the British embassy.'

'Do you have business with them? You could have secret contacts concerning your presence in our country.'

'I am being accused of murder. I want legal and consular help.'

'Are you sure you do not work for the British secret service?'

'No.'

She sucked in her lips while she considered his denial. Was the No too quick? Too emphatic? Too shrill? Too whatever-it-is that means Yes?

'What is your occupation?'

'I am a wine merchant.'

'A merchant.' Something about this enchanted her. 'There is no shoe merchant or fish merchant or book merchant but there is a wine merchant. English is a language with many wrong turnings. Devious I would say. Explain please.'

The captain had fallen quiet, glowering at them. The questioning was by the woman.

'I import wine and sell it in England.'

'It is a big company? You are an important man?'

'It is a very small company. I run it with a partner. We employ one other person, a driver-cum-warehouseman-cum-guard. Also he drinks the bottles that fall off the back of the lorry.'

'Surely they are broken. I do not understand.'

'It is a joke.'

'Why do you joke? Do you find the situation you are in funny?'

'It is an English habit. It lowers the tension.'

'You are a people apart.' She contemplated him severely. Jokes were in poor taste at such a moment. 'Did you come to Latvia to buy wine?'

'There is no wine grown here.'

'But there is, Mr Cloff. At Sabile there is a vineyard.'

'This is not possible. It is too far north. The wine would be terrible.'

'It *is* possible. They said it would not be possible to be free of Russia but we have done that too. The vineyard has been replanted. That shows faith in our future though I agree with you it would take great faith to drink the wine. What is the name of your company?'

'In Vino Veritas.'

She put her head back, looking at him, frowning. Another joke? She shrugged. 'What is the name of your partner?'

'Lewis.'

'Give me the telephone number. I shall speak to Mr Lewis.'

You are in enemy hands. You are being held captive in some Lubyanka. There is a break in the interrogation. The tormentor has left the room. This is a deliberate tactic so you have time to reflect on the hopelessness of your position.

A murder has been discovered. You are the suspect.

But it is more than that. The captain can be left to deal with sordid crimes. What does the woman do?

The typewriter made the same clatter as the one in Birznieks' office. Would nobody answer the telephone? The captain sat like a prison warder. When Clough rolled his shoulders to ease the tension the captain edged forward.

She'd been gone a long time. She couldn't just be talking to Godfrey, she must be consulting someone else. She was from a different bureaucracy, a different world. And he found her a most attractive woman. He imagined there was something Parisian about her, her direct stare showing a hint of challenge. He liked that idea. She would be the French woman that every English schoolboy fantasised about. When their passion was spent she would lie back with a cigarette and they would enjoy a little intellectual afterplay, discussing the pitfalls of freedom and attempting to escape through the bars of their own failings.

He was accused of murder and he had these fantasies. He was mad.

The woman returned, sat in her chair and got out a cigarette. Once again she handed her lighter to Clough and her eyes held his above the flame. It was a cliché from an old movie, Clough knew, but still…

'Mr Lewis said, "Tell him that God will punish the sinner." It was something to do with tax returns you didn't finish.'

'His first name is Godfrey. God for short.'

She leaned back in her chair. *She's doing it on purpose*, Clough thought, *distracting me*. She wore a pale blue blouse with a rounded collar and it rose and fell with every breath.

'Another of your English jokes, Mr Cloff?'

She raised an eyebrow but Clough said nothing. She turned to the captain and spoke to him. He seemed to object, his voice harsh. She said something else and when the captain interrupted she sat up straight and raised a hand. The captain switched his gaze from the woman to Clough. He gave the slightest nod which Clough translated as: I'll be seeing you some time in the future, pal.

'You are free to leave now, Mr Cloff. The captain agrees that no one can positively identify you as the man who went to Sigulda. There are none of your fingerprints in the house. You cannot be arrested or charged so there is no legal justification for keeping you. Speaking frankly I would say this was a golden opportunity. You may wish to take advantage of it to leave Latvia.'

Clough stared at her. Had he heard right?

'When I get my new passport.'

'When is that?'

'Friday.' He added, 'With luck.'

'Do not involve yourself in any more trouble. Be a tourist. Go to a bar and meet some more of our girls. I am sure a man like you will have no difficulty in amusing himself.'

Clough stood up. 'You knew Krisjanis Kulbergs was my father when I was brought here. How did you know?'

'We hear things.'

'What is your name?'

'Why do you want to know?' she asked.

'It's a small world. Perhaps…' Clough hesitated.

'You will soon have flown away. You do not need to know my name.'

She tilted her head towards the door in a gesture of dismissal. With his fingers resting on the handle, Clough turned and saw she was watching him. Her head was on one side as if considering what she had said and drawn back from saying.

'Lucija.'

When she gave her name – and it was softly spoken – her forehead wrinkled as if she was puzzled by her own behaviour.

'And your surname?'

'It is a secret.'

'Suppose I need to contact you. I might have a problem getting my passport.'

She pursed her lips a moment. '07 21 91 81.'

They had made love though Debbie hadn't thrown a pillow. It is mellowing, Clough thought, maturing. She lay staring at the ceiling.

'Do you think we are free?' he asked, as if the question followed naturally from their love-making.

'Free of what?'

'Do we live in freedom?'

'Sure,' she said, giving it no thought.

'Is it possible to be a prisoner of freedom?'

'I don't understand.'

'Suppose I am living in freedom. Can I look out through the bars…' Clough held a hand in front of his face, fingers apart and rigid '…of my failings and weaknesses? What am I looking at on the other side of the bars?'

Debbie rolled on her side to face him.

'Matt, what the hell is this?'

He didn't answer. *I am responsible for my own acts*, he told himself. *I can regret the things I have done. But at the end of my life it is the things I have not done that I'll regret more.*

I am Mr Cloff, he told himself, *Cloff as in cough.*

Chapter 13

They'd kissed goodbye and then at the bedroom door Debbie paused. What made her turn back?

She said, 'It's tough trying to dig up my roots. It's all gone.'

For the first time she was talking about why she'd come to Riga.

'How come?' Clough said.

She looked straight at him.

'Burned. Bulldozed. Shelled. Knocked down. Shredded. Bayoneted. Gassed. Shot. Hanged. Deported. Finally solved.'

Each word was a hammer blow. A shadow had settled over her face.

'The Holocaust, Matt.' She bent towards him as if talking to a child.

'You're a Jew?'

'Well, Jew*ish*. I wouldn't go the whole hog.' She tried a smile. 'C'mon, you knew, you guessed. The eyes, Matt.' She smoothed both eyelids with her middle fingers. 'The eyes tell you. I'm Jewish through my mother's family. Grandparents saw the hurricane coming and emigrated but great aunts and great uncles and great grandmothers and cousins of all kinds stayed put.'

She opened the door.

'Have you traced them?'

'Hey, what traces? You're a Brit so you have a narrow perspective of the war. You see the lesser breeds of Europe falling down in front of the Nazis. You were taught about Dunkirk and Winnie with his cigar and the Battle of Britain and the few who saved the world from darkness. Other wars were going on but… they're not part of your national myth. Before the starting pistol was fired,' and she pointed a finger at her head, 'forty thousand Jews lived here. When Stalin grabbed Latvia he had some empty huts in the Gulag so he shipped a few thousand off to Siberia. Then the Germans kicked the Soviets out and Hitler's lovelies got to work. When the Red Army returned the Jews had all gone up the chimney or huddled together in mass graves. A hundred came out of attics, no more. They'd been hidden by virtuous gentiles. One hundred Jews left out of forty thousand.'

She stopped. The silence went on a little too long and she shrugged. She took a step into the corridor and stopped again. A stretch of old city wall ran right through the hotel and metal plates made a gangway across it. There was the clang of shoes on iron and the sound of two men out of sight.

'Debbie…'

'Don't say you're sorry. You had nothing to do with it. You want to know more, go to the Jewish Museum. Speak to the old guardian. She's alive because her family fled to Kazakhstan. Latvia to Kazakhstan, that's some journey. Then back again after the war. So maybe she's a bit…' Debbie tapped her forehead. 'Can you blame her? Just be gentle.'

It was mid-morning when Clough knew he was being followed. He had the day to fill and was heading for the Jewish Museum when he had a tickle. A man in a flat cap came out of the café near the hotel then turned to look in a shop window at precisely the moment that Clough swung round to admire a fancy doorway. It was *Jugendstil*, all elegance from the time Germany was famed throughout Europe for its culture not its concentration camps. *Gotcha*, Clough thought, and walked on.

He gazed up at a roof where a pair of rampant black cats raised their backsides at the bourgeoisie. He cast an eye at the river where grey ice floes mirrored the clotted sky. He looked at St John's and

St Peter's churches. He shook his head over the statue of a rooster perching on a cat which balanced on a dog which was standing on the neck of a braying donkey. All right, Clough decided, I've shown I'm a tourist.

The man in the flat cap followed. When a street was empty the man held back. When there was a crowd he came closer. One man. An amateur. A pro would at least swap the headgear.

A department store offered a café on the top floor. There was a lift or a long climb up the stairs. Clough took the lift. He was sitting by a window when his tail appeared and seated himself against a wall.

Clough watched from the corner of his eye. A waitress approached, stood at his shoulder then bent lower. She'd do that for a foreigner, to make out what he was saying.

Clough paid and stood by the lift doors where a grey-haired couple were waiting. The lift arrived, the three of them got in and as the doors slid shut the man in the flat cap went dashing for the stairs. It was four flights down. At the bottom Clough held back while the couple got out. He pressed the button for the fourth floor again. As the doors closed he caught sight of the man in the flat cap. He came down the stairs and ran for the door to the street.

Clough was close to his hotel so he called in to dump his guide book.

'Any messages?'

'No, Mr Cloog.'

She didn't smile.

'Nobody telephoned?'

'No sir.'

Still no smile.

'Nobody came in and asked for me?' Sometimes you needed to frame the question differently.

Blonde curls shook.

It was the blondeness of the receptionists that had been the problem. Clough couldn't tell them apart. Until now. This one didn't smile. Somebody had got to her and bought her smile.

He stood outside his room, key-card in hand. *You never know, do you?* He had been mugged. Twice he'd been followed. A woman with secrets had picked him up. An old woman had been beaten to death. No, you never know. He put the card back in his pocket.

He knocked on the door. He gave three taps, two taps, three taps, like a pre-arranged signal. He waited, checking back over his shoulder he was alone. Was anybody inside, waiting for him? He repeated the knocks, more boldly this time. With his ear pressed to the door panel he heard nothing. He counted to ten. He went 'Waah waah,' like a muffled name, a colleague asking to be let in. Give it another ten and he'd use the card. He was counting and hearing nothing when the door silently unlocked, opened a crack and an eye inspected him. The door eased back further and he came face to face with his onetime controller and confidante Martin.

Martin sat on the desk chair, Clough on the edge of the bed. No room service, Martin insisted. Nobody should see them together. Clough went to the bar to fetch drinks. Martin frowned at the vodka and Orangina. He had slipped back into Cold War operational routine and had the TV on. It was BBC World where Tim Sebastian was interrupting an American senator. Martin leant across to part the curtains and peer outside. He dragged his chair closer to hear what Clough was saying.

'What's so important about Krisjanis Kulbergs? He's dead. Why do I attract so much interest? The Canadian woman picked me up, then I get mugged...'

'You think that's connected?'

'The jury's out. But she chose the restaurant and I got jumped walking back here. Then Finnis. Now this morning's joker.'

'Yes?'

'Picked me up outside the hotel, trailed after me round the sights.'

'What happened?'

'I lost him. If there's only one he sticks out. And he wore his flat cap the whole time. Amateur.'

Martin sipped his vodka and Orangina and frowned.

'He was the best I could do at short notice.'

He waited for a reaction but Clough said nothing.

Martin took another disapproving sip.

'Orange piss. Don't they have Scotch here? His name is Chapman, the man who tailed you. He's in charge of security at the embassy. Checking the guests at Her Majesty's birthday party is his strong suit.'

'You could have warned me it wasn't some thug on my back.'

'Possibly.' Martin cast a doubtful eye at the telephone.

'Why did you put a tail on me?'

'A worry I had. All that attention you've been attracting and that old woman beaten to death. I got as far as Helsinki last night and managed to phone Chapman. Embassy to embassy patched through by London should be secure. But phoning you here...' Again he glanced at the telephone.

Clough thought of the receptionist who had lost her smile. He nodded.

'I told Chapman to make sure you were tucked up in bed last night and come back after breakfast, lend a hand if anything cropped up.'

'Armed, was he?'

'Well, there *is* a pistol in the strong room. Standard procedure is that the ambassador has to give the green light. Being a diplomat there are times when he is looking the other way. So he might have been armed. Chapman I mean.'

'I was pulled in yesterday afternoon by the police.'

Martin had fingered a gap in the curtain again to look out at the yard. He swung back.

'Tell me.'

Clough told him about the Captain, Lucija, Sigulda, the half-identifications. It was Lucija who interested Martin: her authority, her age, her behaviour, her class.

'She smoked,' Clough said. 'Mind you, they all do. She gave me her lighter and had me bow over her to light her cigarette. Of that class.'

'She told you she was Lucija. Surname?'

'No. But I got her telephone number.'

'Did you now?'

'I had the feeling she'd been under the bright lights at some time.'

'Prison? Police? Back room?'

'Interrogation of some kind.'

'Latvian? Russian? Riga is half Russian, I'm told.'

'Latvian. A nationalist. Strong feelings about the Russians when they ran things.'

Again Martin peeped through the curtains. 'This room makes me uneasy. Ground floor rooms always do.'

'Danger?'

Martin raised a hand and tilted it side to side. Maybe. He went to the door, put the security chain on and opened the door a crack. Nobody. He came back to his chair.

'It's why I got Chapman to trail round after you. The danger comes from your father. He worked for us and he worked for them. Dangerous. But after his death? There's something else - but what? It doesn't help that everybody lies. Your bedmate Debbie Brown, for a start. How goes that?'

'It's not for the long run.'

'How short is the run?' Martin asked.

The answer he got was Clough, in his turn, raising his hand and tilting it side to side.

Martin went on, 'You be careful. The *National Geographic* do not know a Deborah Brown and have bought no photos for a feature on the Canadian backwoods. The fellow calling himself Finnis is interesting. I showed your fax to an old colleague. It caused a little ripple in his grey cells so he did a search. Chummy was old KGB. Been at the UN in New York. Holland, no – a fairy tale. Back to Moscow then posted to Leningrad where he targeted a Norwegian consular official. Then he dropped out of sight, presumed retired in the post-Soviet fall-out. No one heard anything about him until now.'

Clough frowned. 'The Soviet Union is history. So is the KGB.'

'Tell that to Putin. Oh, and the man who came to see you in Wallingford – not the copper, the one who gave no name – '

'Sat in the shadows.'

'Name is West. He's Foreign Office. Works for a small unit called Policy Research Group. I don't know his real interest yet.'

'A spy?'

'He wouldn't see it that way. They dig around the political undergrowth, try to find scandals, discover rotten eggs.'

'Me?'

'No.'

'My father then. But they knew he worked for Moscow. He was a double agent. And it was all a long time ago.'

'Ah.' Martin got up, stretching his shoulders. If there was more to say he was saving it. 'Let's have a bite to eat.' At the door he stopped and laid a hand on Clough's arm. 'I'm retired now. After you spoke to me I found out a bit and realised I had to contact my former employers. Certain things had to be cleared with the Fifth Floor because if they thought I was stirring up trouble – well, they could take away my pension. They could do a damn sight more if the mood took them.'

'You're here officially then.'

'Well now.' Martin gave a glance at the door and took a step back into the room. 'The Firm's not the place you remember or even I remember and I've only been gone a few months. Some nasty people have got their feet under the top desks now. I was at the Fortress – yesterday morning I'm talking about – and I never felt the name was so right. It had a hunkered down feel as if the building was under siege. Top Floor wanted to quiz me. An armed security guard took me to the Deputy Director's office. Faces turned to me, none of them friendly. The Deputy is a woman. "Sit there," she said, pointing.'

Martin raised his hand.

'Not good. I was on one side of the conference table, six of them on the other side. Star Chamber. No one said *Hello Martin, nice to see you again.* Straight in. "There's the stitch-up theory of history and there's the fuck-up theory." That's the finger-stabbing Deputy taking control of business. Notice how it is the women who have scrambled up the ladder, stamping on all the fingers in their haste, who do the swearing these days? She went on, "The stitchers say the KGB, never mind what it's called now, is still the KGB and they've got one of their own as President and they're playing a long game and Kulbergs is one move in it, to drop us in the shit. The fuckers say it is just one of life's messes and we have to sort it out before Fleet Street gets wind. What's your view?" I said that you had used an emergency protocol to ask for help and whatever the sins of the father the son had always been all ours and your call was genuine. She called me a fucking romantic.'

'Charming,' Clough said.

'So I said to her, "Listen, you're the ones living in cloud cuckoo land. Suppose Matthew Clough comes to a sticky end. The Rottweilers of Fleet Street will get you in their jaws and won't let go and that would be ten times worse for you and the Firm and your political masters. Can't you see that?" Silence. She frowned and told me to go and cool my heels outside while they had a pow-wow. Then I was hauled back. The stitchers had won: the Firm couldn't be dragged into a Russian trap. But the fuckers had also won: it had to be sorted out so there would be no scandal. Hooray, everybody's happy. So this is how it is: officially I am not here. I am deniable. But in the tradition of the great British muddle I am officially here unofficially. All clear?'

This tidal wave of words overwhelmed Clough but he clung to one thing. *Sticky end? Me?* Murder always happened to someone else.

Martin opened the door. 'I'll go first. You follow in half a minute. Turn right when you leave the hotel and pootle off. I'll watch your back.'

Chapter 14

Martin didn't drop crumbs of information on the lunch table. The controller/agent bond still held. Don't tell the agent more than he needs to know. Keep him focused on the target. Martin paid the bill, squeezed Clough's shoulder and was gone.

Time to try to understand what demon drives Debbie, Clough decided. There'd be more than one demon but *shot, hanged, bulldozed, deported, finally solved* was on public show, a people's suffering laid out in display cabinets.

The street he wanted was in the nineteenth century commercial district. He turned a corner and came to a building with tall doors. A great vestibule had shops along one side, a café, a moneychanger and an information booth with nobody to help him. A grand staircase led up and a sign pointed the way. He climbed up and a sign pointed higher. The staircase dwindled in grandeur. On the next floor he found himself in an antechamber with a choice of half a dozen doors, none of them marked. He waited until a man clutching an armful of files backed out of one of the doors.

'Museum?' Clough asked.

'*Muzejs,*' he replied, nodding at one of the unmarked doors.

Clough went into a poky lobby with posters on the walls he had no time to inspect. A woman seated behind a table crammed with cardboard boxes peered at him over wire-rimmed spectacles. She'd been reading a book and she marked her place in it with a finger.

'Hello, good afternoon,' Clough said. 'I was hoping to be able to… Oh, do you speak English?'

'Most certainly. English, Latvian, Hebrew, Russian. Also German.'

'I wanted to have a look round the Jewish Museum.'

'You have come to the correct place.'

Her eyes inspected Clough's face, perhaps measuring his eyelids whose importance Debbie had stressed.

'There's no sign on the door, that's the trouble.'

'That is true. But I would say that people who have a genuine interest will find the way. Are you staying long in Latvia?'

'A week, more or less.'

'Shalom.' Her eyes moved to his coat. 'You can leave your coat here. It is warm enough, I think.'

There were no hangers, no closet. Clough draped his coat over a chair. In case of attack, he decided, neo-Nazis with aerosol cans hidden in their coat pockets. She was calm as she watched him, maybe a little distracted as if her mind kept slipping away to another world.

'Where are you from?' she asked.

'England.'

'Oh, England,' she repeated, putting her head to one side while she considered England's worthiness. By degrees her eyes lost their focus on Clough. Some private vision held her, a green and pleasant land, a Royal coach clip-clopping down the Mall, a thatched cottage with hollyhocks round the door, a red double-decker bus, Winnie making a V sign.

'Go ahead,' she said. 'There is no other person in the museum. You will be alone with the testament of history. If you have questions, I am here. I will do my best though some questions have no answers.'

Clough went through an arch and it hit him.

Questions, yes, such as why is there no air in here? And no noise? Who has stolen the soundtrack? Who has squeezed all the smells out? And these photographs on the walls, dozens of them, hundreds, why do they show no happy people? Why is there not one smile between them? Why are some photos in black and white and some the colour of sun-dried blood? Why are the children not playing hopscotch? Why are there no lovers laughing on their wedding day? Why do these schoolgirls stare at the camera as if it is stealing their souls? Why are these bankers, lawyers, musicians, dancers, architects, surgeons, teachers stopped in their tracks as if they have heard a gunshot? Which ones are Debbie's great aunts and great uncles and cousins of various kinds?

Four rooms ran together without the formality of doors. This first room showed life up to the First World War. Had Debbie pored over these images for her roots?

The next room showed life between the wars though some argued there was really one long war with a pause for breath at half time. While the important players rubbed their bruises Latvia had enjoyed a make-believe independence. Here was a snapshot of life when Jews had lived freely among Germans and Latvians and Russians. Here were actors who had long ago taken their final curtain call, a *corps de ballet*, swans in tutus, a writer with a thinker's pipe and a creative frown. On his desk was an inkwell, a pen, an ashtray and a magazine. Clough could just make out the title: *Idischer Bilder*. Children stood on the seashore, fully dressed, storm clouds massing on the horizon. Clough peered at a sportsman hoisting a team mate on his shoulders. Centre forward of the Latvian football team, a caption said. 1937 was the date. Didn't he know the final whistle was about to be blown?

A family group posed in a sitting room with an upright piano and a gilt mirror and potted plants and floor-length curtains and gas lamps on the wall. A father in Sabbath best sat to attention in an overstuffed chair, a mother rested a hand on his shoulder, two girls and a boy held their breath. What happened to them, to their home? *Burned. Bulldozed. Shelled. Knocked down. Shredded. Bayoneted. Gassed. Shot. Hanged. Deported. Finally solved.* Clough advanced until he almost touched noses with them but could recognise nothing of Debbie, no free spirit, no laughter. What earthquake can they feel before it happened? What echo do they hear before the gunshot? What screams burst out before they open their mouths?

Some questions have no answers.

Turning, his hip nudged a display cabinet. Fragments of a people's existence were pinned like butterflies under glass. There was a piece of Torah scroll, apparently ripped off. Hebrew writing was chiselled into a slab of stone. Twisted ironwork might have been a candleholder. A yellow star, singed by fire. A gold ring.

'From one of the *shuls*.'

The custodian had shuffled from her desk. She stood behind him like his own conscience.

'*Shuls?*' he repeated.

'Synagogues. Some say from the Soldiers' Synagogue. Entire families from the ghetto, even people passing in the street, were driven inside the synagogue. German soldiers piled up furniture and books. They poured petrol over it all and started a fire and locked the doors. The fourth of July 1941 was the date.'

Her English was excellent, the accent refined. She learnt it from the BBC, he thought.

She pointed to the next room.

'Come. There is more you must see.'

Was this a warning?

'Understand that we had already suffered from the Soviets swallowing our country. That was the Ribbentrop-Molotov Pact. Terrible things happened, killings, terror, deportations. When Hitler invaded many people saw the Germans as liberators. Nobody knew the German plan. This is from the newspaper *Terija*.' She touched the bold headline: *Uzaicinajums*. 'It is calling for volunteers to cleanse the country of bad elements. Some Jews they shot. Some Jews they burnt. Some they hanged. See the photo – they are left swinging in public places. Imagine what it was like for those waiting for their fate.'

Her face showed nothing, as if all emotion had long ago been spent. Did Clough's imagination need more stimulus? She carried on, her voice low. There seemed hardly enough breath to get the words out.

'People were rounded up at gunpoint and sent to the camps

and were worked to death. Thousands were killed in the forest at Rumbulla. There were camps at Mezaparks and Salaspils where many thousands were killed. Look at the photographs.' She closed her eyes and took a breath. 'Today there are people in America and England and Sweden who say that the Holocaust never happened. It is a lie. They look at the evidence and say it is a Jewish invention. Did we invent this scaffold? Are the men hanging by their necks dummies? Did we burn this building ourselves? Did we make our own people disappear by magic?'

She hung her head as history weighed down on her and shuffled away, leaving Clough alone. The wall of photographs showed smashed buildings, ghetto houses locked in behind a tall fence, scarecrow figures glimpsed through barbed wire, Nazi officers in immaculate uniforms, prisoners hanging while a lynch mob looked on, armoured cars and tanks with swastikas on their turrets, skeletons in a pit, a line of women on a beach, naked, with hands covering their sex in the last moments of their lives.

In the end he found he wasn't seeing these images. Instead he saw Debbie's face, thrust towards him in the half light of the bedroom, the middle fingers of both hands smoothing her eyelids. He felt distanced from the horror. There was battle fatigue and compassion fatigue and now he'd experienced Holocaust fatigue.

'Do you have questions?' the curator asked when he returned to the entrance lobby.

Questions about details? Or ideology? Or authenticity? Or numbers? Or heroics? Or betrayals? Or complicity? Or retribution? Some questions have no answers. He had to ask something. She was waiting.

'Are you here every day?'

'Yes, except Saturday and Sunday.'

'All day you sit, this evidence all round you,' Clough said. 'How does it make you feel?'

Her eyes closed and her body rocked forward as if she would collapse on the desk. Recovering she said, 'I can never comprehend

134

it. I try but my mind cannot take it in. No matter how often I reach out there is always something that…' She ran out of words. Her hands made gestures as if she was packing together a giant snowball. 'There is also a video if you would care to see it.'

It was a home movie – how else to describe it? The camera was hand-held, the film poorly focused. It showed a couple of dozen men, naked, standing at the edge of a deep trench. One by one they toppled in as they were shot. There was no sound. Who had wanted to record this event as a souvenir? Finally there were snatches of the trial and execution in 1948 of the SS Chief.

'His name was Friedrich Jeckeln,' she said. 'I had always liked the name Friedrich.'

Clough gathered up his coat from the chair. It was heavier than he remembered.

'Thank you,' he said.

Her face seemed to flinch. Thanks were out of place here.

'Tell me,' he said, threading one arm through a sleeve, 'do you know a woman called Deborah Brown?' He threaded the other arm through its sleeve. 'About thirty years old with short dark hair.'

'The name is not familiar to me.'

'She's Canadian. She came to Riga to trace her ancestors.'

The curator's gaze went cloudy as if a mist had grown up between them. Sometimes there are people or events you simply do not see. What you don't see you can't talk about.

'Shalom,' she said. Clough saw how her hand trembled as she reached for her book. The design on the cover was of a woman's head framed by a black scarf with her mouth open in a scream nobody heard.

He went down the stairs, Debbie on his mind. She came to Riga in search of her roots. Everything was wiped out, bulldozed, burnt, shot, hanged. There was nothing for her. Still she stayed. Why?

It was an evening of Let's Pretend. Let's pretend I'm a wine importer and never been anything else. Let's pretend I'm a Canadian photographer. Let's pretend I'm a lowly Foreign Office flunkey and Matt Clough's uncle to boot. Enough truth peeped out to make the pretending believable. Seven-thirty outside the embassy was agreed.

Martin was waiting, talking to the policeman in the sentry box, when Debbie and Clough arrived.

'Marvellous chap. Good command of our language. He asked if I knew the Prince of Wales. Not intimately. A while ago Chas was in Riga on an official visit. In the afternoon, four o'clock-ish, he stopped on his way out accompanied by his personal police guard. The heir to the throne said, "I say, where does one go to get a decent cup of tea?" The chap in the hut says to me, "Why did he say *one* when there were two of them? Does the bodyguard sit beside him with no tea?" Good question. Hello, you must be Debbie. I've been looking forward to meeting you, my dear. You don't mind me calling you that, do you? I'm Martin. Friends and enemies alike call me that. If I ever had another name I've forgotten it.'

Debbie's gaze rested on him while he delivered all this. Let her see him as a codger on his last lap, a bit long-winded, an old buffer fancying himself as a ladies' man. It wasn't a difficult role to play.

'Matt, you never told me your uncle was a charmer.'

'You be careful,' Clough said. 'He's the black sheep of the family. It's a wonder the Foreign Office took him.'

The policeman in the sentry box had advised against going to the restaurant opposite. 'Full of Russian *biznezmen* getting drunk,' he said, 'and shouting into mobile phones. If we want a Russian restaurant we have to go to the next street. There's one there without the wide boys and their blonde companions.'

A sign in Cyrillic announced it as *Traktieris*. Steps led to a low room with wood everywhere: walls, ceiling, beams, floor, pillars, bar. The only table free was by the entrance to the kitchen. A waiter with wild eyes dropped a menu on the table and fled. Loudspeakers played Russian pop music. Glasses clinked. Voices rose. Martin bent forward to make himself heard.

'Do we want to stay? Find somewhere else where we don't have to shout?'

The menu was a slim volume in red plastic. Debbie was turning its pages.

'Pay heed, you guys. The Cavalry of Cooper Salad – any idea what that is? How about Greengrocery with Fermented Milk? Who made this stuff up? Some copywriter on Ecstasy? Back of the Woods in the Morning Salad – that has a certain promise. Hey listen – Black Spawn. I vote we stay.'

The waiter had chosen to stand close to Debbie. His nostrils twitched every time she leant forward.

'What is *Pelmeni*?' Martin asked.

'*Pelmeni*? You ask what is *Pelmeni*?' The waiter looked up to God for inspiration. '*Pelmeni* is *Pelmeni*.'

'Good. I'm glad it's not something else. Is it fish, flesh or fowl?'

'Is meat. Sometimes.'

'Let's hope it's one of those times. I'll chance my luck on *Pelmeni*.'

To the great wine importer fell the duty of choosing. The wine list could have been the Shanghai telephone directory so he stabbed a finger at the page. 'Kindzmarauli?'

'Kindzmarauli good,' the waiter said.

The bottle was brought and banged on the table. The waiter disappeared. Clough poured a little in his glass, swirled it round to release the bouquet, took a mouthful, closed his eyes and swallowed.

'So? How does it score?' Debbie asked. 'Ten out of ten?'

'No.'

'Nine? Maybe eight? Seven? Come on, forget the countdown. What is it?'

Clough tried another mouthful and wondered what to say. There had been a time in Albania, he remembered, when he had tasted disaster after disaster. Four men with folded arms and sharp eyes had watched him. More men with rifles slouched outside the warehouse. How had he got away?

'What a wine!' he said.

Debbie studied the label and poured glasses for Martin and herself. She took a swig and some emotion passed across her face.

'OK, it's red and sweet. But it's got alcohol. You're just spoiled.'

'Now look here,' Martin said, 'we never ordered a starter. Where's the waiter? We should have Black Slush.'

'Black Spawn,' Debbie said.

'Exactly. And vodka. With no orange piss. Pardon me, young lady.'

'That's OK. The good Lord preserve us from orange piss. When you piss orange that means bilharzia.'

Vodka was sold by weight. Was two hundred grams the right amount? Martin poured the vodka into wine glasses 'so we can see what we're getting'. It looked 'mean' – Martin again – so when the caviar arrived he ordered more.

'Now, Sir Martin,' Debbie began.

'I turned down the knighthood. It's plain Martin.'

'Going for Lord, are you? I want the story of your life so far. Particularly I want the dirt.'

There was something about this room built of wood, hot and noisy. It could be a chalet or a sauna or an Alpine refuge on a winter's night, perfect for confessions. There was something about Debbie too, the way she bent low when she spoke to him. He held her eyes and gave a wry smile as if his days of looking down a woman's cleavage were long past.

'I just beaver away in the Foreign Office. You've heard of high fliers, chaps who are destined to run empires? Well, I am a low flier. It's safer. High fliers have jealous folk taking shots at them. Or they soar too high and the sun melts the wax and their wing feathers fall out.'

'What do you actually do?'

'I'm on the internal security side.'

'Wow, sounds glamorous.'

Martin allowed himself to cover Debbie's hand with his own.

'Is your idea of glamour checking that the combinations on the embassy locks are regularly changed? And the ambassador's desk isn't visible from a window across the street? I doubt it. Or the closed circuit camera in the ladies' toilet is functioning? And...'

'Hey, no kidding.'

'I made that one up. Cheers.' He took his hand off Debbie's to lift his glass in a toast.

Their main course arrived. *Pelmeni* turned out to be ravioli. The noise level in the restaurant rose a notch.

'And you truly are Matt's uncle?'

Martin tipped his head. 'Why shouldn't I be?'

'You being here at the same time. That's some coincidence.'

'I'll let you into a secret. I think he steals my travel plans. I go to Budapest to test the shredders work, Matt arrives to check out what the flying Australian wine makers are doing. Or we run into each other in Sofia. Or Bucharest. Remember Bucharest, Matt? Dinner at the Premiera? Wonderful swordfish. And better wine than this. Remember?'

Clough had eaten there, though not with Martin.

'That pianist at his white piano, smiling like Liberace.'

'He misses out when I go to Lisbon or Madrid. Why did you choose central Europe to buy wine?'

'Because there are gems nobody knows about. They're going to surprise everybody and the Sunday papers will rave. And I got there first and have the contacts.'

Debbie wasn't interested. Her eyes were on Martin.

'And Matt's mother was your sister?'

'Yes.'

'So Matt's father – your brother-in-law?'

'They never tied the knot. I never met him, never knew who he was.'

'Your own sister never talked to you about it? What was her name?'

'Valerie,' Clough slipped in, sensing a hesitation in Martin.

'Valerie didn't confide in her own brother?'

'My dear,' and Martin gave an amiable grin. 'He was Russian, I was a young puppy at the Foreign Office, it was the Cold War. It wasn't long since Soviet tanks had crushed the Hungarians, Krushchev was thumping his shoe at the United Nations. If it was known that my own sister…'

He broke off. Three men and a woman erupted from the service door into the centre of the room. One man tucked a fiddle under his chin, the other two grasped balalaikas. They wore black trousers stuffed into leather boots, red shirts with leg of mutton sleeves, embroidered waistcoats and gold earrings. The woman was dressed in a floral blouse and a full pleated skirt. With a shout and a stamping of boots the musicians got going.

'Oh God,' Debbie said, 'the Gypsy band. That's Yehudi Menuhin's cousin and he's going to lean over us and drop hairs in our food until we pay him to go away. The dame is going to belt out the *Collective Love Song.*'

'Collective Love as in orgy?' Martin said. 'I didn't know you spoke Russian.'

She swallowed a gulp of wine and it set her going.

'Russian, bullshit. Every woman knows this song. It could be anywhere, a prairie farm, a Manhattan office, an English factory making garden gnomes. OK, this restaurant is called Tractor so the song is about Boris and Olga down on the Hammer & Sickle collective farm in the good old Brezhnev days. The steppes reach out to the horizon, the August sun beats cruelly down, heat is in the air and in the blood. Boris is driving the tractor. Olga is baling the straw. Boris says, "Give me a kiss, my little chicken." Little chicken? Olga has bulges like a hippopotamus. She simpers, as a hippo does, and says, "Not so fast, Comrade Boris. Not until you have completed your daily quota."'

Debbie paused to refresh herself while on the dance floor the balalaikas went separate ways, each screaming for attention. The singer's gaze swept the room and settled on Martin. Despair was in her eyes and Martin was the cause, for laying siege to her, for having his way with her, for being unfaithful to her, for being a man. She rested her hands on her bosom then flung them to heaven while she shrieked at Martin in C sharp.

Debbie had a different tale. She leaned across the table.

'Boris puts the tractor into turbo drive. Up-down-up-down-up-down the field. Olga lolls in the shade of the baling machine. She is painting her toenails in this year's fashion colour: Proletarian Blood. She has never seen someone so urgent on the tractor. The tractor stops. Boris leaps down. He has done the whole field. He takes Olga in his muscular arms and kisses her. Now his horny peasant's hands have found their way inside her dungarees and they're searching for the promised land. Olga slaps his face. "What is wrong?" he demands. "Your hands are imperialist hands," she replies. "They invade honest peasant country. No further advances until we are married." And that, gentlemen, is the Collective Love Song.'

Debbie sank back in her chair while the balalaikas wailed.

During dinner snow had fallen. They stood at the top of the restaurant steps, looking at a street made suddenly beautiful, listening to the muffled sound of the fiddle screeching at the balalaikas. Martin teetered a bit on his feet. Debbie linked an arm through his and her other arm through Clough's.

'That was an experience not to be...'

'Repeated,' Clough said.

'C'mon. It was fun,' Debbie said.

They began walking, like drunks supporting each other. Debbie hummed something that might have been the Collective Love Song. Then she serenaded the night.

'Go back, Comrade Boris, and sit on the tractor.

I shall remain virgo intacta.

Until you have done double your quota,

You shall not touch me one iota.'

'My dear,' Martin said, 'what an aria. I shall alert La Scala. Oh by the way, Matt,' he went on as if it had just popped into his head, 'bit of chat in the embassy. Your passport will definitely be ready tomorrow. Go in and pick it up before midday, my advice. All right, you lovebirds, I'll be leaving you now.'

Taking Debbie in a comradely embrace, he kissed her on both cheeks.

'Hey, where are you staying?' she asked.

'Not far,' Martin said, not quite answering her question. To cover his exit he threw out other comments. 'Fresh air will do me good. Have to get Boris and Olga out of my head. Poor fellow. Did he ever get the red in the bed?'

This was the last chance saloon for serious drinkers. For Martin it was something else. He chose a table by the window. When he cleared condensation off the glass he had an angled view of the Konventa Seta.

Quite a gal, Debbie. He should say woman to be PC but didn't care to. Vibrant, intelligent, sparky, spontaneous. Her sexuality was that of the modern miss – yes please, I'll have it when I want it. Also she was a liar, a schemer, a manipulator, which Martin admired in a professional way. An actress too, putting on a show with Martin as her audience.

He drank coffee. When he thought he'd outstayed the welcome of a single coffee he ordered vodka. He pointed out a lemon peel flavoured vodka from the shelf behind the bar but the bottle was produced from an ice chest. A man with a two day beard and alcohol-smudged eyes came and sat at his table and launched into a monologue. Martin nodded though he understood nothing. The barman said something and the drunk left Martin alone. He paid for his drinks as they came. When Debbie stepped out of the hotel he put on his coat and slipped out after her.

It was the time of night that belonged to crazies and touts and boys and girls together. There were enough people about so Martin didn't feel conspicuous. He walked with care because of the ice, keeping close to walls, ducking into doorways when she paused at street corners. He felt alert and at peace with himself, using skills that had been part of his life.

Abruptly she stopped in front of a three storey building. Martin found shelter in an alley. With half a head round the corner he watched. She didn't ring a bell. She had a key in her hand. As she was putting it into the lock two figures stepped out from the shadows and advanced on her.

Martin started forward. Rape? Mugging? She thought the same, letting out a sharp cry. Then to Martin's surprise she gave a second cry but of delight. As the two men crowded close she embraced first one, then the other, then drew them both in for a hug. All three disappeared into the building. Martin waited until he saw cracks of light appear round the curtains of a second-floor window. He went to the door and ran a pocket flashlight over a panel set into the wall. There were four bells to press and four names, though Debbie Brown's was not one of them.

Chapter 15

It was noon when they reached the lawyer's building, Clough with his new passport tucked into an inner pocket, Debbie peering up at the naked ladies on the facade, voluptuous but unyielding.

'Olga and her sister Volga,' she said. 'They named a river after her.'

They climbed the stairs. The door to Munters Advertising and Design was open to welcome new clients. There was a tiny reception area. A poster was displayed on an easel as if it was a painting. In a tableau like a nativity scene a perfect family adored a bowl of frozen peas. *Enjoy Summer in Winter* was the slogan in English. Miles Davis soothed from hidden loudspeakers. They climbed again and outside the door to the lawyer's office Debbie seemed to see something in Clough's face she didn't like.

'Sure you're OK?'

Who visits a lawyer with a light heart? He could say that. *Why do you lie and what are you after?* He could say that also.

'I'm tired,' he said.

'It's that wine, Matt.'

'The vodka,' he said.

'The more vodka.'

This light exchange masked their doubts. Debbie, with a military squaring of the shoulders, pushed open the door and advanced. The same secretary hammered at the typewriter and showed no sign of stopping. Debbie bent down and pushed her face forward until her chin nudged the letter being typed. The typing stuttered and came to a halt.

'Mr Clough to see Mr Birznieks. We have an appointment. We telephoned earlier.'

Debbie said it in English, the language of frozen peas, of Shakespeare, of international law, commerce, banking, aviation, pop music, espionage, oil, drugs, arms deals, sport, revolutionaries and protesters who hold up signs to catch the TV news.

There was the same feeling of autumn mist in Birznieks's office. He advanced on them through the cigarette smoke. Clough had forgotten how slight he was. He had no smile – a smile was not legal proof of welcome – but he held his hand out. Clough made to shake it but the hand moved away to point to two chairs then dropped. Clough hadn't forgotten the flow of words. He was talking from the moment they entered the room, talking as he retreated behind his desk, talking as he picked up a packet of Millord and put a cigarette in his mouth. Debbie took her chance.

'Mr Birznieks says we have upset Mrs Gerasimova again because she has been obliged to rearrange his schedule. So certain Japanese have been put back by half an hour. The Colombians have been moved to after lunch which means they will smell of beer and be noisy. Though the Greeks, being Greek, had not intended to come at their appointed time anyway. But Mr Birznieks says that notwith-standing all this he is delighted to make your acquaintance once more and trusts you have spent a pleasant few days in Riga. Oh yes.'

'You didn't mention our visit out to…'

'How could I? He's mad,' she said, 'not in the way normal people go mad but in the way lawyers go mad. They look for ways to sneak round the law, sidestep the law, soar above the law, burrow under the law. He has something of yours and won't give it to you and he says that is the law.'

Birznieks was speaking again. Debbie did manage to slip in a question then turned to Clough.

'Now hear this. He had a visit from the police who questioned him about your father. But Mr B kept *shtumm* because your dad was a client and the police were only on what he calls a fishing expedition. Then there was the Russian who claimed to be an old pal of your dad and wanted to become a client. Mr B smelled a rat and sent him packing. This morning someone came from the British embassy. He spoke no Latvian but brought a local to interpret. He'd heard your father had left something to you and wanted to have it transferred to the safe keeping of the embassy. No prize for guessing how that turned out. This has been his week for saying "no" but now you have your new passport he's going to have to say "yes". Right Matt, your moment on stage.'

Clough offered his passport across the desk. Birznieks cupped both hands to receive it. He riffled through the pages. Surname: Clough. Given names: Matthew Leopold. British citizen. So on. At the bottom was an official reference that should satisfy the most suspicious:

7020219458GBR201077MO705132>>01.

Birznieks lifted the passport to get a reflection off the photo. Next he compared the photo with Matt's face, a critical lawyer's inspection, searching for evidence of perjury and malfeasance. Then a reluctant nod. The Great Immigration Officer has admitted Clough to legal existence.

'Something else, Matt. He wants you to sign your name. He's going to watch you do it so do it naturally not like some forger taking immense pains. On that sheet of paper, Matt. Matt? You know your name? You know how to write?'

'All names in full? Just initials?'

'Fuck's sake, whatever's in your passport. Just do it before he invents some more legal hocus-pocus.'

Birznieks leant close to watch him. He raised paper and passport together to compare the signatures. He nodded again.

'You're in,' Debbie said. 'You're kosher.'

Birznieks went to the wall safe, checked over his shoulder that neither had sneaked up to steal the combination, twisted the dial this way, that way, this way, that way, swung open the door and brought out a manila envelope. A typed sheet was produced which Debbie skipped through.

'On this day I have received blah-blah, addressed to me, blah-blah, seal unbroken, blah-blah. Sign again, Matt, and date it.'

Clough signed. Debbie signed as translator. His signature was matched again then his passport and the manila envelope were pushed across the desk. A smaller envelope was produced out of a desk drawer.

'What's this?'

'Keys,' Debbie said. 'Keys to the houses plus their addresses.'

'Let's hoof it before he gets his second wind.'

Outside low cloud pressed down but didn't crush Debbie's spirit.

'Woo,' she said, 'we passed the initiative test.' She looked up at the naked statues. 'Bye, girls. We'll – '

Clough jerked at her arm.

'Come on, for God's sake.'

'We got the goods, Matt,' she said.

'We got a plain brown envelope. Come on.'

They crossed the street and skirted the Latvija Hotel. Debbie gripped Clough's arm with both hands, not because they were lovers, not to stop him making a break for freedom. She squeezed the arm: we've won.

They came to a square with a church clad in scaffolding and beside it a small café. Steps led down to a low-ceilinged room with a dozen square tables. A display cabinet showed winter salads of grated carrot, celeriac and beetroot. There was a choice of cold fish in a vinegary sauce or chicken fillets in aspic.

'I'm having Feather Animal Sleeping in Goo,' Debbie said. 'And beer.'

Clough laid the two envelopes on the table between them. He opened the smaller one and tipped out three keys, labels attached. A typed sheet gave addresses in Mezaparks, Sigulda and Majori, wherever Majori was.

The manila envelope was the prize. It was A4 size. The seal on the flap was hardened red wax. It had been stamped with a design of an owl perched on a bit of branch. Was an owl significant? Symbol of a lawyer's wisdom? Ridding the world of rats and other vermin?

'Do you recognise the handwriting?' Debbie asked.

'I never knew him. I never saw anything he wrote.'

'It could be a letter bomb.'

That was absurd. That was so crazy Clough turned round to make sure nobody overheard. The waitress thought he wanted something and wandered over and Debbie sent her away.

'Here, let me do it, Matt.'

She was trying to take over. Matt shook his head. He used a knife to slit the envelope at the end opposite the seal. Using the knife he twisted the cut envelope and peeped inside. What he saw wasn't a bomb, not to outwards appearance. There was a letter and what could have been a mobile phone.

He leaned back. 'Maybe it is a bomb.'

She leaned forward. 'It's a Dictaphone.'

'That? It's too clunky.'

'If it's from K.K., who knows how old it is?'

'Address in Mezaparks,' Debbie said. 'Dated a couple of weeks back.'

She took a sip of beer while her eyes zigzagged down the letter. It was in Latvian, written in an old person's hand that quavered like an old person's voice. Cross-bars of Ts drifted off to the right, words were crossed out, other words squeezed up as the end of a line took the writer by surprise.

'I'll do my best,' Debbie said, 'but it's a mess. Seems half educated.'

'My father not educated?'

'The writer. Listen. *"My son,"* it begins.'

She took another sip of beer.

"My son,

"'It has come to this, that my eyes are now too weak to be able to read or write. I can see well enough to drive a car or shoot a gun but words on a page look like a line of marching ants. It was de Gaulle…" only

148

spelled G-u-a "…de Gaulle, a fool in international politics but astute in other ways, who said that old age is a shipwreck. My ship is sliding beneath the waves while I cling on by my fingertips to a life raft. Soon my fingers will slip – or someone will stamp on them – and I shall sink into the eternal deep.'"

Debbie looked up.

'Hardly a bundle of fun, is he?'

'Is there much more?' The opening phrases sounded a warning like the distant roll of artillery.

'Sure.' She looked down again.

"'Since I am incapable of writing, the task has fallen to Otilija. Otilija, my woman, my companion, my…" Can't understand this word. Something to do with secret. Perhaps confidante. "… my confidante, my adviser and recently my nurse. She has treated me well, as a woman does a man. She knows about you, about your mother, about the love we had. I do not hide it. And why should I? I knew your mother many years before I met Otilija.

"Otilija is a good woman though she is not one of our intelligentsia. What good are the intelligentsia anyway? Do they grow food? Do they give us children? Do they build houses or protect us from our enemies or make us laugh when the day has been hard? These are the important things in life. The intelligentsia are concerned with crazy ideas and their own egos.'"

Debbie refreshed herself again.

'Goes on a bit. Rambling in his head.'

"'My son, I have seen you only once. Have I been a bad father? It was simply not possible to do differently. My life would have been in danger if I had tried to do better. The one time was when you were a young boy, in 1968. You know about this year. Students decided they could rule the world by rioting – just young intelligentsia. I had some business in Prague and in August soon after the fraternal tanks had restored order I had to visit England on a certain matter. I travelled on a diplomatic passport which confined me to thirty kilometres around London. One morning I evaded our security and then your security.

"*I took the train to Folkestone. I bought a map and walked until I found the street and the number of your house. It was a Sunday, a day of despair in England when one prays for the forgiveness of sins, though the sins most people commit are so small they would bore God. He would yawn and turn away, which in my experience is what He mostly does. I waited and had my reward. You came out of the house accompanied by your aunt. She wore a severe hat and a coat buttoned to the throat, even though it was summer. You wore grey shorts and a jacket that was too small for you. I think she was taking you to church. My own son, I thought, and my heart jumped in my chest. I swear I could recognise the woman I had loved in your hair and your eyes. You walked towards me. I put a cigarette in my mouth and went to light it. I had a special lighter, one of the toys of our profession, that takes pictures the size of a rice grain. Of course they can be made larger afterwards. But how? I could not give this sub-miniature spy's film to a London shop to be processed – I could not trust them not to alert the authorities. I could not give it to our technicians – how to explain that I had evaded security to see the son they did not know about? I watched you pass close enough to touch, then I put the lighter away.*"*

Debbie went on to a new sheet, skipping down the page while she took a mouthful of beer, and another.

"*I kept that image of you in my head always, how your eyes were quick to notice and quick to move away, how a curl of hair fell forward as if you could hide your face behind it. I wonder how you have changed as the century has passed. Sometimes I am overwhelmed by a need to know – what is my son like now?*"*

'What is it?' Clough asked.

Debbie had stopped. She seemed to skim the rest of the page before putting it down.

'A girl's got to eat.'

She took a couple of forkfuls and started again.

"*I feel that my life is drawing to a close. Certain people who bear me ill because…*"* She faltered. 'Can't make the writing out so I'll skip that bit. "*Birznieks is an old rogue behind that legal jargon but*

I have known him a long time. Find my son, I told him, and give him this recording. Actually I started it a very long time ago: 1991. Yes, that long. 1991 was a year of tumult in Latvia, in Moscow, in the world. Everything has changed beyond belief and it is important that you, my son, understand what I have done in my life. Listen! Understand! Do not rush to judgement! Remember many influential people thought as I did. Now they creep out of the shadows, bowing and scraping and washing their hands. What I give you is not an apology, not a defence, but a record of one man's journey along the twisting rocky road of our time.

"*Enough. Time for my medicine. Growing old is a twenty-four hour occupation leaving little time for life.*

"*My son, I embrace you. Your father, Krisjanis Kulbergs.*'"

Clough's eyes were closed so tight he might never open them again.

'Matt, you *knew*. You damn well did.'

His eyes stayed closed. Listen to his father's tape? No. It was an unexploded bomb. Who had his father expected to translate the letter? Perhaps no one. It was enough to hear the 'record of one man's journey along the twisting rocky road of our time'. He held the Dictaphone down at his side, gripping it tight, keeping its secrets from slipping out.

Jab in the chest from Debbie.

'Look at me.'

He refused to come alive.

'Your father was a spy and you knew it and hid it from me. What more do you know about him? Lover, spy, man of mystery, that's you. What else? I want to know.' She stopped. Then her voice dropped. 'Oh God, now what?'

At the door stood Finnis, glancing over the room, catching sight of them, nodding. He was one of those men who could smile and take in everything without moving his eyes. Why him, why now, why here? Whatever Finnis said, Clough knew it would be a lie.

'I was right. Just having a drink in the Latvija and I glanced out of the window and said to my companion, "Can it be? Yes it is, a good friend of mine with a *most* attractive lady." I made my escape but when I got outside you'd vanished and I've spent all this time tracking you down.'

Lies, Clough told himself.

'You were coming from Valdemara iela – isn't that where your lawyer is?' Finnis said.

That's it, Clough decided. Not Birznieks. His secretary Gerasimova. The moment we stepped out of the office she got on the phone. Russians together against the world.

'You've arranged your business with him? I hope so. I'm genuinely pleased to see you again.'

Finnis had put out his hand. Clough had slipped the Dictaphone in his pocket and shook his hand.

'And who is she?' Finnis asked.

'If by *she* you mean *me*…' Debbie got up, raising her hand. Finnis thought it was to shake and extended his but her hand went up to run through her hair. '*She* is just going. Attractive ladies got to keep circulating.' She busied herself with her shoulder bag, holding his stare. 'I'll leave you two boys to it. *Amusez-vous bien.*'

Finnis watched her all the way to the door, admiring the hints of her body moving under her coat. He called out to the waitress for a beer and sat down.

'So who *is* she? Local girl you picked up?'

'She's a friend.'

'Is she French? Why did she end up speaking French?'

There was a scar on Finnis' left cheek Clough didn't remember. It was like a duelling scar an old Prussian officer might have boasted. Probably a knife wound. Clough said nothing.

The waitress put down a bottle of beer and a glass. Finnis was macho and drank straight from the bottle.

'And this is all the lawyer gave you?'

Finnis's hand dropped from the bottle to the envelope pushed to one side. The large envelope and the letter had disappeared into Debbie's shoulder bag. The Dictaphone was in Clough's pocket. Just this small envelope remained. When Finnis picked it up there were the three tagged keys underneath. The typed list of addresses must also have found its way into Debbie's bag.

'Yes.'

'*Three* houses. First there was one, then two, now three. Krisjanis must have been a millionaire.'

'I'll take those.'

It wasn't a struggle but Finnis's hand was strong and he didn't give up the keys until he had turned them round and could read the labels.

'Sigulda… Mezaparks… and Majori. Well, well.'

'Where is Majori? Clough asked.

'Majori is in Jurmala. Jurmala is the seaside, out to the west, not far from here. Twenty kilometres out of town. You can drive it easy. Excellent road. In Soviet days people called it "Ten minutes in America" because so many movies set in the US had scenes shot there. It was the only stretch of highway in the whole fucking Soviet Union good enough to look like an American Interstate.' Finnis smiled. 'They filmed car chases, shoot-outs, hitch-hikers killing drivers, blacks being lynched, girls getting raped, gangsters bribing cops, prostitutes pulling their skirts up, drugs being injected – just everyday Yankee life in the squinty eyes of Mosfilm. The capitalist world was dying, the proletariat was oppressed, the workers couldn't afford cars – yet here was this marvellous highway. *Prieka*.'

He lifted the bottle.

Clough scooped the keys into the envelope and slipped it into his pocket.

'You going out there?' Finnis asked. 'To the coast, I mean?'

'I'm going home.'

'What, now?'

Clough had had enough. He left Finnis without another word. As he went out into the street he saw Finnis staring after him. He'd stared after Debbie too but that had been different.

Chapter 16

I'm free, Clough told himself. He'd got his passport, given Finnis the slip, Debbie was God knows where, Martin was about his own mysterious business. Leave now. Take a taxi to the airport. Just do it.

There was the Dictaphone in his pocket. Drop it in the Daugava. *I'm free*, he told himself again. Except…

He thought of Lucija. Mr Cloff is a prisoner of his freedom.

Like any prisoner he walked to the window to see freedom outside. A pretty girl was standing in the doorway of the shop across the courtyard, staring up at the sky. Clough looked up and saw clouds the colour of lead. When his eyes dropped again he saw the girl was gazing at him. Snowflakes drifted down between them. She shrugged her shoulders, gave him a dazzling smile and returned to her counter of amber jewellery.

No, he wasn't free. He had to know.

Clough tugged the curtains closed, sat at the desk, switched on the lamp and straightened the Dictaphone prised from Birznieks's grip. He stared at it. Did he truly want to? Stupid question. You only knew whether you wanted to when it was too late and you'd done it. So press the *on* switch. Would he need to rewind or had some kind person done that? Press Playback.

Oh my God.

The voice of the father he had never met.

It's war! Those bugles and uniforms – haven't they always made you catch your breath? Doesn't your heart beat a little faster? More thrilling than sex, more intimate than money, more basic even than eating. War! Your life or mine. The Chinese are right – war is the natural condition of man.

This is different. This war is playing in my living room, courtesy of CNN, brought to me in Mezaparks on this 17ᵗʰ day of January. Saddam thought the Americans were bluffing, right? Thought he could twist and lie some more. He thought Bush didn't have the balls. Big mistake. Bush had to prove that he did have balls, the biggest in the world. Here come the missiles again, cruising into downtown Baghdad. Pow! A communications centre has vanished. Thank you, CNN. I am seeing the smart bombs, repeats every half hour. Oh, they are smart. I tell you, they salute before they enter the window on the top floor, take the elevator down to ground level, then blow the building apart. No sound track. One puff and it collapses, reduced to rubble in total silence. With Desert Storm there are no bangs, no cries. We can play a God who has gone deaf.

It is war and I am a young man again. That is the beauty of war. How else does a young man get to play Master of the Universe? I am an old man remembering being young. I tell you, my memories are brighter than my recollection of last night. What did I do? I tried to screw the old bat. And failed. Maybe I got bored and rolled off her. War in the Gulf is not boring. The last war in Europe was not boring.

How old was I when the German army came to Riga? Twenty. The Latvia I had been born into was independent. Sort of. Really a false kind of freedom. Russia and Germany were breathing down our necks. We'd had a bit of democracy and a bit of dictatorship. Then Germany and the Soviet Union did a deal and Latvia was handed to Stalin. Stalin, well, he did what he always did: pack the trains to the Gulag, kill a few thousand. Just a statistic in his view. So when Barbarossa came and the Wehrmacht rolled in, we crept out from our hiding places. The Krauts were saving us from the murdering Reds. How naïve can you get?

The Germans drove their tanks into Riga, right into the centre. We lined the road and cheered and some of the girls blew kisses, the uglier ones. The hatches were open so the leutnants could stand up and salute. Not many looked like the blond Aryan gods of the propaganda pictures.

They looked like drunks who had been on a binge for a week. Some threw cigarettes into the crowd for the sport of it, watching how they were fought over until they were torn to shreds.

Here is a universal rule of war: when the fighting stops the military holds a parade and they pin medals on each other. On the first day of July the Germans chose the Freedom Monument – a rare example of German irony - installed a German guard of honour and everybody clapped. In a flash Brivibas Bulvaris changed to Adolf Hitler Allee. And when the Germans were defeated Hitler's name vanished and Lenin's name was used instead. This is normal in my opinion.

What? Just a minute.

The old bat came in and asked if I wanted breakfast. 'Get me a brandy. This is war.' She is always nagging. Perhaps I didn't screw her last night and that is the trouble. She has brought me the brandy, a small one, and sniffed. She can smell I have had one already.

Let me tell you about my desk. It is so big I don't know how they got it through the door. A president should have such a desk, made of cherry wood with a marvellous grain. It has six drawers, deep enough for stacks of state secrets. In one of the drawers I found this Dictaphone. I don't even remember buying it. But what a day to use this toy.

Who am I talking to? Why choose English? I could be speaking Latvian or Russian, even German. Perhaps my German is fading a bit. But English? For her? But she died long before our love could turn sour. For you perhaps, my son. One day you may hear it. Or not. No telling.

War is war. You are on the winning side or you are dead. That is the meaning of war, so simple it is beautiful. The Germans called for volunteers to help cleanse our country of inferior elements. Mainly these were Jews. Also gypsies, perverts and degenerates, some Poles and Lithuanians who had settled here, Russians who hadn't got out.

I volunteered. You'd think you would be greeted with a clap on the back and a glass of something to set your pulse racing. Wrong. The Germans were keen I should volunteer for a combat division to smash the communists. My guts clenched. It would, I agreed, be an honour but my health was the problem. The sergeant sneered. He had a face like a weiss wurst, the neck of an ox. He said I looked young and strong and if my health problem was a yellow liver he knew a cure. A kick up the arse was wonderful medicine. In those days I had a different name and different papers. In war you learn how to survive. The papers came from a man of my age who disappeared into Stalin's Gulag. He had no need of his documents including a medical report that said he had an irregular heartbeat. This was translated for the recruiting sergeant who spat at the weakness of an inferior race and growled: 'The camps.'

The camps! I was being arrested. But no, I was wildly wrong. I was assigned to running the camps, the best job in Latvia. How can I explain? Imagine being a bouncer at a brothel, with a free choice of the girls, and being given first dip before the evening shift got down to work. I smile to think of it. The smile fades when I think of last night and the old bat telling me to get on with it if I'm going to because she's tired and wants to sleep. I don't love Otilija but she is reality, an old woman who looks after me. If I am honest – and at my age truth has its attractions – do I need more than memories?

Shit, I am tired. I was up early and drank the large brandy, two in fact since I am being so truthful today, and the brandy she has given me no longer feels so small. Now I look at the screen and with each silent bomb blast my head thumps. I hate it. Growing old is the worst thing imaginable except for the alternative. I hate my powers failing. God, why do you do it to us? God doesn't answer. He's growing old too. In old age even God's power fades. So I couldn't fuck the old bat last night. It is two thousand years since God did it.

Silence. Matt's eyes had been riveted to the Dictaphone as if he could see the man talking. That can't be all. He waited. Then…

She woke me. I was stretched out on the settee with my feet stuck over the arm. Did I want something to eat now, she asked. 'What is it?' I wanted to know. 'Breakfast or lunch?' Doesn't matter, she said, you need food. 'Bring me a brandy.' She shook her head. I was helpless, lying on my back while she leant down, lips thin, eyes like buttons. At Jurmala you see jackdaws like that, scavengers poised to strike. As I stared up she changed to a helicopter soaring above me.

She looked away at the TV. 'Why do you watch this stupid war?'

I told her, 'Why did the Romans go to the Colosseum when the lions were hungry?' She doesn't understand the importance of spectacle. She has no culture.

She said, 'You haven't shaved yet,' and closed the door.

You see? She had no answer but she likes to have the last word. She is a woman and now her juices have dried up.

Oh, that American general, the one who's directing it all. Just seen him on CNN. He's not one of those generals who sit behind a desk, he looks as if he gets sand in his boots. Here's the funny thing: his name is Schwarzkopf. German name. He's just like that sergeant who sent me to the camps. Cheers. I drink to you, my general. He could tear Saddam apart with his bare hands.

I was going to tell you about the camps. I don't know what idea you have but I'll tell you the truth. Don't forget, I'm an expert. A prisoner would see one camp; I saw several. Rumbulla was a temporary place for Jews. Kaiserwald right here in Mezaparks was also mainly for Jews. There was the Central Prison in Riga but I was never there. I don't like places like that. There's no fresh air. And where's the sunshine on a summer's day? And the forest beyond the wire? Things like that which lift your spirits is why Salaspils was my favourite.

Leaving the camp – when that was possible – was a tonic. I could walk in the forest. There were pine needles underfoot and the air was fresh. I'd take a path and search the snow for the tracks of hares. It wasn't silent, you understand. When the snow slipped off the branches it was like a sigh. I remember leaning on a wooden bridge over a stream. A noise like a gunshot was the ice breaking. Spring is here!

My son, yes, it is you I am speaking to. The war to kick Saddam out of Kuwait started me off, reminding me of an earlier war. Also the brandy. I feel the need to tell you about the father you have never known. The moment I am in my grave people are going to start saying bad things so I want you to know the truth. The truth is simple: I

DEAD MAN TELLING TALES

SURVIVED. We are born crying, we struggle to get food, we fuck to make the next generation, we die. That is what it means to be human. The rest is fantasy and ego.

I hear voices whining, damning, voices from all sides.

Regrets, Kris, don't you have any? Sleepless nights? Nightmares when you do sleep? The shakes, the horrors, the silent scream? Tears? No to all of it, Kris?

Not a single tear?

My accusers are lined up against me, a firing squad, their fingers pointing.

I say one word: Listen.

Once more there was a pause. It's the Dictaphone taking a breath. That was the idiotic thought in Matt's mind. The Dictaphone needs more strength

Fools! The Americans. They have not gone into Baghdad to finish Saddam off. They let him get away and they'll regret this. Never let your sworn enemy escape or you'll be condemned to fight him again.

Days have passed since I last spoke, my son. You have been in my thoughts but so have many things, stirred up and flying round inside my head as if a great wind had caught them. I have fetched myself a brandy. It is necessary. This war in the desert, memories of the last war.

The Soviets had been bad for Latvia so we welcomed the Germans. But the early days were hard, I cannot hide that. I answered the call to cleanse the country and was ordered to the camps. First there was work of a different nature in Rumbulla and Bikemieki. Oh, oh, you must excuse me.

There was the sound of a bottle clinking on a glass then a pause. Drinking? A hum or a moan.

This is how it was.

Trains would bring the Jews from Riga and further away, even from Austria. The SS would order an Aktion and the Jews would be

rounded up and put on cattle trucks. This was not on Hitler's orders. Hitler was against non-Aryans, no doubt of it, but his mind was on greater things. Hitler was a genius, my opinion. He came to power in a country defeated in war. It was crippled by reparations, its currency just good for toilet paper. Six million men were unemployed. Six million. Yet in a few short years Germany was the most powerful country in Europe. Tell me that wasn't the work of a genius. His mistake was to believe he could bring about the same change to the whole of Europe, then the world. Too much even for a genius.

In Riga the SS general in charge was Jeckeln. He was an expert. No doubt of it. He was the best, but it wasn't a crowded field he worked in. He rationalised everything, made the production line run smoothly. Dig the pits in the woods. Bring the prisoners by train. Make them strip because clothing is too valuable to be thrown away. Men, women and children all stood naked. Women holding babies would turn their backs. Did they think that would protect the infant? Our job was to execute them. We carried out our orders. These were superfluous people but it was hard. It was very hard. Sometimes a baby was still crying, crying for its mother, and had to be finished. The sergeant would shout, 'Don't waste a bullet on a baby. A rifle butt.' A rifle butt. Imagine you were holding the rifle. Then the corpses had to be ranged in the pits. It was Jeckeln who worked out the system of Sardinenpackung.

Clough stopped the tape. Please, no more. But there was more. He knew it. His feelings were in tumult. Horrified, dismayed, stunned. This was his father.

He stood at the window and parted the curtains. The girl in the amber shop caught sight of him and smiled. He remembered standing at the window of In Vino Veritas and watching the young woman across the road arranging fancy sweaters. Wallingford was a different universe.

I was moved to Salaspils. It was not all breezes and greenery. Don't run away with that idea. It was a Konzentrationslager for superfluous people. Some were sent to work; clearing mines on the front line, for instance. Many stayed inside, though not for long as there were frequent Selektions. Some stayed longer; young women, girls even, if they were thought pretty. Myself, well I couldn't see it. Their heads were shaved but you got this hairy triangle between their thighs. To me it was unbalanced. A matter of aesthetics. They should have shaved their pubic hair as well. All right, with young girls there was no bush worth speaking of but then their breasts hadn't developed either, except for Jewish girls. They develop earlier, I swear it. But at eleven or twelve what does a girl know of pleasing a man? Otilija, even five years ago when her juices were running, could have taught them a trick or two. No, perhaps not. You couldn't teach these Jews anything because they knew it already. They thought they were special. It was a shock, a humiliation to find themselves at Salaspils.

YOU JEWS ARE NOT SPECIAL.

Again and again I shouted that.

What makes you think you are special and merit special consideration? You delude yourselves that it is Jew-this, Jew-that, the most gifted, the most God-fearing, the most hard-working, the most family-minded, the most creative, the most wise, the mostest of the most. You are NOT the most special.

In fact not many Latvian Jews found their way to Salaspils. There were Jews from other countries, even from Berlin and Leipzig, though I could never understand the logic of sending Jews a thousand kilometres to wail at us. We had Lithuanians and Russians and Poles – listen, even some Polish Muslims, would you believe, descended from long ago Turkish invaders. Gypsies of course and defectives and communists from everywhere, so Latvian Jews were a minority. But they made the most noise.

Some Levikins or Rabinovics was being taken to the gallows, exemplary punishment for breaking a rule. His shaven-headed wife was crying out and wailing, 'God! God, no. Why do you forsake us? Why do you not listen in our hour of anguish? Oh God, help us!'

I pointed at her.

'Save your breath, woman. Stop calling for God.'
She turned her head towards me.
'GOD IS IN SHORT SUPPLY TODAY,' I shouted.
*She looked and looked. She stared as if she wanted to imprint my
face in her memory for all eternity. Maybe she did. Another guard
clubbed her to the ground with his rifle butt and hit her again. She
moved no more.*

*I tell you, a day like that was hard work. I would make a pretext to
get away from the camp, to go into the forest, to walk through the trees,
breathing air that did not smell of unwashed bodies and shit and fear
and last winter's rotting cabbage. To hear sounds of dried leaves rustling
under my feet instead of shouts and screams. And in summer to turn
my head up and feel the warmth of the sun on my face.*

A bell was ringing. It was an alarm at Salaspils signalling some
Aktion. It was inside Clough's skull. Then it was the telephone on
the bedside table. If you look at a telephone long enough sometimes
it stops. Not this time. He turned and picked it up.

'Yes?'

'Who's there? Matt? Matthew?' There was a pause. 'Who is it?'

'It's Matt.'

'You took your time answering. Everything all right?'

'Yes.' Firestorm in the head, that's all. 'You've rung. Something
up?'

'I want to see you. Meet me by the police hut where Charlie
asked where he could get a decent cup of tea.'

'Got you.'

'Forty-five minutes. Gives you time for a walkabout.'

Bit of jargon, making certain he walked alone.

'Right.'

The line went dead.

What to do with the Dictaphone? He had to hide it. Except
the spy in Clough took over from the shaken son. A spy never
hides something. Putting it under the mattress would be hiding

it. A spy *caches* it. In the bedside table drawer was a Gideon bible. That would do. The text was in German, French and English. The French section was in the middle and he felt it was a sign that the first gospel was Matthieu.

Abraham engendra Isaac; Isaac engendra Jacob; Jacob engendra Juda et ses frères;

Juda engendra Thamar Pérets et Zara; Pérets engendra…

Forty-two generations from Abraham to Jesus, every one of them Jewish. Jesus was a Jew too, he told his father.

Using his spy's razor blade he sliced out six pages at a time, stuffing them in his pocket to dispose of in the trash can outside McDonald's. Now the Dictaphone fitted snugly in the bible. Put it back in the drawer? No. He didn't try to conceal the bible but left it in full view on the bedside table as any troubled soul might. Anybody who came searching wouldn't give it a second glance.

Et Krisjanis engendra Matt…

You can't choose your father.

Chapter 17

Two police were smoking in the wooden sentry box outside the embassy. No sign of Martin. Clough let his gaze wander down a line of empty parked cars, a closed restaurant, a couple of shops and finally a café. A face was angled towards him in the window. Crossing the street he checked for traffic left and right. No one was following him.

Martin got up as Clough entered, nodding his head towards the back of the room. He carried his drink with him, a glass in a metal holder with a Lipton's Yellow teabag sunk in the depths and a slice of lemon floating on top. A table in the corner caught his eye.

The waitress stood beside them and Clough ordered coffee.

'You saw the lawyer this morning?' Martin said.

Clough nodded.

'What joy?'

'He handed over the addresses of three houses – two of them I already knew. The third is on the coast, not far out of Riga.'

'That was all?'

'The keys.'

'Anything else?'

'No.'

There was a pause while Martin considered Clough's single word as an answer. He wasn't sceptical, certainly not accusing. Instead he kept silent. He seemed fascinated by a lemon pip floating on the surface of his tea and he concentrated on lifting it out, then raising his eyes to Clough's face. He noted the pucker of skin to each side of his mouth, the knots of his jaw muscles. Best part of a week the lawyer had kept Matt waiting and wouldn't even tell him it was for three house keys. *Anything else? No.* Some look away after they lie. Some try to outstare the questioner.

A man banged the door open from the street, shouted some cheery greeting to the waitress and left. Clough and Martin both looked away to see what the noise was about. It was enough, this sudden eruption, to break the spell. *It's mine* – Clough took a breath – *the journal is for me.* Martin still said nothing. The silence meant that Martin suspected he was lying. The silence went on just too long so that Clough began to wonder. *Why doesn't Martin accuse me directly? Could be hiding something himself.* That would make him feel a little delicate.

'When I saw the lawyer he said someone from the British embassy had called earlier. The man didn't speak Latvian so he'd brought a local to interpret. The man was after whatever my father had left. It did just cross my mind…'

Clough didn't finish the sentence but he looked up and held Martin's eyes. He could see the surprise in Martin's face.

'Someone from… Oh, me. I assure you…' Martin shook his head. 'I believe the lawyer contacted the Foreign Office in London directly so nobody at the embassy knows anything about him. Who on earth…' He shook his head again, baffled. 'Tell me exactly what happened when you met the lawyer.'

'I had to sign my name.'

'A receipt?'

'Acknowledging I had been given blah-blah-blah. First I signed the receipt, then Debbie signed as translator. Oh, first he made me sign another piece of paper.'

Martin pursed his lips. 'Let me get this straight. He made you sign this paper first?'

'That's right.'

'Why?'

'Wanted to watch me do it, see I did it naturally, wasn't doing a careful forgery.'

'He could have done that watching when you signed the receipt proper.'

'I didn't know when I signed that I was going to have to do it a second time, did I?'

'Oh Matt.' Martin prodded at his teabag. 'Tell me what you signed.'

'A sheet of paper. I told you.'

'A blank sheet?'

Clough said nothing.

'So, a blank sheet.' Martin leaned over the table. 'By now his secretary has typed above your signature: "Being of totally sound mind, I give absolutely and without prejudice all my late father's estate to the admirable Mr B in recognition of the many years of devoted service he rendered dear papa." Signed Matthew Clough.'

Again a silence.

Martin ran a thumb across his upper lip, turning half his mouth up into a wry smile. 'Maybe he won't do anything of the sort. It's just I have a dirty mind. What happened next?'

'Debbie and I went to a café to get something to eat. After fifteen or twenty minutes Finnis arrived.'

'My dirty mind tells me that is not a coincidence.'

'Finnis said he was having a drink at the Latvija Hotel and saw us walk by.'

'Possible?'

'Our route took us round the back of the Latvija. Would the bar have a view of the dustbins?'

'So how would he know where you were? Did he follow you?'

Clough had a clear memory of standing outside the lawyer's building while Debbie chatted to the naked ladies. He'd checked the street both ways before they crossed over. No Finnis in sight.

'Finnis didn't follow us.' He drank coffee while Martin waited. 'It's possible Birznieks's secretary alerted him. I wondered how he knew and that's the best I could come up with. They're both Russian.'

Martin blinked as if dust had got in his eyes.

'What did Finnis want?'

'What the lawyer had given me. He saw the keys. He picked them up and I had to force them from him. Debbie had tucked the paper with the actual addresses in her bag but he saw the tags saying Mezaparks, Sigulda and Majori.'

'He wanted what the lawyer had given you.'

Martin thought about this. Meaning the lawyer was straight. Meaning someone else was dodgy, someone who was aware Clough was going to see the lawyer. Sometimes, Martin knew, you smiled inside yourself when you made a connection. I may be old, he thought, but old is different from senile. For a moment the smile broke through to the surface.

'So Mr B is boring and nit-picking and self-important - just what we expect of a lawyer – but he has protected your father's interests.'

'The police also called on Birznieks,' Clough said, 'fishing around.'

'When was it you were called for questioning by the police? Day before yesterday?'

Clough nodded.

'It was a woman who questioned you. She was the one who spoke English. But you thought there was more to her than being an interpreter.'

'Lucija,' Clough said. 'Surname unknown.'

'She gave you her telephone number. Never ignore a lady who does that. Is that formidable memory of yours still in good order?'

'I wrote the number down when I left the office.'

'Get in touch. Find out what her interest is.'

Had there been an intruder? Clough stopped just inside his room. He was like a fox, alert for anything alien. Curtains closed. Bed linen smooth. Papers undisturbed. He skirted the bed and picked up the bible and opened it. The Dictaphone was there. He hesitated. Yes? No? Then he pressed *play*.

I remember the day the Germans lost the war. Not 8ᵗʰ May 1945, I mean lost the war for me. February 1943 it was. I even remember the exact

*day – the tenth. That is when we heard about the defeat at Stalingrad.
The authorities in Salaspils tried to keep it secret. Hopeless. They knew
there'd be trouble. The news that von Paulus had surrendered spread
like a grass fire. Cheers and arms waving. 'Heil Hitler!' boys shouted
and stuck their arses out and pulled a lavatory chain. This was no time
for rifle butts. The gallows were busy. Half a dozen had a noose tied
round their necks while they called out to God but God was otherwise
occupied. The trapdoors opened and they danced their last in full view
of the other prisoners. You have to show who is master.*

*The surrender at Stalingrad was a shock. The German army was not
invincible. Their discipline broke. They were disloyal to Hitler's orders.
They tried to save their own skins, which not many did. Russian snow,
Russian bayonets, Russian camps saw to that.*

Talk about the road to Damascus – a vision, a conversion.

*You think I exaggerate? Insult God? Believe me, God had his hands
full dealing with the chaos he'd let erupt in the world and paid no
attention to me. I had to plan my own survival. The Red Army was
advancing. No stopping them. Every unit had a* politruk *– a political
instructor – and this is what they taught. 'There is no such thing as a
prisoner of war, there is only a coward. Fight to the last bullet and then
keep fighting. When we finally defeat the Fascist invaders, any Russian
who surrendered will be shot as a traitor to the cause of proletarian
triumph.' So the Ivans fought. If their ammunition ran out they fought
with knives, they fought with their bare hands, they fought with tricks.
Do you know what I heard? They threw snowballs and the Krauts
pulled back thinking they were grenades. Well, that's communism for
you. You've got to admire it.*

*When the Red Army reached Latvia what would be the fate of a
guard in a camp?*

*I walked in the forest and thought about war. Death is for heroes.
To survive you must plan ahead.*

*In autumn I got to know Merija. The railway line that brought
prisoners passed through the forest. Incidentally – you'll find this hard
to believe – the line went on to a place called Ogre. There, I knew you*

wouldn't believe it. Sometimes when I slipped away for a walk I crossed the tracks. There was a clearing in the forest. Just three or four cottages and patches of potatoes and beets.

Picture the scene. I stepped out from behind a beech tree and surprised a woman about my age. One hand held a basket, the other clutched the dress above her bosom. In war women are always afraid of rape. I asked what she was doing and she said gathering mushrooms. Didn't she know it was against wartime regulations to take food for private consumption? She began to tremble. I said I hated to see a woman cry and perhaps it wouldn't be necessary to report her. I would have to consider. I said nothing more, I swear it, but she turned round, bent over, lifted her skirt and we did it right there at the edge of the forest. She wasn't pretty but, by God, she had some flesh to her and I went like a stallion.

I couldn't get away more than once a week but she told me she went to the woods every afternoon, just in case. When winter came we moved inside, lying on an eiderdown in front of the kitchen range. She had a husband who worked as a tree feller. I say 'husband' though they had never married in the legal sense. It was more – how shall I say – more of a barnyard union. Why wasn't her husband in the army? He was as good as deaf, she said. Is this a problem? Do sergeants give orders in a quiet voice? I found out it was true because he came back unexpectedly one afternoon while we were going at it. I scrambled through the kitchen door with my trousers in my hand. The chickens and the dog went berserk but he never came out to find out what the fuss was about. He heard nothing.

It was early 1944. The Red Army was grinding its way closer.

'Do you love me, Merija?'

'You know I do.'

'It's not just the fucking?'

'Don't use that word.'

'As you love me, get me Vitalij's identity card and ration book.'

'Why?'

'He does hard physical labour. I might be able to get him an extra ration of sausage.'

The third evening after that the German military authorities called at the cottage. They were desperate for more men, deaf or not. Vitalijs couldn't be conscripted because it was against the Hague Convention but he could volunteer. They demanded his papers. When he couldn't produce them he was given a choice: go to prison or volunteer.

How did they know he hadn't got his papers? Who could have pointed the finger?

Merija was upset, I could tell. I gave her a gold ring I had got from a prisoner, slipped it on her finger, and told her we were going to live in Riga. Her husband was lost in the war and I was her new husband. She held her hand up, twisting it this way and that, admiring the ring as it caught the light, and her tears dried up. Don't women amaze you?

So we went to Riga, Merija with the gold ring on her finger, me with a new identity. We got a room near the market. It had a table, two chairs, a closet with a curtain instead of a door and a bed that sagged in the middle. When we undressed the first night she clapped a hand to her mouth to stifle a scream. It was the first time we had been completely naked. True.

'What's that?'

A scar ran round my ribcage under my left arm, like the stab of a bayonet. It was fresh, one of the stitch holes infected and weeping. I had drunk half a litre of vodka before I had the courage to do that with a kitchen knife.

'It's my war wound. It is why I am invalided out of the army.'

Planning ahead, you see.

I chose to live near the market because there are always pickings. At one time it was the biggest market in Europe. The meat hall was the size of a football pitch and during the war just as empty. I got pally with a butcher who slipped me little packages - pig's trotters, pig's ears, sometimes a pig's tongue. 'Hell man,' I said, 'is this all there is to a pig these days?' A week later he gave me a bloody parcel with a wink. I opened it – a pig's tail.

Merija got a job washing dishes in a canteen. I did better, a factory making casings for artillery shells. It was working twenty-four hours a day. The manager who interviewed me was German.

'What work did you do before?'

'I was in the army.'

'You?' He frowned. In wartime there are two conflicting imperatives: cut any corners to get a job done, but don't get caught breaking regulations. 'Maybe you are a deserter. Where are your discharge papers?'

'Here.' I opened my jacket, pulled up my shirt and gave him a sight of that vivid scar running round my ribs.

He jumped to his feet to shake my hand. 'You are a brave man.'

Now you know what your father did during the war.

I SURVIVED.

Clough pushed back the chair and went to the bathroom. He filled a glass of water and drank it down. Look at that face in the mirror. Is it his father's?

He moved to the bedroom window and parted the curtains. He wanted to see the girl opposite but she had a customer with her.

He should never have played the Dictaphone. The river was the right place for it. Too late now.

The Allies were sweeping east from the Channel and coming up through Italy but the real menace was the Red Army. Their generals lacked imagination. One idea had been drummed into them at military college: put the artillery in a long line, blast the shit out of the enemy, haul the guns forward, do it again. When they got to Latvia we would be blown to bits, then the bits ground to dust under their tank tracks. No escape.

But yes, there was. A miracle occurred. In the last October of the war the factory was moved to Germany. Everything: machinery, workers, management, the lot. We were loaded on a freighter, shipped to Rostock, sent by rail to Prenzlau, just north of Berlin and got down to business again.

That is to say, I went. Merija was in tears again. In wartime, I told her, husbands are strictly temporary. Don't get me wrong, I looked after her. I took her to the market and showed her to my butcher pal. He nodded. He appreciated a good piece of rump.

Berlin! Seventy kilometres away! I could scarcely believe my luck. You see I had an address in the suburbs beyond Wannsee. I got it from an old Jew who passed through the camp. His name was Rothstein. 'Why, you are half way to being a Rothschild already,' I said to him but he didn't laugh. Shame. You should keep your sense of humour or the camp becomes depressing. I looked after him for a month, maybe less. 'Of course the sausage is kosher. The pigs are all in uniform.' Laugh, well I did. I gave him a couple of bread rolls and he gave me the address of the family home in Berlin.

Just over the horizon it seemed. So close but out of reach.

We turned out shell casings until the steel ran out. First of April. 'Aprilscherz' we muttered, now what. The manager vanished but we were locked in a compound, starving like prisoners in the camp. We ate grass, buds from an oak tree, snails. The war was catching up with us. It was distant thunder, it was close, it was roaring all round us, then it stopped. Berlin had fallen, the Führer had killed himself, the Red Army was triumphant. Prenzlau was in the Soviet sector, my misfortune. Russian soldiers lined us up against a wall. Not good. I speak from experience.

Nobody spoke. The Ivans began fingering the triggers on their weapons. Weren't you afraid, you ask. Well you damn well shouldn't. Bad manners. I swallowed and found my voice.

'We are Latvians.' I spoke Russian which I had learnt when they gobbled Latvia at the beginning of the war. 'We have been forced to work here night and day. We are slave labour.'

'Papers,' the sergeant demanded.

'Our papers were taken from us. The manager burnt them because they were evidence we were foreign slaves.'

'You are lying. You are fascist shits.'

'Comrade sergeant, look at us. Look at the rags we wear. See how thin we are, skin and bones. Do we look like the master race?'

His eyes went down the line until they reached Mohr. Now here was a sad case. Mohr was German but he wasn't an evil fellow, he just obeyed orders. He coughed badly because in 1917 he had got half a lungful of gas. It was German gas, as it happened, because the wind had changed. So here he was, Half-Lung Mohr, second-in-command of the factory, now in sole charge since the manager had handed over the keys and told him to stay at his post. Mohr obeyed.

'Who is he?'

'He is Herr Mohr. He is in charge of us. Or he was until you came.'

'German?'

'Yes, comrade sergeant.'

The sergeant raised his rifle and shot him between his eyes. The woman next to Mohr screamed and dropped to her knees.

'Who is the woman?'

'His secretary.'

'Also German?'

'Yes.'

The sergeant jerked his head and two soldiers dragged her to a corner and raped her.

'Wait here. Do not attempt to run away or you will be shot.'

We could not have run anywhere. We were too weak.

Am I boring you? Too many memories? Don't give up. Now it becomes amazing.

We were moved to Berlin, Well, not really Berlin, more the end of civilisation. Getting the railway working was a priority so there I was, labouring away with a shovel, helping to lay new track. What a waste of my languages, but that's the military mind for you. It took weeks before I could get moved to the Transport Directorate of the occupying powers. I was a clerk but don't think that is a lowly job. It was a position with possibilities. For instance I had to draw up the manifest for transporting goods. The order was then signed by a senior officer of the occupying powers, but since they were busy men I developed another talent: copying their signatures. I was planning ahead as you will see.

No Wall divided the city so it was possible to visit all sectors. Berlin was the world capital of espionage and I determined to join in. How?

*Look furtive, make notes, act like a bad spy until... One day I was
followed by a man in a belted raincoat and a tweed cap – only an
Englishman would dress like that. I dodged round the corner of a
bombed warehouse and as he hurried after me I caught him by the
lapel, knocking his cap to the ground.*

'I wish to spy for England,' I muttered. 'Take me to your colonel.'

*Not sophisticated, but I was a young man in a hurry. He blustered,
even denying he was English. I picked up his cap and brushed the dirt
off it. He had written his name in black ink on the inside.*

'So you are from the distinguished German family of Sidebotham.'

*I let him go and followed him. This made him nervous so eventually
I ended up seeing his superior, a thin man with hair that was dying in
patches. He shook my hand and gave me a cup of tea though a whisky
would have been more welcome. I saw no reason for the dance of the
seven veils so I said directly, 'I want to spy for England.' He drew on
his cigarette and said nothing. Ah, a cunning one, I thought. 'I work
in the Transport Directorate.' 'Da?' he said, raising an eyebrow. He is
interested, I decided. 'No, I am not Russian, I am Latvian.' 'Latvian?'
he echoed. The eyebrow sank. 'Dear oh dearie me, Latvian. Wheels
within wheels and all that.' His voice had sunk to a murmur. 'Terribly
sorry, old boy, but I'm jolly grateful you thought of us.'*

*Useless. So I tried the Cheka. Don't tell me the Cheka went out after
Lenin. The Russians keep changing the name of their spy outfit so I stick
with Cheka. First I was accused of being an agent provocateur and
given a beating. Then they said I had no useful intelligence because they
knew everything. 'Really? Do you know the prefix code the Americans
use when a train is bringing in ammunition?' That impressed them
but I still wasn't trusted.*

*I went to a dreadful social evening run by the communist transport
workers union. We suffered a film about life on a collective potato
farm, drank thin beer and heard a Red Army choir singing songs no
one understood. The evening was going badly so I banged my mug on
the table and said I had a little poem. I still remember it.*

'Vor Turen von Stalin, steht Kirchensteins rot,

Er bittet ihn dringend um Salz und um Brot,
Er macht einen Kniefall, er Weint und wird weiss.
Doch läcbeit bloss Stalin schicht ihn, 'Geb Scheisse.'
There was stunned silence. Then some began to jeer, others to titter.
A union boss stormed over and I said, 'Don't be an ass. Look at the ones
who are sniggering. They are the class traitors. You'd do better getting
their names than raising your fist at me.'
He thought about this and smiled.
So, in a modest way, began my association with the Cheka.
But, you are objecting, what about the Rothstein house? What was
so special about it? Why have…

Enough. It wasn't just the things his father had done, it was the preening and boasting. *But,* a voice whispered in his ear, *this was your father, you followed in his footsteps and became a spy. Didn't you sleep with a woman you picked up in Düsseldorf, betray her and lead to her death? Well, how do you answer?*

Something made him think of Debbie and sleeping with her. That was different. She had picked him up. She wanted to know how good his German was. Let's see.

He rewound the tape and translated.

Kirchenstein is standing at Stalin's front door
Pleading for bread and salt and much more,
Down on his knees, in tears, growing white.
But Stalin just laughs and tells him, 'Go shite.'
Language, rhythm, rhymes, not bad at all, Debbie.

Here was the father he never knew. The more he discovered the more his bile rose. Yet his mother had fallen for him. A farmyard union? Surely more. It was something he would never understand.

Enough.

Time for Lucija, Who was she? Why was she interested in K.K.?
The phone was answered on the third ring.
'*Svieka.*'
'Is that Lucija?'

'*Es nesaprofu.*'

'I want to speak to Lucija. Do you understand English?'

'*Angliski?*'

'Yes.'

There was a series of clicks. How many people are listening? A pause, then a man clearing his throat.

'You want Lucija?' he asked. 'What Lucija?'

She'd said her surname was a secret.

'I'll tell you what she's like. Early forties, elegant, smokes Quattro cigarettes and has a gold lighter. Is that enough for you?'

'Why do you want to speak to her?'

'Do you always ask questions about a lady's private affairs?'

There was a pause, another click, then 'Hello.'

'Lucija?'

'Yes. Who is this?'

Clough paused a moment. Not his name, he decided. He knew what had intrigued her.

'This is the wine merchant.'

'Oh. You haven't flown back to England.'

'Can I see you?'

She made a little noise, half way to a laugh.

'So this is how you make friends with a woman in a bar – the direct approach.'

Clough thought of how she had held his eyes, like a challenge.

'Lucija, I am not in a bar now. This is serious.'

There was silence. Had she put her hand over the phone to speak to someone? When she came back her voice had an answering seriousness.

'Do you know Raina bulvaris, Mr Cloff? It's in the centre of the city.'

'I have a map.'

'Come to number five. I will be waiting.'

Chapter 18

Martin walked into his hotel room and into a trap. A man he'd never seen before was sitting in the padded chair, magazine covering his lap, hand under the magazine. Damn, he thought, where's my tradecraft gone?

'Don't go screaming for mother,' the man said. 'We don't want a tantrum, do we.'

The Spectator, Martin noted. He brought the magazine with him, preparing to wait. Any significance in the choice of *Spectator*? A lively right winger? Martin was searching for any scrap of information to help him assess the situation. He gave a swift glance round the room. Pillow disturbed, wardrobe door slightly ajar, TV possibly shifted. He moved a couple of steps and lowered himself on the bed. Now he could see the pistol pointing at him from under the magazine. He won't shoot, he reasoned. If he'd come to kill me, he'd have done it already. He's in the chair because he wants a chat. That was logical but a gun pointed at your stomach has its own logic.

The man got to his feet. 'Just routine,' he said.

He stretched out his left hand and patted Martin's breast and side pockets. He kept his right hand with the pistol pointing at Martin.

'Good boy, you're clean. Now we can relax and be cosy.' When he sank back in the chair the pistol had vanished. 'I expect you want to know who I am; fellow sitting in your hotel room, waving a firearm at you.'

Martin broke his silence.

'So who are you? What name are you going to give me?'

'I'm from London,' he said, not bothering with a name.

'Big place, London. You and eight million others.'

'Don't play stupid. You know what I mean.'

Yes, Martin knew in a general way. But which department? Or outfit? Or niche? Chip away at the man's confidence, he decided.

'That thing real?' He nodded at the bulge in the man's pocket.

The man stared and said nothing.

'And loaded? Pistols aren't my strong point.'

'What use is a gun that's not loaded?'

'Well, it *looks* threatening. Are you a gambling man? Would you have a go at someone with a gun that might or might not be loaded? There again it might be a replica.'

'It's genuine.'

'I have to believe you. I suppose. But, you see, if it was plastic it wouldn't set the alarm off when you stepped through that security arch at Heathrow. Pack it in your luggage and it would show up when it was x-rayed.'

Sometimes you shut up, gave nothing away. Sometimes you burbled on so the other party lost control of the flow.

'Bit of a poser,' Martin was in his stride now, 'getting a gun past security. Body search, patting you down, unless you have some kind of diplomatic immunity. Of course you might have. You're "from London". Another possibility is you picked it up here. Since you've just flown in that means having contacts in Riga, people on the shady side of the street. You can't just wander into a shop and say "I'll have that nice gun in the window." I mean, even if – '

The pistol in the man's pocket cracked against the chair as he jerked to his feet. Martin swayed back, afraid he'd goaded the stranger too far. No, he seemed to need movement. He turned to the window to peer out at the darkening afternoon. Martin was staying at the old Metropole. In the thirties this had been the hotel of choice for spies, louche diplomats and the kind of woman known as an adventuress.

'Of course you could have got it from Caruthers.'

The man swung round. 'Caruthers?'

'Whatever. I've never met a man called Caruthers but I see him as an old Etonian with an unconvincing moustache. He's Second Secretary at the embassy. Spying is not important here anymore so your coming brightens his day. I'm borrowing the pistol you've got in the strong room, you say, but don't tell anybody.'

'Shut up.' The man stood in front of Martin. 'Listen to me because it's for your own good. You shouldn't be here. You're retired. You're no longer family. Krisjanis Kulbergs worked for us years ago but whatever he did, whatever his death means…'

'Whatever his death means?'

'Listen. What he left to his son is none of your business. You're out of the game. You're digging into things you know nothing about. You know nothing of relations between us and former agents. Nothing. Get it? You come blundering in and sources are at risk.'

Martin nodded. This was what he expected.

'This is the cosy chat you promised?'

'I could be a lot less cosy.'

He jabbed his finger in Martin's face. For a moment he said nothing, letting Martin imagine whatever he wanted.

'I'm not talking about rough stuff. You could face official action when you return to the UK. Let's start with your pension: stopped. Then you could find your passport had died. The police could make one of their dawn raids and turn over your house searching for anything – documents, paperclips, you name it – you'd taken from the Fortress. The Inland Revenue could do one of their Spanish Inquisitions into every crevice of your finances. Understand?'

'You could do that but you're not going to?'

The man's bulging eyes stared at Martin.

'I'm not going to and I'll tell you why. Your interest in Kulbergs is now at an end. You are booked on the 11 a.m. flight to Heathrow via Copenhagen tomorrow morning. Your ticket – whatever it says – will be rewritten when you get to the airport. You will be on that plane.'

Rewriting a ticket, Martin thought, rewriting my life. My interest in Kulbergs finished. On a plane to London. Man with a gun tells me.

'You can do all that? You're the big boss no one has heard of.'

'Don't you understand? You're not in the Firm any longer. Once or twice you ask old pals for favours. They indulge you. Then they wake up. Private crusades, private vendettas - what is Martin up to? He's in competition with the real thing. He's not on the inside any more. He's screwing things up. They won't stand it.'

'"They" won't.'

Martin ran his thumbnail across his upper lip while he considered the man. His tie had discreet stripes – some school? Then there was the pinstripe suit with the slight bulge of the pistol. The black Oxford shoes were spattered with pavement slush. He was dressed for some Whitehall ministry.

'You were never one of us, were you?'

'*You* are no longer "one of us". You are out. You are finished. You are an "ex" interfering for his own reasons.'

I have my reasons, yes, Martin thought. *But there was also the visit to the Fortress and the DD's instruction to find out what the mess was, but softly softly. The man didn't know that.*

Martin had given Heather three names and a telephone number. That telephone number had set off alarm bells and she'd called him urgently. He'd gone to her flat because she didn't trust the telephone. West the man's name was, the man with bulging eyes who 'sat in the shadows' in Wallingford police station.

The bulging eyes were staring at Martin now.

'It's not all stick,' he said. 'Here's the carrot. Drop your interest here and keep your nose clean and you earn your reward. You drive a modest car, Golf, bit dented, quite old.'

'Volkswagen make sturdy cars.'

'You park in the street outside your house where any fool could back carelessly into it. Or, your part of London, joyriders could steal it. Insurance would pay up but not much on a ten year-old car. Maybe it's time you got a new one, moved up market for a bit of comfort in your retirement. A BMW would do you nicely. One morning in, let's say, a month's time you could find one parked outside your house with the keys popped through your letter flap. Provided you've been a good boy, that is. You know what the cocaine barons say in Colombia? *Plato o plombo.*'

He was speaking slowly, then he stopped. He cocked his head to one side as if listening for a voice.

'Your decision, Martin.'

West, Martin thought, first name not given by Heather. Works for a splinter of the Foreign Office called Policy Research Group who assessed the intelligence the Firm provided and the initiatives proposed. That was part of their job. Also charged with hushing up scandals and keeping an eye on the spies. Who kept an eye on them?

'Check-in ninety minutes before the flight,' West said. 'Allow a quarter of an hour to have your ticket rewritten. Be there.'

West picked up the navy overcoat he had draped over the back of the chair. He tapped his suit pocket where the pistol was, to check it hadn't slipped out, or as a reminder to Martin. He didn't say goodbye.

Martin had the phone number of the Policy Research Group but it was stuffed in a drawer of his desk back home. It took three calls until he charmed the number from a secretary at the Firm. He rang and got a jolly female voice.

'You want to speak to Mr West? Awfully sorry but he's away for the weekend.'

'Already?'

'Already?' she echoed as if that was a hoot. 'Yesterday actually. Lovely long weekend in the country.'

'Out of the country, you said.'

'No, *in* the country. You know, green stuff beyond the M25: cows, babbling brooks, frolics behind the barn.'

'When will he be back?'

'Weekends commonly end on Monday morning, you know. But long weekends, ooh la, depends on what delights there are. Will someone else do? Me for instance? I'm available.'

Martin pictured a girl with long brown hair, painting her nails before the assault on the weekend. She was called Sarah, was wearing a dress from Miss Selfridge, and mummy and daddy had a place in Shropshire.

'It was West himself I needed to speak to.'

'A message then? Who's calling?'

'No message.'

West was not in Riga on official business. Martin had never thought he was. The Foreign Office did not do policy research with a pistol.

Martin was in Riga officially unofficially. He needed to keep the Deputy Director on his side.

'Hold on. Are you calling from the embassy?'

'The embassy is too...connected.'

Martin had given thought to how West could have known he was in Riga and at which hotel. Only the embassy knew, so West must have a chum there.

'Then you're on an open line.'

Bad men know it all already, he thought. Aloud he said, 'Everybody here wants something, but something different.'

'Everybody everywhere wants money,' the Deputy Director said, 'and sex and power.'

That's her style, to cut in and be sharp. He started again.

'It's a messy situation, nothing clear cut. Matt is here because his father is dead. His father's body hasn't been released so it sounds as if there's doubt about the cause of death. Father's housekeeper-stroke-mistress was battered to death and the house ransacked. An ex-KGB man is taking too close an interest for my liking. Matt has been mugged and questioned by the authorities and picked up by a woman who lies about why she is here. I have been warned off by a man with a pistol, one of our own side.'

'One of us? Who?'

'Not in the Firm.'

'Well, who then? Come on, give me a clue.'

This is the game we have to play, Martin knew, tiptoeing past the computers listening in Cheltenham. He thought a moment. 'It's where young men in America were told to go.'

She was back like a shot.

'He's a cheeky bugger.'

'He's not here officially. I rang his office. His assistant said he was having a long weekend somewhere in the country. Instead he came here. He was waiting in my room.'

'What did he want?'

'He wants me on a plane home. He wants me to keep my nose clean. He tried to be threatening but it didn't come naturally to him. He belongs behind a desk. In the end he made me the Medellin cartel's offer.'

'Which is?'

'Silver or lead.'

She was silent. She's translating that into whatever jargon they speak in the Firm these days, he decided.

He said, 'Some dirt swept under the carpet is making a big bump. You may want to take action.'

There was a long pause.

'So may you,' she said.

He didn't kill me when he had the chance.

Martin got out his bottle of duty free Macallan and sipped from the bathroom glass.

Gunshot noise wasn't a problem. Old hotel, thick walls. Anyway a single pistol shot? Or was it a car backfiring? Nobody would come knocking at the door.

West didn't kill me because he hadn't got what he wanted. He'd searched the room and it wasn't here. Martin sipped the whisky. *What is he expecting me to do? He didn't kill me but he threatened me. Bad move to kill me in Latvia. Local police get involved. Embassy pushes. London tabloids sniff dirty work. Posh papers point out Latvia used to be part of the Soviet Union and start speculating. Kill me in England and Inspector Plod can be led astray.*

West was worried about what a one-time British agent might have given away, a name, a link. In the Firm? In Whitehall? In the police? That was it, wasn't it?

Another sip of whisky. Martin decided he knew nothing.

He picked up the telephone and dialled the Konventa Seta. He was put through to Matt's room. One-two-three. Counting is what you did when you were worried. Four-five-six. He's lying on the floor, dead. Seven-eight-nine. West shot him and then ran here. His shoes were all dirty. Ten-eleven-twelve.

He put the receiver down.

Matt wasn't dead. He just hadn't returned from seeing Lucija, surname unknown, professional interest unknown.

Chapter 19

Raina bulvaris ran along the north side of the park, classical elegance mixed with brutalist thugs. Big buildings are snobs: only people who already know them are welcome. Which was number five? There were no signs.

'Mr Cloff, you are walking straight past me. Why do you have your nose in the air? Do you not want to see me?'

Lucija's voice brought him to a stop. Turning he saw her face framed by a car window. Like a portrait in a gallery, he thought. The car was a green Citroen Dyane that showed honourable scars: a cracked sidelight, a dented wing, as if ice made roads treacherous and there was no point having it repaired until spring. She lifted a hand to her mouth to draw on her cigarette than dropped the butt in the gutter. An eyebrow was raised which made her look quizzical. It takes a certain class, Clough thought, to look quizzical.

'I wasn't expecting you in that.'

'Oh?' The eyebrow raised a fraction.

'It's…modest.'

'And me – I am not modest?' She frowned. 'Oh, you mean it is not an expensive car. I regret freedom has not made Latvians rich, except for bankers and lawyers and the owners of nightclubs.'

'You are a prisoner of your freedom,' Clough said. When she looked puzzled he said, 'that's what you said when we first met.'

'Also we are prisoners of the past. There is no escape from that. We think the past becomes more distant but it is always inside us.' She touched her forehead and her heart. 'But it is better we don't

185

debate the bigger issues of life in the street. You may not have noticed but it has begun snowing. Come and sit beside me.'

When Clough closed the door she started the engine. It was not to drive anywhere, just for the heater. The car was very cold. She used the flick-wipe to clear snow off the windscreen.

'So why do you ask to see me, Mr Cloff? What is it that is so urgent?'

And you agreed to meet me at once, Clough thought. And I didn't say it was urgent, I said it was serious.

'It's about Krisjanis Kulbergs. I need to find out the truth before I go back to England.'

'You want my advice? It is better you go back to In Vino Veritas now. Safer, most certainly. Search for the truth there.'

'I had an idea you could help me.'

'Mr Cloff, truth is very precious, so precious that sometimes people lock it away out of sight. They say, do not reach out a hand to touch it or you will be shot dead.' She took a deep breath and leaned across him to point. 'Do you see that mound? On the other side of the canal?'

'Yes.'

'There are five stone slabs but they are hidden from this angle.'

He waited.

'Ten years ago five men were killed here. January the twentieth. Very soon it will be the anniversary. There will be flowers, red and white, and candles will be lit. Last year someone brought a tape recorder and played Elton John. You know the song? I hope that doesn't happen again. Our remembrance should not be turned into a pop concert. We want to remember the day in 1991 when Soviet Special Forces stormed the Interior Ministry. Stormed? Is that the word you use?'

'Newspapers use it.'

'Very well, they attacked the Interior Ministry because we were already declaring our independence. Dozens were shot, five fatally. There was a film crew and one of them who was shot, a man called

Slapins, said as he lay dying, "keep filming, keep filming." These Special Forces had automatic weapons and bulletproof clothing and knives with broad blades to cut throats and grenades that can blind attached to their belts and faces painted black and killers' eyes. What did we have?' She brought up her hands and opened them, palms up. 'Nothing. They turn everywhere looking for an enemy and all they can find is people who demand truth and liberty and justice. It is a humiliation for them.'

She stopped. She was here, Clough realised, part of the crowd claiming their freedom.

'The special forces, OMON, were overrunning this building here.' She pointed. 'Where I work is next door, the Citizenship Board. Does that sound boring to you?'

'I don't know what you do.'

'You imagine days spent putting forms in filing cabinets, yes?'

Clough waited. Lucija listened to the idling motor, heard it falter and revved it with the accelerator.

'Latvia is a small country, less than three million people. That includes everyone who lives permanently here, citizen and non-citizen. We Latvians are only just a majority. Here in Riga, Russians are actually the majority. We must be careful we are not outnumbered in our own country. So there are rules about who can live here, who can be a citizen, who can be elected. There are some who can never be citizens, such as former Soviet soldiers, such as former KGB officers. Does our work begin to have interesting possibilities?'

Perhaps the heater was broken. The car seemed no warmer. Again Clough said nothing, not wanting to break the flow.

'Andris Slapins said "keep filming, keep filming." The evidence of Soviet brutality had to be shown to the world. "Keep filming," were his last words. All we wanted was to have control of our own destiny. In a different way it is what I am doing: making sure the future of our country stays in our hands.'

She opened her handbag, pulled out a cigarette, then handed Clough the lighter. Her eyes fixed on his face above the flame as it touched the end of the cigarette. When she accepted the lighter back from Clough her fingers seemed to stay on his a heartbeat longer than necessary. *Am I imagining it? Does she do this with every man? Is there a different etiquette in Latvia?*

'This is why I am interested in your father,' she said, still holding his eyes. 'Your father was a bad man, Mr Cloff.'

The judgement was straightforward but her eyes looked troubled.

'That is my opinion. He was a Latvian but a spy for the Russians. And before that he worked in a concentration camp for the Germans. It doesn't surprise you, what I say? You knew it already? Why do you not answer me?'

'I knew it.'

'How did you know?'

'How did you know?' he countered.

'A telephone call. Usually we get letters. No name of course. You can guess the kind of thing: Mr So-and-so used to be a Soviet James Bond. We look into it and find it's a quarrel between neighbours. Sometimes the letters are written with the left hand to disguise it, or words cut out from newspapers. Telephone calls definitely less often. But about two weeks ago we had such a call. Krisjanis Kulbergs had been a Nazi collaborator of the worst kind, also a spy for Moscow. I did not answer this call myself. It was that captain you have already met.'

'The one who wanted to hit me.'

'In a very painful place, Mr Cloff.' She drew on her cigarette and let the smoke out slowly. She reached over to pat his knee. 'The captain went to the house of Kulbergs. There is no secret about the house in Mezaparks. Kulbergs is known to the telephone company. The captain spoke to an old woman; your father's companion, I suppose. The captain was, in my view, indiscreet, but that is his nature. You have noticed how quickly he can become angry. Perhaps he made certain threats about prosecuting your father for war crimes, removal of citizenship, confiscation of property. So it goes.' She sighed. 'Before we could take any action your father died.

Now there is a coincidence, a neatness you might say. Kulbergs is well enough to go out about his business, the captain calls, and two days later he is dead.'

'How did he die?'

Lucija was surprised. 'You don't know?'

'I was told there is some confusion about it.'

'He was found in the Daugava river, in the suburbs. But was it suicide? Accident? Murder? The pathologist said he drowned so it could be any of those. Did he slip on the ice? Was his head held underwater? I saw the pathologist's report and there was no mention of cuts or bruises. The pathologist is called Stepanov, which is not a Latvian name. He is in his sixties. Age and name show he most likely had the same job in Soviet days. The police inspector who investigated and signed various forms was called Celmins, late fifties, also a left-over from the Soviet era. We are a free country, Mr Cloff, but such freedom is precarious. A mouse runs free and so does a cat. You look again and the cat is licking its lips. I would say the mouse is not as free as the cat. Right here in Riga we have networks of people from the old regime who look after each other. It's like a club. Maybe not a club, more like a castle. They are inside and have thick walls to protect them and if you get too close they drop big stones on you. According to a document I have just seen your father's body was released to his companion Otilija Stunda. The date on the form was two days before she was killed. The signature of the authorising officer is Inspector Celmins.'

'My father's lawyer doesn't know the body has been released.'

'Well.' Her shrug was weary. 'I would say the form leads a secret life and it was just brought out of hiding to impress me.'

Clough stared through the windscreen at a policeman outside the Interior Ministry. He stamped his feet against the cold, then took a pull on the cigarette cupped inward in his hand. He glanced in their direction and away.

Clough felt it was like a dream that dissolved when you opened your eyes. The captain's visit to the house in Mezaparks, the death that followed so swiftly, the officials still in place from the Soviet era, the forms they signed. And Finnis.

Only connect. There was a pattern but…

The thought slipped away.

'One more thing.'

He noticed the change in her voice, a tightening that warned him: no charming evasions, if you please, no double-speak.

'The telephone call saying that Kulbergs was a wartime collaborator and then a Soviet spy was recorded. I have listened to it. A woman, speaking good Latvian but not Latvian born. There were certain intonations such as ending a sentence with a rising tone? Like this? It made me think she was American. I remembered the ticket inspector on the train to Sigulda who said there was a foreign couple and the woman spoke good Latvian but possibly with a Swedish accent. She won't have heard many Americans talk. I could get the ticket inspector to listen to the tape to see if she recognised her. Maybe I will. But voices sound different on the telephone. Sometimes more harsh, like giving orders. Or more intimate, someone whispering in your ear on a pillow. Have you noticed, Mr Cloff?'

What Clough had noticed was Lucija seducing him. From the beginning she had set out to win him not to fight him, making him do little things like light her cigarette, holding his eyes, reaching over to touch him. Sitting in the half-light of the car was another step, the isolation from the outside world. The heater was working now and Clough felt cocooned in warmth, close to her.

'We did take the train to Sigulda,' he said.

'Who? You and…'

'A woman called Debbie Brown. Canadian she says but with Latvian roots. I have only known her a few days. She was scouting out Kulbergs' house in Mezaparks – I'm almost sure she was – and she followed me back to town and picked me up.'

'So she went with you to the house in Sigulda. Go on please.'

He wondered if she had a tape recorder in the car but decided he didn't care. Sam had said he wouldn't share but telling Lucija was the most natural thing in the world.

'The door wasn't locked so we went in.'

'Like burglars.'

'Not like burglars. My father was dead so the house belonged to me. That was what I decided. When we got inside we could see someone had been searching for something. Chaos everywhere.' Her eyes held his, testing for lies or evasions. 'In an upstairs room was the body of my father's companion.'

'Already dead?'

'Yes.'

'You didn't report it to the police? Why not?'

Clough took a moment to consider.

'Because I thought the police would suspect me?'

He was hesitant. Debbie and he had left the house and simply walked away from the scene of the crime.

'It seemed a good idea at the time.'

People said that when they had been stupid.

'Your girlfriend went all through the house with you?'

'Girlfriend?' Clough frowned at the description of Debbie and shook his head. 'She followed me, taking photos.'

'When she saw the body she didn't cry out? She didn't want to inform the police?'

'No.'

'When she saw the body did she take photos?'

'I don't remember. Just a minute, yes, she did.'

Lucija faced forward. The warmth in the car was melting the snow on the windscreen so it slid in rivulets down the glass. She used the flick-wipe again then ran her hand over the glass to wipe away condensation. Dusk spread out from the buildings but daylight lingered in the park.

'I am not a police detective,' she said. 'All right, you didn't report a crime but that does not concern me. Bad men concern me, men who committed wholesale crime, killing a whole country.' She looked away towards the mound. 'It's not revenge. It's justice, that's how I see it. I don't want men with bad pasts to live in Latvia, become citizens, vote, have influence or power. It's not easy because these people – police officers, lawyers, ministry officials, executives in certain companies, former army officers, KGB agents – look after each other.'

'They watch each other's back.'

'They don't talk. It's like *omerta*. So when the captain went to the house in Mezaparks and questioned the woman…' She paused a moment. 'Perhaps they thought your father was breaking *omerta* and the old woman had talked.'

'You think Kulbergs was murdered?'

'I think…' Once again she paused, her eyes on the mound with the memorial stones. 'I think you should be careful.'

'I can give you one of them. Russian, ex-Soviet Foreign Ministry, admitted spying for Moscow, knows about Kulbergs.'

'Who is he?'

'I don't know his name. "Call me Finnis," he said which means his name is something else. I can give you a photo.'

'That's a help.'

'And his telephone number.'

'That's all we need.'

'I haven't got it with me. It's in my room at the hotel.'

There was a silence and as it grew longer Clough had the absurd thought that he'd issued an invitation to her.

'I have things to do,' she said. 'How long will you be in Riga?'

'I should be leaving soon. I can bring you the photo and phone number tomorrow.'

'Excellent.' She clapped her hands. 'Then we shall see each other again.'

Clough reached out, maybe to shake her hand to seal a deal. She took his hand in both hers and squeezed it. I've given her Sigulda, he thought, I've given her Debbie, I've given her Finnis. What more can she want? The Dictaphone? No, that was his.

On an impulse he asked, 'Where did you learn your English?'

She looked at him, eyebrows raised.

'Why do you ask?'

'You speak it as well as I do.'

Except for Cloff, but why spoil a compliment?

'Some years ago I worked for Intourist. I wasn't a guide. I was an interpreter for visiting businessmen and politicians.'

'Didn't you have to be politically sound to have a job like that in the Soviet Union?'

'You have no experience of what it was like. How can I explain? Have you noticed how many husbands are not faithful? And yet they stay married. I would say that marriage was like life in the Soviet Union; you had to learn survival skills.' She was quiet a moment. 'I naturally met many businessmen who were married. In life you can eat at home or at a restaurant. These businessmen were eating at a restaurant far from home and they were always inviting me to join them. I quickly learnt that I was to be the sweet course at the end of the meal.'

'And…' Clough paused. Her closeness was a pull like gravity. 'Are you married?'

She looked away from him, across the stretch of park, over the canal, to the mound with its five stone slabs in memory of the men the OMON troops had killed. She gazed at it like the last sight of land before a voyage into uncharted waters.

'At one time I was.'

Clough had a hand on the swing doors into the Konventa Seta when he heard a shout. He saw a figure on the step of the bar across the road.

'Over here,' the man said.

The light coming out of the bar made a silhouette of the man, his face dark and featureless.

'What's up with you, man? You'll catch your bloody death. Come inside.'

Clough recognised Martin's voice and crossed the road.

'No, sit there,' Martin said as Clough pulled out a chair. 'I want a clear view of the hotel entrance.'

'Who are you watching for?'

'Everybody,' Martin said with a generous spread of his hands. 'You, the cops, Debbie, Finnis if he puts in an appearance, Uncle Tom Cobley.' West too, but Martin didn't mention him. Nor the two men he'd seen greeting Debbie. 'Pure luck you're the first I've caught. What's Debbie doing?'

'No idea,' Clough said. 'She doesn't answer her phone.'

The waitress had wandered over to their table. She was standing, one hip cocked and her hand on it.

'What are you drinking?' Clough asked.

'Scotch.'

'Two whiskies.'

'OK.' The waitress sauntered to the bar, one hand behind her to smooth a skirt that had no wrinkles, as if she knew the men were watching.

'I've had the chat with Lucija,' Clough said. 'She works for the Citizenship Board. Her job is to stop people with bad pasts, as she puts it, settling in Latvia. She seems to target former Red Army soldiers, KGB spies and their like.'

'Russians,' Martin murmured. The Latvian lawyer had done his duty by his client but his battleaxe secretary was Russian and could have tipped off Finnis. Look for the Russian connection just like cold war days. Was he being unfair?

'Krisjanis Kulbergs wasn't Russian,' Clough said.

'He spied for them. Makes him double the baddie.'

The waitress brought their drinks but didn't get a glance.

'Also she said they'd had a tip-off about K.K. Anonymous but sounded like Debbie. Why would she do that?'

Revenge, stir up trouble, prod the authorities; any number of reasons. Debbie had her own agenda. And she wasn't answering her phone. Martin treated the question as rhetorical.

'Where's your father's third house?'

'Majori.'

'I meant: do you know the address in Majori?'

'Debbie took the sheet with the addresses.'

'I know she did.' Martin spelled it out. 'But do you by any happy chance remember the address? Because we should go there. Sooner the better.'

'No, but Lucija can find out. She'll have a contact on the council or know the police chief. I'll ring her. She gave me her mobile number just in case.'

Martin ran his thumb across his upper lip.

Just in case, my eye.

Chapter 20

Taxi drivers outside the Hotel de Rome spoke English.

'Jurmala? Why you go Jurmala?' The driver sounded insulted. 'Is winter, is night, is nothing to do, is shit place. I take you nice place here, plenty girls, very clean, make friends easy.'

'We want to see a man about a dog,' Martin said.

'What dog?' the driver demanded. 'Is special word I don't know maybe? Like grass, hash, pot? Dog like that? Dog you smoke?'

'Just a dog.'

'Is crazy.'

'This is a taxi,' Martin pointed out. 'You're the driver. Why don't you just take us to Jurmala?'

'A Jurmala dog.' The driver started the engine. 'Jesus Christ.'

For five minutes there was silence while the driver negotiated city centre traffic. After they crossed the Daugava the driver slapped the steering wheel and jabbed to the left with a thumb. ''Here is Cheryomushka.'

They looked at a dispiriting stand of apartment blocks.

'It's not Jurmala, is it,' Clough said.

'Is Cheryomushka. Didn't I tell you so? You understand English?' The driver's eyes were fixed on them in the mirror. He spoke loudly to the foreigners. 'Cheryomushka is typical part of Moscow, OK? So when Russia is boss of Latvia many Cheryomushkas were built here. Every town got to have a Cheryomushka just like Moscow.'

You had to love concrete to live here. Eight concrete buildings were divided by a straight concrete path. A concrete wall at the end had a basketball hoop. Local lads had decorated the concrete with graffiti. There were goggle-eyed faces, a swastika, Mick Jagger's lips and tongue, a dinosaur with a saw-toothed back. The most widely understood word on the entire planet leapt out of the basketball hoop: FUCK.

'Moscow.' Martin pursed his lips. 'It's not my idea of Red Square.'

'Jesus Christ.' The driver hunched round to glare at them while the taxi steered itself. 'Is not Red Square. Cheryomushka is part of Moscow where peoples live. Workers, girls, peoples, yes?'

He banged the back of the seat and glared some more before facing front. In the back seat the two men looked at each other. Martin raised his eyebrows: What did I do wrong? Clough shrugged: Search me. The traffic thinned as they drove down a stretch of broad highway. They overtook a beer delivery truck and a Land-Rover marked *Policija*. A Mercedes passed them with two men glowering in the back seat and a chauffeur wearing a peaked cap. Lucija should be here, Clough thought. She would have a context. It used to be party bosses who owned the road, Mr Cloff. Now anyone with a million can be his own commissar.

'Ten minutes in America,' Clough murmured.

'What?' the driver shouted.

'Ten minutes in America.'

'Jesus Christ.'

The taxi stopped outside Jurmala station. Clough paid and the driver inspected each note for forgery.

'You want a drink? You want girls?'

'No thank you,' Martin said.

'You want boys maybe?'

'You're very kind, truly no.'

'What you want with a dog?'

'You'd never believe it.'

The driver's mouth puckered with disgust. 'Jesus Christ.'

The taxi did a squealing U-turn. They watched its red lights disappear in the direction of Riga.

'Did we do something to upset him?' Clough asked.

'I hope so,' Martin said. 'I hate to think he's like that normally.'
'Jesus Christ.'

They stood in front of the station with railway tracks to the left, a band of trees to the right, brightly lit shops behind them and the highway in front.

'Lucija gave you the address,' Martin said. 'Did she tell you how to find it?'

'She said to get the taxi to drop us by the station.'

Martin nodded. Nobody pays attention to a taxi letting people off at a station.

'Then walk? Which way?'

'Down the highway parallel to the beach.'

'How far?'

'A kilometre? She wasn't sure.'

There were streetlights every hundred metres. Between them were pools of darkness.

'She said the house wasn't really in Majori at all but on the edge of the next village. I couldn't catch the name, Dub-something. Maybe a Majori address has more class.'

'Maybe it's meant to mislead.'

The breeze blowing in from the sea felt raw on their faces. It had snowed during the day but it had stopped now. The path beside the highway had been swept clear but only in patches. In between black ice invited a fall. The sound of breaking waves was a muffled roar. The sea was hidden by high dunes topped with trees. Summer villas showed darkened windows. The only lights were ahead and they walked in silence until they reached them. The lights turned out to be the next station. A train must be due. Four or five cars were parked by the entrance and people were standing about.

On the seaward side of the road was a parking lot. White globes of lamps gave a false sense of tropical glamour. In a space half the size of a football pitch there was a car, just one. A dozen cars they would have ignored but a single car was a magnet.

They detoured to it in silence, both laying their hands on the bonnet. It was cold but bare of snow. Anybody could have parked the car but there are times when your brain hops round and says: watch it, that's near our goal. Martin pointed to the tracks the tyres had made, the lines of the treads showing sharply in the lamp light. There were footprints but they got lost in the general scuffling where kids had built an igloo. At the far end of the parking lot was a church, cement rendered, with a clock just visible. Its hands had stopped at ten minutes to three.

'And now?'

'A small road leads off the square opposite the station towards the beach. That's what she said. We take that.'

'How does she know? Who did she speak to?'

'No idea.'

He had asked her to find where the house was and then had to wait until she rang back with instructions. *Are you going to this house, Mr Cloff? You must be careful. Men with bad pasts can be bad now.* But he's dead, Clough had objected. *Stalin died,* she said, *the evil didn't. Take care, Matthew. Your name is Matthew, isn't it?* Yes, Lucija. *Matthew, Matthew, Matthew.* She seemed to be testing the name, judging it.

The narrow road was partly tarred, partly frozen mud. Footsteps had trampled the snow, more than one pair. The road led straight towards the dunes. On the right was a shack built of bricks and clapboard but Lucija had said the house they wanted was on the left. The road started a gentle climb. Now they were walking beside a picket fence. On and up. Then they saw it: a house with shuttered windows. Trees dotted the garden and a viewpoint had a table and benches.

'I want to go further,' Martin said.

They climbed the flank of the dunes. The track dwindled to a path through pine trees and birches. Clumps of coarse grass were bent over with snow. They reached the top and a broad beach lay before them. They could make out children's swings and a climbing frame. A long sweep of sand led down to the sea, waves pawing the beach. At the horizon dark grey met light grey and there were the pinpricks of lights on a ship. To the right was a glow, presumably Majori, to the left there was darkness.

They returned to a gate in the picket fence. Sea air had rusted the hinges and the gate screeched as Clough pushed it. *What does a banshee wail like*, Clough wondered, *and what exactly is a banshee?* He thought it warned of a death to come. He didn't want to repeat the shriek and left the gate open. Looking back he found Martin rooted to the spot, staring at the tarred path. Then it struck Clough: tarred path. The snow hadn't been shovelled aside, it had melted. Someone had put down salt.

They walked up the path and when they reached the house Martin pointed to the right. Clough went that way, Martin to the left. They crossed at the back of the house and returned to the front.

'What do you think?'

Why was Martin hesitating? Was it because the house belonged to Clough's father?

Clough rubbed his shoe on the tar.

'Someone's taking precautions. No snow on the path means no footprints, no evidence of anyone coming and going.'

'Such as someone living here who wanted it kept secret. Your father's companion is dead. Did he have another girlfriend tucked away here?'

'The lawyer never mentioned it.'

'That lawyer…' Martin paused. He'd been too soft with Matt and now was the time – when they were standing at the door – to probe harder. 'That lawyer gave you something. It was more than just house keys. Well, it was, wasn't it?' When Clough said nothing Martin laid a hand on his am. 'I have no intention of walking into any bloody surprises. People have been killed so before we go into this house you're going to tell me.'

Martin had been his Controller and something more. At times it was as if he was the father he'd never had.

'A tape,' Clough said. 'He started it years ago. The Gulf War prompted memories in him. He found a Dictaphone and everything tumbled out. He talked about the Second World War, the Soviet occupation, then the Germans. He was a guard in a concentration camp. Then he worked in a German munitions factory. After the war he was in Berlin and the KGB recruited him. He called it the Cheka.'

'Well, thank you.' About bloody time Martin meant. 'A confession was it, what he did in the concentration camp?'

'The tone of voice is matter of fact. Killing Jews, burying them in pits. Raping female prisoners. Hangings. Beatings. Black market dealings. Cheating prisoners out of jewellery. Seducing a peasant woman. Shopping her husband to the military. Nothing out of the ordinary. That's how it sounds. Just… you know…'

Clough's voice slowed and stopped.

'Dear God.'

Martin closed his eyes. Two nightmares unfolded. First was the public nightmare. Kulbergs, willing cog in a Nazi death camp, had worked for the Firm for decades. Here's a good 'un, they said, forget his shitty past, let's have him. Then there was the private nightmare. What had the discovery done to Matt?

Clough said, 'At the start it was an outburst of excitement. Then it changed as if he was recording his memoirs, telling me everything, making it seem natural. I survived, he said, others were killed, I survived. Survival was his moral principle.'

'So the KGB recruited him,' Martin said, 'and we recruited him. Is there a list of horrors? Operations against the West? Dirty tricks against Moscow Centre to even the score? KGB games to keep them sweet? Double dealing all round? A murder here and there?'

But Clough had withdrawn.

'I didn't know about Kulbergs,' Martin said. 'Others did. The high-ups. The Director. It is Burgess and Maclean and Philby only worse, because we knew. Imagine the headlines: our man sends our spies to their death with our blessing.'

Clough turned aside, concentrating on a pine tree crippled by wind. Martin ploughed on.

'Does he give names and dates? Who his British Controller was?'

'I don't know. I haven't had time to finish it.'

'Is it safe?'

'It's in my room at the hotel.'

Martin was appalled, remembering how easily he'd persuaded the maid to let him in. 'Dear God,' he whispered again.

Well yes, it was in God's safekeeping or at least between the covers of the Gideon bible. Better not tell Martin that. He fished in his pocket for the keys.

'Let's go in.'

This was the house of a dead spy, maybe murdered. For the second time Clough felt he was grave-robbing.

First impression: not darkness but complete blackness. Not a glimmer of light came through the shutters. Never lock the door. That had been drummed into him. You may have to leave sharpish. He moved the little catch of the Yale lock up.

He was blind but his sense of smell was more acute. This wasn't the dead air of a summer house closed for winter. There was nothing so definite as coffee but something. The ghost of a smell.

He caught the sound of movement.

'Wait,' Martin murmured. There was a click. A small torch cast a sharp narrow beam. One swift circuit to check they were alone. Four doors led off the hall, all closed. At the far end was a staircase. The beam searched until it found a switch by the front door. Clough pressed it. Nothing. Martin moved the torch until he found another switch. Nothing.

Martin doused the torch. They stood in blackness. No creaking boards, no footsteps. Waves were a murmur, deadened by walls and shutters. Faintly there was the hum of a truck passing on the highway. Nothing else. Martin touched Clough on the shoulder, a gentle push to stand by the front door.

'Matt, we should leave. I don't like the lights not working.'

'It's winter. The electricity could be…'

Clough didn't finish. The house was warm so it hadn't been shut for the winter.

'We'll come back in daylight and bring help from the embassy.'

Chapman, Clough thought. Big help. This was *his* house and they were here. Stubbornness gathered in him.

Clough opened the door to the right. Martin swung the torch round the room: dining table, chairs, sideboard, all in the heavy style of the house in Sigulda. Under a glass dome a stuffed owl, wings outstretched, gripped a mouse in its talons. *I would say the mouse was not as free as the owl.*

Next was the kitchen. The light didn't come on in the fridge but Clough could make out margarine, beer, ham, vodka and a jar of gherkins. Sigulda all over again.

Martin directed the torch up the staircase. They couldn't see beyond the landing where the stairs turned. Ground floor first, then upstairs.

The third door opened into the study. The desk was a monster, as K.K. had said. On the wall above was an erotic drawing by Schiele. To one side was the TV where the Gulf War had played.

The last door. Clough turned the handle and let Martin go first. Side by side they stood. The beam did one sweeping check for immediate danger. Then, like a camera panning in a film, the beam came back. Martin took his time, halting, lingering, until he'd made a full circuit. He took a deep breath and held it, and held it, saying nothing.

Clough's head throbbed. This was K.K.'s secret, the big one, why Clough had had to show ironclad proof of identity to the lawyer. Here was… what? Evidence of another extraordinary episode in a roller-coaster life? Some shameful crime? No, K.K. had never felt shame. The explanation must lie in the Dictaphone hidden in the Gideon bible.

'You had no idea?' Martin said.

'None.'

'Not an inkling? He kept this hidden how long?' Martin's voice was low. 'Years? Decades? Even when Latvia was part of the Soviet Union? How did he get them?'

Clough had no answer. This was a fact beyond comprehension. Nazi memorabilia he could have understood. K.K. had thought Hitler was a genius. Only later had he turned against the Nazis. So swastikas, photographs of Hitler, Iron Crosses, caps and uniforms, that would be K.K. reverting to type.

This?

Martin's torch was making the circuit a third time. Except where curtained windows made breaks, the walls were covered in oil paintings, a couple of dozen. It was Krisjanis Kulbergs' own, heart-stopping, mind-fizzing, pulse-racing, breathtaking, eye-stretching private art gallery. Two settees were placed back to back in the centre of the room so you could collapse when the impact was too much. The paintings were from the second half of the nineteenth century and the first half of the twentieth.

Martin's torch explored three Toulouse-Lautrecs. One was a self-portrait, the artist sheltering under a hat indoors, probably in a brothel with a woman in a corset, bending to roll down a stocking. The second showed a gross man in a bath robe, cigar in mouth, watching two half-naked women kiss. The third showed a drunk slumped over a table with a knocked-over wine glass while a naked woman brushed her hair.

Van Gogh had painted an olive tree on a Provençale hill against a sky swept clear of clouds by the mistral. A dog lay in deep shade under the tree.

Two Monets of his favourite subjects: Rouen cathedral backed by stacks of clouds, the other of willows weeping over waterlilies at Giverny. Monet had cataracts – didn't he? – hence the fuzzy pinks and misty greens.

There was no mistaking the styles. There was Picasso. Next was Renoir. That one had to be Munch: a woman's head on a pillow, eyes and mouth open, dark brush strokes curving round her face radiating some violent emotion, maybe a shuddering orgasm.

The beam flicked to a Dali. A rooster with a dinosaur's saw-toothed back last seen on the graffiti-covered wall in the Riga suburb. A cannon, sporting a moustache modelled on Dali's own, was aimed at the rooster. Finally the silence was broken.

'Old fraud,' Martin muttered, 'pompous, self-opinionated…'

Abandoning art criticism he moved to a Mondrian with rectangles as precise as slices of supermarket cheese, of red, yellow and a green that was almost black. 'And here's ano…' His voice faltered, the torch darted to the floor.

'Oh God.'

Was that old fraudster Dali playing a prank? At the end of a settee a leg jutted out, a woman's leg, skirt twisted up to the knee.

'Martin,' Clough began.

Words wouldn't come. Martin shuffled forward a step. Clough stood beside him. The other leg was folded under the first as if she was swinging round as she fell. Martin swept the torch round the room. Instinct told him some danger they couldn't see was waiting in ambush. The torch moved back to the body. Its beam lit up short dark hair and staring eyes. The mouth was open in a Munch scream. Clough could hear the scream in his head. He knew the voice. It was Debbie Brown.

Chapter 21

Martin knelt beside the body. 'No pulse.' He let go of her wrist and stood up. 'She's not been dead long.'

Clough looked down on his bedmate. As a lover she had never been still, never been quiet, encouraging herself to go, go, go, telling Matt what she wanted. She was somebody who... cold reality stopped him. Don't bring on the violins. She had her fun but I was just a step on her journey. This was what she was after, this address.

The torch beam moved and found a bullet hole in her chest. A single shot to the heart. Someone well trained or very close or very lucky.

'Why?' It was muttered more to himself but Martin picked it up.

'Why was she here? Why was she killed?' Martin sounded angry. 'Better ask who. The front door was locked, wasn't it?'

'The deadlock wasn't used. The other lock would give up if you breathed on it.'

All these canvases, shouldn't there be a burglar alarm? With the electricity off it might not work. Had the murderer been here or did he slip in after her?

'What was she doing in the dark?' Clough said. 'She must have had a torch.'

Martin sent the beam of his torch darting across the carpet. He found no torch but a camera half under a settee where it had been flung in a violent gesture. The torch continued round the room, discovering new things. They'd been overwhelmed by the paintings, then Debbie's body. Now they saw a coffee table and a glass.

'We get out,' Martin said. 'Now.'

'She carried the camera in her shoulder bag – where's that?'

'For God's sake, we're not…'

There was no warning. The lights came on. It was dark, then it was light. They turned towards the door. No one at the switch. The door was open to the hall. No light there. But beyond that was the open door to the study. A desk lamp created shadows everywhere.

'Come on,' Martin said.

His urging acted like a signal. A shadow moved. There was no sound. As it came forward the shadow changed into a man. Hardly anything to him. A phantom. Phantom with pistol.

'Ka jus sauc?'

He took a step into the room, nudging the door closed with his hip. The pistol was pointing at Martin's midriff.

'Russki togda?'

'No, old chum, I'm not a bloody Russian.'

'You're English?' the man said. Another step closer. He tilted his head to one side to inspect Martin. He was old but the hand holding the gun was firm. 'You expect me to believe that?'

'Believe what you like.'

'So who are you?'

'Name of Martin.'

'No. *Who* are you? *What* are you?'

'From the British embassy.'

Martin wore a charcoal grey suit, a white shirt, a dark blue tie with silver fleur-de-lys. In contrast the man with the gun wore grey slacks and a baggy maroon sweater. They looked leftovers from communist days.

'What are you? The ambassador? His chauffeur?'

The English was faultless, the accent could have come from the leafier suburbs of Woking.

'Somewhere in between.'

'You.' The pistol jerked to Clough's stomach.

Clough had lost his voice.

'Why are you frowning?'

You smile at the improbable. You frown at the impossible.

'Who are you?'

'His assistant.'

'You're here on work? Your name.'

Clough studied the man's face with its fuzz of grey bristles. Enough of his questions. Clough said, 'Did you shoot her?' He pointed at Debbie's body, half hidden by the settee.

The man's gaze never moved.

'You think a trick like that fools me? I turn to look where you're pointing and you jump on me. I don't fall for rubbish.'

Just listen to him. He's not angry, he's not threatening, he's matter of fact. Killing Debbie, killing anyone, wouldn't worry him. Clough was frowning again. Listen to him. Listen to that voice threatening me. This is not possible.

The man jabbed the pistol at Clough. 'Who are you? Come on.'

'Matt.'

'Like a rug? Something I step on?'

'Matt as in Matthew.'

Silence. It was the old man's turn to frown. His eyes patrolled Clough's face.

'Your surname?' Clough wasn't quick enough replying. 'Tell me your family name. Well?'

'Clough.'

The old man's eyes dropped to Clough's feet then worked their way up. The pistol jabbed forward again.

'You are Matthew Clough?'

Clough nodded.

'You have proof? Your passport? If you're lying I'll shoot you.'

'It's in here.' Clough tapped his breast pocket.

'I'm watching. I can pull the trigger quicker than you can pull a trick.'

Clough believed him. He would shoot. What was one more death? Slowly he produced the passport.

'Open it to the page with your name.'

Clough did this, holding the passport forward, name and photo together. But the old man didn't reach out to take it or even look at it. He shook his head as if just the act of producing the passport was enough. The hand holding the gun dipped. Again he shook his head. I believe you but it is unbelievable. Finally, dropping the gun on the table, he advanced on Clough, arms wide for an embrace.

'Matthew, you've come. Matthew, son.'

Clough stared.

Dead.

K.K. was dead. The police superintendent, the man who sat in the shadows, the lawyer all said it. There'd been an autopsy. Everybody agreed. Dead. This was impossible.

But the voice. It was the voice on the tape but slower, older.

It was a con, had to be. Some old actor had recorded the tape, playing the part, a monstrous con.

Clough half closed his eyes. Imagine the bathroom in the morning. Go on. Steam from the shower blurring the mirror. Whose face is that, forty years down the line?

No. Clough refused. No.

Arms drew Clough to the old man's chest. Right cheek kissed, left cheek, right cheek again. The unshaven whiskers tickled. The old man rested his hands on Clough's shoulders and like a veteran Russian general held him at arm's length, put his head to one side and peered to see the marks that life had left on Clough's face.

My son, his lips formed but no sound came. Then he found his voice. 'My son.'

Clough gazed back. Not possible. And yet…

'Matthew, Matthew, Matthew,' the old man murmured. The hands fell from Clough's shoulders and he took a step back. 'I thought this would never happen. Come on, haven't you got a word for your old man? Aren't you amazed we meet at last?'

'You can't be my father,' Clough objected. His voice sounded funny in his ears. 'My father's dead. His body was found. There was a death certificate. The lawyer told me... K.K. is dead. The Foreign Office was told. I was contacted. Man drove down from London to tell me. It's just not possible.'

Clough's rambling came to a stop.

'Son, that was a deception. Had to do that because of her.' He waved at the body. 'But I am your father, hand on heart.' When this still failed to win the smile of Clough's acceptance he tried another tack. 'I loved your mother. Do you understand? I loved her as she loved me. It was just politics that separated us. I did love her.' A peevish tone had come into his voice. 'Why do you look at me like that?'

How did he look? Bewildered? Numb? Angry? Appalled? Fearful? Sickened? Baffled? Panicky? Maybe a goulash of the lot.

'You killed her.'

'Who's trying to poison you against me? She died giving birth.'

'Her.' He gestured at Debbie. Out of the jumble of feelings anger was rising. 'Killed her, murdered her.'

'Oh her. Well now.' K.K. took another step back. 'Maybe I need to teach my son how the world is. It was the law of the jungle, kill or be killed. Her or me. We're never far from the jungle, you know,' he said in his mock Home Counties tones. 'The jungle's not just in Borneo, it's in this house, it's all round us, in Riga, on Wall Street, in London, on a football field, in politics, in the bedroom, everywhere. You want to survive? Then live by the code of the wild. You understand that, don't you?'

'You had a gun, she didn't. You shot her in cold blood.'

'Yes, I carried a gun. I had to because of her.' K.K., remembering he'd dropped the gun on the table, picked it up and jammed it in the waistband of his trousers. 'Two weeks ago, three weeks ago, I can't keep hold of time, she came to the house in Mezaparks. I was out but Otilija let her in. How could she be so stupid? I don't know why I've put up with her all these years.'

'You won't have to any longer.'

K.K. went still, catching a warning in Clough's voice.

'She's dead,' Clough said, 'murdered.'

'Murdered? Did she…?' He ducked his head at Debbie then shook it. 'No, all she was interested in was the paintings.' He broke off again. 'Dead? You're sure?'

'I saw her in Sigulda. Your house there. Someone had gone through it, ransacking it, gone upstairs and killed her.'

'Shit.' Whatever else he muttered Martin and Clough didn't understand. 'That was a prayer to any gods who are listening: give me the man who killed Otilija. How was she killed?'

'Blow to the head.'

'Her fault.'

He moved over to Debbie, put a shoe under her chin and nudged it. Now unseeing eyes were staring at Clough and he looked away.

'Bitch. It was to do with these paintings. Remember? I told you on that tape. I wanted you to know about them in case…' He drew a hand across his throat. 'We all have secrets. The more secrets you have the more successful you've been. This was my secret. Imagine.' He swung an arm round the room then pointed down at Debbie. 'She got to know about the paintings but couldn't find them.'

K.K. nudged her foot, straightening it in line with her body.

'Don't do that,' Martin said. 'Show some respect for the dead.'

K.K. swung round. 'Have you seen many dead?'

Martin didn't answer.

'Let me tell you, once they're dead they give *you* the greatest respect.'

He poked with his shoe at the leg Debbie had twisted as she fell. Clough remembered what K.K. had said about packing Jews in a trench like sardines.

'God, she was trouble. See there?' K.K. pointed at a space on the wall. 'I had a Miro which I sent for auction. I chose Sotheby's in Geneva and I airfreighted it. I like a little joke so I put Commercial Sample on the customs sticker. I gave my name and a fax number.

I got a fax in return wanting to know about me. References? Me? Bloody cheek. I am Krisjanis Kulbergs of Mezaparks, Riga, Latvia. My eyes are not so good any more. To write I use a big magnifying glass. But if I must, I must. I gave them my bank and my lawyer. Damn them, they sent another fax, demanding the *provenance* of the painting. Provenance? You know what it means?'

He was talking to Martin but Martin was not responding.

'I acquired the painting from a certain Rothstein, no auction, private deal. Rothstein bought it in Paris before the war, receipt from a dealer in rue de Seine glued to the back of the canvas. So what's the problem? They were quiet for a week so I faxed them. Hello Geneva, what's happening about my painting? I got a fax saying they had a spring auction of modern masters coming up and did I have other paintings I wanted to auction? I told them *no*, and frankly my Swiss cuckoo clocks, next time I do you can go and yodel up your Alp because you're too slow. Shit, it was my brain that was slow. Next thing she turned up in Riga. Otilija said she saw her peeping through the curtains at Mezaparks. I ask you, what business was it of hers? Who was she?'

K.K. raised his foot for another prod and Martin stepped forward.

'She was connected to the Holocaust Investigation Bureau,' he said, 'based in Tel Aviv.'

'A Jew. I should have guessed. They always caused the most trouble.'

Clough frowned at Martin.

'You never told me.'

Since when did a Controller tell everything he knew? Martin hesitated then went on.

'I watched her meeting two buddies outside her apartment building. Middle of the night, freezing cold, they must have had a long vigil, so I decided it was for work not a cup of coffee. She was a mystery and she was a Jew so I presented myself at the Israeli embassy. Our embassy had given me the name of the officer who dealt with security.' Martin raised a hand as if plucking a name out of the air. 'Let's call him Moshe. Mossad I guess, an old veteran with eyes that looked inside you. Riga was a quiet place, a sort of pre-retirement rest. We saw something in common in each other.'

Martin paused and shook his head to get himself back on track.

'I told this Israeli one or two porky pies – excuse me if that's not kosher – about NATO officers staying at the Konventa Seta and that she'd been seen going in and out. I needed to check on her and Moshe said he was very sorry but he couldn't help. Then he pressed a switch under his desk – cutting the recording, I suppose - and told me, yes, the embassy was a liaison link but they didn't have the resources to provide security.'

Martin's eyes dropped to Debbie.

'You don't last in the spy trade if you spill secrets but this Moshe was quite open. Forget those NATO officers, he said, she's not interested. Moshe told me she was not Canadian but had dual Israeli/US citizenship. She didn't work for the Holocaust Investigation Bureau proper but a separate outfit called RESTART which is short for Restoring Stolen Art Treasures. "During the Nazi years a quarter of a million artefacts went walkabout." That was the word the Israeli embassy man used: walkabout. Debbie was a RESTART researcher. Her family had escaped from Latvia and she had the language so it was natural she came here. "RESTART's relations with the auction houses are excellent," Moshe told me, "so when Sotheby's said a known painting from the Rothstein collection had surfaced…"'

Whatever else the Israeli said was lost in the eruption from K.K. He was swearing in Latvian or Russian. He looked about to kick Debbie's legs again and Martin grabbed his arm and swung him round. For a moment K.K.'s hand hovered over the pistol jammed into his trousers.

'Get hold of yourself.'

'I saved these paintings. Look at them.' He flung off Martin's grip and swept his arm around. 'I brought them here. I built this place. Without me they would have been lost. They'd have been destroyed, used to light fires, buried in some Soviet cellar. Then she sneaks in like a thief.'

He picked up the digital camera from the floor, stabbed at a button and up came the Salvador Dali rooster. He tossed the camera on a settee.

'She must have been spying on this house. I went out for half an hour for food. When I got back, here she was. Right here. Thief, blackmailer, I didn't waste time asking.' He pointed his hand at Debbie, two fingers making a pistol barrel. 'It was a shock. Do you understand? I wasn't safe in my own house. I sat a while wondering what to do when I heard the gate opening; my burglar alarm. Quick, cut the electricity. It's the rest of the gang. First the pretty one, then the hard men. Instead…' His voice dropped. 'I found my son, last seen wearing short pants and a jacket he was growing out of.'

He'd come full circle back to Clough. His arms opened to embrace his son but seeing the distance in Clough's stare he held back.

K.K. sank on one of the settees, tapping his chest. 'Doc told me to take it easy. I asked him, my age, what is there to get excited about? He said, you're not in a wheelchair yet so if some old girl agrees to go upstairs with you, just don't try to carry her.'

His laugh turned into a cough.

'Sit down.' He patted the seat. 'I want to tell you how it is.'

Jump on K.K. Phone the police. Phone the embassy. Phone London and ask the Deputy Director what she wants doing with their one-time asset. Possibilities jumped in Martin's mind. But yes, he did want to know how it was. Slight nod to Clough and they sat either side of the old man.

'You've got to understand this: she started it. After she came to the house in Mezaparks there was a visit from somebody else. A captain, Otilija said, but she never checked. Jesus, you ring the bell, say you're a captain and she says come in, sit down, have a drink. Captain of what? A boat? A football team? Police captain, she thought. You *think*? Didn't you ask for identification? Don't shout at me, she said, which is just a woman's way of admitting she's been stupid. What did he want? You, she said. He wanted to know what you did, what you'd done when Latvia was in the Soviet Union, in the war, everything. Otilija told him she was the housekeeper and knew nothing. Captain growled a few threats and left.'

K.K. stood up. To do this he had to put his hands on his knees and push. Upright he squared his shoulders like an old soldier and wandered over to a table in the corner. He picked up a bottle of Courvoisier.

'Want some?'

Clough shook his head.

'So the visit from that girl plus the captain's questions… better I move here, I decided. You'll love it, son, the sound of the waves, wind in the trees. In summer I sit at my look-out table and watch the sailing boats fly over the sea. Wonderful.'

His eyes turned to a wall and he nodded to the paintings as his gaze went round. They were his friends.

'This is my country in here and I am king. My subjects line the walls and every one is a genius, or should I say the creation of…' He lost the thread of what he was saying and shook his head. 'Nobody in Riga knows about this place. Here in Majori they see a lonely old man. With a few drinks and these pictures, who could feel lonely?'

There was only one glass on the coffee table. K.K. bent down to sniff it then poured some brandy in.

'So I moved out here. When I next spoke to Otilija it was on the phone. She said two men had come to the house, Russians. God, more people after me. Russians, I said, so you invited them in for vodka. No, she said, they pushed me back and walked in before I could say anything. They looked round everywhere, even under the beds, and asked where you were. Out, she said, gone away, gone to the devil. Otilija, I said, the moment we finish talking you're to leave that house. Don't argue, go to Sigulda because you'll be safe there. I was wrong.'

He looked at his glass and decided he hadn't poured enough. Now he had one of his hero-sized drinks and knocked it back.

'Who were the men who called?' Martin asked.

The words came slowly.

'Colleagues, I would say. Yes, colleagues of mine from the old days. That's what they said to her. Tell Krisjanis his old colleagues came to see him. We don't like to be forgotten. We need to talk. Make sure you tell him.'

'Colleagues from the old days?' Martin thought about this. 'Old KGB colleagues? Or working for us?'

K.K. stared at Martin. 'You said you were at the embassy. What work do you do?'

Martin didn't respond, just ran his thumb across his upper lip.

'I get it,' K.K. said. 'No answer is an answer. Listen, it's not the KGB anymore, got a new name. Every few years they change its name but it's still Lenin's Cheka. Well, a number of Cheka officers didn't like the way things were going in Russia. Moscow was going to the devil. Billions of dollars were being stolen from the state and sent to Cyprus and Switzerland and the Cayman Islands. Then there are those mansions in London that get used two weekends a year. Not patriotic. Better it stay in Moscow. So these Cheka officers set up a joint venture with the Mafia to promote growth businesses. These growth businesses were in import-export, banking, entertainment, street trading in high value goods, security and insurance. I became agent in Riga and to this day I swear on my mother's grave I do not know where the product went.'

'Just a minute, hold on.' Martin was sitting bolt upright. K.K. had suddenly gone fast, skipping over the trickier bits of his story. 'You were an agent and your product went missing. What do you mean?'

'I was concerned with import-export. The customs in Russia have got too greedy, the Moscow boys said, you don't pay duty now you pay a ransom. Better to import it into Riga and get it unofficially over the border. When Latvia was in the Soviet Union there was no frontier. There are still tracks that wander across the border where a farmer has fields on both sides. What you need is local knowledge plus contacts with the relevant authorities, which is where I proved my worth.'

A pompous note had entered his voice like a lawyer justifying his fees. Martin was not impressed.

'What was your product? What are we talking about?'

K.K. wasn't talking at all. He raised a hand and cupped the fingers and thumb so they formed a C.

'Colombia to Venezuela,' K.K. said. 'Banana boat to Gdansk. From Gdansk in a fishing boat. Customs don't like searching fishing boats. Market's over that way, St Petersburg.' He jerked his head. 'Only, you see, a shipment went missing and they say I stole it, which is crazy. Nobody double-crosses the Mafia; especially not the Moscow boys. And nobody in their right mind waits for them to come knocking at the door. Have a word with the fishermen, I told them, but they said I was the local boss, I was responsible. So a lot of money is owed and it's become urgent. That's why I was selling the Miro.'

'You went dead,' Clough said, 'because the Mafia were after you?'

'They've got Chechens working for them.' He shook his head as if it was something Clough would never understand. 'Even when a Chechen is dead you don't want to make him angry.'

'And you got me to come over from England.'

'I hoped you'd come. Yes.'

'To help you. You expected that.'

Clough couldn't think what to say. K.K. had tricked him into coming, killed the woman he'd been sleeping with, wanted him to deal with the Mafia, all to protect paintings he had looted.

'It's yourself you'll be helping. I won't live for ever and then all this…' K.K. gestured at the paintings again. 'They believe I'm dead so they'll be realistic and settle with you. Me they want to punish. They want it known I've been punished *pour encourager les autres*. You're familiar with Voltaire? He knew a thing or two. But you can deal with them, give them the house in Mezaparks, maybe Sigulda too. If they know I'm alive they'll be after my blood. It'll end up with the Chechens having a Saturday night party with me. No thanks.'

Dear God, Martin thought, this is a madhouse. We have to get out.

'I'm going to have a drink after all. Am I mistaken or did I see a bottle of vodka in your fridge? How about you, Matthew?'

Clough held his eyes. He'd said Matthew not Matt. Be prepared, change of course, action ahead.

K.K. was enthused.

'We'll drink a toast to the future.' he bustled to the door. 'It's Finnish vodka, not local,' he said. He pulled the door open, took a couple of steps and halted.

Then he took a step back and another and another.

'Dobry vyecher, tovarich.'

Chapter 22

K.K.'s chest shrank with every prod from Finnis' pistol.

Clough stood up, eyes slipping from Finnis to the figure behind him. It was West, the man who had sat in the shadows in Wallingford. Leather blouson was leading the way, pinstripe suit following in his slipstream.

Finnis pointed the pistol at Clough.

'Good footwork, my friend, you got here first.'

'Friend?' K.K. wheeled round to look at Clough.

'Mezaparks, Sigulda, Majori. Any more houses in your hip pocket, Kris?'

It was the opening statement of a man who had a lot more to say. His right hand held the pistol; his left hand came up as if he was begging for something.

'So why do you steal from your pals? You're a naughty boy. Money is an addiction, is that it? You always need one more fix.'

K.K. began some reply. He did it in Russian as if that would bring him closer to Finnis.

'Speak English.' Finnis cut across him. 'We have British guests. Remember your manners. Speaking of which...' he stepped forward and lifted the pistol from K.K.'s waistband. 'We're all friends so you don't need this. And you...' He switched his attention to Martin. 'You have to be the spy I have been hearing about. Fought communism all over Europe. Brought the Berlin Wall down single handed.'

'Retired spy,' Martin said. A wolfish grin spread on Finnis' face. Martin thought he should add emphasis. 'Out to pasture now.'

'Sure. Just here on holiday. Makes a change from Majorca.'

West muttered something. In Wallingford, West had kept in the background to let the superintendent do the talking. Here he was behind Finnis and then he was sidestepping and advancing on a course of his own, gazing at the wall, a frown growing. Something here he didn't understand. He came to an abrupt halt as he stubbed a foot on one of Debbie's legs.

'Hello, what have we here?' West said, surprised but acting even more so. 'Having a bit of a knees-up, were we? Girl had a drop too much?' Another step brought the rest of her body into view. 'Lordy. Party got a tad out of hand.' The bantering tone left his voice. 'Do we know who the lady is? Or was?'

Nobody answered him.

Finnis had finally looked away from Martin and K.K. and Clough to the paintings. Like West he was frowning, eyes darting left and right. He slipped K.K.'s pistol into a pocket of his leather blouson and his own into the waistband of his trousers. Five or six steps brought him to one of the Toulouse-Lautrecs. Finnis gripped the painting with both bands to tilt it so the varnish and brushstrokes caught the light. It wasn't a print. He did the same with the next Toulouse-Lautrec. He wheeled round and suddenly he was back confronting K.K.

'Are these real? They're not fakes?' K.K. didn't answer. 'How long have you had them? Did you steal them?'

West looked stunned. 'They're not copies done in Taiwan?'

Stepping over Debbie's legs, West crossed to the Munch canvas. He licked a finger and ran it across her face, then tasted it. 'There's a chap, name like van Dongen, who used to paint Old Master look-alikes. Fooled the experts. These some of his? Bloody good if they are.'

Getting no answer, West walked the length of the room. He straightened his shoulders and turned back to Finnis. 'Christ.' He took a breath. 'Oleg, we're rich.' He didn't have complete control of his voice. 'Stinking disgusting filthy rich, know what I mean?'

Finnis stepped away from K.K.

'How much?'

West hesitated.

'Got to sell them on the shady side of the street. Even so, that Picasso, fifty million, sixty, maybe more.'

'Dollars?'

'Dollars.'

The prospect of unexpected huge wealth brought a change in the atmosphere. Fifty million? For each canvas? West's bulging eyes couldn't leave the paintings, skipping from one to the next, adding, adding. A billion?

'And the sneaky little bugger was holding out on us for a few hundred thousand.'

K.K. broke his silence.

'I demand to see Birznieks.'

'Who?' West said.

'His lawyer,' Finnis said.

'I demand the right to legal representation. I demand he comes here now.'

'Small problem, old man. Birznieks doesn't want to see you.'

'He'll see me. We're old friends.'

'A friend doesn't pay the bills. He's a lawyer. He thinks like a lawyer.' Finnis looked round at the paintings. 'Helping you pretend you were dead? No, no, no. So shut up and sit down.'

Finnis laid his palm on K.K.'s chest and the old man toppled onto a settee.

It was a tight squeeze on the settee, the three of them, with K.K. in the centre. West placed two chairs four paces in front of them. He fetched goblets of clear-cut glass on tall stems. He poured brandy and passed it round while Finnis stood off with the pistol at his side. Finally, Finnis and West sat down. The pistol lay on Finnis' lap. He caught Clough's eyes measuring the distance and shook his head.

'All right,' Finnis said. 'First we'll have a nice drink and then a nice chat. So, a toast.' He raised his glass. 'I give you Krisjanis Kulbergs, a man of many achievements. He was kind to the Jews during the war, making certain they never suffered starvation by shooting them first. He put in heroic labour to produce a greater Latvian nation by screwing the girls. Let us not forget the part he played in universal understanding by spying for everybody. Finally he created a place of great artistic beauty but modestly never boasted about it.' Finnis emptied his glass in two swallows. 'Drink up, Kris. Give you a bit of courage. Your face, you know, it'd turn milk sour.'

K.K. held his glass rigidly in front of him.

'I expect you're worried about the money that went missing but it'll be all right.'

'What money are we talking about?'

When K.K. started in Russian Finnis stopped him. 'In English so everyone can hear you.'

'The shipment that was lost. You know?' Finnis said nothing so K.K. went on. 'I didn't steal it but I'll pay you. I don't want bad blood between us. You'll get every dollar. Five hundred and eighty-two thousand.'

'Six hundred and fifty six thousand.'

'You said…'

'Interest, Kris.'

'All right, six hundred and fifty-six. Not tonight but you'll have it by March.'

'March? Krisjanis old friend, it'll be up to… let's see…in the region of seven eighty.'

'Don't get carried away,' Martin said. 'You won't get it.'

'Nobody asked you,' Finnis said.

Martin ignored him. He was leaning towards West, in his view the weak link. Maybe in London he could pull strings but this was a long way from London.

'That Picasso that caught your eye. Fifty million you told your chum? One painting. You did the maths. Twenty times fifty million. You see penthouses looking over Central Park, yachts, a dazzling future. Oh dear, what a shame.'

Martin stopped. West broke the silence.

'You're trying to tell us something, right?'

'Yes. All these masterpieces, all those dollars.' He leant forward. 'Not for you.'

'You're going to stand in my way?'

'Not me.' Martin managed a smile of sorts, sad about the news he was bringing. 'I'm just saying, not one cent.'

West was listening closely.

'All right, I fall for it. Why not?'

'He can't sell even one,' Martin said, nodding at K.K., 'and he's desperate to get you off his back.'

'Why not?' West said again.

'See that space on the wall? He tried to sell one. Trouble with paintings like that is you have to prove ownership and give a history of where it came from. These all belonged to a someone who Kulbergs processed through a Nazi death camp. When one comes up for sale, alarm bells ring. That's why that lady on the floor was here. She'd tracked him down. She's got colleagues in the city waiting to jump.'

Finnis broke in. 'Where were you trying to sell, Kris?'

'Sotheby's in Geneva but I can…'

'Sotheby's? Kris, auctions are for second hand furniture. My friend, I respect what you've done in your life. You learned to live with Nazism, you learned to live with communism, you must learn to live with free markets. A painting is a painting. You've got to be quick on your feet. There are all these houses in Florida owned by – let's call them new Russians. They're not tied to Moscow, they're global players. Their money moves as quick as they do. They don't want Moscow snow, they want palm trees and swimming pools. In Florida they are buying big places. Big places have big *blank* walls. Opportunity, right? People with their background, are they going to say, Show me the history of your Miro?'

K.K. said nothing. Finnis looked at Martin.

'You heard of Zhitomirsky?

'Tittle-tattle at the watering holes. Zhito used to be in Moscow Centre. He went private, had political protection of course. It was the Yeltsin years. When Putin took over that was even better because they'd both been KGB. Then Zhito moved to Budapest. Usual rackets. You may have read about money laundering in Belize.'

'Nothing proved,' Finnis said.

'Quite.' Martin gave Finnis a long stare. 'Not easy to get witnesses in those parts. Lot of hungry sharks in the sea off Belize.'

Finnis felt he was losing direction and he took back the lead.

'What I do is get on the phone to Budapest. "Zhito, how's screwing these days? Listen, I heard you bought a nice chunk of real estate in Florida. Zhito, I've got a Cézanne your lovely wife Ludmila will adore – special price for you, fifteen mill." Zhito doesn't say, "Show me some seventy-year-old receipt." He says, "Done deal. And while you're at it I want a Gauguin for little Natasha's love nest, something with nice tits." That's how it is these days. All these canvases here, I visualise them…' He raised his arms as if acknowledging the roar of a crowd. '…hanging on the walls of Spanish style haciendas in Miami Beach and Fort Lauderdale. Beautiful vision. That's what's needed, vision. You used to have it, Kris, but…' He shook his head.

'There's an honest crook's account.' Martin looked at West. 'And you? Happy with that vision? A few killings along the way but all those millions in the bank ought to stifle most doubts.'

Debbie farted.

They hunched round, all of them, in surprise. It was just her body settling, her sphincter relaxing.

'The lady has spoken,' Finnis announced. He clapped his hands. 'All right, time to move her out.'

He jammed the pistol in his waistband and lit a cigarette. Martin recognised someone used to being on the street, lighter in his left hand, right hand cupping the flame from unfriendly eyes. *Time to move her out.* This was the end.

Nobody spoke. In the distance was the sound of waves breaking on the beach, a muffled roar.

Chapter 23

This can't be happening. Clough thought of the Jews in Krisjanis Kulbergs' camp calling out to God to help them. He took a breath. *Stop. Stop right there. Don't think like that.*

This is real. Finnis has a gun, we do not. Our job is to be pall bearers. The social chat is over and we move on to the final act. Unless. Unless what? Clough couldn't think. He glanced at Martin but from the expression on his face he had withdrawn into a private world.

Even the blackest scene can have its moment of farce.

They were standing, all of them, West and Finnis a little apart, when K.K. pushed forward to Debbie's body. Pure luck meant he had shot her in the heart. Not much blood on her clothes but a spattering on the carpet. He peered down then straightened and started for the door. Finnis was quick to stand in his way.

'Where the hell do you think you're going?'

'Bowl of water. There's blood on the carpet. Rub it off before it dries.'

'Jesus Christ, it doesn't matter.'

'Stains. Don't want that. Dirty.'

Their concerns went different ways. K.K. didn't want his carpet ruined. Finnis thought of forensic evidence. Granted, if fibres were taken away for analysis they'd show Debbie's DNA. But if the surface evidence was sponged away no one would notice. Finnis muttered an instruction to West and followed K.K. out of the room. West produced a pistol.

This roused Martin whose eyes darted round the room, the shuttered windows, a fire extinguisher standing in a corner, the table

226

near the door where their coats lay, to West, to the patch of floor between them, four paces, maybe five.

'Don't,' West said. 'Don't even think of it.' He angled the pistol at Clough's chest. 'Either of you moves, he gets it first. Then you.'

Martin might chance his luck but wouldn't put Clough at risk.

'All your life you're going to regret this,' Martin said. 'It's like backing the wrong side in a war. Switch sides.' Martin was suddenly urgent. 'This is your last chance to make good. When Finnis comes through that door, shoot him. Don't try to bargain or argue, just shoot him. I've got the connections, I'll make it all right for you. West? Do you hear what I'm saying?'

Would it work? Would West have the guts? There was a chance, Clough thought, a slight one. K.K. came back into the room holding a plastic bowl. Finnis was behind him. Then Finnis stepped to one side. West had a clear shot. Clough held his breath. West's eyes were on Finnis, then they slipped to Martin. Martin was nodding. *Now, do it now, shoot him.* And West did nothing.

K.K. was kneeling on the floor, kitchen sponge in hand. He began rubbing at the carpet, little circular motions. He said something in Russian, Finnis replied and West asked what it was.

'He wants soap. Can you believe it? Expects me to fetch it?'

The water in the basin was taking on colour. Each time K.K. squeezed the sponge it changed, from palest pink to something darker. K.K. stopped, peering at what he'd achieved. Before there'd been a scattering of spots of blood. Now there was a sodden grey patch the size of a doormat.

'Well,' Martin said, 'no one is ever going to notice that.'

'Forget it,' Finnis said. 'Let's get going. We'll move her outside.'

Aware that Martin's eyes were on him Clough turned his head. There was nothing he could put a finger on – no nod, no wink – but something in Martin's face held him. Was it the way his head was tipped upright? Or cheeks that were fuller as if he was holding back a smile? Perhaps it was the intentness of the eyes that saw the way ahead even if Clough didn't.

'It's going to be like this,' Finnis said. 'West goes first to check against surprises. Then Krisjanis. Then you two carrying the girl between you, one to her feet, one to her shoulders. I bring up the rear so I can keep an eye on everything.'

K.K. had the truculence of old age.

'I'm not going outside. This is my house and I'm staying.'

'Krisjanis, old man.' Finnis shook his head in wonder. 'You killed her, not me. You can't have her body stinking the place up so we're doing you a favour. You're coming with us to see we do it right.'

'The ground's frozen so you can't bury her.'

'Sure. You know about digging pits, you're the expert. I have a better idea. We're going to take her down to the beach and these two gentlemen are going to send her for a swim. Which way does the current run?'

'Uhh.' K.K. shook his head.

'Does it go that way towards Majori, or down the coast towards Valvari?'

K.K. followed Finnis's pointing hand but it confused him further.

'Why have I got to come? I'm not carrying her.'

'Because you owe six hundred thousand dollars, more every day. Because you might take it into your head to run. Because we tell you to and we have the guns. Where the hell do you think you're going?'

His pistol swung on Martin who stopped short and lifted his hands in a calming gesture.

'Coat.'

Martin's and Clough's coats were near the door.

'You mind a bit of cold?'

'Well, do you want them lying about the house?'

Martin stared at Finnis. We're not coming back, his steady gaze said, we'll be joining Debbie. Finnis stared back then nodded.

Clough zipped Debbie's jacket so the spots of blood were hidden. He was younger and stronger so he took Debbie under the armpits, Martin gripping her ankles. They moved to the front door. West pulled it open, took a couple of steps and stopped.

'Wait.'

Twisting round Clough could see West with a hand up. He was looking away towards the dunes. The sea was out of sight but the rumble of waves was louder. West's head swung round to the right, towards the main road and the station.

'OK,' West said.

He began down the path. K.K. came after him, short steps, almost trotting.

'Come on,' Finnis said. 'Move.'

'Easy now, Matthew, nice and easy,' Martin said. 'She's a weight.'

Interpretation: don't go fast, let West get a distance in front.

Martin began to whistle *Yellow Submarine*. It was their code: I'm making contact, I need help *now*.

'Bloody song,' Finnis said. 'Shut up.'

Clough stepped out into cold night air. Light from the house caught Debbie's face. He'd seen that face full of life, singing the Collective Love Song, hurling pillows against the wall.

'You're going too fast. Matthew, do you hear me?'

He wasn't going fast. West and K.K. had drawn ahead.

Then it happened.

'Mind where you're going, Matthew. You're going to trip.'

Martin gave the body a shove and Clough fell. As part of the same movement Martin stumbled in the doorway, dropping the body. He reached behind, got a hand round the door and heaved it shut. Finnis' shout was muffled. Clough heard Martin urging him – he caught an 'ay' sound, 'lay down', 'get away', something – and he rolled off the path into the snow. West stopped in his tracks, ten metres ahead, turning round towards the house. K.K., with his nose for trouble, veered away towards a pine tree. Clough's head swung back to the house as the door was pulled open. Light flooded out. Finnis came out a step and halted. His pistol was raised. The only person in his sights was West. Debbie's body lay on the path. K.K. had reached the darkness of the tree. Clough was half hidden by snow. And Martin?

'Don't move,' Martin shouted. 'I'm armed.'

Martin scrambled to his feet and stood pressed flat against the side of the house. Clough had glimpsed him struggling with his overcoat pocket. Now he held a pistol, a two-handed stance.

'I've got a gun,' Martin warned again. But the wind was blowing and the sea growling and his voice sounded weak.

Finnis, not believing this bluff, began to swing round and Martin shot him at point blank range. Finnis staggered back against the doorpost and began a slow slide to the ground. Martin shot again because Finnis still gripped his pistol but most likely he was already dead.

'Oleg!' West called out. He was facing back to the house, gun in hand, but in the mayhem – the shouts, the gunshots, the two figures so close together, the light through the open door turning them into silhouettes – he didn't shoot.

Seconds passed and nobody spoke, nobody moved.

From the main road down by the station came the muffled sound of a car horn, then a second horn joining in, a long angry blast. West swung away from the house as if afraid of an ambush. What he saw was the dark figure of K.K. There was another blast from a horn and closer to a sudden fall of snow from a tree branch as K.K. brushed against it. He was moving, maybe sideways, maybe backwards. West shouted but the wind tore the words away. Was K.K. raising an arm? What did the gesture mean? *I hear you*, or *stop*. No telling. West shot at him, shot again, and this time got a cry of pain.

Martin was on the path, pistol raised.

'Drop your gun. Do it NOW. I'll shoot you before you can turn. Drop it, West.'

Martin took a step forward, another, another.

'Do as I say. Drop your gun.'

West had frozen. He couldn't drop the gun. He couldn't turn towards Martin. Step by step, Martin walked right up to him, laying the muzzle of his pistol against his cheek, close by his ear.

'West, listen to me. Pay very close attention. You're under arrest. Kidnapping, menaces with firearms, collusion with a foreign intelligence agency, accessory to drug dealing. Have you got that? I'm arresting you.'

West tried to tip his head to the side but Martin kept the muzzle pressed tight.

'Idiot. You can't arrest me. We're in Latvia.'

'True,' Martin said. 'So let me tell you why I'm making it formal and legal. Because if I don't I'll just shoot you. I could do it easily just like you intended for us. There'd even be an edge of pleasure. Tomorrow my conscience would stir a bit but that'd be too late for you. You'd be dead.'

Clough came close behind West who still held his pistol.

'He'll do it,' Clough said. 'I know him. He used to be my Controller.'

'He's out of it now. He's not a spy. He's nobody.'

'For you, I'm in it.' Martin's hand turned the pistol, screwing it into West's cheek. 'You have a choice. Listening? I shoot you now or I take you back to London. Which is it?'

He stopped, waiting, twisting the pistol for emphasis again.

'Are you a gambling man? Want to take a punt I don't have the stomach to shoot?'

West said nothing. He held the pistol rigidly towards where K.K. had cried out and fallen silent.

'All right, this is how it is.' Martin paused a moment. When he spoke again his voice was deeper and slower, a judge passing sentence. 'You are a British subject, a member of the British Foreign Service, and I am arresting you in the name of Her Britannic Majesty for treason. Pompous but so be it.' The formality was helping Martin keep control of himself. He drew a breath. 'Don't start bleating about a lawyer and your rights. You've got no rights. You've got me and this pistol. I'm going to count to five but I'm going to do it to myself, silently. When I get to five, if you haven't dropped the gun, I'll shoot you. There'll be no warning. It's known as resisting arrest.'

In the silence Clough found himself counting. One, two, three…

West's fingers opened. The pistol made a clatter when it hit the tarmac.

Clough found a length of cord in a kitchen cupboard and they tied West's wrists behind his back. 'Now his ankles,' Martin said. 'So he understands.' West was trussed on the floor in the entrance hall, bulging eyes switching from one to the other. They carried in K.K., took him through to the art gallery and laid him on a settee. He had been shot in the chest and was breathing but unconscious.

'Doesn't look good.' Martin shook his head.

'Martin.'

Martin looked up. 'What is it?'

'Suddenly you had a gun. It was stuffed in your overcoat pocket.'

'Thank chummy in the hall for that. He was waiting for me in my room at the Metropole and he poked a gun at me. It brought home how naked I was. I did what I should have done at the beginning. I had serious words with Chapman at the embassy who got the pistol out of the strong room. Nobody asked the ambassador. Possibly he'd lain down with a migraine.'

'So,' Clough thought about it, 'a gun from the British embassy killed Finnis.'

'Look, West is my priority. I've got to make phone calls, London and the embassy. You deal with the Finnis problem.' He was rubbing his shoulder which he'd bruised when he threw himself down. 'Work out what our story is.'

The story couldn't be just about Finnis. There were Debbie and K.K. to explain. Clough sat on the settee with K.K. behind him. It was an impossible story. He stared at a Gauguin of a bare-breasted woman against a background of jungle. What had K.K. said? The jungle was everywhere, in politics, in the bedroom, in this house. The breathing behind him was bubbly, the sucking of a pool hidden in jungle undergrowth. He stared at the bare breasts for inspiration.

Martin came back. 'Number two at the embassy is on the ball.

I told him about West but nothing more. He's not troubling the ambassador. The security man Chapman is coming with a van and I'll go in the back with West. The RAF is being told to come and fetch us. I don't know how pleased they are at being used as a taxi service.'

'And if West screams he's being kidnapped?'

'We're not using Riga airport, we're flying military. Latvia is in NATO now and they can be deaf when they want to be.'

'You spoke to the Firm?'

'The Deputy Director.'

'He's pleased?'

'He is a she. Pleasure is not a concept she fully grasps. She sees an opportunity.'

'Can you hear that?' Clough asked.

'What?' Martin listened. 'I can't hear anything.'

'He's stopped breathing.'

Now there were three people shot to death.

Clough and Martin sat in the art gallery, waiting for Chapman with the van. Reaction had set in and they didn't talk much.

'What are you going to do?' Martin asked.

'Ring a friend.'

'Three bodies. Shot with three guns.'

'I'll work it out.'

Martin turned his head towards Clough. He didn't say anything.

'Sweet milky tea is what they recommend after a shock,' Clough said. 'Fancy a brandy?'

'Good thinking.'

They clinked glasses.

'What'll you do in London?'

'It's not just West,' Martin said, as if this answered the question. 'He's part of a network and I don't know how wide it stretches. This is not spying, it's organised crime.'

Finally they heard three beeps on a horn down by the main road, a pause, two more beeps.

'Chapman,' Martin said. 'Help me take our guest down to the road then you can come back and ring your friend.'

'Lucija?'

'Is that you, Matthew?'

'I need help.'

A pause. Is she about to tell me she can't help? Impossible. He never questioned the impulse to ring her. He thought of the mound and the five stone slabs and the OMON troops with blackened faces. That was her battle, this is mine. She'll understand.

'Where are you?'

'K.K.'s house.'

'Understood. And you need help. From me. Is the trouble very bad?'

'Yes.'

'I thought so or you would not have telephoned.'

'Three people are dead.'

'Matthew!' She paused. 'And you… are you all right?'

'Yes.'

'Matthew, I can't work miracles. There are certain situations…' She lost her way. 'What I mean is that if it is you…'

'I didn't.'

There was another pause. He could hear cigarette smoke being blown out.

'Still, *three* dead.'

'One is K.K. Those people who signed documents that he had drowned are going to be in bad trouble.'

'Who else?'

'Another is a Russian ex-spy who was involved in a gang. Drug smuggling. The third is the woman I met.'

'I see.'

'I'm sorry,' Clough said. 'There's no one else I could call for help. Just the fact that I am alive and three people have been shot dead makes it look bad. For me, I mean'

'I'm sure you have an explanation.'

'Not on the telephone.'

'All right,' Lucija said. 'I'll ring the police chief in Majori. He was the man who told me where the house was. I will come of course. It's best I bring that captain who wanted to do terrible things to you. He's a good man to bring because no one likes to argue with him. Stay where you are.'

Chapter 24

This is a voluntary statement made by the undersigned,
Matthew Leopold Clough, of In Vino Veritas, Castle Street,
Wallingford OX10 9DL, England.

The deceased, Krisjanis Kulbergs, is my biological father
though I never saw him from birth until tonight. A week
ago in Wallingford, a police superintendent informed me
that this father I did not know had died (information that
proved to be false). He was a Latvian citizen so I came to
Riga to wind up his affairs.

A lawyer in Riga, by name Birznieks (first name
not known to me), gave me the address of this house in
Majori. Late this afternoon or early this evening I came by
taxi from Riga and with difficulty found the house. I had
come uninvited and the scene I encountered was a terrible
shock.

The gate to the garden was open. I walked in and the
first thing I noticed was someone lying in the snow. I subse-
quently learnt this was Krisjanis Kulbergs. It was the first
time I had seen him in my life and he was unconscious with
a gunshot wound in his chest.

I decided I must go into the house to call an ambulance
but on the path was the body of Debbie Brown. I recog-
nised her because we had become friends during the week I
have been in Riga. She had told me she was a professional
photographer and she had come to Riga in search of her

Latvian roots so I could not understand why she was here.
She too had been shot and she was dead.

Then, by the door to the house, was a third body, a man
whom I later learnt was someone called Oleg (last name
unknown), a Russian.

The door to the house stood open and I carried Kulbergs
inside and laid him on a settee. While I was looking round
for a telephone he regained consciousness. He explained he
had returned to his house and surprised Oleg carrying out
the body of Debbie Brown. He knew Oleg slightly, having
met him in a bar a couple of times. He did not know how
Oleg had found out the address of the house in Majori. Why
was he carrying out the body of Debbie Brown? Kulbergs
assumed they were thieves who had fallen out – perhaps
on how to divide the art treasures – and Oleg had shot the
woman. Perhaps he intended to dispose of the body in the
sea. But this is conjecture.

Kulbergs said he had been carrying a pistol since his
companion had been murdered some days earlier. He told
me he drew it from his pocket. But Oleg had dropped the
body and drawn his own gun. They both shot at the same
time. Oleg was killed instantly and Kulbergs was badly
wounded.

I told Kulbergs who I was and he was full of joy. He said
he had invented the story of his death in the hope that I
would come to Latvia and he could get to know the son he
had never seen. He didn't get to know me but he did at least
have the comfort of seeing me for a few brief moments.

He died before I could call the ambulance.
Signed
Matthew Clough

It had been a question of matching bullets in bodies to guns then
getting the right fingerprints on the guns. Debbie had been shot

with K.K.'s gun, K.K. had been shot with West's gun and Finnis had been shot with Martin's gun from the embassy. Clough had wiped the pistols clean and then clamped the hands round the right guns. With a dead man's hand that was nearly impossible, but he got some of the right fingerprints on even if not in the right places. It meant that Finnis had two pistols but, well, he was the type. He was a thug and he was a Russian and nobody was querying it.

The police had come in force: local police, the captain from Riga, technicians with cameras and evidence bags, men in boots and chunky sweaters, a doctor who went through the motions of checking that the dead people weren't acting, men in suits who stood apart and looked over each other's shoulders at the paintings and glanced at Clough and at the bottle and glass (Clough had washed and dried all but K.K.'s). Everybody stared at K.K.'s body as the ambulance men took it out on a stretcher.

Lucija spoke to the suits and the captain and came over.

'We can go now,' she said.

'We?'

'Specifically *you* are free to go. I thought I would drive you back to Riga unless you prefer to take a taxi.'

Clough stood up.

'Tomorrow I will do the official translation of your statement,' she said. 'I am glad to say they accept your account.' Her gaze was straight and unblinking, and if one of her eyebrows twitched none of the suits was close enough to notice. 'I would say what actually happened must remain a mystery since everybody except you appears to be dead. If there is a different version of events I advise you to keep quiet about it.'

'I shot no one.'

She put a finger to her lips.

'That is enough for me.'

Clough gave one final look round the paintings on the walls. His eyes fixed on the Gauguin of the woman on a beach, holding a bunch of bananas. The painting – just this one - would make him a multimillionaire. The captain from Riga had turned his way. His face had an expression Clough could not work out. Hint of a smile? Not of friendship, perhaps understanding.

'My passport,' Clough said.

'Tomorrow,' Lucija said.

Clough frowned. That new passport, the futile struggle with the lawyer, the week's delay, it had resulted in this: three dead bodies here, one in Sigulda.

'Matthew, it has yesterday's date. Such a new passport worries them. Three murders is too much for them, I would say. It is not in Stalin's league, for sure, but they are accustomed to crime on a smaller scale. A drunken husband beats his wife or neighbours come to blows over a noisy television. Crimes of a capitalist dimension are too much so they will reduce the scale of their enquiries to your passport.'

'I told them I had been mugged.'

'And you reported it. Excellent. They will intensify the search for the hooligans who did it. Many drunks will be questioned. They will redouble their efforts. Criminals – small ones naturally – will have to account for their activities. They will be seen to be busy. Unfortunately there will be no arrests but everybody will be satisfied.'

Outside, tape quarantined the areas where the bodies had lain. A cop guarded the tape but not before the snow had been trampled by the local police and ambulance men. Alien footprints – such as those made by Martin and West – were lost.

He heard the distant thunder of the waves. It was like a lion purring. No, he told himself, it was nothing like a lion purring. Stop flying so high.

They left the car in a parking lot two blocks from the Konventa Seta. The streets were narrow and cobbled, snow hiding ice. In the hotel lobby three army officers in combat gear were waiting for someone. American voices were talking about sun-up and cloud ceiling. A NATO exercise?

They passed the desk with its unsmiling blonde receptionist and went through to the bar. It was late. The pianist had gone home and only one other couple sat at a table. They crossed to the far side of the room, ordering whisky from a bored waiter.

Lucija picked up her glass and paused.

'You're worried.'

Clough dipped a finger in his whisky and traced the outline of a pistol on the table.

'K.K. owed money. He's dead. So now I owe the money.'

'Your father…'

Clough cut her short.

'We shared some DNA. Nothing else.'

He drank some whisky. Talking about K.K. was not easy.

'The paintings, Matthew, how did he get them? I was overwhelmed. Then when I considered their value, I was appalled. No normal person has that much money. How did he get it?'

'It'll be on the tape.'

She raised an eyebrow. Of course, he'd kept it secret from her.

'He had a Dictaphone and talked about what he did in the war and afterwards. A confession? I don't think so. An apology? No. A justification? He wouldn't think of it like that. It was a record of what he did to survive. How he got the paintings must be on the tape.'

'You mean you don't know?'

'I haven't finished it. There hasn't been time.'

'Don't you want to know?' she said. 'I do.'

She drained her glass.

Clough unlocked the bedroom door and stood back to let Lucija go first. She stepped inside and came to an abrupt halt.

'Matthew…'

There was a warning in her voice.

His clothes were emptied from the closet; suitcase upside down on the carpet, bed stripped, pillows out of their cases, mattress hauled on the floor, drawers pulled out of the desk. When the Mafia was breathing down your neck they wanted you to know.

'Looking for money?' Lucija asked.

'K.K. owed half a million dollars, maybe more.'

'Did you have any money here?'

'No. But I'd seen K.K.'s lawyer. Finnis and his chums knew that. So the lawyer might have given me money.'

'They weren't interested in the tape?'

'They didn't know about it. I hid it in…' He stopped. The bible. Where was it? *Jesus!* It had been on the night table. Now he saw a copy of the *Baltic News*, a tabloid that carried racy tales of increased timber production. He moved the newspaper…and there was the bible. Inside was the Dictaphone. He pressed the playback button.

But, you are objecting, what of the Rothstein house?

Clough stopped the playback. Brandy hadn't affected K.K. The voice wasn't slurred. No ranting. He had done what he had done, no concessions.

Lucija was beside him.

'This is it?'

'They weren't the kind to open a bible.'

The mattress was on the floor so they squatted on that.

'Ready?' Clough said.

What was so special about it? Why have I told you nothing?

My son, war is capricious. After years of slaughter, the opposing generals meet, open a bottle of schnapps and arrange an armistice. Peace will break out next day; eleven o'clock exactly. At the appointed hour you climb out of your trench, throw away your rifle and cheer. Alas, your watch is two minutes fast. The sniper in the church tower kills you with the final bullet of the war. Somebody has to die last – why not you?

Also the war has to be lucky for somebody.

July 1948. Berlin was blockaded. Stalin's orders. No trains were running. I was bored so I dug out the address I had been given all those years ago, set out by tram which didn't take me far, then on foot through

a desert of bombed buildings and rubble. Thin faces with the alert eyes
of rats watched from cellar doors. I asked the way from an old hag.
On through devastated suburbs until ahead I saw an extraordinary
structure, a building rising like a cliff from a sea of destruction. Agreed,
upper windows lacked glass and chimneys had toppled, but the building
had been lucky. Like me it had survived.

I drew closer and saw the number chiselled in gateposts crowned with
stone pineapples. I had arrived. I called it Schloss Rothstein.

On the gate was a sign in German, Russian and English: Leprosy
Isolation Centre. The ground floor windows were boarded but who says
lepers need to see the sun? Or possibly experiments were being carried
out. Germans know about experiments, know not to poke their noses in.
I walked along a crumbling wall topped with barbed wire. Barbed wire
is an invitation, something valuable is being protected. I just needed to
find where some desperate Berliner had cut the wire. I scrambled in,
circled the house, then shot the lock out of the back door. I carried a
pistol. In Berlin where the streets were dark, of course I did.

Don't tell me that house is impossible. Going to the moon is impos-
sible. Giving someone a new heart is impossible. A house that survives
the war, has no squatters and is not confiscated by the authorities is
impossible, but there it was.

The Rothsteins had been rich and bought protection as the Nazis
terrorised the streets, burned books, smashed faces. Even when the Reich
was at war and Jews were being exterminated Rothstein had bought a
life. He built the Nazis a factory to make uniforms. He built a hospital
to nurse the wounded. Then he built a gallery, named it The AH Centre
for Modern Art and sacrificed his personal collection to it.

Fatal error.

The Führer arrived for a private viewing and was spitting with rage.
The paintings were the creation of sick minds, the vomit of sub-humans.
The artists were Impressionists and Dadaists and Cubists and Fauvists
and Modernists of every kind. Can you hear the stamp of jackboots,
the shouted orders, the rattle of handcuffs? Rothstein, his wife and three
daughters were arrested.

I know this because Rothstein told me when he passed through Salaspils. He was in despair, reduced to nothing because he could no longer buy himself a life.

'My downfall,' he said as if he had given it much thought, 'was the Gauguins. Those breasts were not Nazi breasts, they were not disciplined, they promised freedom, they hailed joy through pleasure and not through strength, they celebrated living not dying for the Fatherland.'

The Führer gave orders the paintings were to be burnt. Put the ashes in a bomber, he told Göring, and drop them on London to corrupt the enemy.

I looked round the house. There was no electricity but I had my torch. There was a reception room grand enough to hold a New Year's Eve ball, a billiard room, a library with empty shelves, a kitchen with a spit to roast a sheep. People had camped here after the Rothsteins, most likely German soldiers before the final defeat. Furniture had been broken up and burnt in the main salon. Empty bottles of Jägermeister had been hurled against a wall. Chairs had been knocked over and I imagined a desperate retreat.

Then I came to a study with a desk that could do battle with a tank, gilt-framed mirrors, the stuffed head of a boar snarling at the world. And there they were, four crates with their lids levered off, filled with the paintings that Hitler had ordered to be destroyed.

I told you war is capricious.

I lifted a canvas out of each crate: a Gauguin with the corrupting breasts, a crazy Picasso, a Montmartre street empty of humanity by Utrillo, a shimmering Seurat. With the paintings propped against the wall I sat behind the desk to contemplate…what? Works of genius? Crates of gold? This was half a century ago before paintings like this soared in value to the stars but they were still worth a fortune.

Prost! I am toasting the paintings, Gauguin's languid tits, Picasso's tits that would stab you, Toulouse-Lautrec's well-handled tits, Dali's tits that would melt over you. I saw them then. I see them now.

The blockade of Berlin was total: no trains, no trucks, no barges, no work for me. Supplies were coming in by air but that was in the hands of General Clay and Curtis LeMay, known as Iron Pants. So every day

I went to Schloss Rothstein, an afternoon lover, slipping in the back door, stealing by torchlight to the study. I gazed at the paintings one by one, getting to know every brushstroke, every nuance of colour. What should I do about this treasure trove? I loved the paintings. I also loved the idea of the money they could bring. Everybody had looted Berlin after the war, Americans, Russians, everybody. Now order was imposed, by gun if need be. How could I spirit the paintings away?

Now pay attention. One week after my discovery. I went to Schloss Rothstein, crept in as usual, went to the study and stopped short a step inside the room. On the desk was a candle. It was burning.

I felt a dampness on my trousers and realised I was wetting myself. It was more than fear, it was dread. I was facing the unknown, a burning candle in an empty house. I had crazy thoughts. Rothstein's ghost had come to protect his art. I unbuttoned my flies and let loose against the side of the desk. A noise made my head jerk up. In the mirror behind the desk was the reflection of a mirror on the opposite wall, so I saw not one but a whole battalion of men, phantoms in the light of a single candle. Buttoning myself, I turned round. He faced me, pistol in hand.

There were no words. We were taking measure of each other. I'd been a fool but getting sudden riches does that to a man. The sign on the gate was in Russian and English as well as German so it had been put up when the war was over. Was this the sign writer? He wore a belted raincoat and a hat, even indoors. No, he was not like the Englishmen I had seen who looked as if they were dying of consumption. This man was built like a tree stump. He was the product of a diet of cabbage and potatoes, so I murmured a tentative 'Zdrastvootye.'

He nodded, acknowledging he was Russian and we spoke that language always after that.

'I made a grave mistake,' I said. 'I should have pissed on the candle. Then we would have been equals in the dark.'

He raised the pistol a notch, up from my stomach to my heart.

'Where I work we have a saying: the dying man can piss where he likes.'

I knew I was very close to death, my bowels told me that.

'May I ask what work this is?'

'The interrogation cells, Dzerzhinsky Square.'

'Bravo,' I cried, feeling life flood back into me. 'Then we both work for the Cheka.'

'Are you Rip Van Winkle? Been asleep for quarter of a century? The Cheka no longer exists.'

'My friend,' I said, 'the Cheka always exists. Only the name changes.'

This piss-awful beginning was the start of my association with Piotr Kirov. It transformed me from small time purveyor of scraps into a respected agent entrusted with foreign missions, entrapment of NATO officers and playing the double game. But how nearly it ended by the light of a single candle that afternoon.

It wasn't a conspiracy that bound us. A conspiracy means a crime but the real law in Berlin at that time was the law of the jungle. No, it was the plan we devised over the days we met so we could continue to enjoy the paintings. He was due to return to Moscow after his posting in Berlin. As an intelligence officer surely he could ship home whatever he liked? No. Someone had tried to smuggle back a Degas statuette of a dancer and was executed for acquisitive bourgeois tendencies. The statuette, so the rumour went, had been taken by Beria, who lusted after anything in a tutu.

The plan was crazy but it was the best we could do. Kirov should not try to smuggle any canvases home. Instead I would issue a mandate for transport by rail to Riga of four sealed crates of files. Kirov brought headed stationery, examples of his Head of Station's signature plus his stamp of office, and I created documents authorising me as the accompanying courier. Imagine my nights and days of terror as the train bound for Leningrad jolted through Warsaw, Bialystok, Grodno and Vilnius where the wagon was detached and left to cool for hours in a siding before being hooked onto another train. As it crossed the Daugava and crawled into Riga station I peered out over a grey war-damaged city and saw my new Jerusalem, my golden future.

Enough. I can't go on. Pardon my yawn. I look around and cannot even tell how long I've been talking. My fogged brain pleads: stop, stop.

Is it morning or evening? When I peep through the curtains I see a sort of grey half-light that could be any time.

The tape went silent.

'Is that it?' Lucija said. 'But what happens –'

She got no further.

Well, I have found this little toy again, shoved at the back of a drawer of the desk. I blinked my eyes and months have passed. Right, nothing but the facts or I'll never be finished.

Kirov visited Riga to collect his half of Rothstein's legacy. He said Moscow was a snakepit and the Cheka was in uproar. Stalin would frown and an entire Directorate would vanish into Siberia. Kirov himself had been in Berlin so was no part of the plot. What plot? The imperialist-Jewish plot that Stalin had invented. Get a job, Kirov advised, anything, so long as it doesn't draw people's attention. Patience. Our time will come. I was taken on at a factory making radios. My job was to take the completed radio and place it in a box. And again. And again.

1953. Stalin died. Kirov was well placed in the section called NATO Attack. I left the factory and attended the spy school at Dietskoye Selo. Do you think spying is fun? Well, this was. I learnt about invisible writing, sub-miniature cameras, radio transmitters in olives, all the toys of spy novels. The only part that was not fun was resistance to interrogation. No fun at all, but necessary. Once I had passed that... just listen to this. My English was already good and this was built on: language, culture and customs. I had my own personal instructor – are you paying attention? - 24 hours a day. Think about it. Yes, that's right.

Her workname was Dorothy and in bed I called her Dot. She was dark haired, a Georgian beauty, in her prime, passionate and experienced. Once I heard her mutter in her sleep, 'Arkasha'. In the morning I asked, 'Dot, who is Arkasha?' 'My husband,' she replied, staring at the ceiling. I was stunned. 'You are married?' 'Between assignments, yes.' 'But surely your husband objects to... well, this.' She jerked upright in bed, despising my bourgeois weakness, showing her fiery Georgian spirit and impressive breasts. 'My work is a state secret. He knows only that I am helping bring about world revolution.'

Such was life in those mad days.

As introduction into British culture she taught me many terms: shag, screw, a bit of the other, knee trembler, soixante-neuf, roll in the hay, hump, have it off with, nooky, hanky panky, fuck, blow job, how's-your-father, rumpy-pumpy, leg over, bonk, shaft. How did she learn them?

1958. I was flown to Bratislava for a talk by a politician from London on the class system. His name... got it. Driberg. Having a beer afterward he put a hand on my knee. I said, 'If you think I fancy a bit of the other you are barking up the wrong tree.'

Driberg raised an eyebrow.

'And I thought music hall was dead.'

I met other politicians from Britain, trade union officials, reporters, academics. Oh academics! Have you noticed how stupid very clever people can be? One professor told me the best way to make Moscow trust the West was to send the Kremlin all the West's secrets in a big brown envelope. At that time Bulganin and Krushchev were in power. Bulge and Krush he called them, making them sound cuddly. 'Bulge and Krush are not demons like Stalin, they're decent chaps. Once they know all our secrets they'll realise they have nothing to fear. We can give up the arms race and live in peace.' What was Lenin's term? Useful idiots.

I'll tell you some of the British who came on 'fraternal visits' behind the Iron Curtain and then spent a quiet weekend with the Cheka.[1]

A surprise or two, yes? And then there is [2]. He is a rising star in the Firm.

1964. About your mother and me.

Talking about matters of the heart with children is not easy. Even here – where I have been speaking openly about so much – I sense a <u>block. Make no mistake</u>. I loved her from the moment we met. There

[1]   Names omitted for legal reasons.

[2]   Name omitted for legal reasons.

had been a flickering start to détente; flickering because it could have easily been snuffed out in the Cuban missile crisis. But now bureaucrats were meeting at some diplomatic beanfeast in Helsinki. What a dreary evening until I found myself face to face with Valerie. When you meet a woman for the first time her eyes look at you, look away, look back and in those first moments you know the plot of what will happen. Not the details, not the...

Without a word Clough pressed the *Off* button. They were kneeling side by side on the mattress. Clough put a hand on Lucija's shoulder and when she turned to him he pressed a finger to her lips.

'Did you hear?' he whispered.

'Hear what?' she murmured past his finger.

'Something.'

But what? You've taken shelter in a room and you know the dogs are after you. Fragments of training flitted through his mind. He gestured Lucija to stay still. He rose up, crossed to the door and pressed an ear to the wood. There are times when nothing is something. There are times when something is a sound you didn't quite hear. He waited. Now he caught it. In the corridor, voices, male, two, hushed. You've always got a weapon, his instructor had said, pen in your pocket, coins. Suppose you're bollock-naked. Then spit in his face, he'll flinch and there's your chance.

Clough's eyes dropped. The security chain on the door was missing.

The clothes closet was on the hinge side of the bedroom door. He opened the closet door then fetched the chair from the desk to act as a brace. Now the bedroom door would open a crack but not wide enough to squeeze through. A couple of shoulder rams would splinter the chair's frame but it was the best he could do.

He skipped round the bed to grab the telephone. At night it was the receptionist who handled calls.

'Did you just let some men come to my room?'

There were two receptionists: one who smiled and one who didn't.

'I...I don't know what you mean.'

Her voice was frightened as if she knew perfectly well what he meant.

'Get the police. Do it now. The police.'

But the phone was dead. She'd cut the connection.

'You want the police?' Lucija said. 'Why didn't you say?'

She scrabbled in her handbag for her mobile phone. A bump brought their heads round. The bedroom door was open as far as it would go, jammed against the closet door. A face, two faces, were visible. A hand was holding the key-card that had swiped the lock. The hand dropped the card and now it held a knife, broad blade, commando issue. The time for getting help had gone. Clough swung round and jerked back the curtains. Then he remembered.

'Dictaphone.'

'Got it,' she said.

Clough opened the window, clambered on the desk, stepped on the sill, looked down at the soft whiteness of snow. Martin hadn't liked the room, thought the ground floor window wasn't secure. He jumped. Martin was wrong. Clough looked back up to the window. Lucija was a silhouette against its brightness.

'Jump.'

She landed in the snow beside him.

He took her hand and they ran together over cobbles to the exit facing St Peter's church. A concertina gate barred it. They ran back across the courtyard to the hotel's rear door, through the lobby to the front entrance. At the kerb were the same three army officers in combat uniform last seen in the foyer half an hour ago. They were stamping their feet on the frozen pavement, wondering where in tarnation their transport had got to. Running footsteps made them turn. Clough pulled Lucija to a stop.

'You're American?' Three pairs of eyes fixed on Clough. 'If two men come out of the hotel looking for us, tell them we went that way.' He jabbed his arm to the right.

'What the hell's going on?' one of the officers said.

'Her husband's after us. And his brother – he's got a knife.'
They headed left towards the darkness at the end of the street.
Run, Clough ordered himself, *faster, you only have seconds.*
A voice behind them cried out, 'Go, lady, go.'

Chapter 25

'Don't move. Don't switch on the light.'

His instructor had said: when you enter a suspect room, stand absolutely still. If any adverse party is waiting, he'll be tense. A tense person cannot stay still in the dark. A tense person will always make some movement, cannot help it.

Clough and Lucija stood still. No sound, no breathing. His eyes moved round the room. *Don't rush it*, he told himself. *Look for shoes under the curtains. Look for shadows within the shadows.* The orange glow from street lamps made the room full of ghosts. But he could see no danger. Nothing. He crossed to stand beside the window. They hadn't been followed, he was positive, but he checked the street, the doorways, the parked cars, and checked everything again. Tonight was a night for paranoia. Looking up he had a glimpse of Aunt Mona hauling her dress over her head. He closed the curtains.

'Matthew, I don't live in Buckingham Palace,' Lucija said, turning on the lights.

Something of an apology shaded her voice but his impression was not so much of clutter but of abundance. Books were on tables, on shelves, on the floor. There were CDs, videos, magazines, a globe. This was also her garden: spider plants trailing youngsters, a vase of freesias, a philodendron yearning to reach the window. Paintings of poppies and tulips made bold splashes of colour. As ever in countries that had slumbered behind the Iron Curtain, furniture was the let-down. The bookcase looked glued together from plywood, chairs could have been bent from curtain rods. The desk was the exception: a dark German antique swamped with papers, a pot of pens, a telephone and a man's photograph in a silver frame. Clough had the sense of a life interrupted, a normal evening abandoned for the dash to a murder scene.

'Better than Buckingham Palace,' he said. 'It's home, it's your life, it's you.'

She stopped watching him and looked round the room, seeing it through his eyes. On the floor was a brown and white rug with the pattern of a maze. On the chairs were blue cushions printed with a line of fir trees that looked as if they were holding hands.

'Yes,' she said, 'it's my home. Will you have a drink? I have beer. There's sherry a friend brought from Spain. Coffee, maybe?'

Coffee, Clough decided, and while she was in the kitchen he crossed to the window again to peek out through the curtains. Buildings hid the street where they'd sat in the car this afternoon but he could see the mound with the memorials to the shot demonstrators. He turned back from the window when the telephone began ringing. She was standing in the archway to the kitchen, frowning. She could have been counting the rings because when it reached eight she said an angry word and stepped over to the desk. Before she could pick up the phone it fell silent.

'I don't want to speak to anyone tonight,' she said. 'I don't want us to be disturbed.' Possibly she replayed in her head what she had said because she added, 'It's not every day someone comes after me with a big knife.'

The coffee was served in black cups which she placed on a low stool.

'We haven't finished listening to the Dictaphone,' she said.

'You took it.'

'Did I?'

Shock had driven it out of her head. She fetched it from her jacket pocket and without a word she put cushions on the floor. They knelt side by side. Clough hesitated. What's coming next? With K.K. there is always more. And then more. He pressed the button.

* * *

Not the details, not each scene. But deep inside you know that you are the hero and she is the heroine.

I hope you are fortunate to know a love so intense. For us to meet was hard: my travels, my work, her position at the embassy, the security checks. When a meeting was impossible we exchanged messages slipped into a copy of Beethoven's Fifth Symphony in the record department of a store. Crazy risk!

Your birth was no accident. She wanted our child, was overwhelmed by the urge. And you were created. What should we have done? Fly away to South America? My service would have tracked us down even a thousand kilometres up the Amazon and killed me. Love is private, love is a denial of the collective. Our love could not be tolerated, neither by my country (which never knew) nor by hers. When the British authorities did find out, the grey men decreed our passion could not exist. They snatched her away from Helsinki. She became that Stalinist creation: an unperson. She died in childbirth. Their punishment, that's what I felt.

But they could not prevent the fruit of our love: you.

Yet I came to spy for the people who had divided us. How can this be? I'll whisper the truth.

I spied for everyone.

I spied for Moscow.

When London found out I spied for them.

I told Moscow I had been approached on a trip to London, told the Cheka my orders from my British controller, was given disinformation to feed back to London.

I told London that Moscow had given me disinformation.

I reported back to Moscow that in order to cement my relationship it had been necessary to tell London it was disinformation. So new disinformation was prepared for me.

I warned London that the previous disinformation I had given them had been superseded by new stuff.

What did I then tell Moscow?

It doesn't matter. Picture some extravagant Viennese pastry where there is

always another layer, cream for the British, meringue for the Soviets, chocolate for everyone. It became so complex that I could say to my controllers
on either side whatever came into my head and at some level it was true.

In Finland I met a communist millionaire – now there's a double
agent – and sold him a Miro canvas from the Rothstein collection. I
never cared for Miro but he said it complemented his Sibelius record-
ings. With this money I set about acquiring my house in Mezaparks.

The procedure for doing this was more devious than I had anticipated.
One rainy autumn day I was taken to the KGB headquarters in Riga
and into a room used for interrogation. Three apparatchiks sat on hard
chairs. They shared a desk with a bust of Lenin. Lenin was a warning
because bad things are always done in his name. I stood while the three
grey men stared at me. Thin fellows, all three of them, with a lean and
hungry look. Oh yes, I know my Shakespeare: let me have men about
me who are fat. These men wanted to share the glory of nailing a traitor
and accused me in turn. Why did I need such a house? How could I
afford it on my salary? Was I taking imperialist gold?

'Comrades, is this why I have been brought here?' I stared back at
them. 'Then I advise you to listen closely, very closely.' I paused. Give
them time to understand they were confronted by someone on a higher
level. 'I need the house on the orders of Moscow Centre and it is for the
most secret of conspiracies. You must divulge the address to no one. You
must delete it from your files. Any recording of this meeting,' and I waved
a hand at the listening walls and ceiling, 'must be destroyed. I will tell
you no more. To ask further questions would incur the displeasure of
Moscow, I would even say the most severe displeasure. Have I made
myself clear? Comrades, I wish you good afternoon.'

Have you noticed how loud silence can be? I walked out in silence
that thundered in my ears. I had become the double-treble-quadruple
agent. I floated above everybody.

Enough. I come out with the old man's bleat that I am just setting
the record straight; as straight as any man in my profession can. Now
it is time the old man bowed out.

Except… well, there is one more thing. There always is.

1968. Prague. Why did the Cheka fall so in love with Prague? For its art and music and theatre? Don't make me laugh. They liked it for its dark alleys and dungeons, its Gothic gloom. They liked it for its hard men and for its soft women. That hustler who falls into step beside you and hisses 'Deutschmarks? Dollars?' Just you and him, you think, until you glance behind and see the leather jacket boys hovering beyond the lamp post. In Prague even the shadows had shadows.

But 1968 was the Prague Spring, socialism with a human face. Dubcek with his sad smile as if he could foresee the defeat to come.

Go to Prague, I was ordered, go now, go in secret. August 1968, middle of the month. Riga was my home because in the world of smoke and mirrors Moscow was a hard fact but Riga was ambiguous. My controllers in the Cheka were content because it was in the Soviet Union. My controllers in London were pleased because Moscow's grip never quite strangled Latvia's free spirit. But go to Prague? I knew nothing about our fraternal ally. I don't speak Czech, I have no contacts.

Go to Prague. A plane leaves in eighty-five minutes. Here is your passport. You are Ludwigs Kaposts, commercial representative of the amber industry. Register at the Ambassador Hotel. You will be contacted by someone from the Committee for the Protection of the People.

Aeroflot to Prague, with stewardesses who had trained in hospitality in the Gulag. I registered at the Ambassador and wandered the streets in late afternoon sun. Was I being watched? I never checked. I didn't want to seem worried. Prague was a city of young people. There were boys in blue jeans though that was frowned on as Western decadence. And look at those girls in mini-skirts. How could you fulfil your proletarian duty with such a distraction? Posters shouted 'Mir a Socialismus'. No. It was freedom they wanted. These weren't just Czechs but idealists from the West. Marxism had taken a wrong turning but Dubcek was putting it right.

The basement of the Ambassador had a restaurant that served game even in mid-summer. I looked down the menu. Hare with redcurrant sauce sounded good. It came with bread dumplings of course. I chose a bottle of red from Moravia. The waiter had just poured the wine when a man appeared at my table; square face, pitted skin, boxer's shoulders, fists instead of hands. I could see the bulge of the pistol under his jacket.

'Comrade Kaposts?'

'Yes.'

'Comrade Ludvigs Kaposts?'

'I am Kaposts.'

'Show me identification.'

He spoke English as if he was punching it into submission.

I handed him my passport which he stuck in his pocket.

'Show me your identification,' I said.

'It is not necessary. Come.'

He made a gesture with his hand as if he was sweeping dirt off the table.

The waiter arrived with my hare but Pock-Face said something sharp and the waiter walked backward with bowed head. You'd think he was leaving royalty. I swear conversation died as we made our way out but possibly I was listening to different sounds. Outside a car waited with its engine running. The driver and another man were in front, Pock-Face and I sat in the back. The car drove down to the Vltava, crossed the bridge and I thought: that's nice, the president is inviting me to dinner. But we set off away from Hradcany, raced past the trams and out into the country.

'Where are we going?'

'You'll see.'

'What for?'

'To have fun.'

The passenger in front sniggered. We drove on in silence.

Fields of sunflowers with their heads drooping gave way to pine trees, row after row. There'd been pine trees at Salaspils too but they had grown wild and free. These were in lines like the crosses in a wartime cemetery. When I thought of Salaspils images flashed: a girl's shaven head, a man swinging at the gallows, a woman's face turned up, God is in short supply today. Why should I be haunted by the past? But as the car turned off the highway I knew that the past was not past, it was just that my role was reversed.

We halted at a gate while soldiers checked with our driver. Glancing back I saw the first lights coming on in the distant city. Ahead, rolling hills covered in pine forests stretched into the dusk. The car braked in front of a mansion put up by some nineteenth century industrialist. At places like this there is always the sound of dogs.

Even in summer the house had a coldness about it. A hand shoved me in the back and I stumbled into a reception room. The door closed behind me. Whatever old furniture the salon had once contained had gone. Now there was a trestle table with three men behind it. Three is the ideologically correct number of interrogators. Never mind the other two, my eyes were riveted on the man sitting on the right. It was Sebastian Conrad, a deputy director of the Secret Intelligence Service from London.

I heard the click of the door being locked and walked slowly forward. A half-glimpsed movement made me check over my shoulder. I hadn't heard Pock-Face locking the door as he went out. What I'd heard was Pock-Face snapping the safety off his pistol.

You know, in the world in which I lived we deal not just with facts but with mood. It wasn't just this house that was cold, the mood in that room was icy.

I'm just going to give highlights though in fact the confrontation was not long. I had been summoned for what was intended as a formality. And yet in just a few minutes the mood changed.

You are face to face with three accusers. First, though, focus on the one in the middle because he is in charge. He was military, fitting his uniform like a pig fits its skin. On his chest were ribbons for more wars than were ever fought in his lifetime. He cleared his throat.

'I am Colonel Eapak. This is Comrade Hrzanov. You know the Englishman.' There was a curt military nod in the direction of Conrad. 'We will speak English.'

Speaking English, right. First chink of light. Conrad obviously didn't understand Russian or Czech. I didn't know him in the sense of having worked with him but I'd seen photos. Colonel Eapak was nominally in *charge but Hrzanov had security written all over him. Danger man unless I got him on my side. His features were as spare as an Indian fakir's and his grey suit hung on him like a bat's skin.*

'You travelled here,' still the colonel, 'on a passport that says you are Ludvigs Kaposts but you are in fact Krisjanis Kulbergs. Comrade Conrad has shown us damning evidence that while working for the organ of state security of the Soviet Union you have been passing secret intelligence to the British.' The colonel cleared his throat again and glowered at me. 'This is of course a capital offence.'

So, my son, there we are. The simple soldier is laying out the facts before giving the order to have me shot. What should I do? Most important, don't rush the fences. Don't plead innocence. Don't be caught lying. Don't look worried because worried means guilty.

'That is correct.'

I nodded and managed a small smile. I am a man at ease, never mind the churning in my belly. Conrad frowned. The colonel blinked. The security officer was biding his time. My ready agreement was so unexpected that for a moment they were at a loss how to proceed so I stepped in.

'For years I have been spying for the British and Conrad must have known. Yet it is only now he has come forward. It makes me wonder about you, Comrade Sebastian. Got yourself in a bit of a pickle, old boy? Think accusing me will earn you Brownie points?'

Step one towards survival: question the integrity of the accuser. Throw doubt on his motive. I used what I have been told is my Disgusted of Tunbridge Wells voice and saw his cheeks colour.

'What is this pickle?' the colonel asked.

'A mess, a...'

But Conrad couldn't contain himself.

'You admit spying for the British?'

How bizarre hearing a deputy director of the Intelligence service phrase it like that, so I needled him a little more.

'For your crackpot outfit? Absolutely I spied for them.'

'What is crackpot?' the colonel asked.

Conrad jabbed his finger at me. 'You admit to betraying the names of certain Soviet agents?'

'Spot on.'

Far from making Conrad exultant my agreement seemed to infuriate him.

'So, do you admit giving Moscow Centre false information about British targets?'

'Bravo, Sebastian, you are making my case for me.'

The colonel was dumbfounded. Why was I not behaving as a devious man should and trying to wriggle out of the mire? In theory it was the colonel in charge but the security officer had the real power. He broke his silence.

'You say you are an officer of Moscow Centre?'

'Yes.'

'Passing information to the British?'

'Yes.'

'You have done this to bring back intelligence of greater value to Moscow?'

'And more. Since the British believed I was their double agent they wanted to know how their material had been received in Moscow. It was necessary to devise new layers of deception in Moscow to pass back to London. Then...'

The colonel was lost so Hrzanov gave a shortened version in Czech.

Patience was what I needed until Conrad made a tactical error: he gave a specific case.

'He was responsible for the betrayal of Lyubov.'

Lyubov had been a Soviet spy in Singapore. I told London, they tipped off the Singapore authorities, Lyubov was deported, then – nice twist – he was arrested in Moscow, tried for crimes endangering national security, and sent to prison. That must have left them confused in London.

'Poor Lyubov,' I said. 'But you will agree, Colonel, that to win a victory it is sometimes necessary to sacrifice a man. Indeed if the prize is great enough, even a battalion is not too great a price to pay. The British trusted me even more after I gave them Lyubov.'

It was an argument the colonel understood and he nodded. 'Sit down,'
he barked. He was a man who spoke in orders. And to Pock-Face, 'Chair.'

Note that. We were all on the same level now. The mood had changed.
I faced Conrad,

'Why have you come to Prague at this time?'

Taken aback he said, 'Mind your own bloody business.'

But the good colonel briefed me. 'He came to tell us what advice
British Intelligence have given their government concerning any Warsaw
Pact action to restore normality here.'

'What Warsaw Pact action?'

The colonel lifted a stubby finger.

'What do you hear?'

I listened.

'Nothing.'

'In forty-eight hours you will hear the sound of metal tracks on the
tarred highway.'

'Tanks?'

'They are grouping at the border.'

'And you needed Conrad to tell you that Harold Wilson will suck
his pipe and do nothing? I don't know how much you pay Conrad but
you could have learnt that by buying a copy of The Times.'

Finally I succeeded in breaking Conrad. He was on his feet ranting.

I said softly in Russian which I was sure such senior officers had to
learn, 'Is he to be trusted? Have you considered he might be a triple
agent? What does Moscow Centre say?'

I suspected this was some local initiative. My speaking Russian which
Conrad didn't understand increased his fury. He was half over the table,
grabbing at my jacket and it took Pock-Face's raised pistol to make him
subside. The trestles had shifted, glasses of water crashing to the floor.

'Comrade Hrzanov,' I was still speaking Russian, 'you agree it is
always wise to consider the wider implications of one's actions. Let me
telephone Comrade Kirov, the Director of NATO Attack in Moscow.'

It was summer and I tracked Piotr Kirov down to his dacha. I
have visited it; charming place, lake and silver birches of course, and

a stunning art gallery. It wasn't late in Moscow so Piotr hadn't gone to bed. I handed the telephone to Hrzanov and it was a wonder to see the way his back straightened. First he asked about me, then about Conrad, finally the political/military situation.

He spoke Czech to the colonel then Russian to me.

'You are a highly valued fighter in the struggle against imperialism. The Englishman produces little of value. There is a question mark over his reliability which today's events make more serious. And the situation? They know what the West will do. Nothing.'

As he was led away Conrad was screaming abuse and calling on God to damn me. I kept a stern face but inwardly I had a little smile because I remembered how memories of Salaspils had haunted me on the drive here. God would not damn me, I could have told Conrad, because God was in short supply today.

And why had I been brought to Prague from Riga?

'Western revanchists have infiltrated Czechoslovakia which is the reason for the coming Warsaw Pact action. You are known to have made clandestine journeys to London. Certain documents incriminating British Intelligence would have been found when your body was discovered in a Prague alley. There would have been outraged Soviet speeches at the United Nations.'

It had been Krushchev who started the dramas at the UN. Remember how he hammed for the cameras, taking off his shoe and banging the desk?

'May I respectfully suggest,' I said, 'that Conrad's body is found crushed by a tank track.'

'That would turn him into a hero against the invasion,' the colonel objected.

'So much the better. No one should ever suspect he had any connection with you. It starts people worrying about other double-treble-quadruple agents.'

I laid a hand over my heart.

The streets were still lively when I was driven back to Prague. A huge red star shone above Wenceslas Square, a beacon lighting the way to the future. At the Ambassador I went down to a nearly empty restaurant.

'I'll have my hare now,' I said. 'You had better open a fresh bottle of wine.'

The waiter stared at me as if I had risen from the dead. He was right, of course.

Should I get on to the British and warn them of the invasion? That would lift me in their estimation which could only be to my good. I drained my glass and poured another while I turned the matter over. I had no contact in Prague. I could go to the embassy but that would mean showing the police on guard outside some identification. The Kaposts passport hadn't been returned so it would have to be my Krisjanis Kulbergs identity card. My details would be noted. Not a good idea. Telephone? Hmm, not secure. But there was another consideration. There would be uproar in London and an emergency session at the UN at the prospect of an invasion. Questions would be asked in Prague and Moscow. Who warned the British about the Warsaw Pact action? In the scramble to duck the blame someone was sure to say, hang on a minute, K.K. was privy to that information.

The Falklands, the downfall of the Iron Lady, the attempted assassination of the Pope, there are tales I could tell. But enough. Matthew, if you hear this I have a feeling it will not be in my lifetime. You may find yourself puzzled by the twists of my life. Yes, yes, you say, in a turbulent century you were able to survive. You grappled with the swinging fortunes of the war, you endured the ravings of the world's maddest mullahs, you did some extraordinary things. You were dazzling to the British and made the Cheka see stars. But in the final analysis, father, where did your fundamental loyalty lie?

An excellent question, my son. Let me have a last glass while I consider my answer.

The tape kept running. It was silent for five seconds, maybe ten, while Lucija and Clough knelt. There was a noise.

'Huh.'

What did that mean? Then the tape stopped.

'I have a little brandy,' Lucija said. 'I keep it for emergencies.'

Chapter 26

'Do you want me to tell you about men?' Lucija asked, as if it followed from what they had just heard.

No, Clough didn't want that. Men always got a hammering when women talked in this way. She was going to tell him anyway.

'A man wants women,' she said, holding his eyes. 'Oh, a woman wants a man but that is different. You see, a man wants women, plural. He makes love to one, he rolls over in bed and goes out in search of another. Look out of the window and what do you see? Men rushing everywhere. They are hurrying from one bed to the next. They look at their watches – do I have time? They jog with a cellphone clapped to their ear – is the coast clear? How long will we have?'

'Lucija.'

She raised an eyebrow. Clough stopped. There was more to come.

'All right, I exaggerate. I want you to imagine a speeded-up film of reality. It is the truth about men. All women know this. It is not what women want so how do we cope? I will tell you: each in her own way. Some play the same game as men. Some weep. Some buy a gun. Some develop blindness to what is going on. Some become devout and call upon God to help them.'

We have been at the scene of three murders, Clough thought. *Two men have tried to kill us with a big knife. Yet here we are squatting on the floor like students discussing love and the meaning of life. There had to be a point. Be patient.*

'Each woman must act according to how she is.' Lucija sounded as if she was delivering a lecture. There was a little brandy left in her glass and she drained it. 'I do not like to kiss a man goodbye, look out of the window to watch him. There he goes, the man who has just left my bed. He reaches Brivibas Bulvaris – Freedom Boulevard, please note – and stops. Now I see him take out his cellphone and his little black book and call the next woman. I am diminished. Do you see?'

Was this her life or her imagination? Clough didn't know.

She got to her feet to fetch the framed photograph from the desk. She crouched beside him again. Clough saw a man in his early thirties seated on a sofa with one arm draped along its back. The pose was relaxed but the expression on his face was intense as if he had just been asked a searching question.

'Guntis,' she said. 'We were only just married when…' She nodded her head towards the mound with the memorial to those killed by the OMON troops. She was silent a moment or two, twisting the photo in her hand. The light from the lamp reflecting off the glass switched Guntis' face on and off.

'Once, when Latvia was part of the Soviet Union, I was sent as interpreter with a businessman to Siberia. It was the minerals he was interested in; me too, of course. He wanted a photo of us together so he handed his camera to the waiter in the restaurant. This was in the region of the Khant people. The Khant waiter wanted me to know he was not Russian. So…' She drew a breath. 'The Khant man said words in his own language. Then he translated them into Russian. Then I, a Latvian, put them into English for this Swedish businessman. This was the United Nations working, or how it should work. You wonder why I am sharing this with you.'

'You'll tell me,' Clough said.

'Yes. Yes I will. The Khant people have a word for a photograph which translates as "a pool of still water"'. Again she twisted the photo of her dead husband, catching the light. 'I look at this photo of Guntis and I think, yes, a pool of still water. But,' she put the photo down, 'is that all there is to life? Staring at a pond? Surely there is more. Isn't there?'

She was quiet but Clough didn't answer.

'Tell me, Matthew, are you married?'

'No.'

'A woman waiting for you in England?'

'No. There was, but…"

She shook her head. She didn't want to know more. She rocked back on her heels and tilted her head up so she was talking to the ceiling as much as Clough.

'Tomorrow, maybe the next day, you will leave and fly back to England. I will not see you taking out your little black book and calling up the next woman. I will not be… diminished. That is why, for me, you are the perfect man. I will remember you with affection and gratitude. And you, I think, will feel the same about me.'

She reached out to him on the rug with its pattern like a maze, touching his cheek.

'We will make love,' she said simply, as if it had long ago been decided. 'You will show me yourself and I will show you myself. That way we shall never forget each other.'

With a finger she tipped his chin so that his eyes and hers were locked together.

'Now,' she said.

She undressed him and he undressed her. They forgot all about closing the bedroom curtains. The lights were switched off but the glow from the city lit up their world. There was a neon sign just across the road. It switched from orange to mauve and back to orange, daubing a patch of ceiling like flashes from a distant battle.

Get a grip, Clough chided himself. There is no distant battle. I'm flying too high.

They made love and he had shown her himself and she had shown him herself, just as she had said.

'Except one thing.'

'What is that, Lucija?'

'I will not tell you.'

'Why not?'

'Because,' she said.

'Because?' he said. 'Because what?'

But she put her fingers on his mouth to stifle his protest at this most childish of answers. They slept an hour or two before a car's alarm in the street disturbed them.

'You are awake, Matthew?'

'Yes.'

'It is bad to be alone at night. It is good we are awake together.' She ran her fingers down his body, the very lightest touch on his skin. 'You are a quiet man, Matthew. Your English word is reserved, is it not?'

'Sam, who left me…'

'Sam is a man's name.'

'Samantha. She said that I wouldn't share.'

'Perhaps she and I say the same thing in different ways. But I would also say that she did not know how to make you share.'

'Tonight I am overwhelmed.'

'By your father, by the murders, by the men who came to kill us.'

'That and more.'

She waited. He stared at the ceiling. K.K.'s tape – he didn't want to think of it – but there was that bit about a hero and heroine in the drama of life. Lucija had faced dangers but had stayed strong. She'd lived in a system that demanded compromises but stayed honest. Lost love but not despaired. She'd climbed a mountain of experiences. She was a heroine. And he, well, he had tripped over a molehill. She seemed to want him but only for a night.

He was still putting his feelings in order when the telephone rang and the moment was lost. It was her mobile phone which she'd dropped beside the bed. 'Shit,' she said into Clough's shoulder. The phone on her desk she wouldn't answer but her mobile was different. On the third ring she swung her legs over the bed, picked up the phone and wandered over to the window. She spoke and listened, spoke and listened, gazing down at the street below. The neon glow switched her naked breasts orange-mauve-orange.

'That was the captain,' she said. She lay at his side again. 'He said the police have not caught the two men who tried to kill us. But they have arrested the receptionist who has confessed she was paid – naturally she does not know the name of the man who paid her – twenty US dollars to say when you returned to your room.'

'Twenty dollars?' Clough said. 'Three people have been killed, a gang of drug smugglers has been uncovered, hundreds of millions of dollars of looted art has been found, two men tried to murder us, and the police have arrested a girl who accepted twenty dollars?'

'I would say it was twenty dollars well spent, Matthew, or else you would not now be here.'

She turned to him. Her eyes caught some of the neon reflection, glistening like Greek olives.

'Matthew, Matthew, Matthew.'

Her lips were close to his ear. There was no fumble in their lovemaking, no nervousness, no holding back. It was as if they had been friends for a long time and couldn't understand why they had never taken this decisive step.

'What is the one thing you wouldn't show me?'

'Hush.' She put a hand on his mouth again. 'There must always be one final secret or love will lose its magic.'

His ears hadn't tricked him, had they? She'd used the word 'love'.

There was no way of holding the morning back. The orange-mauve glow from the neon sign was fading and the window turning grey. Clough had to speak to Martin.

'Use the cellphone,' Lucija said. 'It is my latest toy. With luck no bad people know about it. I'll go and make coffee.'

It wasn't yet eight o'clock, a time unknown to embassies. Martin himself answered the telephone.

'I had the line switched through to my room. There were telephone calls from London I was expecting.'

'They gave you a room?'

'Matt, this is not the Ritz. It's somewhere a visiting spy can catch his breath. It has a sofa-bed, a telephone and a bottle of Scotch. What else does one need?'

'Company?'

'Ah.' There was a pause and perhaps Martin was listening for hints of company at Clough's end. 'I've had West for company. He's down the corridor and he was noisy for a time and then quiet as the grave. I went to have a look. He's in the stationery store-room, lashed to a chair and the chair tied to the shelving. Remember Chapman, like a bank clerk in the days when banks had clerks? He had gagged him quite viciously.'

Clough was standing by the window, watching the street. Nobody was taking an interest in the building where Lucija lived.

'Have you had a talk with our friend before he was gagged?'

'He won't say a word, or at least nothing you'd like your aunt to hear. You'll find this hard to believe but he demanded to see a lawyer. You're in no position to demand anything, I told him. The passport in your pocket was in the name of Winstanley so you're not here at all. You don't exist, you're a non-person and that's how you're leaving Latvia. You're being put out the back door with the rest of the rubbish. Later this morning we'll be taken in a closed van to some military airport with an unpronounceable name. His eyes looked like marbles, you know the ones schoolboys used to play with. They were hard, glittery and crazed. How about you? You're not calling from the hotel?'

'No. We left my room through the window. We had visitors. They'd searched the room earlier and were coming back with knives, big ones.'

'Did they find it? K.K.'s bequest?'

'No, I've got it.'

'Interesting?'

'He names names, people who were friendly with the KGB.' Clough's voice had slowed down. 'One or two shocks.'

'In the Firm?'

'Yes.'

'A problem?'

'Yes.'

Neither would talk about it on the phone but Clough's plain 'Yes' meant the problem was serious.

'Also he told how he came by the paintings. And he could have given a warning about the Warsaw Pact invading Czecho in '68 but he had a good dinner instead. You can't tell who had the last call on his loyalty. Actually, I don't think anybody did.'

'Where are you now?'

'Her apartment. I have to make another statement to the police.'

'So you're all right?'

'Yes.'

'What are your plans?'

'I'll come back to England and contact you.'

'When?'

Clough took his time answering. 'I don't know.'

'You must understand there is not one great conspiracy but several small ones,' Lucija said. 'It depends who they knew in the old days, who they did business with. Krisjanis Kulbergs was in one group, the man you know as Finnis was in another, then they got together. You know the symbol for the Olympic Games, how one circle is linked through another? They were like that.'

'Some games,' he said.

She looked at him over her coffee cup and smiled.

'Now, about today,' she said.

'I have to make that statement about last night's attack in my room.'

'I mean after that.'

They were driving in her Dyane. Lazy snowflakes drifted down from heavy clouds packed with more. The flakes rested on the windscreen until the wipers batted them away. The heater had a will of its own. Clough remembered it from yesterday, either blasting out a tropical heatwave or sulking and refusing to work at all. So they had it on full blast with Clough's window open a crack. They were on the road to Salaspils.

'The journey is necessary in my opinion,' she had said, 'in order to throw out certain demons. I do not know the right expression for "throw out demons".'

'Throw those demons out is what we'll do,' he had agreed with a cheerfulness he didn't feel. What demons possessed him? Krisjanis Kulbergs? God damn it, he had only met K.K. for a couple of hours. That was enough.

'If prisoners were coming from Riga,' she said, 'they would have been transported by truck along this road.'

Clough looked out at land that had once been fields. It was the same on the outskirts of all cities: the land died while it waited for the bulldozer.

'If they came from further away – Lithuania, Poland, even Germany – they would come by train. So we start from the station.'

Like Rothstein, Clough thought.

The station was yellow brick and looked post war, as if the old station had been flattened by the Red Army or by vengeful citizens obliterating a landmark in their troubled history. Lucija parked the car and said the station was actually called Darzini. But there was a sign that promised Salaspils with an arrow to point the way. They walked down a track that disappeared into woods. When the track became tricky with ice hidden under the snow they detoured through the trees. Pines made it sombre, fallen branches made them stumble. Was this the forest K.K. had wandered through as a break from the camp? He supposed it was. He was walking in K.K.'s footsteps when he had come across Merija hunting for mushrooms. She had turned round and lifted her skirt so he could take her from behind. No pressure on her to do that. Honest, he protested.

Clough had read that at the place of a great killing no birds sing.

It was silent here. Now, on the far side of the track, was something surreal. In the middle of these woods, in the middle of nowhere, with no village in sight, there was a football pitch. Between the goalposts at the far end was a snowman with a woollen cap to keep out the cold and a pine cone for a nose. The goalie had stumps of arms stuck out, waiting for the penalty shoot-out. Dali would have approved.

The track branched and an arrow pointed to the left. Tractors hauling logs had left deep ruts and the mud had frozen. A small bridge crossed a stream which was still running.

'It's not far,' Lucija said, as a promise or a warning.

'You've been here before?'

'It was necessary. We have to understand past evil so we know when it threatens again.'

The woods thinned. They passed something like a gatekeeper's cottage but there was no gate. Then, without warning, they had arrived. But where was the camp? There was nothing, just a flat area that had no limits, bleak, lacking humanity. On their left was a concrete block pierced by holes, a couple of dozen of them, as if prisoners had been lined up and a machine gun had opened fire.

'You see it?' Lucija pointed. 'A poem has been cut in the concrete.'

Lichen the colour of bile had spread over the concrete. A ditch had been dug in front of the memorial and a flat stone laid to kneel on. But the words that had been chiselled were hard to make out. Lucija jumped over the ditch so she could trace out the first line with a finger.

'"Beyond this stone the earth groans…" A poet called Ververis wrote it. Maybe your father met him. Ververis was a prisoner here.'

She caught up with Clough as he was striding down a paved path flanked by more concrete blocks.

'Don't be angry with me.'

'Maybe he met the poet, maybe he didn't, but he's not my father.'

They walked in silence before she spoke again.

'There were thirty-nine barrack huts. Prisoners were employed in building roads, digging peat and constructing airfields.'

'They were sent to clear mines.'

271

'That too. They were told to walk across the minefield. If they refused, they were shot. If they got to the far side of the minefield alive they were promised their freedom. A lie, of course. Prisoners who were executed were buried beyond the wire.'

'Sardinenpackung,' he said.

'In winter when the ground was frozen they used dynamite to blast holes. Sometimes it was frozen too deep so the bodies were left lying on the surface. The crows...' She made pecking motions with a hand. 'In the centre, near here, was the watch tower. I forget how many metres high but tall enough to see to every corner of the camp. It is one kilometre from end to end. On that side were the gallows. They faced east. The last sunrise.'

K.K. had talked about how busy the gallows were when the defeat at Stalingrad became known.

They were walking again, at a funeral pace. A central area was covered in squares of concrete paving. On one side was a slab of polished stone. As they got closer they heard the tock-tock-tock of a metronome. It came from under the stone.

'It is the heartbeat of the earth,' she said.

Clough listened – tock-tock-tock – and said, 'Blood dripping.'

She looked at him. His jaw muscles were clenched, his brow was in furrows, white half-moons showed in the skin under his eyes. She took his hand to lead him towards a group of huge figures. They were a world out of scale with humanity, built of unforgiving concrete. Concrete was everywhere, blocks, structures, statues. This must be a legacy of the communist era. The Soviets had loved pouring concrete. It set so hard. It boasted of eternity.

'These statues represent Mother, the Humiliated, the Unbroken and Solidarity,' Lucija said.

Someone had cleared the snow off the central area and pushed it into heaps. A fresh snowfall had covered these heaps so they looked like the mounds of newly filled graves.

'I don't know where the guards' quarters were so I can't tell you where your...'

He snatched his hand away from hers and she flinched as if he was going to hit her.

'He's not my father. Why can't you understand? I have had nothing to do with him. I never lived with him. I never knew him. I didn't even know who he was. Look at this. Look at it.' He swung his arm round the desolate wasteland, the concrete, the pine trees that pressed against the fence. 'I have nothing to do with this. Oh God.'

His face took refuge in his hands and he started to shiver as if a cold wind had got up. The cold wind was inside. Lucija wrapped her arms round him and pulled him to her so that they stood, a single shaking body. He lowered his head and buried it in her neck. His shoulders heaved, dry sobs, deep gulps of air. He was muttering, first curses, then words of denial, calling on God and damning K.K., damning Hitler and Stalin and the war that had swept back and forth over this land, damning the spy lords who had lied and twisted and invented a world to fit their own purposes, making use of the father, ensnaring the son, damning the madness that had overtaken him, on and on. He looked in her face and she seemed to be sharing his pain but no – this was his own pain – and he closed his eyes again. K.K. had been his father – a biological fact. Had he inherited more than an art gallery from him? Was there a gene for trickery and deceit? A gene for lying? For spying? For not sharing? He thought of Düsseldorf and the Irish woman he had made love to before pointing her out to the executioners. He had resigned but the K.K. of the journal wouldn't have. K.K. would have exulted: SHE DIED BUT I SURVIVED. The morality that he, Matt Clough, lived by was not the amorality that flowed through K.K.'s veins. K.K. was someone entirely self-centred while he reached out to connect with the world.

It took time until calmness settled on him. What had she said? Throwing out demons.

Snow had started and Lucija said, 'We must get back.'

* * *

At Darzini station they found the Dyane wearing an overcoat of white. Lucija started the engine and they sat waiting for the heater to blow out a tropical breeze. The windows were three-quarters covered in snow so they seemed to be sheltering in a cave.

'Do you speak German?' he asked.

'I never had to learn it.'

'The Germans have a word – are you ready for it?'

She nodded.

'Vergangenheitsbewältigung. It means coming to terms with the past. I prefer *throwing out demons*.'

'Poor Germans. With a language like that weighing them down, no wonder they keep breaking out of their own country.'

She took a cigarette, gave him the lighter and as he held the flame to the tip of her cigarette she touched his hand, steadying it with her fingers. The air in the car was warming, melting the snow on the side windows. Anyone on the station platform who turned their way could see them, a couple, sometimes talking, sometimes silent. A marital tiff, you might think. Or they could be lovers at cross purposes: part forever, hide their passion, run away together? Just look at the man – how troubled he was.

'In my apartment, before we made love, I said that soon you would be flying back to England. We would have our moments of pleasure and there would be no time to become disillusioned. But that was last night and this is now. I very much regret my remark. I was not serious.'

Lucija stabbed out her half-smoked cigarette.

'What are you going to do?'

He opened his mouth but found he had no voice. The tumult of the past days had scattered his thoughts.

'Do you want me to take you somewhere?' She sighed. His silence was a burden to them both. 'Matthew, we can't sit here all day. You must decide. Back to England? Back to In Vino Veritas? Or…'

He wanted to ask her what was the last secret of love that she hadn't shown him in case the magic faded.

Again she sighed.

'Where are you going in your life? Do you want me to come with you? You must tell me.'

Where?

At last he said, 'I want to go back to your apartment. Nothing makes sense here.' He nodded out of the window. The woods were a winter wonderland but beyond, out of sight, was Salaspils. 'It casts too long a shadow.'

England, February 2001

Chapter 27

This is what came next. This was nearly the end.

Matt Clough was back in Wallingford but everything that happened in Latvia had a tight grip on him. The weather was foul, the Thames flooding knee-deep over the path. Out running, he took a detour through backstreets, past the boathouse and over the by-pass bridge. He paused, jogging on the spot, looking down at the surging Thames. He remembered stopping on the bridge in Riga to look down at ice floes, Finnis at his side. At the end of the bridge he turned right. A Jewish school used to be here but it had closed abruptly. He made a circuit of the grounds while rain dripped from the trees. The place was abandoned as if staff and boys had all been shipped off to Salaspils. Coming back he went through the centre of town, down an alley with an artists' supply shop. In its window was a poster of one of Monet's Waterlilies. *Hello, I recognise you. I may even own one of your cousins.*

Everything took him back to Latvia

He was at the traffic lights, twenty seconds from his front door, when it happened. He set out across the road when the car, turning the corner with a squeal from its tyres, was on him. He dived just in time, tumbling on the pavement. If he hadn't already had momentum from jogging the bumper would have caught him.

He was dazed, no breath in him, couldn't speak.

A small crowd gathered. He caught snatches.

Bloody maniac, jumping the lights.

Kid on drugs.

Two of them.
Hit and run, never stopped.
Did you get the number?

It was Liz who helped him to his feet, Liz who owned the office supply shop across the road from In Vino Veritas, Liz with her pale intelligent face. She rested a hand on his shoulder to steady him.

'Licence number was 51 something, the rest covered in mud. I was just going to cross too. The car was crawling up to the lights until you stepped off the kerb then it accelerated.'

'Let's face it – we've got to sell up while the going's good,' his partner Godfrey said. 'I'm the entrepreneur but you're the wine buff. If you get bumped off I can't carry on here.'

Godfrey's tone was jokey but his frown was serious. He hadn't taken kindly to being abandoned with no notice, having to do the tax paperwork, dealing with tardy suppliers who battered him in German while Clough was off, as he put it, fighting World War Three.

'Come on, God, this is England. Who's going to kill me?'

'You mean apart from hit-and-run drivers? Let's see. Who have you got on the wrong side of in your life?' He held up a hand and grabbed hold of a thumb. 'The IRA or its descendants have a score to settle. The Hungarian army feel miffed about certain business near Eger. Some of Ceausescu's boys bear a grudge. There was an awkward encounter in Albania.' He tugged at his fifth finger. 'How about Latvia? Any dicey moments there? Any jokers with knives? Any international gangs wanting their money and if they don't get money they want blood?'

Every day Clough phoned Lucija. He had rejected his mobile phone as being untrustworthy. He had stared at the telephone on his desk. It was an alien. Look at it: grey as a bureaucrat, silent as a spy, wired like a bomb. *This is more than flying too high*, he told himself, *this is going mad*. But the real world was mad so he crossed the river to a callbox in Crowmarsh Gifford or drove to Didcot. They spoke in the evening when she had returned from the Citizenship Board.

She picked up the phone but seemed to listen before speaking.

'I love you,' Clough said.

'I love you,' Lucija replied.

I love you was the safety signal. *I love you* meaning all is well. *I love you* meaning I love you. He avoided using a name which in his mind had become insecure. They tapped phones. Computers in Cheltenham latched on a name in a nanosecond. Who were they? The enemy, whoever they were. He was behaving in England as he once had in the Soviet satellites.

'It's snowing,' she said. *Snow* was another trigger word. *I'll always talk about snow if everything is well with me*, she'd said. *No snow, not well.* 'It reminds me of walking through the forest to Salaspils and the snowman who was too fat to dive to save the penalty.'

'Does the captain make progress?'

'I would say no. Or…' There was a pause ended by the snap of her lighter. 'Maybe he makes progress backwards. The pistols that were found at the house at Majori, used for the murders… you said you found them close by the bodies and didn't touch them. The serial number of one of them, according to the manufacturer, shows it to be part of a consignment sold to an arms dealer in Birmingham. This is Birmingham in England.'

Clough closed his eyes: he could see Martin, holding the embassy gun, shooting Finnis.

'The arms dealer will not co-operate. He says the pistol was sold legally but he won't say who to. The captain was not happy. Then he had problems with the people involved with K.K.'s death; the first time he died before he came back to life to die again at Majori. The pathologist who is down as examining the body of the drowned K.K. denies it. Look, the captain points, here is your signature – Stepanov - and your official stamp. Stepanov looks closely and pronounces the signature a forgery. There is talk of a pogrom against Russians living and working legally here. Moscow has lodged an official protest. Putin behaves like a spoiled teenager. He can't crush the Chechens so he kicks us instead.'

* * *

The meeting with Martin was arranged like a textbook exercise. Clough used a telephone box near the base in Benson where the RAF trains its helicopter pilots. He whistled *Yellow Submarine* then waited for Martin to reach his telephone kiosk. A crash meeting, Clough said. Time: the following day. Place: a Turkish restaurant in Camden Town.

'It's what Greek food is going to be when it grows up,' Martin said. He didn't bother with the menu. 'We'll have the *mezze*,' he told the waiter, ordering for both of them. 'They'll bring a lot of dishes then leave us alone.'

The wine list was very short, typed on half a sheet of paper which was tucked in a cracked plastic folder. Clough ordered Buzbag.

'Were you followed?' Martin asked.

'I don't think so.'

'I was. Or they wanted to. Two heavies were parked down the street from my door. Yesterday it was a different car. So it's surveillance by an outfit with resources. This morning when I left home I went and rapped on the window. It worries watchers when you do that because it's not playing the game. "I'm going to have lunch," I told them. I gave them a restaurant name. "Would you gentlemen care to join me?" If it's the Firm snooping on me they are employing some low grade watchers these days. One of them told me to go forth and multiply, except he didn't use biblical language. At the corner I looked back and the passenger was on his mobile. Putting jokers like that on me is an insult.'

'They're not here?' Clough nodded at the two tables by the window.

'I told them a restaurant in Notting Hill. All right, I make it sound like a joke but it's not. When your own side, or people you always thought were your buddies, start breathing down your neck, then it's trouble.'

Clough told him about the hit-and-run in Wallingford, using knives and forks to make a diagram of the streets. They had to have been lying in wait.

'Do you run every day?'

'Yes.'

'Remember what we tell diplomats in hardship postings: vary your route, vary your time.'

'Has West talked yet?'

'His lawyer has. This lawyer demands his release because there is no case to answer. The Latvian authorities accept your account that K.K. and Finnis killed each other, ergo West didn't. Dictaphone recording? Tittle-tattle. Where is the evidence that K.K. recorded it? Since K.K. is dead he can't be questioned or verify it. An obvious fake. It is not evidence, it is unsupported allegations. Produce one concrete proof, one live witness.'

Their food was untouched. A waiter came over to ask if anything was wrong. Delicious, Martin assured him. They ate several mouthfuls to reassure him.

'The deputy director who sent you with her blessing,' Clough said, 'you've seen her?'

Martin broke off a piece of pide, then dropped it.

'She's away on leave. In February? I asked myself. Has she gone to the Alps? She doesn't ski. The Caribbean? She's not one to flop on a beach. I still have one or two people there I trust. She's on leave because she is suffering from stress, been overworking. There is only one cure for overworking. She won't come back. Also,' Martin needed a strengthening swallow of Buzbag, 'she is not the only deputy director. The other is the one who K.K. named as a rising star all those years ago. He said it on the tape but this is so patently ludicrous that the whole tape is discredited.'

'They think K.K. was making it all up?'

'They don't think K.K. was making it up at all. They think other people were. Nevertheless, some honest spark tracked down that ex-KGB type Kirov; like the ballet but without the tantrums. The idea was to ask him, "Piotr old chap, is it true that [1] is a wholly owned <u>mole of Russian I</u>ntelligence?" This bold seeker after truth was at

1   Name omitted for legal reasons.

the Moscow embassy so his idea was to go out to Kirov's dacha. Kirov is some kind of big crook who lives in a mansion; in Russian it is called a *kottedz,* which I find sweet. It is grand enough to be guarded by thugs with assault rifles. This spark reported back to the embassy which duly sent a note to London. The mandarins who processed this report had a hissy fit. They said it was preposterous to postulate (good mandarin phrase that) that old Soviet spies and people in British Intelligence and high-ups in the Foreign Office and Special Branch and the Mafia were all in bed together. They said it was a conspiracy theory too far. They flagged the report: inaction this day.'

Lunch over, they stood a moment outside the restaurant, Martin hoping for a taxi, Clough about to walk to Camden Town tube station.

'I was deniable, you see, that's why they used me.'

Martin seemed to think he hadn't explained enough.

'Before I went to Riga I was summoned to the Top Floor at the Firm. I faced the faceless men. They didn't like me, didn't trust the story, but they went along with my flying out to join you because I was deniable. Well, now they are denying me.'

Martin had paid for lunch, just like old times. Clough thanked him, though the food had made no impression.

'Go well,' Martin said. 'Be careful. This time conspiracy theorists may just have a point.'

It was the last time Clough saw him.

'I love you.'

'I love you.'

'Last night I dreamed of a tropical island,' Lucija said. 'Can you think of a tropical island without sand and palm trees? It's not possible. We were on the beach, naked and making love, quite shameless. Little waves were breaking on silver sand, a warm breeze was caressing our skin, parrots were shrieking. It happened for both of us at the same moment. Ecstasy. You said, "Did you feel the earth move?" Yes, yes, oh yes. Then we saw it – the coconut that had thumped on the sand beside us, like a big brown snowball.'

I love you, snow, all was well.

But all was not well.

Coming through the door he darkened In Vino Veritas. It was Bruiser, the superintendent from Oxford. He chose his time well. It was a Wednesday when Godfrey visited his invalid mother in Worcester. And it was midday, a little on the late side to produce coffee.

'A glass of something would slip down a treat.'

Superintendent Beckett ran his eyes along the display of bottles.

'Lucky you being able to offer visitors hospitality from your work, as it were. What can I offer? The hospitality of the cells. That's not the same thing at all.' He paused a moment and then said, 'Is it, sir?'

Why had he said that? The policeman's tone had been flat so it didn't come across as a joke. Clough poured the wine and handed the superintendent a glass.

'Your good health, Mr Clough.' The policeman took a mouthful. 'More of a beer man myself but this hits the spot.' He picked up the bottle. 'Murfatlar. Where's that when it's at home?'

'Romania.'

'One of your Iron Curtain jobs.'

'There hasn't been an Iron Curtain for years.'

'Ah, but you were in and out of those workers' paradises in the old days, if I remember your passport correctly.'

Clough took a sip of wine then kept his mouth shut. He didn't like Murfatlar. He sold it but didn't like it. Perhaps that was why he gave it to the policeman.

'You'd been to Romania, also Hungary, Czechoslovakia and Yugoslavia. And Bulgaria. So your passport said. All countries in the former Evil Empire. Nothing illegal in that, of course, but it does rather tell a story.'

'What story is this? It was my work. Still is.'

'Ah, what story indeed.'

What was the purpose of the superintendent's visit? It hovered in a grey area between social chat and interrogation.

'Why have you come to see me?'

If Clough expected another bit of flannel he was wrong. Beckett jumped straight to the point.

'To ascertain if you have been in touch with your boss Martin, or perhaps I should say your former boss. I don't mean in Latvia. We know all about that. I mean since your return.'

'I telephoned him when I got back. Home safe and sound, I told him.'

'That was three weeks ago.'

'Getting on for four.'

'Have you had a meeting with him, a face-to-face?'

'No,' Clough lied.

'Now, you remember Mr West who you met at the police station…'

He seemed to need Clough's agreement so he nodded.

'…and met again in very different circumstances in Latvia? Your ex-boss Martin kidnapped him at gunpoint and hustled him back here on the grounds that he was a murderer and a spy. I confess I am no great fan of the gentleman but those seem wild, *wild* accusations, the delusions of the lunatic fringe. Mr West, I may tell you, has a very different tale. He says your father was a Soviet spy and so were you – which accounts for your many visits under cover of being a wine buyer in Eastern Europe – and so in all likelihood was Martin. West says the Soviet Union may have gone down the plughole but Russia has risen with an ex-KGB man as president and old loyalties are being dusted down. He says Martin has tried to discredit a very senior intelligence officer. Mr West says further that he went to Latvia, collected a one-time British agent as back-up and went to your father's house to detain you. In the shoot-out you killed this agent and there has been a cover-up. That's what he says. What do you say?'

Nothing. Say nothing. Don't even say '*nothing*'. Clough stood up and turned away because he had had enough. He heard the superintendent pushing himself out of the chair.

'I don't know how good the Latvian police are. Don't know if they tried very hard. Maybe they were given orders to accept whatever story the Englishman tells. Don't test his hands – your hands – for powder.'

'My fingerprints aren't on the gun.' Clough couldn't let this go unchallenged. 'It wasn't me.'

'Their forensic methods leave a lot to be desired, I've no doubt. We have asked for the gun to be sent over here. It could be a dead hand was wrapped round the butt. But there's always the chance a stray print wasn't wiped off. Did you think of that?'

Clough said nothing.

'How much of this has Martin told you?'

Clough didn't answer.

'Too late now.'

Clough turned to look at him.

'Haven't you heard? Mugged he was, almost outside his own front door. Just last night. His assailants – I would guess there was more than one – must have been disturbed because they didn't even take his wallet.'

'What are you trying to tell me?'

'Blow to the back of the head. Killed outright. Didn't you know, sir?'

He telephoned Lucija. 'I love you.'

'I love you too. When I see snow I want to be warm in bed with you.'

He asked his question.

'Yes,' she said, 'certain British authorities have requested that the murder weapons be sent to London for further tests. The captain rang to tell me. He was indignant, maybe very indignant, even slamming-the-telephone-down indignant. They think we are some former colony they can order about, he said.'

From the telephone box he kept an eye on the car that had parked half over the kerb fifty metres away.

'Will you send the pistols over here?'

'Moscow is still making angry noises. We cannot afford to have Britain cross too so probably the pistols will be sent.'

Clough felt his life was disjointed, days fragmented, events spinning out of control.

The car down the road hadn't moved. There were two men in it. One had a phone in his hand.

Clough had told Godfrey about the visit to Latvia but he had been selective. Now he filled in certain gaps: the tape's list of people who had been Moscow fellow travellers or worse ('Jesus'), about wiping the pistols clean before pressing other hands to them ('Jesus Christ'), about West's accusations, about Martin's murder, about asking for the pistols to be sent over to England, about the superintendent's visit and the glass of wine, about the men in the car watching while he made a phone call.

Silence. Godfrey stared at him. Clough wasn't certain what reaction he expected from his partner – concern? sympathy? – but the frown seemed angry. At length Godfrey said, 'This copper stole a glass?'

'Must have. When I cleared up after he'd gone one glass was missing.'

'Yours?'

'He must have pocketed it while my back was turned.'

'Matt, clever technicians can lift fingerprints, you know, and lay them somewhere they weren't before.'

Like the grip of a pistol. They looked at each other and Godfrey nodded.

The sign on the door of the office supply shop said *Closed* but Clough could see a light on in a back room so he knocked and kept knocking until a figure appeared. Liz waved her hands – closed – but when she recognised Clough she came over to unlock the door. He looked both ways down the street before coming in.

'Can we go in your back room? It's urgent.'

The store-room had shelves crowded with cartons. Clough could see the printer paper he'd bought from her. At the end of the room was a desk with a slew of papers.

'I was doing the VAT returns.'

Clough nodded. 'Good luck.' He laid an attaché case on the desk. 'You know the people who tried to run me down? They've come back, or they've sent some chums. I'm followed when I go out. They're choosing their time. That's what it feels like.'

'That's awful.'

Clough nodded. 'Next time they might succeed so I'm taking precautions.' He tapped the attaché case. 'If anything happens to me, don't give it to the police. They can't be trusted. Give it to the *Oxford Herald.* They'll recognise a good story.'

Liz gave him a long look.

'I think I have to know what I'm getting into.'

'Fair enough. I told you once that I was Matt Clough, bastard. I never knew who my father was. It turns out he was a bad man, a really bad man, a criminal and much more. I found this out last month. Can you imagine what kind of shock this was?'

He waited until she nodded.

'The man who was my father fell out with a criminal gang. It was over money. The gang were after him for the money he owed. Then he died so the gang have come after me.'

She thought about this. 'But killing you...' She stopped and frowned. This did not seem a normal conversation. 'Sorry. If you are dead they won't get their money.'

'I understand that and you understand that but these are gangsters. They live by a different logic. Killing me would send out a message: don't mess with us.'

In the end Liz found a place on the shelves for the attaché case. It had K.K.'s Dictaphone, Debbie's photo of Finnis on a park bench, photos of some of K.K.'s paintings. Clough had scribbled a two-sheet summary of K.K.'s involvement with criminals in Latvia and Russia and also with certain people in British Intelligence, the Foreign Office and the police. He read over what he had written and it seemed deranged. He almost added *this is all true*. Almost. As a precaution he put in his passport and as much money as he could get out of his bank's cash machine.

Superintendent Beckett phoned but it wasn't to explain how a wine glass got into his pocket.

'By the purest chance I heard your friend Martin's funeral will be on Monday at the Golders Green crematorium. Know it, do you? North London.'

'Do you, by the purest chance, know what time?'

'Three o'clock sharp.'

'Do you happen to know what name he is being cremated under?'

'Good question,' the policeman said and cut the connection.

On Monday Clough went to London. He took the Northern Line to Golders Green, asked the way to the crematorium and set out. It was ten minutes' brisk walk. A cold wind from the North Sea cut through his coat and made early daffodils in front gardens shiver. He climbed a gentle hill thinking: *I owe him. It was because of me that Martin was killed. If I hadn't telephoned from Riga, Yellow Submarine, he would be alive today. He was killed so the truth wouldn't come out. There is a web that spreads out from the Firm to Latvia and Russia and beyond. Who are the bankers who move millions with a couple of clicks on their computers? Who are the lawyers who twist the truth? Drugs are part of it. What else? People smuggling? Arms? Maybe further – skewing foreign policy? Meddling in elections?*

I am deranged. Again he thought it. *Or I am dangerously sane.*

Big stone gateposts guarded the entrance to the crematorium. It was close to the hour of the committal. People were moving inside but Clough stood and stared. Who were they? He had known Martin on a one-to-one basis. He had no idea of the rest of his life. Those two women weeping together – were they cousins, colleagues, old lovers whose rivalry was over? At a funeral you didn't put your hands in your pockets so the men had them clasped behind their backs. Who were they? Minor royals? They all had solemn faces in common. They could be comrades in arms from the Firm, members of his clubs, his chess society, church, ramblers, pub? Had he played bowls, raced a greyhound, slapped on make-up and done amateur dramatics? Too late to find out what made him a man.

Everyone had gone inside. Only Clough remained. Why had he come? I'm not part of his other life, he decided. Goodbye old friend, I mourn the man I knew. We liked and trusted each other, worked together for the good of the country though we never talked about it that way.

Clough didn't want to sit shoulder to shoulder with strangers. He started the walk down the hill and saw he wasn't the only person who skipped the service. Or possibly the man had pulled his car over and parked when his mobile phone rang.

In our trade, Martin had said, if you believe the comfortable explanation, you're in the wrong trade.

Suburbs gave way to countryside slashed by motorways and slip roads, culverts and bridges. The bus was crowded but nobody talked. Ploughed fields and dusk-grey woods flashed past. He remembered the snowy landscape on the way to Sigulda with Debbie.

Debbie was dead. And Otilija and Finnis. Weeks ago Martin was celebrating a great victory. Now Martin was dead. West denied that he had killed anyone and Clough himself had wiped his fingerprints off the pistol. K.K. had named certain traitors in Britain but K.K. was dead. Where was the proof? A deputy director had been accused but again where was the proof? Instead his rival at the Firm was pushed into a black hole. In Riga the captain was on the defensive;

Russians were on the attack. Superintendent Bennett came heavy-breathing, with hints and threats.

Clough went through the names again, counting them on his fingers. Five dead.

At Oxford he found he'd just missed the bus to Wallingford so he took a taxi. Is there a taxi driver in the land who doesn't moan about cheating politicians and the swamping of England by immigrants who were scroungers? This driver was Indian, which Clough found interesting.

Coming into Wallingford a barrier cut the road and a constable ordered them to detour through a housing estate. Why? Because of a fire. They drove past lines of identical red brick boxes but when they turned into the Didcot road they found the way blocked again.

'I'll walk,' Clough said.

'Good as Diwali,' the Indian driver said, 'or Guy Fawkes. Mind how you go.'

Low clouds were touched with orange and yellow reflections. Clough was near the library when he caught the first smell of smoke. He passed the fish and chip shop, a couple of curry houses and then the dread started. On past the charity shop and the fitness centre. He reached the corner where someone had tried to run him down. Clough forced his way through the crowd to the policeman who was holding them back. Clough tapped his shoulder.

'That's my place. Don't you understand?' The policeman turned to him. 'My place, my home, my business.'

'Off licence, is it?' A solid arm barred the way. 'You'd think it was an ammo dump. Lethal it is. Glass flying everywhere.'

That's my life going up, Clough knew, my house, my shop, my office, my job, my savings, my papers, my order books, my tasting notes, my addresses, my contacts, my memories, my hopes, everything. Gone.

They did it. Clough knew. Was it to destroy evidence? Scare him off? Kill him? If he'd driven back from the crematorium and not gone by tube and then bus he'd have been there, in that building. He'd be dead.

'When did it start?'

'Half hour ago.'

A crash of glass released a new sheet of flame, blueish and pale yellow, like a blowtorch. Two fire engines blocked the street, water arcing from their hoses.

'Why aren't they using foam? Get a team from Benson. They must have foam.'

The constable just stared at him. A movement caught Clough's eye. At the entrance to an alley Liz from the office supply shop was talking to Godfrey.

'There's my partner.'

The constable was distracted and his arm was limp and Clough brushed past him to join the others. Godfrey looked at him and said very quietly, 'Fuck.' What did his face show? Not quite anger, not quite despair. Little flames danced in his eyes. His mouth was compressed into a line of bitterness. Godfrey saw himself as an entrepreneur, in his element with a phone in his hand, not interested in wine and its infinite possibilities but in the margin of profit. At that moment Clough saw him in a different light, his handsome face, the ski-slope tan, the tousled hair of a film star. Godfrey spoke directly into Clough's face, 'Fuck, fuck, fuck.'

'What happened?'

'I'll tell you what happened,' Godfrey said. 'You swanned off to London for the funeral of your chum, I was here holding the fort. Phone call to say my mother had been rushed to hospital with a suspected coronary. I shut up shop and raced to Worcester. Mrs Lewis? Hospital denied knowledge of her. Is this another NHS cock-up? I charged into A&E and shouted her name and no one had heard of her and I was chucked out. So I went round to her flat and found her in her slippers, early gin in her hand, watching telly. I drove home to Cholsey and I'd been back about ten minutes when the cops rang to say the shop's gone up.'

A fireman was shouting as he jogged over: 'What've you got in the cellar? We need to know.' A black smear shaped like a boomerang went down one cheek.

'Bits and bobs.'

'No barrels of brandy? We don't want nasty surprises.'

'Nothing like that.'

Clough watched him jog back, yelling some order and making an encircling movement with one arm. The noise level was rising. Above the snap-crackle-roar of the fire was the whoop of a siren. An ambulance pulled up on the far side of the fire engines. Injured? Just in case?

'Matt?' A hand pulled Clough round to face Godfrey. 'That's the business gone, up in flames. And why? Because someone's out to nail you. Get us both out, break in, rig a bomb and wait for it to blow up. Blow you up if they're in luck.'

'Didn't you set the alarm?'

'Alarm?' he shouted. He took a breath but when he spoke his voice was not much more than a whisper. He was trying to be calm, laying the facts out to a mentally retarded child. 'Burglar alarms, Matt, are to scare off the kids. Your pro bypasses them, deactivates them, sticks a bloody great magnet on them, whatever.'

There was an explosion. Godfrey looked away and when he turned back his voice was normal.

'Finito. The other side of your life has brought this on and I'm not doing it again. We collect the insurance and we split.'

There was another crack of splintering wood and a roman candle of sparks. The roof was collapsing, tiles falling through burning rafters. That's into my bedroom, Clough thought. They nearly got me.

Perhaps that was the decisive moment, though Clough wasn't conscious of it. He was aware of images slipping into his brain, flames here, his home and his business burning, the synagogue in Riga that the Germans packed with Jews and set on fire, K.K. shooting Jews and lining the bodies in pits. Was there a difference? In scale yes, in intent no. I am their Jew, he thought.

With a hand on her shoulder he guided Liz out of Godfrey's hearing. She was staring at him, her serious eyes looking shocked.

'That bag I gave you, is it safe and sound?'

'Locked in my office.'

'Any chance of getting it?' He sounded so cool, no panic at all. 'In case the fire spreads.'

'There's the back door down the alley.'

Liz paused to see if Clough was following. He was standing a moment longer. His life was burning before his eyes. He thought again of the Jewish Museum in Riga, the old woman telling him of that *shul* which the Nazis crammed with Jewish families before torching it. *Today there are people who say the Holocaust never happened,* she'd said, *it is a lie. They look at the evidence and say it is a Jewish invention. Did we burn this building ourselves? Did we make our people disappear by magic?'*

The alley was dark, no light from the flames reaching it. There was smoke that made Clough cough. Mr Cloff, Lucija had said. He could just make out where Liz was, stopped by a door, fiddling with the lock. He went forward on tiptoe as if that would stop anyone noticing him.

'I love you,' he said.

'I love you,' she said.

'Have you still got snow?'

'Of course.'

'I'm coming to see it.'

Was this a new part of the code? She was silent.

'It's not safe here anymore.'

'Oh.'

'I don't know which route is best. They could be waiting at Heathrow, Gatwick, any of the airports. They could be at Dover. I've decided not to get Eurostar from King's Cross. I'll try driving to Ashford, paying cash for a ticket and catching the first train to Lille. You see, if I get to Lille they'll be at a loss. I could go anywhere: Germany, south of France, Belgium.'

'Take a train to Brussels. You can fly to Riga from there. Are you all right?'

'They killed Martin. They had a go at me. They've blown up In Vino Veritas. But I'm all right so far. As long as I can get to Lille. Do you have a key to the house in Majori?'

'Are you going to live there?'

'There's something I need to collect.'

'The captain has a key.'

'See him tomorrow.'

It was up to Lucija to get it. Clough thought of his route: Wallingford, Ashford, Lille, Brussels, Riga, the world. But he had to lay a false trail first. British Airways. Heathrow to somewhere in the Gulf; Dubai or Doha. This evening. It was absurd. His whole life was absurd. He had walked back to the Didcot road and was using a public phone box. But he'd use his mobile to book the ticket. Hope they'd pick it up. Looking behind him he could see the glow on the clouds. That showed where the war was and he hoped to God he was leaving it behind.

'Listen,' he said, 'if all goes well I'll be with you tomorrow.'

'And then?' she asked.

And then.

Cuttings,
March 2001-April 2003

Oxford Herald
Under the Carpet
GREAT BALLS OF FIRE!!

by Baz Faz

Where there's fire there's smoke – that's what your reporter has found. Whether it's a T-shirt factory in Bangladesh or a mansion in Hampshire, as soon as the press starts sniffing round then great clouds of smoke are puffed out to hide the truth about the fire.

Take that blaze at Wallingford's snazziest wine emporium, In Vino Veritas. There was a mighty explosion and up it went. The shop, the flat above, the precious stock made an inferno worthy of Dante.

Your reporter went to the scene on Wednesday to inspect the damage. Well, you've seen the photos so you know what the damage is like. What do the police say about the cause of this mighty explosion? Wallingford's finest say they are investigating and for the moment have no comment. Was it a gas leak? Maybe it was a bomb? No comment. How about the mysterious phone call that prompted one of the owners to drive off to Worcester on a false alarm? No comment. How about…? But your reporter was firmly escorted out of the cop shop.

Hmm. Something is being pushed Under the Carpet.

Is there dirty work at the crossroads? Matthew Clough, one of the owners, was seen at the scene of the fire on Monday night but has since vanished. A little bird tweeted to your reporter that he had just returned from Latvia on a mysterious mission to find out about the father he had never known. It turns out his dad had been a Soviet citizen. Suddenly this began to smell fishy.

It took four phone calls to Riga's better hotels to find where Matt Clough had been staying. A charming girl at the reception desk remembered our Matt – even though it was a month ago. He certainly made an impression but for the wrong reasons. He and a lady friend left the hotel pursued by men with knives. So what had… *Cont p.3*

ARTS SMARTS
WOW! WOW! WOW!

by Brie Saddler

The boys and girls at RESTART have pulled it off – a mega coup. Your reporter from Arts Smarts (OK, also there were guys from the New York Times, the Guardian, the Beeb, all the usual suspects) was summoned to the Opera House in Tel Aviv.

Tel Aviv? WTF? Buy a plane ticket to have surprises pulled on us? You bet. And it was 8 in the morning because they wanted us before the day had jaded our senses. Yeah, yeah, yeah.

So, some of us were bleary eyed, some jetlagged, and we just wanted to collapse in seats. But no, we were led to the orchestra pit. We stood and looked up at red plush curtains with a sign hanging: RESTART – Restoring Stolen Art Treasures. It was like a presentation by some boutique advertising agency.

Now what? The main man strutted on stage to make his pitch. For years they had been searching for the Rothstein collection, named after the German Jewish industrialist murdered by the Nazis. It had taken clever sleuthing plus the dogged persistence of Deborah Brown who sadly lost her life at the moment of her triumph. The paintings were traced to Latvia. Hey, give him his due, the man didn't rabbit on but pressed the button that rolled the curtains back.

WOW! WOW! WOW! WOW! WOW! WOW!

The canvases were lined up on easels as if the artists had just finished varnishing them. Let me first headline what we saw: a Munch, two Monets, two van Goghs, no less than three Toulouse-Lautrecs, two Cézannes, a Miro, a Pissarro, four – yes count

301

them – four Picassos, two Renoirs, a Dali, a Mondrian, a Gauguin, two Utrillos and a Seurat.

Silence. Stunned silence. We were all holding our breath. Think of the zillions it was all worth. No wonder there were guards with Uzis at the entrance. Then the *More* >

AGENCE FRANCE PRESSE
(Google translation)
Treasure from the jungle

AFP correspondent

'He lived here and he died here and he came to life here again,' said Jeannot Lebrun of the Espace Culturel Paul Gauguin in Atuona, on the island of Hiva Oa. 'A mystery? Yes, but the jungle is full of mysteries. That is the fascination it had for Gauguin.'

A painting by Gauguin has just been displayed to the world. It wasn't in Tahiti or Hiva Oa where Gauguin fell ill and died. It was shown off by Hong Kong billionaire Li Cheung. Mr Li says he bought it when his yacht put in at Atuona. He was having lunch at a little restaurant near the port when the owner called him to a back room, locked the door and produced a canvas.

Mr Li was told that an Englishman and his fiancée had booked an island tour. When the guide didn't show up they hired a 4 x 4 and drove themselves to the Tahanku valley and then hiked into the jungle. Visitors are warned about this as it is easy to get lost. That is what happened to the couple and they ended up at a hut that was being reclaimed by the jungle. They went in to rest and found it had been an artist's refuge with brushes, paints, and an easel – everything smashed as if the artist had lashed out in despair. But, face to the wall, was this canvas.

'The moment I saw the painting,' Mr Li said, 'I knew I wanted it. Price was no problem. I paid twenty-five.' Twenty-five dollars? 'Twenty-five million. US dollars, not Hong Kong. One or two of my friends here are going to be very jealous.' Mr Li smiled.

'Girl on a beach with bananas.' That is the title Monsieur Lebrun gave the painting which he viewed before Mr Li sailed away. 'It is surely one of Gauguin's masterpieces. The sky in the background - is that dawn breaking or some apocalyptic future? The colours he achieved - incredible. The girl's hair is black but it seems there are colours within the black. She is naked to the waist and the brushstrokes on her breasts are beyond belief. You might say they are a caress. And her eyes - they look at the painter — that is to say at you because you see her as Gauguin saw her. What do her eyes show? There is no final telling. Sometimes you think you see lust in her directness, other times temptation, or power. She seems to be saying: enough of your painting, monsieur, let me show you what life is really about, woman and man together.'

And the Englishman and his lady friend who brought this master-piece out of the jungle? They have completely vanished. Nobody has any idea where they have gone.

'Do you know what my given name is?' Mr Li said. 'It is Cheung. Cheung means Good Luck. And that is what I wish the Englishman and his lady. I hope there is a happy ending for them.'

AFTER EVE

By David Brierley

Coming Soon from Safe House Books

'I can't write this story,' I said.

In my voice I hear the echo of a boy protesting to his mother and stamping his little foot. Jozsef could hear it too. He rubbed his knuckles along his chin as if it was tender from a punch.

'You can write it,' he told me.

'I can't. They'll find a way to stop me.'

'You can write it,' he said again, more force this time. 'You'll find a way.'

Jozsef stared at me, Jozsef my cousin, the cop, the killer, the cuckold, the survivor.

All right. I took a deep breath. 'This is a true story. Only the facts have been changed.'

Jozsef's smile was slow to come but worth the wait. 'Isn't that the Hungarian way?'

Chapter 1

Have you ever seen with your own eyes something that is impossible? I have.

Date: Thursday 8 April. Time: 6.19 pm. Location: Oxford. My life is about to change forever.

See how precise I am. The facts are absolutely clear. It's important you know that. I glance at my watch as I press the button on the television. It's tuned to BBC1, coming up to the final stretch of the national news. I am standing in the centre of the sitting room, glancing at a couple of pieces of junk mail. Got it? Then it happens.

Out of the corner of my eye I see her. Eve. On the TV screen. My wife.

She's been dead for four months.

My name is Bazil and I am a journalist.

They use that formula at AA meetings. Let's face it, it's not a bad comparison. Working in newspapers is an addiction. Highs when you've got a scoop. Your pulse races. Your blood sings. Then the lows when you are disgusted by the job. Doorstepping. Phone hacking. No need to spell that out. There's a hunger, a dependency, a need. And maybe, just maybe, it will kill you.

So here I am, Bazil Potter, this journalist who's finished his shift at the wordface, standing in his living room, staring at his wife who was dead and is now alive. She's changed a bit, hair cropped, furrow between her eyes. I don't care. It is her. A man *knows* his wife. There is no disguising the spirit, the soul, the self. But her hands… damn it, her hands are hidden.

I pick up details. That's the reporter in me. Eve is standing at the shoulder of, but a step behind, a man I have never seen before. You wouldn't say they were a couple, an 'item' to use the jargon. The man is wearing a charcoal grey suit. Expensive? I'd say so but I only caught a glimpse. White shirt. Interesting about his tie: a snake with an apple in its mouth. So he's got a wild side. The camera is focused on him. My wife is not the story, this man is. Is he angry? More irritated, I'd say, with a snappy answer to some question. Look at that hard stare he gives the camera. Don't mess with me, those eyes say. He turns and walks out of frame. The camera is hand-held and whips round. The man gets in the front passenger seat of a black Mercedes. My wife gets in the back and the car moves off while she is still closing the door. It joins traffic crossing a bridge and disappears.

All in silence.

How long did that snippet last? Twenty seconds, maybe less. Of course there was more of the story before I switched on. I stand still, shocked. Then I unfreeze, cast round for the remote control. Last night I'd muted the sound to cut off a politician. Where's the bloody remote? I find it in the fruit bowl. By now the news has moved on.

I grab the phone and stand in the centre of the room with an eye on the television in case there is a recap. I punch in Josh's number.

'Josh? It's Baz. I've just seen Eve. Have you got the news on?'

Josh Banner, friend, colleague, shoulder to cry on. He has helped me through the bad times of Eve's death. News of her resurrection troubles him. He thinks my sanity has finally cracked.

'Eve? Seen her?'

'I just bloody said that. On the Six O'Clock News.'

'Baz…' Blown it, haven't I? My obsession has become a bore.

'Listen. Her. Alive. On the news. Five minutes ago.' In my urgency I am speaking like a tabloid. No verbs. Short sentences in case the reader's attention span can't stretch to the end of the line. 'Josh, she's done her hair differently but it was her.'

'You do mean Eve? Not – '

'Eve.'

'Well, er, that is…amazing.'

'What do you mean amazing? It's wonderful, fantastic. Well. Isn't it?' But Josh is silent. I cut the connection.

Think, I order my brain, think. What was the story? Wife of journalist rises from the dead? No, she wasn't the story; the snappily dressed man was the focus. If she'd been the story my editor would have been shouting at me to follow it up.

I've got to tell you about my editor, name of Dexter Lincoln. Dexter has buzz words and one of them is 'real'. Get real. Is this for real? A real drink. That is what is in my hand: a real drink. It's a tumbler of Scotch, darkish. 'We print real news or we are nothing.' Dexter stabs his desk with his finger. Get the message. We're fighting a never-ending war against lies, mush, spin doctors, official secrets, no comment, the old boy network, Freemasons, PR, PC, deep background, deep shit.

I nurse my Scotch and hop between the channels.

Dexter is not a dwarf but he's not tall and wears a bow tie as short men often do. He has the habit of slipping his hand inside his shirt while he is concentrating on something. 'It's his Napoleon complex,' Josh says. Dexter would read your copy and say, 'Order of the Golden Spike. Get round to the Council offices and ask awkward questions. Trouble about living in Oxford is that it's become a one-party state.'

Why is ITV ignoring the real news? My wife who was dead is now alive. I have seen her with my own eyes. God damn it, she was there, behind some unknown man. Twenty seconds. That was how long that clip lasted. I replay it in my head. Camera whipping round to follow him. Eve coming into frame, hurrying. She had to. Scrambling into the car. The car driving off. All in silence. What was it all about? If only I hadn't muted it.

My glass is empty. Someone has stolen my whisky.

* * *

The telephone rings and I wheel round. *Darling, it's me, I'm alive, I'm at the airport. I almost didn't make it – some crazy TV crew thought I was a film star.* That voice of hers, the rush of her way of speaking, a certain impatience, excitement, happiness.

'I watched the news, the whole menu.' The telephone is in my hand and it's not Eve, it's Josh. 'Eve didn't put in an appearance.' So he has taken me seriously. I think. Silence for a bit. 'Let's meet for a drink.'

'Got a drink,' I tell him.

'It'll do you good to get out. You're alone too much.'

'I can't. Speak to you later.'

I can't because of the flow of news. Six: BBC1. Six-thirty: ITV. Seven: Channel 4. Early evening is a news junkie's heaven. I leave it on all the time, Dexter said, it's the air I breathe. He's younger than me, only thirty-three. Editing a provincial daily is his stepping stone to London. One of the Sundays, most likely. There's always one in trouble. A Sunday gives you the luxury of time to get the real story, like the great Harry Evans did with the *Sunday Times*.

I sip and stare at the TV. I'm waiting for my next fix. I'll tell you about me and Dexter.

'I'm giving you a column, Fridays only, op-ed, so you've got a week to dig out the facts. Under the Carpet, we'll call it. Look under the carpet and what you'll find among the dirt is the truth they tried to hide – that's how we'll trail it.'

'Which particular "they" is this?'

'Anybody who thinks they are our masters, our superiors, our guardians, our jailers, our censors. While we are just plebs, proles, grockles, cannon fodder, *untermensch*.'

Hold on a minute. That little exchange between us makes him seem the caped crusader, which was never the whole truth. I was to be the means to his end. 'All journalists are investigative journalists,' Dexter declared, 'or they are nothing. Your job is to add bite. You'll need a name.'

'Got a name.'

'Your byline. That's what I'm talking about. Not the Man They Couldn't Gag. Not *Custos*.'

'Dexter, I've got a name.'

'Bazil Potter? No.' He shook his head. 'Cross between Basil Fawlty and Harry Potter. The ungodly won't tremble in their socks. More sparkle, more punch, more…'

I cut him short. 'Baz Faz.'

He frowned. You see politicians doing that. What's the trap? 'Explain.'

'Baz – OK?'

'And Faz?' he asked.

I kept quiet, smiled, the man of mystery.

'Baz Faz. Baz Faz.' Dexter rolled it round his tongue. Was it to his taste? Will it be the Order of the Golden Spike or a magnum of champagne? He shrugged. He was reserving judgement.

'Could be stupid enough to intrigue. Give it a whirl.'

So I'm Bazil Potter, also Baz Faz.

Channel 5 ignores the story about Eve too. What's wrong with everybody?

The phone rings. Do I want to listen to Josh hectoring me? I don't answer and wait until I hear his voice on the speaker while his message is taped.

'Baz, me old mucker.' Note how chummy he is now. 'Nothing on Channel 4 news or 5 either. Er…' Don't hesitate, Josh, out with it. You think I'm unhinged. 'Are you one hundred per cent sure it was the real Eve? Even the Queen has a double. See you. Cheers.'

Dear God, why has he brought the Queen into it? Have I been married to the Queen? Taken the corgis for a royal wee? *It's Eve*, I shout at Josh. In my head. I am married to her. I know her. She has the kind of allure that draws men's eyes. She doesn't relish it as a power over men. But she doesn't belong to that branch, correction, that little twig of women's lib which argues that it is degrading when a man sees a woman as a woman. Or that Dracula's blood-sucking was a revenge on women for menstruating. No, I'm not making that up. Eve is an achiever, a strong character. But you cannot pretend that you do not react to her as a woman. I never could. Other men felt the same draw to her. And I have seen her.

There's a lasagne in the freezer. I am giving it the kiss of life in the radiation box when the telephone rings. I have discovered that glaring at a telephone makes it shut up. No one leaves a message. Bastard. Who was it? I punch in 1471. It was Mary Monroe. Do I want to speak to her? She works for the *Oxford Herald* too: a snapper. Now there aren't many women press photographers. You can hear a dozen explanations: they're not aggressive enough, too cautious, not tall enough in a crowd, not visual. I've even heard their mammary equipment gets in the way of their technical equipment. Blah-blah-blah. OK, Mary is short but she's full of energy, bustling. Also, busty. Oh yes. Round the office she's known as Two Boobs. Just don't say that in her hearing.

'Mary, you rang,' I say.

'And you didn't answer.'

'And you didn't leave a message.'

Pause. Jesus. This exchange is veering towards a marital tiff. Why are people so difficult tonight? Give me a reason. She breaks the silence.

'Josh told me? About Eve? About your saying you saw her on TV?'

Why the questioning tone? Come straight out and say it. I'm deluded.

'I did.'

'Baz, Baz, Baz, that is simply not possible. Eve died four months ago. Accept that. You've got to. Josh watched ITV news and she wasn't on that. I watched Channel 4 and *nada*. It couldn't have been her. You saw someone who looked like Eve. It just ain't her. Facts are facts. You've got to move on, Baz.'

Move on. Life is a dance floor? Time to change partners? Life is not like that. Life is playing poker with God. How can you win? He knows what's in your hand, knows when you are bluffing.

'Mary, I've got to go. My lasagne is cooling. I'll speak to you.'

'When?'

Hanging up is my answer.

I'm in the trade – print, TV, radio, it's all reporting the news. I know how it goes. Whatever it was has stopped being 'real news'. It could have been a filler in the early evening slot, cut when something big came up. It was one of the pains of working on a national paper. First editions come out. Shit, the competition has an exclusive. Thirty minutes to do a rewrite. Rejig the front page. Some other story gets the elbow to make space. It happens on TV too: vote in parliament, a bomb, plane crash, whatever. Out with Eve Potter, in with the biggie. I know that. In my head I know that. But in my guts...

The doorbell rings.

Eye to the spyhole. It's Josh, head tilted, trimmed black beard, puckered brow. Think Toulouse-Lautrec. He is not so much frowning as trying to peer back at me through the little glass eye.

'Are you alone?'

'No. You're here.'

'Smarty pants.' Josh stares at me, searching for signs of madness. 'We're going out for that drink.'

'I'm waiting for...'

The telephone cuts in. We both go still, listening to it. Why? It's just a telephone.

'I bet that's her,' Josh says.

'Her? Eve?' I look at him and see his grin. The answerphone kicks in and I hear a familiar voice. I pick up my coat from the hall chair and we go out.

'Two Boobs,' Josh says. 'That husky croak, courtesy of a hundred thousand fags. Is romance in the air? I can just see the movie: When Two Boobs met...'

'Shut up and walk faster.' I don't want to see her. She's too much. I lengthen my stride. 'Where are we going?'

'The Temporary Sign.'

315

'As if I need ask.'

The pub, a block and a half away, is a victim of profit-seeking in the brewing industry. It has been a plaything of Big Beer. Here's its story. Sold from one multi-national to another, sign taken down and replaced. Next a change of marketing strategy meant a fresh sign was painted. Then subject to a management buy-out. New sign needed. Finally sold to one of those thrusting new chains – you know, the Dog and Bone, the Bull and Shit, one of those. Somewhere in the midst of this turmoil despairing workmen hung up a board reading Temporary Sign. Good enough name, sticks in your memory better than whatever it's called today. I like the pub in moderation. It's not city centre so it misses out on tourists and the university buzz. It's a pub. That's all it is. A pub.

From a back room comes the clack of bar billiards, a darts match is in progress in this bar and there is that defining mark of the traditional English boozer: people standing with their pints. But we take our drinks to a corner table.

'Sexy Dexy called me in,' Josh begins as if recounting this was the whole purpose of his coming round to my bijou non-des res. 'When he first arrived to sit on the editorial throne he had that five year plan: pick the *Old Hag* up, shake it until its teeth rattle, make waves, get noticed, get a reputation as being a hot 'n' happening editor, move on to the metropolis as the conquering hero. Remember that plan?'

'Strikes a faint tinkle.'

'Right. Two years have flitted past so it's become a three year plan. More urgent, right?'

He pauses to drink some beer. The *Old Hag* was Dexter Lincoln's name for the *Oxford Herald* when he rode to the rescue. Sexy Dexy is our name for him though not to his face, no more than Mary is called Two Boobs when she is around.

'Truth is,' I say, 'the boss doesn't have plans. He has a few drinks and goes wild.'

'He brainstorms.'

'Brainstorms,' I echo. That's about it. There's a Hollywood B movie streak in Dexter. He paces the room, throwing off ideas, and minions run in all directions. That's not the modern style. He should be cool, computer-literate, no alcohol, able to chop logic better than the house lawyer.

'All right, the Sexy one says to me – just this pm – we need to make national news,' Josh goes on. 'Note that – make news, not report news. He says we have the most prestigious university in the solar system squatting in the middle of town. He says it's stuffed with retired diplomats and government ministers. He says they have a hundred secrets, scandals and bombshells waiting to be exposed – if you can expose a bombshell. Think big black headlines and screams from the government. Think threats of prison for the brave reporter. Which is me.' He steadies his nerves with a swig of beer. 'So as of this evening I am officially sniffing round for a bombshell.'

'Eve,' is my response. There's a quiver in his beard.

'Baz, can't you put that to rest?'

I lean in to Josh as you do when you want to say something important, something urgent, something private.

'The whole scenario is very, very weird. It's one of Dexter's bombshells. I can smell it. Journalist's nose.'

I tap mine for extra emphasis.

'A disfiguring disease.'

'I saw her. I *did*. She was on the news with some unknown man. It was in Budapest.'

'Budapest?' Josh straightens in his chair. 'How do you know?'

'How do I know? For God's sake. The car drove away across the Chain Bridge. In the background, other side of the Danube, was the parliament building. Of course I bloody know.'

'Baz, our parliament is on the river too. Don't they look alike? Gothic monsters.'

It's in some people's nature to act devil's advocate. I can't be cross. I shake my head.

'The Palace of Westminster is like a village hall. Believe me, there's no comparison. What I want to know is what the news story was, why my wife was there, how she rose from the dead and where she is now.'

Josh is staring me straight in the eyes. Then, by degrees, his eyes drop until he is focussing on his tankard, tipping it from side to side, watching foam slide down the glass. He can no longer hold my gaze so I know that what is coming is painful.

'Bazil, excuse me but I have to ask.' Using my full name - now he is really intense. 'Could you see her hand? I mean...' He swallows. 'her left hand?'

Between us there is silence. There are the usual evening pub noises in the Temporary Sign, voices raised, laughter from the darts players, clack of billiard balls. But I hear other sounds. Have you ever woken at night in a terrified sweat, sounds echoing inside your head, tyres screeching, metal rending, a single voice screaming, screaming? God, I have. The sounds don't exist so why are they so real?

'Listen, bloody listen.' I take a breath like a sob. 'Eve was standing behind the unknown man, part hidden by his body. Then I had a back view of her scrambling into a car in a flurry. So no, I didn't see her left hand. I couldn't have. It was never in shot.'

'Bazil,' he says again then seems to lose heart.

Because, you see, the wreck of Eve's car was found in the Danube on the outskirts of Budapest, a bit to the north of Margit Island. But my wife's body was never recovered.

Only her left hand.

About David Brierley

David Brierley was born in Durban. He moved to Canada, then England and back to South Africa all by the age of thirteen. Travel and curiosity about different countries is deep in his nature. After Oxford University, he taught at a lycée in France followed by work in London advertising agencies. Once his career as a novelist was established he moved to France. As well as writing, he was a prison visitor. Together with his wife Jill he created a garden that won first prize in a regional competition. Now back in England, they live near Bristol in a small market town whose name - Chipping Sodbury – always raises a smile.

Safe House Books is an independent British publisher of spy fiction which is reviving quality espionage for a new audience.

Printed in Great Britain
by Amazon

26836105R00189